About the Author

Rachael was born in 1999 on the Wirral Peninsula, where she's always lived, apart from the three years when she attended university in London. *A Second Chance* is her debut novel. When she's not writing or reading, Rachael loves spending time with her family, friends and pets, having adventures and travelling. Somehow she manages to bring books home from almost everywhere she goes. Her dream is to have a room with floor-to-ceiling bookcases with a secret door leading to an even more secret library.

Follow her on social media at *RachaelBradleyWrites* – she'll be delighted to hear from you!

A Second Chance

Rachael Bradley

A Second Chance

Olympia Publishers
London

www.olympiapublishers.com
OLYMPIA PAPERBACK EDITION

A CIP catalogue record for this title is
available from the British Library.

ISBN: 978-1-80074-960-3

This is a work of fiction.
Names, characters, places and incidents originate from the writer's
imagination. Any resemblance to actual persons, living or dead, is
purely coincidental.

First Published in 2024

Olympia Publishers
Tallis House
2 Tallis Street
London
EC4Y 0AB

Printed in Great Britain

Dedication

This book is dedicated to my parents, Gareth and Sara, and everyone who has a lucky duck.

Acknowledgements

This book was two years of writing and my whole life of reading, writing, and dreaming of being an author. Publishing books take a lot of time and effort from a lot of people. Writing the actual book is only the first step and there are a bunch of people who deserve recognition and thanks for their part: My family, especially my parents, who bought me every book from the Mr Men series when I was too small to pronounce the word 'library'. For all those trips around the local libraries and carrying at least ten books home every week. For my bookcases and the start of my home library, for the shelf where my own novels will go. For party days and late-night pep talks. Most importantly, for the eternal love and support, and for not laughing when I announced aged eighteen, my plan to be a writer, with no concrete plan on how I was going to do that. Also, to my siblings Sophie and Jack, who are my forever besties. Shoutout to my nan Sue and grandad Bill, nan Mary, my aunties and uncles, and my cousins, who are as invested in this book as I am. Extra shoutout to the ones who said they'd buy multiple copies – I'll hold you to that! Also, to my friends, extended family, and everyone who has been part of my writing journey. Every person who said they're going to tell their friends, neighbours, colleagues, etc. Thank you! Thank you for being my champions and spreading the word, and to the ones who hassled me to keep writing, always. Thank you to the entire team at Olympia who helped make my dream a reality. To you, the reader, who I am so thankful for, and who I can't wait to meet and hear from. A shoutout to Roehampton University, where I did my degree and where this book was started. Special thanks to my tutor Ariel and my fellow novel-writing students in the class of 2020, who gave me feedback on the first three chapters. I finished it! I'd also like to thank my year 10 English teacher Jennifer Robinson, who was the first person to say she couldn't wait for the day to see my books in a bookshop. Jen knew I was going to be a writer before I did. A final thanks to all the authors whose books I've read over my life, whose words were devoured, and whose books will sit next to my own in the library.

Chapter 1

While her great-grandfather was being rescued from the side of the highest mountain on Earth and declared legally alive, Evie was reading a '*Take a Break*' magazine and cheating on her diet with a sharing bag of Maltesers in the kitchen of her family's house in Chester. After she finished the article about a woman whose baby was stolen, she started to flick through the TV channels, idly munching as she ignored several news programmes before settling on MTV music.

"Damn it," Evie spoke aloud to the empty house as her hand reached the bottom of the bag, she'd only planned to have a handful after having the worst Friday in sixth-form. The term had only just started, and she couldn't imagine it getting any worse than it had been today.

At five o'clock she left the house, scowling at her car which was mocking her from the driveway. She really expected to have passed her driving test the other day, they told her three times was the charm. Feet dragging, she trudged to the bus stop at the end of the road.

Evie looked ready; her long hair was sensibly secured in a ponytail. She was dressed in an extremely baggy t-shirt which hid her stomach and designer jogging bottoms. Her trainers looked new, the white soles gleaming and particularly standing out against the dirty pavement. The shoes were actually almost a year old, but Evie wasn't one to wear trainers in muddy places. Or any places really.

Almost forty minutes later Evie disembarked just outside the town centre. The bus-stop was conveniently located right in front of the leisure centre which held the self-defence classes Evie had signed up to for a ten-week course. With a casual turn on her heel, she briskly walked two shops down, sat in her usual booth and called hello to the friendly, blonde waitress, Oline.

Oline was from Norway and was working in Chester while she researched local history for her book. They'd become something like friends over the months Evie had been a frequent customer, and often shared writing tips with each other.

"Busy day?" Evie asked as Oline brought over the menus.

"Normal for a Friday, we'll pick up in an hour or so. How was your week? Did you finish that review?" Oline paused by the table; it wasn't too busy so she could stop for a little chat.

"Awful. It's no wonder I'm here every week drowning my sorrows in ice cream. And I still haven't finished the review, how will I ever make it as a famous critic if I can't write anything good?"

Oline murmured sympathetically and returned to the till.

Evie scanned the whole menu, reading each dessert description and almost salivating as she imagined each one. There really was too much choice. It was a little game she liked to play, where she'd be adventurous and order something different every week, maybe even get two if she had a bad day. Last Friday she got a hot waffle with chopped banana, strawberries and caramel sauce drizzled on top.

Today, Evie figured she deserved something special to make up for an especially rubbish morning. Either a super chocoholic feast or a sharing cookie dough and ice cream platter. In fact, she was debating getting both and decided to ask Oline for her expert opinion, when her rubbish day was well and truly ruined by her dad throwing the door open and bursting in. It was almost comical, the way he did a dramatic double take when he spotted his daughter.

"Evie? This had better be a joke. You would think, after swearing to me that you not only were learning some valuable skills that could save her life, but that she was starting to finally lose some weight, that she'd have the decency to at least go to the class she had her poor parents pay in advance for," Evie's dad, Jason, started off talking at a normal volume but reached shouting level by the end. He paused for dramatic effect, savouring the wide eyes of his fifteen person audience before he started questioning them.

"Do any of your daughters disrespect you like this? Do any of you have to drive into town to check on your lying daughters?" Jason paused again briefly but no one answered him.

He had a habit of talking about her in third person when he was really angry. His ears flushed red and he glared around the parlour, daring any of the staff to contradict him. Oline had paused by the till, torn between offering assistance and minding her own business. Evie smiled sadly and shook her head.

"If she's ordered, cancel it. I don't care if she's paid already. We're leaving." He stalked out, wrenching the door open and striding towards the car, knowing Evie would be hurrying along after him.

Jason shoved the car into gear and drove home, radiating anger and ignoring his youngest daughter. The tension was thick, Jason immediately knocked off the radio that was reporting breaking news. Evie sat stiffly in the passenger seat. She didn't think it was that big of a deal, she only signed up to the stupid classes to try and learn some real, useful self-defence. After the first time she went, when she'd paid upfront, she'd told her parents that it was a load of fitness mad, middle-aged men punching each other and throwing their legs up so high they could kick each other in the face. No, thank you. She's not having some aggressive man punching her and shouting because she couldn't do a proper press-up.

Evie was fuming when they pulled into the driveway, parking neatly in between Evie's black Corsa which was waiting for her to pass her test and her sister Tilly's blue Peugeot. Tilly had, of course, passed her driving test first time with no minors only a few months after she turned seventeen. Tilly had been driving for three full years now and Evie had failed to pass her third driving test last Monday. She'd been waiting at a junction when a red Mazda had slowed to a stop and flashed her, indicating that they were letting her go. Evie checked all her mirrors and in both directions before carefully pulling out. It would've been a kind gesture, if the Mazda driver hadn't changed their mind and carried on, almost crashing into Evie. It was an instant fail for causing another driver to change their speed because of her. Her examiner was quite apologetic and encouraged her to try again in ten days.

Evie was truly fed up with the whole thing, it was as though there was a worldwide conspiracy to prevent her from passing. She'd had an unfortunate incident where she drove in a bus lane after mistaking her left turn, and an embarrassing first attempt where she'd accumulated sixteen minors after working herself into such a state that she vomited right before and did silly faults that she'd never done before or since that day.

Jason glanced at the Corsa as he sidestepped towards the door between the two cars, gathering some more ammunition for the argument that was brewing and about to explode. He shouldered open the door to the modest two-storey semi-detached house they'd lived in for eighteen years and bounced straight into the kitchen where Evie's mum, Maria, was waiting. Jason launched into the evening's events before Evie had even taken her shoes off.

"I was right. She was stuffing her face in a dessert parlour.

14

Can you believe it? Right after that cute little speech she did about wanting to lose weight! It would be funny if it wasn't so disappointing." Jason gestured wildly as he talked, pointing at his daughter, the source of shame and disappointment.

Maria sighed, holding her hand to her temple, gently rubbing. There was a long pause before she spoke, they all knew how awful Maria's migraines could be, and this was a classic sign. Maria would be especially short tempered with her headache, and Evie was the obstacle stopping her from retiring to the darkness of her room and sleeping away the pain.

"Why, Evie? Your sister has never stolen from us or lied to us. Why do you think you can? Could you not be an adult and talk to us rather than going behind our backs? My grandad climbed Everest and my daughter can't even run for a bus. You're a joke, I almost can't believe that you're *my* daughter!" Maria spoke softly but every word punched Evie in the gut.

"But, Mum, I told you about the horrible men at the self-defence! Remember? I said—" Evie burst into her explanation but was cut off by Jason speaking over her.

"I am sick of this, Evie. You need to grow up. I'm not having one of my children lying and sneaking around behind my back. Take a long look at your sister and take a page out of her book. Get upstairs, you're skipping dinner, I'm sure you're full from all that crap earlier. You're grounded for the rest of the month!" Jason spat out the punishment and abruptly turned away from his youngest daughter and made towards the TV which had been silently reporting the news.

Evie turned to appeal to her mother, who was already drifting up the stairs.

"I didn't eat out, we left before I ordered. Please let me have dinner. I can explain. You wouldn't have stayed either! Mum! Mum?" Evie's words echoed off the walls, leaving an awkward silence which neither parent decided to break. She sighed in defeat and traipsed upstairs to her room, passing perfect Tilly on the landing.

Sometimes it felt like Evie was set up for a loss before she even started, like she intruded on what was a perfect family of three. Tilly was a model daughter and Evie's biggest rival without putting an ounce of effort in. She even looked wildly out of place, Tilly was blessed with their fathers' genes, resulting in her long caramel blonde hair and bright blue eyes in contrast to Evie's dull brown eyes and reddish brown hair. Tilly was tall and toned, captain of the local netball team in the winter and rounders in the summer, she had dozens of friends and a chaotic schedule. Life was all lined up for Tilly as she continued her extended pre-university gap year.

There hadn't always been such a fierce divide between the sisters, it was a change in dynamic that haunted Evie in the middle of the night when she couldn't sleep. Especially since they'd been inseparable when they were young, playing endless imaginary games with their Barbies and Sylvanian Families and sleeping over in each other's rooms. In recent years they'd grown so far apart that they barely spoke. The more successful Tilly was, the less time and attention everyone seemed to have for Evie.

"I'll bring you a bowl up," Tilly murmured as she danced past, she said it smiling, not maliciously but indulgently as one smiles at a toddler's tantrum over spilt milk.

Evie slammed her door, muffling an angry shout from her mother. She looked around her lilac room, her prison cell for the next month, and picked up a marker pen, slowly crossing dates off her calendar for the rest of September. Early screening for Tarantino's latest film – cancelled. Deadline for her subsequent review, failed due to lack of submission. A couple of tears dribbled towards the floor as Evie continued to cross off plans and resigned to her grounding.

Chapter 2

Day three. Evie didn't mind too much, she just stayed in her room and watched films. If anything, it gave her time to complete some reviews which she'd been intending to write for a while and to get ahead with her homework. Maths wasn't Evie's strongest subject, but with nothing else to do she was really getting the hang of quadratic equations. Family life continued without her, but that was nothing new. She was eating cold potato wedges that had been left over from the night before when her door flew open, crashing into the wall and revealing Maria on the threshold.

"Sorry, I didn't mean to do that." Maria's eyes darted to the bowl balancing on Evie's lap and she took a deep breath.

"Why don't you come down for a bit, I'll make some toast. We need... a family meeting." Strangely, the word family brought tears to Maria's eyes, and she turned and fled.

Evie was perplexed. Normally eating on her bed was breaking a house rule and eating outside of designated meal times while grounded would garner at least a ten-minute lecture. Her parents had been ignoring her all weekend, and Tilly had left on Saturday morning for a long beach trip. Evie realised she had barely spoken in the last few days, aside from chatting to her rabbit Toby C as she cleaned his hutch.

Never before, had Evie been asked to come downstairs and talk in the middle of being grounded. Something very good or very bad must have happened to create such extreme circumstances. It's bad news. Someone must be ill, Evie thought,

17

that's why she's not shouting at me. They're trying to break it to me gently. Evie felt her stomach drop. She carefully put the bowl of wedges on her bedside table, her appetite suddenly non-existent.

Acting braver than she felt, Evie headed downstairs, taking each step slowly. Dozens of scenarios raced across her mind. She lingered in the hallway, still out of sight of the living room, and glanced longingly towards the sanctuary of her bedroom. She would much rather remain grounded until she moved out than hear bad news.

"Evie? Are you coming down?"

She started guiltily at her mother's strained voice. It still wasn't too late to run back up and lock her door. Whatever this was, she didn't want to hear it.

Tilly's return home prevented that. She dropped sand covered bags next to her kicked off sandals and surprised Evie by enveloping her in a hug.

"What's going on? I got out of the shower to see that Mum had called me about ten times and all she said was that I had to come home straight away, because there was an emergency!" Tilly let go of her sister and darted into the living room. Evie trailed reluctantly behind.

"Mum? What's going on?" Even in a crisis, Tilly conducted herself with confidence.

Evie perched on the edge the sofa next to Tilly, looking up at her parents who were standing awkwardly in front of the fireplace. They both looked weary, shoulders slumped as though they were being pulled down by the weight of the news they were about to share.

"So, I, er—I—have some… news. It'll be a shock but bear with me," Maria's voice shook as she started speaking. Her mascara was streaked down her high cheekbones and her usually straight hair was mussed. Cancer, Evie decided, and her eyes welled up as she considered losing her mother.

"You know, of course, that I never knew my grandparents. My grandad was always ridiculously competitive, and it killed him in the end. He thought he could conquer Everest..." Maria started to speak before both Tilly and Evie interrupted her.

"But in the end Everest won," the girls said tonelessly.

"Right, my grandmother Margaret pretty much gave up after she heard the news and passed a year later," Maria continued.

"And they left behind their eighteen year old daughter," Tilly filled in. "We *know* this story, Mum!"

"Be patient, girls, this is relevant. So, my mother, your nana and namesake, Evie. Just imagine, she was due to give birth to me any day and she lost both her parents within the year." Both girls shifted restlessly. With a reassuring nod from Jason who took her hand, Maria ploughed ahead.

"Well, you see... I don't want either of you to get your hopes up, but I also want you to hear this from me before you see it in the media. Long story short, a very confused man was rescued from Mount Everest. He was one of eight people who have been found in the last few days up there. And, I know this will sound crazy, but he's claiming to be my grandad, Charles."

Evie was too stunned to react. All she could think was thank God it's not cancer. There was a pause before Tilly leapt up.

"Is this a joke, Mum? Obviously, it's not your grandad. He died almost half a century ago! I can't believe you're taking this crap seriously. I saw this on Twitter yesterday, that a bunch of people got rescued and were confused, but we all ignored it. It's clearly a hoax. You dragged me home to tell me some nutter is claiming to be my great-grandad?" Tilly started pacing.

"Dad, come on. Tell her she's being ridiculous." Tilly could usually charm Jason into anything, but he only shook his head and turned on the television.

"Breaking news," the TV voiceover announced. "Zombies, reanimated or liars? This story is brought to you live from Everest Emergency Room in the Himalayas." A news reporter wrapped up in several scarves and a puffy red winter coat, was standing in front of the hospital, she was nodding as the correspondent asked her questions.

"I can confirm that there are eight people so far who have been rescued from the death zone on Everest. For almost fifty years these people have been frozen in time. Until now, with the unusually warm temperatures thawing the ice. Eye-witnesses claim that they were wearing outdated gear that was dangerously short of current health and safety regulations. The first man is reported to have thought that it was still the seventies. He was asking if he's missed the Eurovision in Brighton. Next of kin are being contacted as we speak, I'll be back this evening with more information on this remarkable but chilling tale. Andrea Cabot, live from the Himalayas." The newscaster returned to the headlines and was muted by Jason.

"Is that the nutter claiming to be your grandad? I don't doubt that this guy believes what he says. He probably got lost up there, got oxygen starved and got confused. You watch, his family will get in touch and they'll laugh about him thinking it's the seventies. Or it's someone doing a publicity stunt or something." Tilly turned to leave but Jason stopped her.

"This is a strange situation, no doubt about it. Your mother has been asked to do a DNA test in a hospital in London so the truth can be established and then we can move on. Whether this is true or not, this poor man has clearly been through a traumatic experience. I don't want either of you putting this on social media and, Tilly, no telling your friends. This is family business and let's keep it that way." After laying down the law, Jason turned the volume back up and settled into his chair.

Tilly left the room, shaking her head. Evie dithered briefly before following Maria who had drifted into the kitchen. Evie had been quietly thinking since she heard the news and concluded that she mustn't have all of the information. Her parents were a lot of things, but she'd never thought of them as conspiracy theorists. Maria put four slices of bread into the toaster and didn't look at Evie as she started loading the dishwasher.

"Mum? Is there a reason why you think this man is your grandad? What did they tell you on the phone?"

Maria let some table spoons clatter to the floor and turned towards Evie. Her eyes were bloodshot and leaking tears. She looked unusually pale and had a minor tremor in her hands as she reached for the dropped cutlery.

"My mum used to talk about her parents a lot since I didn't get the chance to know them and I had endless questions. For some reason, she always wondered where his pocket watch went. It was very distinct – silver with the silhouette of a duck engraved onto the top. Over forty years later and it's turned up, in the pocket of this man who was found on Everest! Apparently, it's the only distinct thing about him – no tattoos or piercings I could identify him by," Maria stared straight through Evie. "Did you know that when someone dies on Everest, if they're above twenty-six thousand feet then their bodies can't be recovered? It's too dangerous and expensive – they call it the world's largest open-air graveyard. Climbers will walk past them on the way up and use them as signposts."

"Why didn't you mention the watch in the family meeting? That would have persuaded Dad and Tilly!"

"Because it doesn't make any sense! What if it is him? What

if he's been left there all this time?" Maria was wringing her hands as she spoke.

"It doesn't make sense! But that doesn't mean that it isn't true! That would make him…how old?"

"If he was alive today, he'd be eighty-three. But the man identified was about forty years old. So, that makes him younger than me! My head feels like it's about to explode. I know people can't come back to life but who is this man I'm meeting tomorrow with my grandad's watch who thinks that it's 1974? The media haven't reported it yet, but once the eight survivors were warmed up and hydrated they were flown back to London for specialist rehabilitation. Most of them were—are British citizens." The toast popped up, startling both of them. Maria ignored it and continued to load the dishwasher.

Evie buttered her toast and took it up to her room. She was convinced, seeing Maria's shock and hearing about the watch, that there was some truth to the story and that her life was about to change. After wolfing down the toast, Evie wondered about this possible new relative. How strange, she mused, acquiring a new relative who wasn't a squealing baby or marrying into the family. Had she inherited any traits from this great-grandfather? Maybe he used to watch and review shows and was absolutely thrilled when he spotted a plot hole and could expose it to the directors. If he even watched shows back then of course. He could've passed on the genes which meant they had matching reddish hair with muddy brown eyes. For the first time, Evie might find herself with a family member who looked like her and understood her.

The more Evie thought about it, the more appealing the idea of this new great-grandad was. In fact, Evie now hoped this mysterious guy with the pocket watch was genuinely related to her. A tiny voice whispered that it wasn't possible, and she shouldn't be so ridiculous, but that voice was easily ignored in favour of imagining a lovely elderly relative to discuss films and drink cups of tea with. After a quick few hours of wondering and Googling if people watched shows in the 1970s, Evie got into bed and dreamed of ducks marching to the beat of a ticking clock.

The harsh tones of angry voices disturbed Evie's sleep the following morning. Hearing Jason shout was a common sound inside the house but hearing Maria and Tilly's higher pitched angry responses was unusual.

Evie resolved to show her support for her mum, assuming the fight was about her upcoming trip to London. She'd already heard 'London' and 'Ridiculous' shouted several times between being woken up and going downstairs so it was a safe assumption. Entering the tense kitchen, Evie immediately regretted her decision to leave her bed.

"Nice of you to join us, Evie," Jason sneered.

"Like I was saying, Mum, me and Dad think this could even be some sort of practical joke and they'll film you for YouTube or if not then it's surely some sort of con for money!"

Tilly had clearly been working on their dad behind the scenes and had recruited him to the anti-Everest group. Maria's bottom lip was badly chewed, and red lines were etched across the whites of her eyes. Evie had been tempted to swipe some breakfast bars and retreat, but after seeing Maria's tear stained face, she decided to be brave and voice her opinion.

"I-I think you should go, Mum. To London, I mean, and to see if this man is your grandad. If that's him, he'll need his family, us, to help him. It's the right thing to do. At least we'll know the truth and won't be always wondering." Evie glanced around the room; her gaze lingered on Maria before she studied her shoes.

For a long moment, her family members were too surprised to respond.

"Stop. End of discussion, Evie's right. I'm going. This is my choice, and I won't hear any more on it. I'll be leaving within the hour." Maria swept dramatically out of the room.

"For God's sake, Evie! I almost had her persuaded before you burst in. You shouldn't have gotten involved!" Tilly followed her mum's lead and stormed out, leaving Jason and Evie to avoid each other's eyes. Jason made to open the fridge and then spun on his heel and also left the room. Evie felt she should've just stayed in bed.

Evie was back in bed, writing in her diary when the door banged open. Maria leaned in, looking better than she had in days. She had fresh make up on and was dressed in a floral blouse and knee length black skirt with matching black stiletto heels.

"Right, are you coming?" she asked with forced brightness.

"Me? Where?"

"To London, of course."

"But, Mum, I'm grounded. What about school?" Evie protested.

"I don't think that applies any more. These are exceptional circumstances. You can be grounded again when we get back. Now, hurry up. We need to be on the train in thirty! Oh, make sure you bring your passport or provisional with you." Maria then swept out, calling behind her, "I'm making a flask of coffee, we'll get lunch in London."

Chapter 3

Maria's toes were tapping on the train floor. The closer they got to London, the faster the taps. Evie turned away from Maria and opened a chocolate bar, gazing out the window at endless green fields. Every so often Maria would check the email on her phone confirming the details for the day, her lips silently mouthing the words as she repeatedly read them.

"Well, it's not often we spend the day in London, is it, Evie?" Maria was meeting Evie's eye in the reflection on the window. The tapping slowed almost to a stop as Maria chatted.

"No, I haven't actually been to London before." Evie smiled at the window. "It's nice. Isn't it, Mum? Just me and you together!" Evie said impulsively.

"It would be a lot nicer if it were under different circumstances. I'm half tempted to turn around. It's just the *watch.*" Cue the tapping again.

"I know. I understand. That's why I'm here and not Tilly or Dad, isn't it? Where are we going when we get off the train?" Evie turned so she was looking directly at Maria.

Without needed to so much as glance at the email, Maria answered. "The Regional Neurological Rehabilitation Unit. North East London. We'll be getting the tube, Victoria line and then Overground."

"Wow, I wonder if he'll look like us at all. Do you think he remembers dying on Everest? What do we say when we meet him? Maybe we shouldn't talk about Everest yet, he might be traumatised." Evie couldn't imagine what the man would look like, never mind how to speak to him. She hadn't had a grandad before, never mind a great-grandad.

"Evie," Maria started.

"Normally if it's family, you would hug but he's also a stranger so a handshake might be more appropriate. Should we have brought him something? Maybe we can pick up a box of chocolates. Worst case, I have half a Cadbury's Dairy Milk in my coat pocket. I don't even know what to call him. My great-grandad. Or possible great-grandad anyway." Evie failed to notice Maria's expression.

"Evie! You're being ridiculous. Let's wait until I've done the DNA test first before you throw my money at him. This is probably a waste of time, the guy probably looted the watch from my grandad's body. Now shut up, all that babbling has given me a headache. And you better not pipe up when we get there." Maria leaned back in her seat and closed her eyes, ending the conversation.

"Do you want it to be him, Mum?" Evie asked quietly.

Maria didn't answer, but squeezed her eyes shut tighter.

"What if it is him? What will that mean?" Evie whispered. She watched Maria for a few seconds, noticing a lone tear roll down her mother's face before she turned back to the window. Evie spent the rest of the journey watching the green fields turn to grey buildings. A few times her hand strayed to her coat pocket, but every time she abstained. Just in case.

The mother and daughter duo didn't speak as they disembarked. They silently scanned their tickets and walked into the centre of London Euston.

"Do you want lunch now then? We need to hurry; they're expecting us in forty-five minutes, and it takes thirty on the train," Maria asked to the air to the left of Evie.

"I'm not actually that hungry right now," Evie muttered back.

"I bet it's because you've been scoffing chocolate for the last two hours. You're just being awkward for the sake of it now. You're always hungry. What do you want? Burger King?" Maria seemed to think Evie was purposefully trying to wind her up.

"Really, Mum, I can wait until later. We can eat at the hospital even," Evie suggested.

"For God's sake, Evie! I'll give you money, go to Burger King while I run into Smiths and then we're going. And don't you dare try to be petty and not get anything. You'll be the one whinging in an hour that you're starving!" Maria snapped as she pressed a twenty-pound note in Evie's hand.

One large Chicken Royale meal later and Evie and Maria were on the Tube. Evie felt sick, her stomach was churning the fast food around like a washing machine on the fastest setting. As they approached their stop Evie felt like she was about to simultaneously throw up and pass out. She took deep breaths and stumbled after Maria, a few steps behind.

They were buzzed straight into the building and had to wait at reception for their identification to be extensively checked. Then they both had to sign a disclaimer to not alert the media before they could go further into the building, but not before going through a metal detector. Evie tried to catch Maria's eye, but Maria was staring at the chips in her pastel pink nail varnish.

They were introduced to a lovely man in a white lab coat called Dexter who had to stay with them the whole time that they were in the building. He led them through a maze of corridors and through two more ID stations before they arrived at the section of the hospital for the Everest Eight. The area was split into ten labs, and Dexter showed them into lab number eight.

"Okay, Mrs Monroe, the first thing we need to do is the DNA test. We'll take both a blood and a saliva sample from you, and it'll be fast tracked through the lab. You'll also need to fill in a few questionnaires for us and we'll do an informal interview at the same time," Dexter said, as soon as they got to the lab. Maria sat on a stool opposite Dexter, while Evie stood behind her and surveyed the room.

The room was a large rectangle shape, full of tables with microscopes and chrome covered cupboards. There were two doors leading from the room, as well as the one they entered through. Several people in white coats were striding around and comparing notes.

"Don't DNA tests take weeks to get the result?" Evie piped up, her curiosity of the room satisfied.

"Evie, remember what I said to you on the train? Sorry, Dexter," Maria grimaced at her daughter.

"No, no, please feel free to ask me any questions. I know how strange this must be. Usually, samples take at least four days, but with the whole world watching and wondering we have been given a lot of resources to work this out. So, we should know by the end of today!" Dexter's face was animated when he talked. He seemed excited to be involved in such a mysterious project.

Evie still felt sick, her stomach was tossing the burger around, somehow faster than before. As her mother talked and had blood taken, Evie sat on the floor with her back against a table and closed her eyes. This wasn't what she expected. She focused her thoughts on the great-grandad she'd imagined and tried to ignore the urge to throw up. Dexter was talking about accuracy and reliability to a nodding Maria, nothing Evie cared to pay attention to. She could picture a man in a winter coat, with a heavy bag over his shoulder. She wondered if he complained about the weight or carried it with a smile.

"Evie! Get off the floor! He's here, we're going to see him!"

Maria shook her shoulder, startling Evie. She must have accidentally fallen asleep while Maria was filling in all the boring questionnaires.

Evie leapt up, thankful that her stomach had settled. She followed her mum and Dexter down two flights of stairs and into a long hallway before they stopped. Dexter was standing half-way down, beckoning them to join him. There were sets of two doors all the way down the hall, five sets on each side. As they approached, Evie saw that the door on the right was fitted with several locks and had a camera focused on it.

They followed Dexter through the door on the left, into a small observation room. The whole wall on the right was a window looking into the other room. Several chairs were set up with people who would look up and then make notes on what they saw. There was also a video camera on a tripod recording through the window.

"We have twenty-four-hour monitoring on the Eight. If you look on the monitor you can see that we're tracking his vitals, and our team are regularly interacting with him and making sure he's okay. Their health and wellbeing is our number one priority. How much do you know about what happened on Everest?" Dexter spoke quietly, as he endeavoured to not disturb the scientists. From the doorway, they couldn't see through the window.

"Just the basics. Eight people rescued off Everest. Only they have been dead for decades. That's all on the news, and I know from you guys that they were flown to London for further testing and treatment," Maria rushed through her words, while Evie nodded beside her.

"Okay, I'll give you some context. The first man was rescued six days ago. Rangers thought he was oxygen starved and confused. Potentially amnesia – that's when someone has memory loss. Then came number two. Same story, different place and circumstances. A very odd coincidence maybe. By number four, alarm bells were ringing, and there were four more before the week ended. Your man in there was the last one we found. They were able to give us their whole life story, like the name of the priest in their local church and what the football score was…and it was all accurate information, from the 20th century. That's when we realised something bigger was going on—" Dexter paused, waiting.

"Wow! So how did you verify it? How did you know he was related to us?" Evie responded eagerly.

"We checked their dental records, then cross-referenced with the records of death. We denied it up until there was too much evidence. Somehow, these people died on Everest and are in the room next door alive today. It got leaked, and the media is all over it. Only a few select people know that they're in this facility in addition to the immediate families of the Eight like you two. It was easy enough to check the census and find the living relatives. We want to give them as much adjustment time as we can before the media hound them. Speaking of adjustment, do you want to see the man claiming to be your ancestor?"

"Yes! We won't tell anyone, will we, Mum?" Evie could not wait to see her great-grandad. She was sure that it was him, Dexter seemed to think so anyway.

"Evie, calm down. It might not even be him. It's almost definitely not him. Dexter, will he be able to see us in the window?" Maria was hanging back. She looked overwhelmed, and not the slightest bit happy.

"No, it's a one-way window. And you're right, the DNA test will confirm or deny it. It'll be 99.9 per cent accurate as I was telling you earlier. For now, you'll just be able to take a look, we can't let you meet him unless it's confirmed that you're his family. But we'll cross that bridge as and when we come to it." Dexter led them further into the room. They stopped when they were in the middle of the window. One of the scientists looked up and grunted in annoyance until Dexter explained that it was the possible family. Then the scientists exchanged looks and decided to go for their lunch break. Leaving Evie, Maria, Dexter and the huge camera alone in the room.

"You'll notice the decoration of the room is—" Dexter began to explain.

"Shhh! Please. Give us a minute," Evie whispered, moving until her face was right next to the glass. The room was designed to look like an old living room. There was a coal fireplace, emitting an amber glow into the room. A radio was atop the mantle, with a carriage clock and an ornamental set of horses.

The man, who Evie now thought was Charles, was sitting in a brown armchair. There was a jam sandwich balancing on a plate beside him. Evie couldn't see his face because he had his back to the window, inspecting the tassels on a lamp that was next to him.

"Dexter, why is the room so weird?" Evie enquired, without moving her gaze from Charles' back.

"That's a great question. As you can imagine, we have a lot to tell him. A lot of news will be a shock to him, so we're trying to make sure he's surrounded by familiarity as much as we can to ease the transition. Each person has their own living room like this, and an en suite and bed, so it's like a little flat for them. We bring them food that they'll recognise and soon we'll start filling them in on the twenty-first-century world. We're hoping that the families can help us with that part."

Evie nodded and turned to look at Maria, who was standing further back looking shell shocked.

"Mum, have you seen the carpet from the seventies? It's so

brown! It's all brown and tassels – tassels everywhere!" Evie called over, she hoped it might entice her mother to come closer. She laughed with delight, it was like a set from a film, but real life and only Evie and her mum got to see it.

Maria didn't respond. Her eyes were glued to the mantlepiece. Looking closely, Evie realised that next to the clock and almost hidden by a horse, was a little pocket watch. It was open so the time on both the clock faces was visible. Evie couldn't quite make it out on the little pocket watch, but it didn't look like the same time as on the big clock.

"Mum, that's the watch, isn't it? Dexter, has the man said anything about that pocket watch? It is his, isn't it?" Evie looked right at Dexter for his answer.

"Hang on, I know his file is here. Aha! Yes, male eight had on his person outdated climbing equipment, Kendal Mint Cake wrappers, a pencil, three matches and a distinct pocket watch. It is believed that he must have had more equipment in a bag which is lost somewhere on Everest. So yes, he had the watch on him, and apparently looks at it *a lot*," Dexter read from one of the many files and then summarised.

When Evie looked back through the window, Charles had settled into the armchair and was slowly eating. For the first time, they saw his face. Maria gasped and moved right up to the window, next to Evie.

Maria's hair was bleached blonde but her natural roots were brown that turned into a lovely golden red in the sun like Evie's. Both of them had brown eyes, but Maria's sparkled where Evie's were dull. His reddish brown hair was peppered with grey and stopped just above his brown eyes. He had a strong jawline and a slight bump on his nose. He wore a grey t-shirt with short sleeves that showed large biceps and matching jogging bottoms.

As they were watching, he finished the sandwich and shuffled over to the fireplace where he scooped up the pocket watch and sat back down. He was still as he gazed at the clock face. The expression on his face suggested heartache.

Maria wrenched herself away from the window, grabbing Evie's shoulder and digging her nails in as she pulled them both out of the room. Dexter hurried after them.

"Mrs Monroe, perhaps you can explain your reaction? Was it too upsetting seeing him? I dare say it was a shock at the least. I'm sure you'll have seen photos and—" Dexter for the first time looked distinctly uncomfortable and trailed off.

Maria didn't reply. She sat back in the chair she left earlier and took a few deep breaths. Evie anxiously hovered next to her.

"Evie? What did you think? You're actually the first potential family members who have arrived at this facility. Did we do something wrong?" Dexter prompted them.

"I'm fine! I think it's my great-grandad for sure. We even have the same hair colour! He looked sad though. Really sad—" Evie paused thoughtfully.

The silence in the room settled. Dexter was discreetly texting someone. Evie was looking between him and her mother, who was blankly staring at the table.

"Okay guys, how about we go up to the café and have a cup of tea, and then we'll work out what happens next." Dexter put his phone away to address Maria.

"No, I don't think we'll go to the café," Maria said.

"Our treat! There are lots of things we can discuss until the DNA results come back. It won't be long. I think the cake special today is carrot cake. It's lovely! And then—" Dexter began confidently.

"Thank you, but I'd rather go home. I've got a lot to process and a migraine coming on. I trust you can contact me and verbally report the results. We can discuss any further steps as and when necessary. Thank you, Dexter, you've been very helpful." Maria headed towards the door out, Evie in tow.

"Thank you, Dexter! I'll try the carrot cake next time," Evie called, waving towards a bewildered looking Dexter.

They retraced their steps until they were back on the train heading home. Maria put on a pair of sunglasses and shushed Evie every time she tried to talk. There was no option to pick up food, and no conversation on the train.

By eight o'clock that evening Evie was back home. Jason and Tilly had questioned Evie extensively since Maria went to bed to sleep off her migraine. When they were finished, Jason went into the living room to watch TV and Tilly wandered upstairs to her room.

Finally, Evie was able to retreat to her room, with the day's events weighing on her mind. It had to be her great-grandad, the family resemblance was uncanny. She wrote about her day in her diary, pouring out all the emotion and turmoil until her mind was empty and she settled down with Netflix on her laptop. At the very least she'd had an extra day off school.

Evie was woken up early the next morning with Tilly shaking her. She'd been up until the sun had risen that morning, every time she thought about turning Netflix off, she'd remember the man's sad face and start the next episode, it was only when her eyes were burning that she surrendered to sleep. Evie blinked at her sister sleepily and murmured for her to leave.

"Evie, wake up. Mum's had the call. Come on!" Tilly ran out of the room when she saw Evie's eyes snap open as she suddenly sat up and launched herself out of bed.

Tying her dressing gown as she went, Evie raced downstairs, shaking off sleep as her bare feet stumbled on the cold floor. She found her parents sitting at the kitchen table, Maria looked like she was in a trance, swaying slightly and staring at nothing. They both had full cups of stone cold coffee in front of them. Tilly was leaning against the fridge, biting her nail.

"Mum? Did they call you? Has your migraine gone?" Evie broke the silence.

"Dexter rang me just past seven this morning. I just got off the phone. It's him. My... grandad," Maria replied, her voice barely audible.

"Unbelievable!" Tilly murmured.

"I knew it! As soon as I saw him, I knew it! He has the same hair as me, Tilly! We have to go back, to meet him properly and not through a window. This is crazy! But I knew in my heart it was him when I saw him. Can we go back today?" Evie asked.

"*You'll* be going to school. Don't think you can play truant again young lady, if she wasn't already grounded I'd ground her again!" Jason laughed to himself before he continued, "your mother and I will be visiting the hospital every day and slowly introducing Charles to the twenty-first century. It's nothing to do with you. The doctors will decide what happens next," Jason smirked at Evie.

"But, surely, I—Mum?" Evie was so shocked she could barely formulate an argument. Even with her parents, with Jason, at no point did she expect she'd have to go to school. In none of her daydreams did she sit in class writing essays and doing daily quizzes while this was all happening.

Jason leaned over to Maria and whispered to her. Knowing Jason, he could just be asking if she wants a new cup of coffee, something entirely irrelevant but somehow he looked like he was talking about Evie, plotting something unpleasant. His eyes never left Evie's, and Maria nodded once in assent to what he had said.

"Mum, you need me there. I was the only one who believed you! Please, I really want to meet him, Mum, you've got to let me! How can I go to school and pretend it's a normal day when

I know you're in London?" Evie was tripping over herself to plead her case.

"You'll be going to school, Evie, end of discussion. This is a matter for the adults to arrange. Go to school like a good girl and keep this quiet, Dexter said we aren't to discuss the situation with anyone," Maria finally chimed in, after exchanging a look with her husband.

Evie stalked over to the cupboard to retrieve a couple of cereal bars, she couldn't force herself to wait for the time it would take to make toast or pop tarts. Just typical she thought, she had been the only one who supported Maria, who stood up for her even when she was belittled by her father and sister, and she didn't complain at all. Then, she had traipsed all the way to London and put up with Maria's anxiety and Dexter had said she should try the carrot cake – she had never tried carrot cake, it always sounded too healthy, but she was willing to give it a go! Right when everything got exciting, she was sent off to school. They can't have it both ways, she's either old enough to look after herself and make her own decisions like whether she attends martial arts classes and keeps huge secrets about the Eight, or she is a child and has no say at all and goes to school. It is so ridiculously unfair. Once again, Jason was ruining everything. He probably didn't care one way or another if she was there, he just liked upsetting her. Once she'd grabbed enough food, she glared at her parents as she left the kitchen to go and get dressed. On her way out she heard Tilly pipe up from by the fridge.

"Can I come to London with you, Dad?"

"Of course, Till."

Chapter 4

Evie could barely force herself to listen in school. Her form tutor had to call her name twice before she responded. She was in shock. Evie hadn't heard whatever nasty comment her ex-best friend turned biggest bully, Kendall, had made as she stumbled into the classroom twenty minutes earlier. It's as if the sound she heard was going into her ears but never connecting to her brain. Even when she concentrated it was like everyone around her was speaking a language she couldn't understand.

She could imagine it perfectly, the door opening up in the brown, old fashioned room with all the tassels, and her great-grandad's eyes lighting up as he saw his family. He'd make the hugest fuss of Tilly, his firstborn great-grandchild. By the time he met Evie, whenever that may be, the novelty would have worn off and he wouldn't be interested. Tears started quietly rolling down her cheeks. Evie felt so stupid for letting herself be so hopeful and excited prematurely. Of course, she'd be pushed aside. Why would this be any different to any other time?

For the first time, she thought that it was lucky that most people maintained the charade that Evie wasn't there, so no one noticed her crying. As registration drew to an end and the rest of the class started chatting and sweeping pens and papers into their bags, Evie subtly wiped her cheeks and gazed into the light above her until her eyes were watering for a different reason.

"Evie? Are you all right?" Evie barely glanced in the direction of the voice. She mumbled that she was fine and started gathering her belongings before she had to leave for her first class of the day.

Evie managed to sleepwalk through the day. She responded when directly spoken to, but her ears were ringing so loud that she couldn't hear her own voice. If she fiercely concentrated, she could understand the words being spoken around her. A couple of teachers discreetly checked in on her, the obvious turmoil in Evie's mind was unusual and Evie was grateful that they let her off lightly and didn't punish her for the lack of attention.

At lunchtime, Evie didn't want her packed lunch. For the first time, she didn't want any comfort food. If anything, she felt sick, a feeling that was quickly becoming all too familiar. Her insides felt like they were squashed, her stomach was squeezing in on itself, pushing her breakfast upwards. Her throat constricted to only allow the tiniest amount of air in, it was like she was silently suffocating, and no one noticed or cared.

On her way out of her film class, Evie paused outside the door, letting her classmates surge ahead before she made a beeline for the toilets. She locked the cubicle door and crouched down, oblivious to the smell as she leaned over. Once the retching started she couldn't stop, only bile was coming up and her eyes watered until she finally stopped and could breathe normally again. The relief was short lived as the sick feeling returned before she had lifted her head from the toilet.

For a short while, she didn't want to get up from the grimy floor and try to pretend she was fine. She wondered where her family was and what they were doing. Despite the overwhelming instinct not to look, Evie went on to Instagram and looked at her sister's page. The last post was a few days earlier, of Tilly and her best friend, who just happened to be Kendall's sister, Katie. They wore the same bikini in different colours and looked tanned and happy and carefree as they posed in front of a pink streaked sunset on the beach. Evie saw a twenty-four-hour story had been posted, and she should've stopped there but now she had to look.

There was a selfie of her parents and sister as they held up their fancy drinks and the hashtags #Qualityfamilytime #Myfamily #Roadtrip #Fun #Summer. Evie knew it would've had hundreds of views, and not one person would notice or remark upon the fact that there was a family member missing.

Eventually, a group of girls came into the toilets and banged on the door of the cubicle Evie was in. She rolled her eyes but got up and made her way out of the bathroom. She still had half an hour of lunch left.

She ended up sitting by herself in the sixth-form common room, a can of Coke on the table in front of her, unopened and on its side as Evie absent-mindedly rolled it across the table.

It was only the word 'Everest' that caught her attention and had her suddenly focus and listen to the conversation on the table behind her.

"Don't you think it's crazy though? They were literally dead and now they're not. Like what if I blinked and fifty years passed? It's like some Hollywood film. Maybe everyone who ever died will come back to life too, or maybe we'll never die."

"Guys, they're in the UK! I follow this page that's all about the Everest people and they're not in that hospital and apparently they're here!"

"They'll be in America. Or Russia. Or somewhere less rainy. Why would they be here? To have tea with the Queen?" A girl laughed.

"What's that page you follow? I want to see and maybe I'll be inspired to think of an idea because I've heard that we'll be doing a fundraiser."

"Just Google E8Updates, I don't know who runs it, but they have info faster than the news does sometimes!"

"You're all dumb, it's not real. People haven't come back from the dead like a corny zombie film! It'll be some new film promotion, and all you suckers are giving them exactly what they want, attention and followers online." A boy she vaguely knew from maths class cut across all the chatter, his confidence broking no argument and once his friends chimed in, the conversation was over. It was clear most people believed as Jason and Tilly had, that it was all fake.

Evie stayed very still as she listened to the idle gossip as it drifted over to plans for a beach party the following weekend. After she counted to one hundred, she reached into her pocket and carefully typed the name E8Updates into her phone.

If she couldn't be there, she'd keep up to date her own way. For the first time, it occurred to Evie that she was one of very few people who knew the truth and had actually seen one of them in real life.

Evie's heart was pounding so loud she thought anyone within ten feet of her would be able to hear it. If she turned around and said she knew for a fact that they were in London and one of them was her relative... she'd be popular. Everyone would be hanging on to her every word and they'd forget about the embarrassing fiasco from Friday. For once she had something interesting to say. She turned, mouth open, to spill the tea. And then froze, the image of Charles, in his brown room with his jam sandwich sadly looking at his pocket watch flashed across her mind. Evie immediately decided she wouldn't betray his trust by inviting in strangers who would sell the story. Her cheeks heated as she realised the people behind her were waiting for her to speak, eyebrows raised and smirking at each other.

She fumbled for something to say, and said "Hey… does anyone have a charger? For an iPhone?"

Then she was stuck sitting there, pretending to charge her phone when it was on 95 per cent already. After twenty more minutes of waiting, she made a show of checking and thanking them, handing the charger back and escaping to the library.

The rest of the day crawled along, she stayed in the library for her free, intending to update her film review blog but instead, she obsessively refreshed social media to see if Tilly had put anything new online. Her English class was no better, she couldn't focus on the discussion and barely managed to look like she was paying attention.

Once school had finished, Evie hurried home. She broke into a light jog when she got to her road and by the time she fished her keys from her bag, sweat was dripping down her back and collecting above her lip.

"I'm home! Hello? Mum?" Evie called, listening to the sound of her own voice fade to nothing as her words were devoured by the silence.

Evie dropped her bag by the door and walked around the whole house, making kissing noises at her rabbit Toby C as she searched the garden. She didn't pause until she'd thoroughly searched the entire house. They were still out.

Evie was pacing up and down the kitchen. She knew how long the journey was, and it would have been too quick for them to be home before she arrived back from school, but this now meant she had no idea when to expect them.

In a burst of productivity, Evie scribbled down a to-do list in the back of her school planner, giving herself some tasks to keep busy and stop watching the clock. She sent a message to the family group chat.

Evie: Hi, hope all is well. Msg me when on way home. Been thinking about it all day. Let me know how it's going – xx

Evie checked the clock, four p.m. She examined her list and started gathering kitchen roll and sawdust. She missed cleaning the rabbit hutch yesterday, so she really needed to do it today. Evie put Toby C in his outdoor run to snack on the grass, dropping a ball in there to keep him busy once he eventually finished eating. There was a metaphor there about eating and distractions that she didn't want to think about. She scrubbed the hutch from top to bottom, restocking it with hay, and then stroked Toby C on top of his head as he ate, apologising for not seeing him yesterday.

After a while, the wind picked up, causing the temperature to plummet. Evie scooped up Toby C, holding him close for a cuddle before putting him back in the hutch. She waved to him as she locked the hutch up and smiled faintly as he dived into the hay.

After going in and washing her hands, Evie poured a pint of Coke, adding several cubes of ice and a slice of lemon. She sat at the kitchen table, savouring her drink as she checked the next thing on her list: nails.

Evie went upstairs to get her nail kit and pulled out the remover, some cotton pads, and a burgundy colour. Evie removed the chipped remains of the polish she had on, filed and cut her nails down and carefully painted four smooth layers – one basecoat, two burgundy coats and a shiny top coat. Once her nails were perfect, Evie grabbed another drink and finally looked at the clock. 16:35 p.m. She checked her phone to make sure the clock was right and looked at her messages too, and even though there were no notifications, she checked the family chat to make sure there were no updates.

Evie banged her hand on the table, then immediately checked her new nails to make sure she hadn't chipped any of them. With a sigh, she checked her list again. It was going to be a long night. She was also starving since she couldn't manage lunch but was holding out, for the first time hoping that the four of them would eat together at the table.

Eventually Evie decided to cook a meal and made a bargain with the universe that if she prepared and cooked a family meal, they'd arrive home before it got cold. She chose lasagne, and carefully made it. It was one of her least favourite meals, she much preferred potato-based food than pasta. But it was Maria's favourite, so she made an exception. Too soon, the homemade lasagne was prepared and in the oven. Evie carefully made sure the kitchen was spotless as she wiped every counter and washed the dishes as she went along, and she had even refrained from sampling any of it once it was made.

By the time four plates were served and steaming hot, Evie collapsed in the chair. Her stomach rumbled as she waited, she checked the clock and was disheartened to see it was only just quarter past six. She sat there and waited, thinking and worrying. The only movement she made was when she carefully put the plates in the oven and closed the door to keep the warmth in. When sixty minutes had somehow dragged by, she moved the now cold plates into the fridge. No sign of them, and she only had lengthening shadows for company as the sun set and still, her family hadn't come home.

When she couldn't take the waiting any more, she retrieved one of the plates from the fridge, not even bothering to heat it. She barely tasted the cheesy pasta combination as she shovelled it in. Once her plate was merely red smears of sauce, she reached for a second plate. Even though she wasn't hungry, and didn't particularly enjoy the lasagne, she couldn't resist the urge to keep eating and to be doing something. When that plate was cleared, she washed the dishes and went upstairs to clean and tidy her room before she settled down to do all her homework.

By the time Evie finally got into bed, she was physically exhausted. Her arms ached from cleaning her room. Her bedroom light hung like an artificial sun, but instead of gentle beams, harsh rays emitted in every direction and hurt her tired eyes. She lay on the bed, eyes shut and as still and serene as if she was in an eternal slumber, but underneath the calm exterior, her mind furiously raced, speeding up with every lap.

She opened her eyes and leaned over to check her phone again. Nothing. She tapped her finger on the side of her silver glittery phone case, willing the three dots that indicated typing to appear. Still nothing. She plugged it into the charger and checked the volume was on high before she put it down. Evie debated whether she should call. It had gone midnight; she'd waited and tried to keep busy and for a while that had worked. Time slowly moved on, as it always did and somehow she'd gotten to nightfall and was faced with spending the night alone.

She argued with herself, on one hand, they must have stopped to eat and by now be planning to sleep, so surely, they'd check their phones. They wouldn't be staying overnight without letting her know. Unless the battery on all three phones had died, maybe they hadn't realised they'd be gone all day or how late it had gotten. They might have forgotten to take a charger. And she never usually called them, and it wasn't an emergency or anything. She was just lonely and worried. It might even panic them if she just called out of the blue.

But then an unwelcome image of an overturned car on the motorway, bathed in flashing blue lights and accompanied by a symphony of screaming and sirens crossed her mind. They hadn't mentioned an overnight stay. What about her parents' jobs? They wouldn't have just upped and left, surely. She considered a whole range of accidents and events that could have kept them in London. Maybe it was her great-grandad, his health could have taken a turn for the worse and they had to stay there in case he didn't make it. There were infinite possibilities, most of them equally terrifying.

"They're fine!" she said out loud, feeling comforted to have noise. She flicked on her radio alarm clock for some background noise and felt slightly better and then quickly decided she didn't like not being able to listen out so turned it back off. The innocent sounds of a house settling and rain on the window were far more sinister when her ears strained to place the sound over the music. At least in silence, she could listen out for any noises, like a key in the door or a car pulling into the driveway.

A thought suddenly occurred to her, she quickly typed her sister's name into the search bars on various social media sites, looking for any update. Though nothing had been posted, there was another selfie on her sister's Instagram story from earlier that afternoon with another coffee cup and the London location tag, and on Facebook she'd last been online forty minutes ago. She was fine, clearly, if she had been on social media.

Evie felt her eyes well up and didn't even bother trying to contain her tears. She was used to stuff like this happening, but she thought they would have at least text. If her sister had been on Facebook on her phone, she would have seen the notification from the family group chat. They all probably would have. And they knew she'd be at home by herself wondering and worrying and waiting. Evie didn't know exactly what time she fell asleep, but she knew her pillow was soaked through and damp on her cheek and her dreams were full of giant clocks and blue flashing lights.

Evie opened her puffy eyes and squinted into the brightness. She'd forgotten to close her curtains, so the morning sun streamed into her room with warmth and promises of a new day. She felt terrible, she'd lost track of the number of times she'd woken up in a panic, disorientated and with her heart pounding before she could rationalise that it was only a nightmare and lie back down.

Evie felt very uneasy but couldn't put her finger on why. She listened for the usual noises of the house on a weekday morning, but no kettle boiled, no doors slammed, and no pipes creaked. Somehow it was the morning, and it was clear that her family hadn't returned home in the night.

She thought about it for a second before scenarios started materialising in her brain. Maybe they'd decided not to come back, and she'd be forever waiting and wondering what happened to her family. She'd read a book like that once, and there hadn't been a happy ending.

She didn't have any extended family; Maria was an only child and so was her mother, Evelyn. Jason did have a sibling out there somewhere but unsurprisingly his family wanted nothing to do with him. She couldn't even recall what Jason's family had looked like, she was very young when they'd parted on the worst of terms and declared that they would never see each other again.

Evie gasped into the silence as she realised that if her family didn't come back, she was too young to be legally independent and would probably end up having to be adopted or fostered and what if the new people didn't like her or wouldn't let her keep Toby C. She didn't like her family much, but she might like strangers even less. *Calm. Stay calm. No need to overthink and panic until you know what happened,* she chanted to herself.

Evie hurried out of bed and had a cold shower to wash away the worry. It didn't help much but it did kick start her into getting ready for the day. She didn't know what a better option was – to go to school and spend the whole day wondering if her family would be there when she got back or stay home and risk the school noticing after her absence earlier in the week and falling behind in her classes.

Another day passed in a blur of trying not to let her emotion spill out and though she had decided going to school was the sensible option; she resented every second that dragged by and her mind was entirely somewhere else. The only thing she paid attention to was the growing talk of the Eight that swept around the entire school.

Almost everyone was discussing it, offering opinions and making bold claims. She'd heard dozens of people swear it was real and their uncle's best mate worked for the government and had inside information. Even louder were the sceptics who proclaimed the reporter from TV was in front of a green screen and more and more conspiracies were born and spread. No one knew for sure, and no one knew what Evie knew. She kept her head down and as usual, blended into the background. She sat quietly and alone, already turning her thoughts inwards and waiting for the day to be over. Time would inevitably pass no matter what, it was just a case of waiting.

By the time Evie trotted around the corner of her street, she knew the house would be still and empty. Despite running most of the way and before pausing to catching her breath, she tore through the house, checking every room and even left a voicemail on the house phone to check it was in full working condition. She still had the sinking feeling as she confirmed that her family had still not returned or contacted her.

Once again, Evie compiled a list of chores to keep busy and wear herself out until she could go to bed and wait for the following day to arrive. She also ate the other two plates of lasagne as she wrote, but even heated up and served with bread it tasted wrong. It was like cardboard, chewy and flavourless. Her list spanned two pages by the time it was finished.

Before she started working through her list, she brought Toby C indoors to stretch his legs and run around the kitchen. Evie pulled an unopened packet of chocolate digestives out of the cupboard and took one, and then another.

Toby C loved being in the house, she'd had grand plans of bunny proofing her room and letting him free roam, but when Jason threatened to get rid of him unless he was kept in a hutch in the garden, she reluctantly accepted it and settled for getting him out as much and for as long as she could manage. She sat on the floor with her legs crossed, watching him investigate the room. When he came up to her, she patted her lap and smiled as he settled down on her. As she ran a finger over his soft fur, she thought about how much she loved the rabbit, and how big of a reason he was for her to get out of bed. No matter what, she had her faithful companion by her side. She'd rather run away than live somewhere that wasn't pet friendly, if her own family didn't return that is.

All that remained of the biscuits was the discarded wrapper on the floor and a few stray crumbs. Evie sat for quite some time, gently stroking Toby C as he dozed and tried to think of nothing beyond her rabbit's weight and maintaining the rhythm of stroking him. That was how her family found her when they burst in over an hour later.

Evie hadn't even heard the front door, it was only when Toby

C leapt up, ears vertical, and preparing to sprint away that she looked up, just in time to see Jason stalk into the room. She was so relieved that she didn't argue when she was told to 'put the damn stinking rabbit away' and then reprimanded for not having tea on the table after their long journey.

Maria joined him in the kitchen, looking bone-tired. As Jason phoned the local Chinese and arranged delivery, Evie made her mum a cup of tea and settled into the seat next to her.

She didn't know where to start. She wanted to burst into tears and hug her mum and throw the mug that was in front of her and shout until her throat was sore. She wanted to hate her parents for not caring and not replying, but she also desperately wanted to know about her great-grandad. She took a deep breath as she considered the options.

Jason had left the room, still on the phone. So, Evie leaned forward and began talking.

"Mum? I missed you. I was so worried last night when you didn't come home. Didn't you see my message? What happened?" Evie asked, fighting to keep her voice soft.

Maria didn't even blink, she was just holding the mug of tea and staring at nothing.

"Mum?" Evie asked again, and at the same time she reached out and touched her mum's arm, causing her to startle, and a few drops of tea spilt over the edge of the cup and onto her hand.

"It's really him." Accompanied by a sigh, it was the only reply she got from Maria. She didn't react to the hot tea on her hand.

"I know. I knew it when I saw him, and then we had it confirmed by the DNA. But why were you gone overnight? You have to at least tell me next time! Mum, I thought something terrible had happened! I thought I was alone and would have to be adopted by a family who didn't like pets!" Evie tried, eyes welling up as she saw the words glide over her mother with no effect.

The kitchen was silent until Jason barked from the doorway where he had been leaning and listening.

"God help any poor family who got burdened with you. It is none of your business, despite what you may think you are not rightfully owed any of this confidential information. You are a child, a silly crying child and every word that comes from your mouth proves me right, and proves you are too immature and emotional and quite frankly, too dumb to understand what's at stake here." Jason kept his tone low and his voice quiet, but each word was a punch to Evie's ribs.

She didn't try to speak again and kept her head down as Jason put the TV on. He flicked through channels until he stopped on the news and watched with a faint smirk.

The same news reporter who had been live when the case first broke, when Evie and Tilly had learned about Charles being potentially related to them, was back on the screen. She was in the UK now, and wearing a smart navy skirt suit, glowing as she talked to the camera.

"Our sources now report that the Everest Eight have been relocated and we believe they are in the United Kingdom. One of our inside sources has revealed that the Eight are in rehabilitation and subject to many tests, none of which can explain how this impossible return from death has happened. Though some still dispute and disbelieve, we have experts around the world weighing in. The experts have varying theories, but one thing they do agree on is that it's one thing to be declared legally alive again, but it's another to stay that way and re-join society." She was thrilled, this news reporter. Absolutely delighted to have landed on probably the biggest story of her career, and she was the face associated with it. "Join us at eight o'clock this evening as we delve into discussion about the Everest Eight, we're covering science and facts, and looking into just how much has changed since the 1970s."

"In other news, a global climate strike, join us in Thailand, Greta Thunberg has spoken and scolded world leaders at the United Nations Climate Action Summit in New York City and UK parliament is suspended for five weeks. Back to the studio, I'll be bringing more updates as I get them. See you all at eight, I *snow* you wouldn't miss it."

While more mundane news flashed across the television, the focus in the room shifted. Jason muted the sound, and drummed his fingers on the table, uncharacteristically quiet for a change.

Only after the food arrived, and dishes of golden fried rice, chicken bathed in curry, sweet and sour, satay and a range of brightly coloured and heavenly smelling sauces were laid out on the table, did he speak.

Evie immediately noticed there were only three plates and sets of cutlery on the table. As her sister joined them and started heaping rice onto her plate, Evie realised she had been excluded. She brushed off the familiar sting and headed to the cupboard to retrieve her own utensils when Jason spoke.

"There's nothing for you. She doesn't need any, not when she's been inhaling biscuits by the packet and gorging herself on snacks the entire time we were out. She even ate the cheap biscuits we keep for when guests we don't like come round. So, I'm sure she's full." He laughed, not noticing Maria was too distracted and Tilly stony faced as he continued, "I'm doing you a favour really, if you can't control yourself or have any restraint then it's a blessing that I withhold the very food that's feeding your problem. I can see the plates over there, you clearly ate already. You're selfish for not saving any for us anyway, and greedy for having a second dinner. Sit down and shut up."

Evie didn't argue. She knew it would only infuriate her father and result in her getting sent out of the kitchen. If she stayed silent she would a least learn a little more about what was going on.

It was Tilly, who had put her phone down for a minute and initiated the conversation. Her plate of Chinese food was full still, with only a small dent in the mountain of rice.

"I was talking to one of the technicians yesterday, and he really made me think. It's like travelling into the future in the blink of an eye. He climbed up Everest with his Kendal Mint Cake and old fashioned equipment, and then he opened his eyes and almost fifty years had passed. Now he's returned to a world where every home is full of technology he couldn't have imagined back then. I can use my smart watch as a phone, to pay contactless in shops and loads of other useful features that are more than just telling the time. I probably don't even know the full extent of what I can do on it. His weird pocket watch could only tell the time, and apparently, it's broken now anyway. It's so wild!" Tilly said, with an unusual amount of tenderness and wonder in her tone. No one replied so she continued.

"He left a world where contacting someone who didn't live nearby was sending a letter. Where most people didn't travel abroad, and cars were huge and loud and didn't have computer chips in. I don't think twice when I connect my phone to my car to play music and follow a built in sat-nav. I take weekend trips to Europe for hardly any money and read books on a Kindle and he probably never saw our capital city never mind spent every weekend of summer in a different European city. I can't get over it, how can someone just learn to live in a totally different world?"

"He's like an alien. He looks like us and is in fact related to you lot by blood, but he doesn't recognise this world any more. If you ask me, they should be kept locked up and away from the rest of us. It's not right. He's like some charity case who will probably sponge off the government for the rest of his life. However long that may be." Jason clearly had not taken a shine to Maria's grandad. "I've had enough listening to all the scientists gushing over these freaks, I don't want to hear any more of it, got it?" Tilly nodded, her face expressionless as she started dragging rice in listless circles across her plate.

Chapter 5

Within weeks of finding out that her great-grandad was alive, the decision was made that he should immediately move in with the family. He was tested several times and proved to be healthy and well, a fact which was still perplexing scientists around the world.

The illogical yet irrefutable facts were that his body, when frozen, hadn't suffered any ill effect from death. All his vitamin levels were acceptable, his muscles were sore but had not wasted away. His hair was rather thin and didn't seem to be growing at all, prompting a conclusion that the hair follicles did not survive the freezing. But apart from that, he could eat and drink and defecate and urinate normally. His mind was sound, or as sound as it could be after the trauma of dying on Mount Everest almost fifty years ago and then returning to life.

Charles quietly consented to all the tests and was evaluated by a psychologist who later stated that while he was understandably shocked by some of the things he was told about the current world and devastated when he realised his wife and daughter were gone, he was nonetheless in a sound mind and suffered no apparent lasting effects from his death.

This was all explained by a patient Dexter who had made some home visits and interviewed Evie's family individually to ensure that this was the best place for Charles. Evie was shocked, so much that she could barely form sentences as she imagined and sympathised with her great-grandad. She was desperate for him to arrive, and then she could get to know him and help him navigate his new life. Before Dexter left, he had given them some very strict orders, on what they can and can't say, and who they can or can't speak to – or rather that they can't speak to anyone. Dexter tensely attributed the world's fascination with the Eight, and given how popular they are with the media, it would be a frenzy.

Dexter had murmured about leaders who wanted to learn how to come back from death and maybe even live forever. But their means to discover such things would mean a life of being experimented on and perhaps the discovery of knowledge no human had the right to learn. Not even Jason commented, all four members of the family were horrified by the picture Dexter had painted. Dexter had again reminded them they are sworn to secrecy and departed after giving Evie a box with some carrot cake in. It was surprisingly delicious.

Though many doctors and scientists believed that they should be closely monitored for the foreseeable future, there was an outcry from the media to 'Free the Everest Eight', leaving the government no choice but to let them leave. Luck and portrayal in the media left the Eight labelled as victims of an untimely death and unexplainable event, but these people were human beings, and if there was no concern for their health or safety, it was only right to grant them freedom and not treat them inhumanely. Although the media didn't have details, they had caught on to the fact that the Eight had been held in secure facilities while they were assessed, and with little else to go on, the media had spun a story of imprisonment and some loud and weighty voices had demanded their freedom.

The rescued people were quite quickly rehabilitated back into society with an envelope of crisp twenty pound notes and a list of numbers they could call if they had any questions or issues. In such unprecedented times, there was no guide book, everyone was making it up as they went along. Dexter had left small, white rectangle cards with his phone number all over the house, emphasising to them that they should call if there's any issues at all.

The family had received a pamphlet from the government, warning them that Charles would most likely have extreme mood swings as he adjusted to living again. He would also be disorientated, so they should be prepared to give him space or gently explain things to him. Discretion was also advised, as the media met Dexter's prediction and were in a frenzy trying to track down the Eight survivors, and there was no need to advertise their locations. They had expressly been told to avoid the media completely and signed some scarily detailed paperwork that legally bound them to keep the secret. There was quite a lot of extra information highlighting the importance of keeping their new relative a secret, and several intense phone calls with Dexter's boss's boss. This information had been explained already, it was just to remind them going ahead. Evie had read it twice through, determined to do everything right.

When Charles had arrived at his new home, Evie, Tilly and Jason were positioned in the hallway, ready and excited to graciously welcome him into their family. They all wore ironed outfits and had tidied the house in preparation. There were balloons in the kitchen and a banner across the front door. Evie had neatly printed the phrase 'Welcome Home' and hung it up so it would be one of the first things he saw.

All inter-family feuding between Evie and her sister, and their dad had been put aside for a temporary truce. Maria had been a nightmare for days, flying into fits of anger when anyone left a bowl in the sink or didn't put away their shoes the second they crossed the threshold. She'd driven all the way to London to pick him up and had stubbornly insisted that she needed to go alone. After making her husband and daughters swear to have the house immaculate by the time she returned the following day, she set off, and the only communication they'd had was a text to the group chat to confirm she had arrived safely and what time she planned on leaving.

Although it was unprecedented circumstances that none of them could possibly accurately imagine, Evie had spent the whole night dreaming of and planning the big reunion. She prepared a few lines she could say to her new great-grandad and she couldn't wait to run over and give him a huge hug and welcome him to the family. No one knew exactly what would happen, but Evie spent a lot of time playing through various scenarios and debating whether she should bake some muffins to present to him. It felt right somehow, to give him something upon his arrival. Just to be on the safe side, she set her alarm an hour earlier and made one of her favourite baked treats, cinnamon buns. She left them stacked on a plate on the kitchen table, alongside some flowers which Maria had arranged.

What they expected, as they waited in the hallway, was a bewildered old man who would be overjoyed to have gained a family and have another shot at life. Instead, Charles strode into the house and his first comment, before anyone had introduced themselves, was "it's a bit small, I thought you would have worked your way up the property ladder by your age, Maria. My house is far superior than this, and I was younger than you."

"G-Grandad, a three bedroom semi-detached house is a respectable—" Maria started to defend her home but was abruptly cut off.

"Don't worry, I'll help you sort your life out. It's not like I have anything better to do with my lousy life. You two! Girls! Why are you standing around? My bags need bringing in!" He snapped his fingers and continued further into the house, taking his hat and shoes off as he crossed the threshold.

For once, Tilly and Evie were united. They were equally shocked and outraged by the cheek of this man. Following a nod from their father, they struggled to drag Charles' boxy suitcase into the house and followed the procession into the kitchen.

"Chicken casserole is what I want, and a thick piece of bread with butter on. Real butter. It's the least you can do after I've been eating that miserable hospital food. And move all these ridiculous balloons, they're in the way. This isn't some happy birthday or homecoming like that cheap banner on the door suggested. It's an unfortunate turn of events, and I don't intend to stay here for a minute longer than I have to." Charles had only been in the house for a matter of minutes and had settled right into the role of a tyrant. He and Jason would either be the best of friends or the worst of enemies.

The following day was a rainy Thursday, the furious grey clouds closely mirrored the tension in the house. It was already apparent that Charles was not the great-grandfather Evie had dreamed of. He was nothing like what any of the family expected, and no one knew quite how to act towards him. Evie was determined to be kind to him, but her patience was already strained. Last night was a disaster, and Evie felt like she'd failed already. Mood swings were one thing, and Charles was quite another. Despite her best intentions, there had been no warm, welcome environment. Maybe she should've made the muffins after all.

The first problem was when Maria called her down before dinner, much later in the evening than when any of them usually ate. Evie usually scavenged for herself and ate alone, she tended to heat up a frozen ready meal not long after she returned from school, and then she would have some supper before bed. But since it was Charles' homecoming, they were to have a family meal, and Maria was actually going to cook. With fresh vegetables, nonetheless. Evie was concerned whether the finished meal would be safe to eat, as far as she could remember, Maria had never been a natural cook, and any attempts over the years ended in fire alarms or arguments. Jason's favourite phrase to say on the rare occasions when they had dinner guests over was 'luckily for my wife, I can order food on my phone because I didn't marry her for her culinary skills'. Though Evie's parents usually got along just fine, Jason seemed to have made it his mission to destroy any confidence or enthusiasm anyone but especially Maria, displayed in the kitchen.

They had all been shooed from the kitchen and instructed to 'get to know each other'. They dutifully trooped into the living room where Jason flicked through channels and complained out loud that he'd rather be playing golf. Evie and Tilly took turns to answer Charles' endless questions, while Maria attempted to cook casserole. Evie was finding his rapid subject changes and judgmental looks after they answered to be rather tiring.

"Do either of you work? I had a full-time job at your ages and a house of my own."

"No. I'm still in school, I have a blog though, and I'm—" Evie tried to explain.

"I should've guessed. Do you know how to cook? Don't you think it would be good manners to offer assistance to your mother?"

"She told us to give her space actually. I didn't see you offer," Tilly said back to him.

"I am a guest. Speaking of which, I'd like a drink," he said with a pointed look at Tilly. Both of them got up and went out of the room. Behind them, they heard Charles complaining about the poor quality of the shows Jason was flicking between.

"God, he's a lot isn't he?" Tilly whispered to Evie.

Evie shrugged in response and retreated to her room.

When Evie finally entered the kitchen later that evening, nose wrinkled at the distinct smell of burning, she immediately spotted trouble. Charles had positioned himself at the head of the table and looked quite proud as he sat up straight and waited for his meal to be served. Anyone would mistake him for a rich man in a posh restaurant, in fact, he could be the owner of the restaurant. Jason was trying to loom over him, childishly refusing to move until he got his way.

Evie dithered in the doorway, not wanting to evoke any anger by drawing attention to her arrival. It was only when Maria deposited a plate of thickly sliced crusty bread that she noticed the one sided standoff. She tugged her husband through the kitchen door into their small garden. Words were hissed, the hostile tone leaking through gaps in the door and then the door opened again, and Jason stalked back over to the table. He was glaring at Charles, jaw set as he took a new seat, delegated to the other end of the table, right next to the door. A vein pulsed under Jason's hairline and he helped himself to the red wine Maria had picked up earlier. Only once the brimming glass had been gulped down and a second glass poured, did he speak.

"Since it's your first night here, I'll make an allowance, pal, but I always sit there. It's *mine*. The man of the house belongs at the head of the table. Even if you're the only one in the house you need to choose a different seat. You can sit in that one." Jason clearly pronounced each word, speaking slowly and gesturing towards Evie's vacant chair.

Charles didn't even glance in his grandson in law's direction. He appeared thoroughly bored, and his face only changed when his gaze drifted to the doorway where Evie stood, cringing in anticipation of the fight. After he looked her up and down, he furrowed his eyebrows and moved to study the floral pattern on the cutlery instead.

Jason tensed, getting angrier and angrier as he was treated like a piece of distasteful artwork. He wasn't used to not getting a reaction from one his targets.

"Are you deaf, old man? I'm waiting for a thank you. You don't sit in my seat, eating my food under my roof and not even reply when I talk to you. Who do you think you are, huh?" Jason guzzled some more wine in between sentences. "Oy, stop being an eavesdropping creep in the hallway and sit down!" he shouted at Evie once he realised who Charles had been looking at minutes earlier. His shoulders rapidly rose and fell as he wound himself up more. Still, no one took the bait or retaliated.

Evie silently took her seat, directly to the right of Charles. Tilly sauntered in and sat on Jason's right, pouring half a glass from the nearly empty bottle of wine and retreating into the virtual world of her phone. God help her if she looked away from any of her group chats with all her best friends for more than a minute.

They sat in silence until Maria shouldered her way across the room with rosy cheeks and presented a dish of burnt gravy and unidentifiable lumpy shapes and a smaller dish with some crispy oven chips in. The room was silent as each one of them observed the meal. Charles was gazing blankly into the gravy, Tilly and Jason wore identical expressions of horror which Maria missed as she tried in vain to catch Charles' eye. Evie saw it all and smiled at her mum, who looked right past her to Charles.

"Sorry that it's late everyone. Grandad, welcome—" Maria dropped into the seat between Jason and Evie, starting to talk as she peered into the bottle that contained only crimson dregs.

Jason's lip curled as he studied the meal. He interrupted Maria before she'd even finished the sentence.

"Well, Maria, this is a prime example of exactly why you should listen to me and not try your hand at something you've historically proved to be terrible at. You didn't need to prove how inadequate you are at cooking; we could've just told dear old grandpa. Then we could've ordered in or at least hired someone who could make something edible. Well, we have to be grateful for small mercies, at least Evie was kept far away from it. It could have been worse I suppose," Jason retorted.

Maria bowed her head but didn't comment, she merely reached for a new bottle of wine and generously filled her glass.

"Mum, I'm going out tonight remember? We're actually grabbing pizza on the way, so I don't want to spoil my appetite," Tilly smiled sweetly at her mother, and offered the serving spoon to Evie.

Evie swallowed, ignoring the cramp in her stomach and began spooning sloppy gravy coated potatoes, chunks of carrot and other barely recognisable vegetables onto her plate. She silently returned the spoon to the pot, and took a slice of bread, choosing one with extra butter.

Charles shifted his heavy gaze towards Evie for a long moment, and then reached for the spoon and filled his plate up.

"I'm very sorry, Grandad; she should've let you get yours first. You know better than that, Evie!" Maria hissed the last part to her daughter.

Neither Charles nor Evie replied, and the only sound was the metallic clatter as Charles dropped the serving spoon, sending small droplets of gravy in every direction. On that note, Tilly gasped and excused herself, murmuring something about her already straight hair needing straightening and running late.

Evie looked up towards the light, praying no tears would betray her. Her glassy eyes gradually glazed over, and she returned to the meal, glumly spearing what she'd finally realised to be chicken chunks and chewing endlessly to try and break it down. The longer the silence lasted, the faster Evie chewed. At least when she was ignored and fed herself, though it was lonely, she didn't have to deal with the killer glares and suffocating tension. And with sorting her own meals, came freedom of what she fancied eating on that night, all of it pre-prepared and properly cooked. Not to mention the unlimited choices for dessert, her favourite part of any meal.

Jason lifted the bottle of wine, holding it up and shaking it for too long before he realised that it was empty. Maria's lips settled in their signature straight line frown, but she offered no comment. When Jason slammed the bottle back down, Evie startled and swallowed the chicken, feeling it scrape down her throat and restrict her air flow. Her eyes once again watered as she gasped for air, eyes bulging and silently screaming for help.

In the corner of her eye, Evie saw shadows leaking across the table and narrowing her vision to a tiny circle. Heart hammering against her rib cage, Evie knew she was about to pass out. Her hand jerked out, meaning to smack the table, for someone to realise what was happening. For a second she felt only air before her fingers closed around something cold.

Gripping the cold thing, Evie thought of everything she wanted to say. She'd probably start with something like *Hello? I'm choking! Do you hate me so much you'd all just sit and watch me suffocate to death? Why is no one helping me? I'm going to die right here, and I never even got to drive or go on a date or make a best friend. Who will feed the rabbit?*

Evie couldn't focus any more, she let her grip on the water glass relax, before it occurred to her to use it. She frantically lifted the glass to her lips, forcing herself to chug water until the chicken blockage got swept down. And then the coughing started.

By the time she composed herself enough to look around, she saw that only her father was looking up, the other two were moodily looking at their plates. They didn't even realise the person sitting next to them almost died. Evie almost laughed, she was invisible at the dining table apparently, unless being critiqued.

Jason sat with his arms folded and watched the table, stubbornly refusing to take any of the food. He wouldn't even take a slice of the shop bought bread, so stubborn about his food strike that he would rather go hungry. And then probably sneak out for fast food later.

Meanwhile, Maria had taken a small serving of the chicken casserole and was chasing a potato around the plate, but when she eventually caught it, she didn't make any effort to transport it to her mouth, instead it was a boat on the end of a fork, splashing around the gravy sea and neatly avoiding the carrot and pepper islands.

Evie wasn't used to sharing a dinner table with her parents at home, she didn't know when she could politely retreat upstairs, or if it was normal in these situations for no words to be exchanged. The closest experience she had to compare to, was when she was occasionally forced to attend a meal in an expensive restaurant for some anniversary or occasion, though at least she could people watch and order delicious food until the meal ended and she was free until the next one.

Sometimes in the restaurants, she pretended to be someone else. Anyone walking past and glimpsing her might assume she was a minor celebrity – since Jason always bullied his way to the most desirable table and without fail always ordered the most expensive house wine and the largest steak. The people dining would steal glances at them and wonder who they were. She would discreetly smile at passers-by and take notes on what she'd eaten as if she were reviewing a Michelin star restaurant and needed to keep her first impressions fresh. She was merely remembering the meal so she could make sure she ordered something different the next time. But it made the trips slightly more bearable when she pretended to be someone else. In this situation though, it was almost impossible to do so when in her own house and with no one else around for the family to show off in front of.

If she could get away with it, she'd sneakily read a book on her phone. Jason was wise to it now though; he knew as well as the rest of them that Evie didn't have any friends and had no pressing messages to reply to. Tilly had made that very clear with an unhelpful 'as if loser' comment when Evie had defended her phone use and claimed to be in the middle of an important conversation. She'd delivered the lie with a straight face, until Tilly laughed so hard she almost threw up, and Evie had turned a furious shade of red. Now Jason was quick to confiscate her phone so she couldn't play games or read while she waited to go home.

Apparently, reading a paperback under the table is also unacceptably rude. There was no winning, Evie had to endure every second and smile through the ordeal. Most frustratingly, was that Tilly ignored all of them and took phone calls throughout and that was deemed appropriate. In fact, her parents actively encouraged it. Jason and Maria have always been biased towards Tilly, she could cartwheel through the kitchen and kiss the chef and they'd exclaim about how athletic and charismatic she is. It was clear who the favourite child is and always has been.

Evie risked a glance at the clock, she'd only been sitting at the table for just over fourteen minutes. There was no chance she'd be able to even sneak a look at her phone. She'd have to silently endure and escape as soon as she reasonably could. With renewed energy she began scooping up the food on her plate, eager to clear it and be excused from the table.

The silence was excruciating. The only sound was Evie's fork clinking against the plate and Charles slurping water from his glass. Jason was still shooting daggers at Charles, who was still ignoring him.

Evie sneaked looks at Charles between mouthfuls. She felt like she ought to warn him about the type of family he'd joined. He'd find out soon enough she supposed. He looked so sad, his eyes were dull and although he sat straight, he carried an air of defeat. He still had half a glass of water and was holding it even though it was on the table. Evie felt her gut twist. She was selfishly feeling sorry for herself when the man to her side, her great-grandad, was suffering and adjusting to a horribly unfamiliar life.

None of the rest of them were going to bother to show an ounce of kindness or compassion so it was up to her. She thought about how his family were gone before he had the chance to say goodbye and all of a sudden, he had to mourn them. She didn't have a spouse and child of course, but when her family didn't come home from London, she'd had a brief taste of being alone and didn't like it one bit. Evie recognised that her family didn't have a typical family bond. But she hoped to change the narrative with her own future children, grandchildren and great-grandchildren, that they would be kinder and more empathetic than the people she currently shared the dining room table with.

She wondered if any of Charles' daughter Evelyn's traits were apparent in any of them. If it might hurt him to be around the Monroes, and if he saw the ghosts of the people he loved flickering in his descendants.

Evie had no idea what his family had been like though. She couldn't truly imagine how he felt, and not for the first time she wished history had been different and granted her the opportunity to know her nana.

She expected that all the other Everest survivors had been taken in by happy families and were starting their second lives in far more pleasant environments than the Monroe household. It was no reflection on Charles, just rotten luck that he'd been stuck with the four of them as family. Evie's feelings of obligation increased tenfold, she had to try and make up for the others. She was constantly reminding herself that despite how hostile he was, he was out of sorts and had been through a lot. He might be a much kinder and agreeable person once he settled down and had some much needed time to acclimatise.

Make conversation with him, she thought. *What do I even say? Nothing too triggering. The pamphlet Dexter sent said we had to avoid upsetting topics and only talk about recent events if he asks.* As the silence lengthened, Evie felt her cheeks tint red and her breathing increase as she worried. She felt like Charles was waiting for her, and disappointed in her silence. *Nothing about being dead or stuck. It must've been truly horrible waking up and your entire world has changed, it's no wonder really that he looks so sad. It's like he's cheated fate by having a second chance, but he lost his family on the way. Apparently, he passed out when they told him his wife and daughter were gone. Did he see them on the other side? Does he know what happens after death? So many people would kill to know that! I can't ask him yet though. It's way too soon. Do not talk about his family. Do not mention his death. Ask about what his daughter was like, that's a safe topic and she'd grown up hearing stories about her nana so there was some common ground. Did he think of his daughter when he was taking his last breath? Did he regret not seeing her grow out of her teens or knowing what she'd achieve with her life? Evie wondered if he continued the thought when his heart started beating again, or if it was like waking up. It was so hard thinking of what to say. If there was such a thing as an afterlife, Charles was one of very few people who had experienced it long term and still walked the Earth. And that led to the question – if there was a life after death, was he happy there with his wife and daughter? Would he rather go back there, if it existed and if he remembered it? It was too heavy a topic so early on, but she couldn't stop her mind as it drifted back and continued to wonder and begin to obsess. She had to say something casual, what might she say normally to a family member that she wanted to get to know? She'd never been in that situation, but she could certainly try. Think!*

"Do you like movies?" Evie asked, looking at Charles. Her voice wasn't very loud, but Charles jumped slightly. He stared at her, looking perplexed as if she'd just asked him the secret to immortality or something.

"For God's sake, Evie! You always go on about those stupid films you rot your brain watching. The only thing worse is all that not so secret eating you do. If it's not one it's the other, or both! You need to get a life; you don't see your sister watching so much rubbish on the TV or stuffing her face. Think about the two of you together, Evie, maybe you can compare yourself and try to be more like your sister. Maybe you'll finally stop being such an ugly, fat pig!" Jason's flushed cheeks reflected the full bottle of wine he'd drank on an empty stomach. He was spoiling for a fight and his small smirk revealed just how much he was enjoying it.

Evie looked away, pretending her father wasn't there and that his words were harmlessly bouncing off her. She couldn't let him know how deep his words cut and had fought to make sure he wouldn't for a very long time. She also knew that to say anything in her defence was to pour fuel onto the fire. It's what he wanted and for that reason, she wouldn't engage. With a deep breath, she turned back towards Charles, whose eyes were narrowed and his knuckles white around the glass he gripped so tightly and raised once again to his lips. She had to try again, to say something fast and to furiously hope that her tears didn't betray her.

"When they found you, did you know what happened? Did you see your wife and daughter on the other side or know they were gone?" Evie blurted out.

Immediately, she replayed the words in her own head and shook her head in wordless apology.

"Sorry—I, I just meant—I obviously thought about it, but I wanted to get to know you, I'm sorry, I know it's too soon. I just panicked and said it out loud when—"

Charles slammed his glass onto the table, the distinct crack of glass as it shattered into a million sparkling pieces whipped through the room. Water dribbled across the white table cloth, creating a waterfall when it reached the edge of the table until it formed a pool on the floor.

"EVIE!"

"You stupid little idiot! Get out of my sight before I slap your stupid face."

Her parents shouted at the same time, Maria ran into the kitchen to get a towel and began fussing over whether Charles' hand was cut.

As she hurried out, she glanced over her shoulder. Charles pushed Maria away as he stood up to leave. Maria was crying as she began wiping up the spilt water, her lip trembling and shoulders lightly shaking. Jason was still sitting, lording over the scene with his signature smirk, looking unperturbed by the turn of events as he poured himself some more wine.

Chapter 6

Evie shuddered as she thought about the events of the night before. She prolonged her morning routine as long as she could, repeatedly dragging a brush through her hair and applying several coats of thick black mascara through her eyelashes with more care than she usually bothered with. She reapplied her eyeliner and wiped it off until the wing was perfect. It was a far cry from the usual one and done method she used when she was late. She was reluctant to go downstairs; she'd heard Charles stomping around since before six and was not in the mood for more criticism or conflict so early in the morning.

Eventually, as the minute hand of the clock crept closer and closer to eight, she had no choice but to go downstairs to get some breakfast, the lesser of two evils when faced with having to starve through her morning lessons. Evie opted to pursue a silent and sneaky route, she tiptoed down the stairs and quietly entered the kitchen, where she poured a generous portion of chocolate Weetabix into her bowl and lowered four pop tarts into the toaster. She perched on the edge of a chair at the table while she waited for the pop tarts. Evie thought that she might've escaped notice when Charles followed Maria into the kitchen, clearly in the middle of an argument.

"What am I supposed to do then, Maria? Everyone I know and love is long dead as your daughter reminded me last night and I have no identity. I can't just *pop to the library and pick up a book* when I don't have a card or even a legal identity can I? I don't have any possessions beyond the clothes on my back and a few bits they let me keep from the hospital. I don't care for the rubbish on the television, the people are ridiculously dramatic, and I've never liked it. I was stuck in the hospital and now I'm a prisoner in this house," Charles' tone matched his cold words.

Maria was spared having to answer when Charles noticed Evie.

"You! What are you doing? Have you only just woken up? I've been up for hours! Are you eating chocolate for breakfast? Eat some real food and get moving! The other one left ages ago!" Granted a reprieve, Maria ducked out of the room towards her shoes and coat, not looking back at her daughter.

"It's fine. I don't need to leave for another twenty minutes. And Tilly doesn't even go to school any more. Listen, I am so sorry about last night. Can we start afresh? I understand that you were hurt by what I said, but it was an honest mistake. Do you think when I'm home later maybe we can have a cinnamon roll and get to know each other? I was wondering if maybe I could see your pocket watch? I always wanted a pocket watch when I was younger. I always use my phone to check the time, so I don't need one, but I'd still love to see yours." Evie had plenty of practice verbally sparring with her family members, but she was still trying to be polite to her newest relative, and kindly ignored his insult as she extended an olive branch. The only response she got for her effort was a scowl.

Strangely, Jason wasn't strutting around the place. Evie suspected that her father would clash with Charles the most. The two men both had a stubborn streak and would struggle to co-exist in such a small space together. He presumably left for work early to avoid any drama or conflict. Last night he'd argued with Charles over sleeping arrangements. Charles believed that he, as a guest, deserved to sleep in the finest bed in the house which turned out to be Maria and Jason's king-size. Jason took the opposing view that Charles was lucky to have a home and in fact, to be alive, and suggested that he stop complaining and settle onto the sofa while Jason decided where to permanently put him.

It hadn't even been a full twenty-four hours and it was already a nightmare. The most recent plan to resolve the bed issue was for the girls to share and re-decorate Evie's room for Charles. This was a solution that pleased no-one. At this point Tilly got involved and shouted the place down, an inherited trait from their father. They had all gone to bed angry, and no solution had been reached. For now, Charles would set up camp in the living room. Evie had been grounded to her room after her disastrous comment at dinner, but she and all of the neighbours overheard every word as her family competed over who could shout the loudest.

As Evie started eating her pop tarts, she glanced over at Charles who was still scowling. He was looking down the hallway towards Maria, who stood in the doorway and began calling goodbyes and instructions into the house.

"Stay in the house for today. Help yourself to food, if you don't understand how to use something then don't use it. I'll be back by six. The others should be back earlier than me. I've left some old shirts and pants of Jason's out for you to wear until you can get your own, and there's a box of photos and albums in the cupboard in the living room if you want to look through them. Have a great day, ciao!"

"Bye, Mum, has—" The door closed, cutting off Evie's goodbye. Then the house went still.

"Photographs?" Charles seemed to mellow with the word, shoulders slumping and the scowl melting off his face. He didn't react to Evie suddenly stopping mid-sentence.

Evie was reluctant to disturb the temporary peace. She

deposited her bowl in the sink and edged out the room, bumping into a chair which protested loudly. Evie winced and raised her eyes to Charles who narrowed his eyes but let her leave without comment.

After brushing her teeth, she scooped up her schoolbag, slid on her shiny black shoes and left the house, calling a timid farewell. Checking her phone, Evie realised that she'd actually left two minutes earlier than normal.

On autopilot, Evie walked to school. She kept on thinking about how Charles had reacted to the photos. But when she was in danger of feeling too sorry for him, she remembered that he didn't notice when she was choking and was going to steal her bedroom.

Evie took her seat in the middle of the classroom, close to the windows. Her classmates were mostly people she'd gone to high school with for five years who, like Evie, had chosen to stay at the sixth-form. Despite being in her seventh year, Evie had failed to make a close friend. At first, she was shy, then she had put some weight on, and she got good grades which a lot of people were cruel to her about. High school was miserable, and now she was at a point where she was largely ignored. Evie either scrolled through IMDb on her phone or people-watched to pass time in school. On days like this, she wistfully wished for a companion, she had been sleepwalking through the past few days and had no idea if any homework was due and had no more than a vague idea on what they'd been taught this week.

The door flew open, the sudden movement caught Evie's eye and disturbed her thoughts. Evie looked up in time to see Kendall, the school's popular head girl and Evie's personal tormentor, arrive with her flock of followers. Kendall's older sister Katie was in the same year and best friends with Tilly. Evie hadn't seen Katie in person recently, but from Tilly's social media she knew the girls were together often.

For a while, the two sets of sisters were a group of four until Kendall decided that Evie was not a suitable sidekick, that she wasn't pretty enough and was too embarrassing to be around, so Evie was dropped. Or so Evie had assumed, the day Kendall decided to stop speaking to her was abrupt, and Evie hadn't received an explanation. That was in year eight, and the rest of the year group followed Kendall's lead and avoided Evie, even years later it would be social suicide for anyone to be seen with Evie. Evie knew the classic friend to enemy trope from countless films, but actually experiencing it was worse than in the movies. There was less drama and a lot more pain.

Kendall surveyed the room, looking Evie up and down before settling at the back of the classroom with her group. Evie released a breath she didn't realise she had been holding, her humiliation from a few weeks earlier was still fresh on her mind, and undoubtedly on the minds of her peers. On the worst Friday Evie had had in sixth-form, Kendall had 'accidentally' launched water all over Evie as she'd walked past. Evie had to spend the rest of the afternoon with her hair plastered to her face, with smudged mascara and a see through-blouse on. The third of which Evie hadn't realised until the end of the day when she'd gotten home and happened to see her reflection. Even weeks later, the memory was sore, and worse still that it had led to the events of Jason embarrassing her in the dessert parlour and her ending up grounded.

Not a single person had told her about her fashion mishap, but all of them had seen her and most of them had laughed. Though she'd been physically attending school, her mind had been elsewhere. She'd been so preoccupied contemplating her drastically new home situation and what to do about Charles that she hadn't had any spare attention for anything else. The anger and shame and sorrow were still raw, unprocessed emotion. Now it was the opposite, as she was trying to block out her home life, the school problems all came rushing back.

Evie realised that she had been glaring towards the back of the classroom as she relived The Worst Friday. It was one of many things that had happened recently which resulted in Kendall embarrassing Evie in some way. Kendall seemed to be getting more vicious lately, and Evie had no idea why, she had never intentionally provoked her. The worst part was that there was nothing Evie could do, she didn't have any friends to back her up, she was never brave enough to fight back, and she could never prove that it was done maliciously. The teachers were always suckered in by Kendall's angelic smile. As if hearing Evie think her name, Kendall suddenly turned towards her, catching Evie's glare. Taking it as a challenge, Kendall stood up, and started towards Evie.

Their form teacher, Mr Scott, arrived before Kendall reached her. He ordered everyone to the main hall, as a whole school assembly had been called which would replace their usual twenty minutes of morning form as well as their first lessons of the day. His timely arrival provided a lucky escape for Evie. The class got up and shuffled as a big group towards the main hall. As sixth-formers, they were allowed to sit on chairs at the very back of the hall. Evie was grateful to postpone the verbal attack but quite quickly realised that her day wasn't going to improve. On a PowerPoint on the big screen behind Mr Loche, the headteacher, was the title 'Everest Eight'. There was a few minutes of chatter filling the hall as more and more form groups streamed in until the hall couldn't possibly fit another body in. Once the headcount of teachers was done, he began speaking. His voice was so loud, he didn't need a microphone. It was like he was standing right in front of Evie and shouting, rather than across a hall.

"Good morning! As I'm sure many of you are aware, something miraculous happened recently. Eight people have essentially come back to life on Mount Everest. Since something so amazing has happened, we've decided that our school will get involved and help in any way we can." As Mr Loche was speaking, the slide behind him changed to headlines from various national newspapers. "We'll be collecting donations and raising money through several fundraiser events which will be confirmed in the coming weeks. I want each of you to imagine if that was you or one of your family members, who woke up in a new century, confused and alone. Most of the people you knew – your parents, siblings, boyfriends, girlfriends, would have died, or you've lost touch. You'd have no possessions besides the clothes on your back. Can you imagine not having any possessions? No phone, no bed, no pets, no clothes, nothing. You probably wouldn't recognise the world. These people need help, and we are fortunate enough to be in a position to offer that help."

The audience was silent, many students considering what they had just heard. Evie didn't even need to think about it, and she was one hundred per cent sure that she did not want to share the news of her new lodger with anyone, even if she wouldn't be murdered by Dexter for spilling the news.

"No one knows how this has happened, and I'm sure that we will learn more in the coming weeks. Until then start thinking about ways we can raise money, you can discuss these in your tutor groups. We'll discuss this further as more information is given to us, this is history in the making. To make it more fun, we'll have a competition to see which tutor group can raise the most money and the winning group will be given a prize at the end of the term!" Mr Loche gestured to a table which was now on the screen behind him, all of the tutor groups had zeroes in the columns next to them.

Once the assembly was concluded with some boring announcements, the students were allowed to go on their break. Evie tended to wait outside the room her next lesson was in, fifteen minutes was too little time to go anywhere. Her next class was double English, and they were watching the Leonardo DiCaprio version of Romeo and Juliet, which Evie had seen before. So, she should have been able to sit back and enjoy the film, a nice change from normal day to day gruelling A-level classes. The fact that she couldn't engross herself in Shakespeare or young DiCaprio was an indication of how distracted she was.

Lunchtime came around quickly. Evie normally ate as early as she could in the school canteen before she retreated to the library. Instead of reading, Evie was on the internet on her phone and was daydreaming about what Charles would be doing at home at this time. She wondered if he would want to look through Maria's photo albums and if it would be a happy or sad thing to do, she expected it would be both. It was hard to live with him, but she had to keep on reminding herself that he'd had a huge shock and needed sympathy, not stress.

Movement in her peripheral vision jolted Evie from her thoughts. Roman was sitting at one of the computers, logging out. She hadn't noticed him until he'd moved. Evie had liked him for years now, they used to be friends but like everyone else, he'd drifted away from her. He was also head boy, popular as one of the school's infamous rugby stars and he was good-looking, though he managed to defy the sporty popular stereotype she was sick of seeing in hundreds of teen dramas. He also probably didn't notice Evie. She liked him a lot but didn't entertain any silly ideas of any sort of relationship with him. They just wouldn't look good together. Boys like that always ended up with girls like Kendall or Tilly.

Evie sighed and focused on her phone again, engrossed in an article titled *'Where Are They Now?'* in which the news reporter she'd watched on TV last week, Andrea Cabot, was keeping the general public updated. They had eventually realised that the Eight were in London and besieged the hospital with cameras and reporters. But it seemed that Andrea Cabot had lost the trail after the Everest Eight had entered the hospital. Evie struggled to determine if they were aware that the Eight were no longer there, and eventually decided that they mustn't know otherwise they wouldn't be wasting their time. Then she wondered if all the others had gone to live with family yet, and what would happen if they didn't have any surviving descendants.

Evie vaguely knew that two of the others, like Charles, were living with family, one person suffered from some sort of medical complication and required urgent treatment. She had overheard that at least one of them had been relocated into a hotel until a more permanent home was found for them. The others who were unaccounted for, she had no idea aside from knowing that they weren't in the hospital with the carrot cake any more. Dexter had said they were having problems since death meant their money and estates had been distributed through their wills and returning to life didn't mean they could magically get a refund. Until they worked it out they were like refugees. She supposed some of them might not have next of kin at all, and even if they did, not everyone would be accommodating. She wondered if Charles was glad to have family to live with, even if there was a lot of friction and tension.

A warm hand lightly touched her shoulder, causing Evie to jump in her seat. Roman dropped into the seat next to her and smiled. Evie noticed his dimples and that he smelt of Lynx, and felt herself blush, betraying her thoughts.

"Hey, Evie, how's it going?" Roman had one arm on the back of her chair and leaned towards her, the screen on Evie's phone had caught his attention. Evie was too busy discreetly looking around to check whether she was about to be the victim of another Kendall led humiliation to reply. Evie didn't trust anything or anyone in this school any more.

Roman was so easy to talk to, and one of the kindest people she had ever known, he always had been. Evie was one of many who had liked Roman, but she had been firmly warned off by Kendall, and that was when they had been friends. As far as she knew, Roman and Kendall were good friends. But Kendall wasn't here now. For the first time all day, Evie smiled. Her smile dimmed slightly when she followed his gaze.

"Oh yeah! That's so crazy, isn't it? How they literally came back to life? I wonder where they are. Apparently, they're in London, did you see that?" Roman wasn't deterred by Evie's failure to respond.

Evie could feel the heat as it radiated from her undoubtedly red cheeks. She scanned around her, no one in the vicinity seemed interested in them, so Roman must be talking to her just because he wants to. Evie needed to stop gaping at him and reply like a normal human being, but her heart was pounding, and her mind was blank. She had to concentrate to find something intelligent to say.

"Yeah, it's so mad! I expect they're being well looked after wherever they are. Or they've tracked down the people's descendants and connected them. Or something like that. If they even have any family that is." Evie knew she would keep his attention if she trusted him with her secret about Charles, but she was worried that he would tell other people and it would get back to Kendall who would delight in broadcasting it to the entire school.

"*Hmm*, I didn't think about that. So, if they had family, it would be like their grandchildren probably." Roman was looking straight into her eyes like he was reading her thoughts. His eyes were unusually dark blue.

"Yeah… and their great-granddaughters. Or great-grandsons. There's probably loads of relatives, great-nieces and nephews and cousins and all that." Evie was letting herself get distracted. She had to focus so she didn't reveal anything. She looked down at the table and shook her head slightly.

"That must be so cool! Imagine getting to know your great-grandparents! They'll have seen the World War and lived without technology. I'd never be bored of asking them questions and listening to their stories." Roman was imagining the dream great-grandad which Evie knew to be a false ideal.

"*Hmm*, I don't think it would be like that. That's only if they were kind, storytelling lovely people. In reality, they're strangers. Even though you're related, they might be awful, rude people who don't want to live with you in the first place and resent you because you're not the family he left behind! Or something like that. Maybe that's just how I imagine it, I wonder what we'll do to raise money for our form. Hopefully not a stupid dance or something." Evie didn't realise that her hands were shaking until Roman covered them with his. He was looking into her eyes again, his eyebrows furrowed.

The bell rang, signalling the end of lunch. Roman stood up and the spell was broken. He patted her shoulder and sauntered away, leaving a flustered Evie to gather her books and hurry towards afternoon registration.

The rest of the day was uneventful. Kendall made a joke about losers who lurk in the library to the amusement of the rest of the class, but Evie feigned apathy. She heard Roman admitting he'd been in the library at lunch and his team mates teased him and laughed. Evie appreciated the relief but didn't let it show on her face.

She walked home slowly, desperate to get away from school but reluctant to arrive at her house. Briefly, she considered getting the bus into town to get a dessert to cheer herself up, but the thought of ice cream did nothing to settle her mind.

By the time she got back Evie had a plan; to clean out Toby C and let him have a run around before anyone would be hungry enough to make food, and then to clear off to her room for the night. She knew there was a new film on Netflix that had just been released, and she'd been looking forward to watching it with some chocolate buttons and a cold drink. She figured by the time she'd watched the film, it would be late enough that she wouldn't bump into anyone in the kitchen and she could quickly eat and then escape back to the safety of her room. She was pleased with her plan and hoped it would happen as smoothly as she had imagined.

The house was quiet, Maria and Jason hadn't arrived home from work yet and she had no idea where Tilly was. No music was shaking the foundations of the house, so she assumed her sister hadn't come home yet either.

"Helloooooo!" Evie called into the house. Her voice echoed through the rooms and was met with no reply. Charles must be asleep or maybe even out. With a burst of energy to put her plan into action, Evie gathered what she needed to clean out the rabbit and headed outside, not bothering to grab her routine snack and drink from the kitchen on her way through. She was on a mission, snacking would be for later.

The garden was square-shaped, a combination of grass and patio with conifers lining the perimeter to keep the nosy neighbours away. A discrete gate led to an alley-way behind that Maria liked to call a path. There was various pieces of furniture including a table and chairs, a hammock and a swinging seat. Jason regularly cut the grass but had missed the weekly chore schedule with all the recent upheaval, so the grass was temporarily longer than usual.

Evie gave the garden a cursory glance before settling in front of the double-decker rabbit hutch. A sudden stab of fear caused her heart to contract painfully as she realised that the bottom left door was swinging open, and Toby C was conspicuously absent.

Frantically, Evie stumbled down the garden, eyes darting around as she looked for her fluffy black and white rabbit. The fence behind the conifers was low to the ground but she knew that rabbits could fit into surprisingly small spaces. Her vision became blurry as her eyes filled with tears. She didn't know who to call or what to do beyond searching. She didn't even know where to start looking when he could've escaped in any direction. On her knees, Evie crawled into the long grass, searching through glassy eyes for her beloved pet.

As she strained her eyes to spot his black and white fur amongst the long green grass, she was trying to remember last night when she had fed him. She'd come down after she'd heard her parents go to bed. Starving after only a few mouthfuls of slimy stew, she'd devoured four slices of toast with chocolate spread and a packet of crisps before she'd gone outside to feed Toby C. She recalled how frantic he was when he caught the smell of kale, and she'd quietly laughed as he ate like he was starving. She surely would've locked the hutch door. She always kissed him nine times, which was her lucky number, before she closed him in for the evening. But she had still been upset from what had happened at the table and hurrying before anyone else ventured into the kitchen and crossed paths with her. The guilt was overwhelming, how could she be so careless? Poor Toby C would have been terrified at the mercy of any prowling predators. She would never forgive herself for being so selfish that her sweet baby had paid the price for her carelessness and distracted mind.

The pain in her heart made her want to curl into a ball and never move again, but if there was a slither of a chance that Toby C was alive, that he was out here somewhere, she had to take it. She had to find him no matter what. She was trying to think of who to call, but beyond the vet, she had no ideas. He hadn't been to the vets since his initial vaccinations as Jason refused to pay for the yearly boosters, so there wouldn't be much they could do having not seen Toby C in years. With no one else home, it was solely up to Evie to fix the mess she had so stupidly created.

She was calling Toby C's name and looking under the conifers when behind her, the patio door that led to the kitchen hissed open. For a second, Evie thought it was a cat hissing and blindly reached for the dustpan. A cat is the most likely culprit to have attacked Toby C, followed by a fox or large bird. Evie had to blink a few times when Maria stepped outside, with a squirming Toby C in her arms. Evie was in floods of tears as she ran towards her mother and cradled her shaking rabbit.

"Your great-grandfather was under the impression that rabbits are for pies not kept as pets. He was very surprised when I screamed at him to let go of the rabbit. Now he is furious with me because he fancied rabbit pie and I spoilt it. Apparently, his wife regularly cooked it and it was his absolute favourite. Get a grip, Evie, the rabbit is fine. You are lucky that I got home early, you silly girl. How did you not notice your rabbit was in the kitchen with him? And speaking of the rabbit that hutch stinks, get it cleaned, now." Maria brushed white fur from her black jacket and marched back into the house.

Evie held him for a long time, both of them trembling. Cold sweat ran down her back and her goosebumps didn't go down. She didn't think she'd ever been so frightened.

After Evie had cleaned out Toby C, she spent forty minutes trying to calm him down with soothing words and apologies. He was stomping his foot and grinding his teeth the whole time. It was growing dark by the time she retired to her room. Evie didn't even collect any supper on her way up, she was too angry to see Charles. Her heart would pound every time she imagined what could've happened to Toby. When she finally fell asleep, her cheeks were tear stained and she had dreams that she was running away from a knife wielding man, who wanted to eat her.

Chapter 7

By the following morning, the tension in the house was reaching a boiling point. Evie was actively avoiding Charles. She'd bumped into him in the early hours, seeing him for the first time since he'd attempted to cook Toby C. The worst part was not trusting that he was just being mean. She hoped he wouldn't have harmed Toby C, but she wouldn't bet his life on it.

She'd sneaked downstairs after she'd woken from a horrible nightmare and realised her stomach was rumbling. As she passed the living room where Charles slept, she'd heard his chainsaw snoring, and then all of a sudden he bellowed and the light came on, shining around the edge of the door. It seemed she wasn't the only one plagued by nightmares.

She hurried into the kitchen and was watching the microwave heat a bowl of tomato soup when he materialised in the kitchen behind her. She's been lectured on how delicious rabbit pie was and how ashamed he was that his kin would keep a rabbit caged as a pet. It was all 'shooting his own dinner' this and 'rabbits are vermin' that. Evie had been once again close to tears as she explained that in the twenty-first century, English people didn't really eat rabbits and it was very common to keep them as pets – no different than a dog or cat. She began to explain about free roaming and personality, her voice conveying her passion. Until Charles laughed in her face, and she'd taken her soup and stormed back to her bedroom to hide her tears, resolved once again to stay out of his way.

Every time she thought about how close her sweet rabbit had been from death, she would feel the same panic and anxiety overtaking her body. It was like her throat was closing and she couldn't breathe enough air and she was going to pass out any second. She was determined not to back down on this one, she was used to yielding in arguments and protecting herself from conflict. But if she didn't stand up for poor Toby C, he'd end up on the dinner table and she'd die before letting that happen.

But Saturday, being the first Saturday of October, was the Monroe's monthly pancake day. Evie loved pancakes, she had them with a light sprinkling of sugar, a few drops of lemon juice and a generous drizzling of golden syrup. They were her classic base toppings, and it was optional if she included any other delicacies. Evie's favourites were chopped banana, strawberries and chocolate buttons – not all together though.

Now the dynamic for the pancakes would have to change. Jason was the main pancake chef; he always ate the first one himself 'to test it' and then Evie was second. In day-to-day life, anything ordered went in age order but with pancakes, it was more of a first come, first served situation. And Evie was always ready to be first in line. Then, once all four of them had eaten, the pattern repeated. With the addition of Charles, the line would be even longer. And they would all have fewer pancakes, since the mix was limited. It was a fragile system, that barely worked as it was, never mind adding Charles in the equation.

Evie pulled on her faded pink dressing gown and went down to the kitchen to assume her place in the line. It was more important to eat pancakes than to sulk in her room. She could just ignore all of her family members, but she couldn't ignore her stomach cramps which would have been protesting the lack of pancakes. The ingredients were all out on the kitchen counter but the sizzle of mix being poured into the hot pan was noticeable in its absence, as were her family members.

Evie looked around the empty kitchen and then went to investigate in the living room which was still doubling as Charles' bedroom. Jason and Charles were standing up, facing each other and arguing over how to make a pancake. Before she was noticed, Evie backed out of the room and sat at the kitchen table. She decided to wait rather than get involved.

It was at least twenty minutes later when Jason finally started cooking. He was wound up, slamming cupboard doors and savagely spraying oil as he stared down Charles. It turned out that Charles believed that lard should be used in the frying pan, and the mix should be home made, not from a packet. Evie quietly listened, and ensured that she made no eye contact, lest she be dragged into the argument.

When it was finally her turn, Evie finished her pancake far too quickly, and then had to hover in the kitchen. She held her plate with both hands and studied the tiled floor. If she left the kitchen then she would forsake her place in the queue, but if she stayed, she had to deal with Jason's constant jibes and scornful looks. Charles had taken his pancake into the living room, so all Jason's anger was directed at Evie instead. Only one option resulted in Evie eating, so she squared her shoulders and braved the line. Luckily, that was when Tilly made an appearance, so Jason was distracted by discussing Tilly's weekend plans. Maria had decided to work overtime to make up for the time she took off to go to London, so it was only the four of them in the house.

When the final pancake was plated up and eaten, Jason ordered them all in the living room. Charles clearly did not care for tidiness. There were glasses on the table, each with a different amount of water in, all less than half-full. A jumble of Jason's clothes and coats were piled on the floor next to the closed suitcase, shirts that normally hung neatly in Jason's wardrobe resembled balls. Jason's jaw was clenched as he scanned the room. Evie sat on the edge of the sofa and Tilly leaned against the doorframe. Charles was laying down on the sleeping bag which covered the three-seater sofa and Jason stood in front of the TV.

"Right, Charles. I daresay after finding your feet for the last week you'll be wanting to get some errands done and see the town. New clothes and shoes are a must. You clearly don't respect my property, so I'll be taking it back after it's all been cleaned. I have a great idea, why don't you get the bus to the shopping centre today and get some shopping done?" Jason suggested this like a question, but his eyes laid down a challenge. He wanted Charles out of the house for a few hours. Evie suspected that he'd planned this in advance for a weekend alone.

"Yes, well. While I don't want to be stuck wearing *your* clothes, I also have no idea where to go or even how to shop nowadays. Unfortunately, I haven't even got a new bank account set up yet. I've had these contactless payments explained to me and I don't trust them one bit, what's wrong with cash? I think I'll stay in and catch up on all the Derbies I've missed." Charles danced right around the question and metaphorically squared up to Jason, all the while eating his final rolled up pancake.

"Aha! Well, that's a problem easily solved. I'm sure Evie wouldn't object to being your tour guide for the day. She hangs around the shops enough. And I'll spot you some cash, it was in our emergency fund, but your blatant disregard for my fashionable suits threatens our family's image, which is emergency enough. You have to go, there's no way around it. *Unfortunately*." Jason really wanted a Charles free afternoon. Evie gaped at her father.

"Actually, I had plans for today. Why don't you ask Tilly?" She fired back, inspired by the way Charles spoke to her father.

"*Haha*, as if you have plans, Evie. I'm going back to the beach for the weekend since I had to leave early last month. It's probably the last trip this year before it's too cold. I'm leaving as soon as we're finished here," Tilly smirked at Evie across the room as she spoke. She looked the spitting image of Jason when she smirked like that, it was the only time Evie thought her sister looked ugly.

"Perfect! So, Evie, you can take old gramps here into town, and why don't you get lunch too, and make the whole day of it? I'm sure you're an expert on the food court, *finally* you can offer something useful." Jason and Tilly laughed after Jason finished speaking. Charles was frowning at Jason, unable to refuse the offer. Evie looked down at her clenched hands to hide her pink cheeks.

So, after the dishes were washed and Evie was dressed in unassuming black jeans and a black hoodie, there was nothing to do but to go into town. Charles, having got up and immediately got ready for the day at six a.m., was waiting for her in the hallway. He was wearing the black button up coat and black hat he'd worn the day he arrived from London. He also had on a scarf and gloves, even though it was still mild out. He was absent-mindedly flipping the lid of his pocket watch open and closed, but when he heard Evie coming down the stairs, he dropped the watch into his pocket.

"About damn time! Were you making the clothes yourself?" Charles' tone was stern, but he lacked his signature frown.

Evie didn't bother answering, she just gestured for him to go through the front door which she held open. They walked to the bus stop in silence. Evie scowled at her car, and Charles raised his eyebrow but didn't comment.

The journey was uneventful. Evie was familiar with the

route; it was the same way she went to the dessert place by the martial arts studio. They sat upstairs at the front, Evie stared out the window, watching endless rows of houses morph into a giant blurry terrace as they hurtled past. Charles seemed to be observing the other passengers, noting who was getting on and off. Evie felt the weight of responsibility to make conversation pressing down. Her shoulders hunched under the pressure, but she couldn't be bothered to navigate the minefield that was acceptable topics with Charles.

Once they'd alighted in the town centre, Evie realised that she would have to speak to him and find out where he wanted to go. He hadn't spoken to her since they left the house, though he greeted and thanked their bus driver.

"So… what type of shop do you want to go to?" Evie spoke to the floor between them. She hated standing in the middle of the street and was eager to start shopping so they could go home again. All of the sixth-formers hung out around the shops on the weekends, chatting and flirting and messing around. Not that Evie ever did herself, but she often saw her classmates through the window of the dessert parlour and Tilly had told her about it. Evie glanced over her shoulder, scanning the area before she looked back at Charles. He looked very unsure.

"I… don't seem to be familiar with these shops. Where is the nearest Ethel Austin?" he asked tentatively, he was clearly out of his comfort zone.

"What? I haven't heard of it. What does it sell? Hang on, I'll just Google it. Oh! It went out of business in 2013." Evie looked back to Charles after she finished talking.

"You—you just researched on your little handheld computer. Huh, that's… useful. Well… we can't go wrong with Marks and Spencer's, can we? Check on your computer to see if it is still open!" Charles was taking it all in his stride, but it suddenly occurred to Evie how much of an alien world Charles was living in, where he sees and understands his surroundings but almost everything is new and unfamiliar. Despite all this, he absorbed the new information without blinking and put on a confident front, though Evie suspected his true feelings were lurking underneath and held in a vice like grip until he was safely alone. She knew and recognised the feeling well.

"Yes, good idea. Let's start with M&S. While we're here do you want to look in JD?" Not for the first time, Evie resolved to be kinder to Charles. He didn't make it easy but perhaps that was an even bigger reason to help when he was so clearly struggling and lashing out.

"Don't be ridiculous, we don't need any whiskey! You are too young to be drinking alcohol. I wasn't born yesterday; you can't trick me into buying it for you and your little friends to drink in the park. I won't condone it. Now, put those ridiculous thoughts out of your mind. Where is Marks and Spencer's?" Charles grew more confident as he took the moral high ground.

"This way. And JD doesn't stand for Jack Daniels—" Evie started to explain about trainers and sportswear, but Charles was already striding along the high street. Evie scowled as she hurried after him. He was impossible sometimes.

They spent over an hour in M&S, Charles insisted on trying every article on before he'd commit to buying it. Even if it was the exact same style and size but just a different colour. He ended up with bags of shirts and jumpers and trousers, all very sensible and in neutral colours. They then wasted a good fifteen minutes arguing over whether the slippers he wanted were brown (which is the colour they actually were) or dark green. In the end, Evie had conceded, just to make him let it go and buy them so they could leave the shop.

By the time that he'd paid and they were back on the road, it was fast approaching lunchtime. As they were wandering further down the street, on the lookout for somewhere that sold flat caps, Evie's phone chimed, signalling a text in the family group chat:

Maria: @Evie *Make sure u get smthg nice 4 anniversary meal. Make sure he gets a suit 2. He's not coming if he isn't dressed nice. Not being embarrassed @ steak house. Have transferred u £££. Stay out as l8 as poss plz x*

Evie rolled her eyes, another evening of forced family time. This time, with the addition of Charles and his first meal out in a nice restaurant, Evie expected a disaster. But even so, she would try her best to get him suited and booted. She sighed as she thought about how many hours would be wasted trying on three-piece suits. She was fed up with her role as tour guide, but if she co-operated she'd at least get home as quickly and painlessly as possible.

"Oh, I don't know if my mum told you, but it's their wedding anniversary next Monday. Every year we always go out for a meal. It's always a fancy, dressy place so maybe you can look for a suit or tie or something. I'll look for something new too. Mum *really* likes us to make an effort you see. But let's have lunch first, I am starving!" Evie was conscious to phrase her mother's message more politely. Navigating Charles was like playing with a mine, the slightest pressure could set him off.

"*Hmmm.* Well, it sounds like a waste of money and time to me. I'll expect your mother to pay if she's inviting me. I never saw the point of spending so much when you could buy steak and cook it at home for a fraction of the price. We'll finish our shopping before we stop to eat, if you insist on eating here and you cannot wait until we're back." Charles stopped and peered into the doorway of Hollister, his eyes flicking between the beach front exterior and the gloomy floor within.

"This is a cool place! Very modern of you. It's quite expensive though, it's supposed to be beach vibes, see?" Evie was the difference between Charles stepping into the twenty-first century or being stuck in the past; she had to at least try to educate him.

Charles merely shook his head and continued. Evie was trying to explain shops to him while keeping an eye out for people she knew and also wondering what she could buy for herself that wouldn't make her look absolutely huge. She didn't even know why she tried when she'd be in the same room as Tilly. This was exactly why she didn't go shopping, and she hadn't bought herself any clothes since she'd recently put a few pounds on, so she'd probably have to pick something up otherwise she'd be wearing too small clothes which would only draw extra attention.

They wandered into Matalan and started in the home section, they would do a clockwise loop through the whole shop and end up back at the door and till Evie decided. She turned to inform Charles and paused. He looked quite lost amongst the mountain of homeware. Evie saw him gaping at the brightly coloured towels and novelty shaped ice cube moulds. He scowled as they passed a stand with children's towels that all had various farmyard animals and ABCs.

"Right, we can start with the basics. Bedding and towels and all that, which colour do you like?" Evie asked.

"There is... so much choice. It's all so expensive. What is the difference between them? All I want is cotton. Just cotton," Charles' voice rose barely above a whisper and was only just heard over the pop music being funnelled through speakers that decorated the ceiling alongside the bright strip lights.

"Okay, we can get you cotton. White? Grey? Blue? Patterned? Help me out here," Evie continued. She never knew what the right thing to say would be, and barely knew him so she couldn't even hazard a guess on what he might prefer.

"I don't need much. One towel will do. Blue or something, whatever costs the least really," Charles offered.

After a moment of thinking, Evie dropped two navy towels, a flannel and a hand towel into the basket. She considered picking out some bedding, but then remembered that he slept on the sofa and instead directed him into the men's department.

Charles deliberated for quite a while, marching up and down the aisles several times and inspecting and comparing everything before he chose two pairs of navy pyjamas, aviator sunglasses, several packets of ankle length white socks and some ties.

Evie crossed into the women's section while Charles studied the underwear displays. He really did need everything. Evie wondered if he was choosing things like he'd had before Everest.

She paused to admire a high waisted denim skirt that wouldn't suit her, and she sighed as she sifted through dozens of crop tops on sale, all of them tiny and fashionable. All of them were ridiculously cheap. None of them were styles that she would ever wear.

"Oy! Where's the rest of those tops? Put them down! You're not buying such revealing clothing like that. I'd be ashamed to see you out in a top like that. If you can't choose something proper, I'll have to help find you something more appropriate. Come on." Charles was swinging between a stern, old fashioned father that he used to be and the bewildered man he currently was. He'd caught up with her, and had clearly took himself to the till on the way as he had two huge white bags on either side of him.

"I don't want it anyway. It wouldn't look good on me," Evie said quietly to his back as she followed Charles further into the shop. She'd lost track of what he still needed.

Evie trailed after Charles; she was getting fed up with him bullying her into getting his own way. She was ready to go home, and she didn't care if Maria and Jason wanted them out all day, they could deal with the burden of Charles for a while.

"Excuse me, Miss, might you be able to assist us? I'm looking for a dress for my... companion. I expect it to be at knee length and appropriate for a formal family meal. I don't know what colour would be most suitable," Charles was speaking to one of the sales assistants, who turned to look at Evie. The evil glint in the girl's eyes had Evie unsteady on her feet, with a jolt of panic Evie realised that under the uniform she was looking at Isabel, one of Kendall's sidekicks.

"Of course! Right this way, sir, I have something in mind. We'll find her something suitable, I promise. Have you seen the latest fashion? Appalling, isn't it? I would never go around in those tiny crop tops. And don't get me started on ripped jeans!" Isabel was smiling angelically at Charles, who seemed oblivious to her mocking tone.

Before Evie knew it, she was in a changing room with Charles and Isabel waiting on the other side of the curtain. Both of them were urging her to try on the dress. It was blue, with buttons from the middle up to the collar and it flowed into a tight, knee length skirt. Evie was positive that she'd look like a whale. It seemed small too, though the hanger assured her that it was in Evie's size.

"Do hurry, we still have so much shopping to do, and I want to get it all done and get back as soon as we can, I know your father is awaiting our arrival!" Charles laughed, seeming to snap out of his patronising mood once he started talking to Isabel.

"Charles... I just remembered that I bought something last week, so I won't need a new dress today!" Evie thought her lie was a fool proof way to get out of Matalan. He would take the hint and they could go straight home. She could only relax when she was safely in her room and any potential humiliation had been avoided. This was in a public shop, Kendall wasn't there, and Charles was at the very least an authority figure. Taking several deep breaths Evie assured herself that it'd be okay.

"Nonsense, you can save it for the next occasion. You girls can never have too many dresses! I'll bet your mother seizes any opportunity to show off and go out, so there's plenty of social events in the calendar, am I right?" Every time he spoke it was accompanied by Isabel's irritating high pitched giggle. She was loving this. Evie would bet her life that she was memorising every word to report back to Kendall. Evie knew the gossip in sixth-form would be all about her show off mum and weird grandad who fights with her dad.

"Are you okay in there? Do you need me to help you button it up? The buttons go on the front! The front, okay?" Isabel could barely get her words out without laughing.

"I need the toilet! We'll have to come back later." Evie tried again, not very optimistic that it'd work.

"Well, hurry up then, silly girl! The sooner you try that dress on the sooner we can leave!" Charles was losing his patience, Evie heard it in the flat tone she knew went with an expressionless face. She'd heard it enough this last week. He seemed determined not to show it in front of the shop workers. He would happily slag off the family, but he wouldn't raise his voice in front of a shop worker.

Evie didn't know how else she could avoid it. She was going to have to put the stupid dress on. Charles wasn't going to let them leave until he'd seen her in the dress and wasn't taking the hint. The only other option would be if she walked out, but then she'd be leaving Charles alone in an unfamiliar city and even worse, alone with Isabel. At least if she got it over with, they could leave. Charles was probably causing way more damage out there, so she had to get out of the shop as quickly as possible.

With a loud sigh, Evie pulled the blue menace on, having to tug it down quite firmly to get it over her stomach. Once it was on, she buttoned it up and pulled it into place, where it ended right over her kneecaps. Her legs were uncomfortably stuck together, her thighs rubbing when she moved.

When she reluctantly turned to look in the mirror, her heart was hurting. Tilly would look incredible in this dress, even though it's clearly straight from the 1950s. Tilly could make anything look good with her confidence, though it definitely helped that she was very skilled in how to make herself look naturally stunning with light and make up and also was obsessed with her sports clubs. Whereas Evie made stunning outfits look awkward and uncomfortable. The buttons made the collar like a noose around her neck, and the sleeves dug into her flesh leaving angry red imprints after barely a minute.

She *knew* the dress was a disaster waiting to happen as soon as she saw it. She shouldn't have tried it, barging past them and leaving the shop would've been a better option. Charles could've finished his shopping and she could be feeling better with a pep talk from Oline and a warm cookie dough. She consciously stopped, suddenly aware of the sweat on her brow and the pounding of her heart. She had read online that she needed to actively control her breathing during a panic attack and once she had stopped panicking she could take the awful dress off and leave and then once she felt better she could go home, get into bed and settle down with salted popcorn to watch a film and the day would be over and forgotten.

"Helloooo! Evie? Is everything okay in there? I'll pop in and check on you!" Isabel hadn't finished saying this before she was sliding the curtain across.

"NO! DON'T! Isabel, please! I'm fine—" But Isabel and Charles were peering in at her. Charles' lips compressed into a straight line as he looked at her, the expression uncanny to the one Maria often wore. Isabel's lips quirked up, her eyes widening with undisguised glee.

"Right, take that off, we'll go and find a toilet for you." Charles closed the curtain and could be heard briskly dismissing Isabel.

Evie turned away from the mirror again and struggled to pull the dress back over her head. Her arms were raised towards the ceiling, tangled in the sleeves. She did a little jump and felt her stomach burst from the dress as it scraped slowly upwards and stopped at chest level, but the dress didn't budge beyond that. Evie realised with horror that she had forgotten to undo the buttons in her rush to get it off. Her panic had Evie flailing around, gasping for air as she wrestled with the dress. With a sob, she ripped it over her head, the buttons like claws dragging along her cheeks and leaving red lines. She pulled on her familiar, baggy black clothes and wiped her eyes, before she dumped the inside out dress on the return rail and stalked out, for the first time she walked ahead with Charles hurrying to keep up. He didn't try and talk until they were out Matalan's door and well down the street.

"Ah! Do you know which shop has a toilet in?" Charles ventured, thankfully being tactful for once and not mentioning what had just happened.

Evie couldn't be bothered to explain that she didn't actually need the toilet. If she tried to speak, she'd either scream or burst into tears. She just shrugged. If Charles wasn't such a bully, they wouldn't even be in this situation, he didn't deserve an explanation. He is as much an enemy as Kendall and her group are.

"Look, toilets this way. It makes sense, this is the entrance to the food court. Shall we get lunch while we're here? My treat." His sudden niceness and effort unnerved Evie.

"I'm not hungry. We can just go home," Evie mumbled to her shoes.

"Well, I am. Pancakes never fill anyone up. Wow, there are so many choices! What's your favourite? I'm partial to a burger." Charles was trying to be especially chatty to compensate for Evie's uncharacteristic silence. They were basically swapping roles, all of a sudden Evie saw how much easier it is to say nothing when emotions are so high.

"I don't care," Evie eventually muttered.

"Okay then. You find us some good seats and I'll get some food!" With a nod, Charles strode over to the counters.

Evie could see a group of people she knew eating ice cream by the fountain. She turned away and chose seats as far away from them as she could get without leaving the building. She ended up sitting with her back to them, though every now and then a whoop or burst of laughter reached her, reminding her how close they were.

"Hope you like it, I got two of what I wanted." Evie jumped as Charles appeared, she hadn't noticed him picking his way through the court over to her table in the corner.

He slid into the seat opposite her, depositing a tray of food on the table between them. The shabby red tray held two chicken burgers, large fries, banana milkshakes and two caramel ice creams. Evie was astonished when she realised that Charles had ordered them not only her favourite comfort food, but that he was the only other person she knew who also liked banana milkshakes.

"I—thank you. This is exactly what I usually order!" She smiled, forgetting her annoyance in her surprise, and Charles looked pleased to have made progress with her.

They tucked into their meal, alternating between big bites of burger and handfuls of salty chips, with sips of milkshake regularly. They didn't talk, they were far too busy eating, but for the first time that day, it was a companionable silence, with almost no awkwardness.

Evie was starting to relax, the day was almost over and despite the dress fiasco, it wasn't the worst day she had ever had, not by far. Most days in sixth-form were far more horrible, and at least going out with Charles was a slight improvement over any time spent with Jason.

Now it was over, she was just glad to be out of Matalan. And she had a banana milkshake which she didn't usually get to have. It was fine. Not great, obviously, but the damage was limited. She was in the changing room where it's illegal to have any sort of cameras. As she felt her shoulders sag and her muscles untense, Evie realised how on edge she had been, she caught Charles' eye as he observed her over the top of his milkshake and gave him a small but genuine smile.

She was just trying to decide whether to take Charles to the dessert parlour and introduce him to the world's tastiest ice cream creations before they headed home when she spotted Kendall making a beeline towards Evie's quiet corner of the room, entourage in tow.

Evie carefully placed her half-empty milkshake onto the table, her knuckles were white, and her hands had started shaking. She reluctantly raised her eyes towards the impending storm, feeling suddenly as though all the banana potato chicken in her stomach was moments away from exploding out of her mouth. Charles had been watching Evie, but when she looked up, he followed her gaze. The approaching girls, who he would judge to be around Evie's age, were smiling at him and seemed to be altogether ignoring Evie.

Evie sat there, mind racing. She considered bolting like she wished she'd done in the changing room earlier, but that would leave a clueless Charles alone with Kendall. It would be worse to not know what was being said, so she remained seated. Kendall zeroed in on them like a predator stalking its prey, eyes on the prize and relentless.

"Oh, hi! I'm Kendall, I'm a family friend of the Monroes! I don't think I've met you before, what relation are you to Evie? I didn't think she had any living Grandads." Kendall smiled winningly and didn't even glance in Evie's direction. Evie tried to silently stifle her outrage, or risk letting Kendall know how much she gets under Evie's skin with such little effort. How dare Kendall claim to be a family friend when all she does all day is torment Evie? If Tilly wasn't close to Katie, then there would be no connection whatsoever between the two families. Kendall had made it very clear over the last few years that she's washed her hands of any association with Evie, she has absolutely no business nosing around now when she thinks there's some dramatic family secret or gossip.

Evie looked at Charles and tried her best to discretely convey her despair to him. Depending on what Charles said, this could get very ugly. There was a very important reason why she had to keep her new relative a secret, and Kendall would be ecstatic to expose her. Charles seemed to be thinking carefully, his eyes flicking between Evie and the girls. The other girls who accompanied Kendall were smirking and whispering, no doubt insulting Evie's slow grandad.

"No. It's none of your business, girl. It has occurred to me that if you were chums with Evie and her family then you would've greeted her, rather than immediately question me. You kids run along now, Evie and I have somewhere to be," he spoke calmly, but his eyes were narrowed, and the end of his speech sounded like a challenge. Evie struggled to hide a smile; it was nice to be on the other side of Charles' barbed comments for a change.

"Your *friend* is really rude, Evie. Oh, don't forget that it's *dress down* Monday. It would be a shame for you to be *stuck* wearing boring formal clothes. Roman says hi by the way." Kendall sauntered away, flicking her hair over her shoulder as if she hadn't just been put in her place by Charles.

"That showed her, didn't it! Not one of your school pals I assume?" Evie shook her head in response and Charles was beaming, it was a miracle that he had read the situation correctly and defended Evie. He probably felt bad for upsetting her before, but that incident was almost forgotten about in light of the latest Kendall confrontation.

"Nope, one of my enemies more like. It's strange though, we only have dress downs on Fridays at the end of term, I didn't think there was one on Monday. Maybe it's a charity thing." Evie had no idea what Kendall was talking about, but she suspected that it was something sneaky. She dragged a chip through the tomato sauce while she thought on it.

Chapter 8

They finished their food in companionable silence, Evie robotically ate while she worried about what Kendall had said. She finished the rest of her meal without paying too much attention and had to physically shake herself to focus when she realised her chips were finished.

"Right, are you ready?" Charles asked as soon as he reached the end of his milkshake.

"Yeah, all done. Thank you for lunch. Shall we head home now?" Evie asked, she cleared their wrappers and they left via the closest exit, avoiding any further run-ins with anyone she knows.

"I think that's a good idea. I never enjoyed shopping at the best of times, your great nana, she used to leave me at home when she went. To be frank, I am at my mental limit for new things today. Let's quit while we're ahead," he told her.

On the bus, he kept on rubbing his temples like his head was hurting him. The words 'information overload' came to Evie's mind.

"Another time, you could try online shopping. Once you've got a bank account sorted that is. You can do it from home and arrange to get it delivered for a small fee. You can actually pay extra for next day delivery if you wanted to. But now you've confirmed your size, maybe you can get the rest of your stuff online. It's harder because you don't get to try on or inspect the clothes but it's very convenient," Evie said, trying to recall the instructions she'd been given by Dexter about how to check if Charles seemed overwhelmed and how much technology she can safely introduce him to.

He'd seemed interested in online shopping and how next day delivery worked, wondering out loud how the logistics worked to get items from warehouses around the country to their door in one day. She stopped there though, so as not to overload him with too much new information in one go. He'd still not gotten his head around the concept of the internet, and the convenience of Google. Small steps, she reminded herself.

The sun had surpassed its highest point and began a gentle descent by the time they had arrived home. Evie let them into the empty house and breathed a sigh of relief when she locked the door behind them.

"Have Maria and Jason gone out do you think?" Charles asked, standing formally in the hallway, still wearing his hat and coat and carrying all of the bags.

"Err, I don't know. Their cars are here, so they're probably around," Evie said with a shrug.

After a short investigation, they found Jason and Maria sprawled out on sun loungers in the garden. Jason pointedly looked at his watch and then at Evie, his stern look promised a discussion later.

Neither of Evie's parents enquired about how the shopping trip went or if they'd had a lovely day, so they went back into the house in silence. Charles deposited his new clothes on the floor at the bottom of the stairs and turned to Evie.

"Thanks for today, kiddo! It wasn't too bad after all, hey?" He was as upbeat as Evie had ever seen him.

"Yeah, I had a nice day. In the end." Evie was cautious in her answer. She hadn't forgotten the dress fiasco that quickly.

Though she was cautiously optimistic about her relationship with Charles, she didn't want to push her luck.

"I've got to finish some homework, so I'll catch you in a bit!" Evie smiled when she'd finished talking and started backing up the stairs.

"Okay, well, you come on down when you've finished, and we'll see if we can't watch some television or play a board game. Or whatever the youth of today do for enjoyment." With that, he wandered back into the living room.

Evie went up to her room and lay down on her bed. All in all, the day wasn't a total disaster. Maybe Charles had even realised that he shouldn't be so bossy, and he might start behaving like a proper great-grandad. He had overstepped, but if he learnt a lesson from it then Evie could let it go and move on as long as it never happened again.

Feeling more motivated than she had in weeks, Evie opened her laptop and started a review of a film she'd watched right before the whirlwind storm that was Charles and the Everest Eight had swept across her life. In just a week, her life had become the plot of a sci-fi film. As well as the mundane chores like homework, cleaning Toby C and working on new posts for her blog, she had welcomed her great-grandad into her life. Although she was cautious to admit it, she felt like a little bit of progress had been made today. If she was careful, she might be on the road to a relationship with her great-grandad.

Luckily, she always took notes on any important points she wanted to later explore, and with the film *'It Chapter 2'* playing on a tab on her screen with the Word document taking the other half, it was as if no time had passed since she'd watched it. She felt a blanket of calm settle around her, she really enjoyed writing, and as the word count steadily increased and paragraphs became pages, Evie felt the bliss of doing what she loves spread through her body. Writing was the only time she felt happy and confident, her blog was written under a pseudonym, so she didn't have any pressure or judgement. She had a few hundred followers who debated and discussed her reviews with her. Not super successful and well known, but Evie preferred having a smaller group of people where almost all of them interacted with her and read her reviews rather than have thousands but only a fraction of them actually cared. When she was on the blog, it was like she was surrounded by friends, she probably spoke more to some of her strongest virtual supporters than to her own family some weeks.

Once the review was finished and Evie had proofread it and uploaded it onto her blog with a preface apologising for the delay in posting, she put her laptop away and realised her burgundy nails had chipped beyond the point of repair. Evie removed the colour and re-painted, in no rush so she let the coat dry properly before starting the next one.

The film had run through and started again, she half-watched as she wondered if she should see if Charles wanted to watch a film with her. He might even want to go to the cinema, although she had no idea what genre he liked. Or if he'd even know what the cinema was. She quickly searched it and learned that the first public film show in the UK was in 1896. While he might be familiar with the concept of going to watch films in public spaces, he would surely be surprised to learn of 3D showings, luxury reclining chairs and high definition screens. After some thought, she decided to put the idea on the back burner for a little bit, so as not to shock him too much. She wondered if any of the Eight had been to the cinema yet.

As her thoughts drifted to the Everest Eight, she remembered the E8Updates page. Unable to resist the temptation, she searched it. It was a compulsion to look, she knew she should stay away, and she probably wouldn't like it, but she still clicked on the page.

The homepage only had facts, and links to trustworthy sources, or as trustworthy as anyone hoped the news would be. The information was the same as what the news outlets had reported and had verified. Each update had an option to comment, and the last update was a link to the familiar face of reporter Andrea Cabot. Evie followed the link, tumbling further down the rabbit hole every time she clicked.

"To recap, the Eight received specialist care and treatment for an unknown time period and are believed to have been moved from a facility in London to a new, so far undisclosed location. Thank you to everyone who called the hotline with tips, and a special thank you to our most passionate audience members who could be investigative journalists! So, the question now is: where are they? Many are keeping their eyes peeled in their communities to try and find the Eight. We had expected they would be interviewed, their harrowing turned miraculous stories shared, and their identities revealed, but so far any attempt to work out who the Eight are, remain in vain. I have a list of every person who has lost their life trying to conquer Earth's highest mountain. But narrowing that down to just Eight individuals is virtually impossible. As soon as anything is confirmed, I'll be live on your screens. Until then, remember to call in with any sightings and have an *ice* rest of your day!" The reporter laughed, unable to deliver the last line seriously and then the video was cut off before any other news began.

It had only been posted six hours earlier, but already had comments in four digits. Evie scrolled, scanning each comment as they slowly slid up her screen. Some of them seemed like curious people, asking genuine questions and wondering what was going on. But amongst them, the trolls were demonstrating the dark, twisted potential the internet offered for nasty and cruel people to voice their own opinions. It seemed the public opinion of the Eight, which started off very positive as the media heavily influenced the Eight moving out of the London hospital quickly, was starting to turn. Paranoia and suspicion were running rampant.

Every person who wanted to offer a comment had to make a profile, and when they posted, a screen name of their choosing would accompany their comment. At least it wasn't completely anonymous, Evie dreaded to think what some people would say if that was the case. Even so, she shivered as she read through the most recent comments under the link. Evie refreshed her screen and even more comments appeared on the screen.

Mermaid.Seahorse1411: I think one of the Eight has moved to my community and joined my church. An elderly man came in, and even though it's a bit windy, the weather is still warm – it's only just October – so of course my suspicions were raised when he was wearing a winter coat complete with a hat and scarf. I told him I was praying for him, and no I will not release his location, these people deserve privacy!

Getoffmytail11: Give me the list. I'll find them and send them straight back to the afterlife where they belong.

C.Norris135: I'll join u. Pm me deets. I'll b there to right this wrong.

WilliamKay0904: I'll pay anyone 2 grand cash for their locations. No questions asked, serious ppl only. I'm sorting this problem once and 4 all.

RoaringJaz3: Hi guys, if you want to earn money from anywhere with flexible hours, message me for more deets. I did it and I never looked back, now I can afford a new Rolex every week.

WirralAlien194: I saw someone in Tesco buying Kendal

Mint Cakes. Coincidence? I don't think so!

RabbitMama1: Leave them alone, go back to bed and wake up with some empathy all you internet warriors xo

She ended up closing the page in disgust, and promised herself she would try to stay away, it only upset her to see what strangers were saying. She had only just turned her laptop off when her phone started flashing with notifications. Evie leaned over to her phone, expecting an email with a promotion from a restaurant, or maybe one of the shops inviting her to autumn sales. Seeing that she had been tagged in an Instagram story was like having a bucket of icy water thrown over her. This could only be bad, she never normally got tagged in anything, especially not by Kendall.

Evie had an overwhelming urge to throw her phone, to get it away from her. If she wasn't holding her phone, then she could have a little more time of ignorance. But now she knew that she had been tagged in a post, she had to see what it was.

Before she opened Instagram, she took a deep breath, trying to control her panic. She kept on thinking of what Kendall had said earlier, '*It's dress down Monday… It would be a shame for you to be stuck*'. Everything clicked together, Kendall's friend working in Matalan, Kendall barely repressing a laugh when she'd said, '*dress down*' and '*stuck*'. Kendall must have heard about the dress incident and had posted something on Instagram. Evie was frantically praying that it wouldn't be a picture. Anything but a picture. She hadn't seen Isabel with a camera or phone but that didn't mean much.

Evie was staring at her phone, her thumb hovering over the icon for the social media app but not quite touching. Her chest rose and fell quickly as she clung to the safety of not knowing. Before she had the chance to look for herself, she received a text from Tilly.

Tilly: *Evie! Really? Why would you possibly try and get that on. It was obviously too small dummy. You're delusional. Everyone at the beach is laughing at you and by default me. Nice one [thumbs down emoji]*

Evie felt numb. Once again, she was the victim of one of Kendall's cruel pranks. Isabel must have seized the opportunity to switch the hangars, knowing there was no chance the dress would fit Evie. Then all she had to do was wait and watch the drama unfold. If only Charles hadn't forced her to try on that stupid dress then it wouldn't have happened in the first place. She knew it wouldn't suit her. And she thought that it had looked small. Evie didn't know what was worse, her disgust with herself for not being assertive enough, her hatred for Kendall or her frustration at Charles. Two of those were feelings she couldn't or wouldn't do anything about.

She reported the story to Instagram as quickly as she could, the glimpse she had of the photo was enough for her to confirm how awful it was. Evie just hoped it would be taken down before too much damage could be done. She didn't hold her breath though. Then she deleted her account and removed the app from her phone. She'd be far better off without social media. She then turned her phone off, blocking out the virtual world and just lay on her bed. Too fed up to try and cheer herself up, she simply wallowed in her despair.

At dinner that evening, Evie glared into her green beans. The four of them were eating the roast beef which had been cooking all afternoon. She had no idea who had cooked it, and didn't care enough to find out, it was the least of her worries. Tilly was still at the beach having an amazing time and showing everyone how different she is from her weirdo delusional sister, at least according to Evie's imagination.

Evie couldn't contain her anger; she slammed her cutlery and emitted hostile vibes in every direction. Maria, looking tanned and relaxed, finally asked about their day, seemingly oblivious or apathetic to her youngest daughter's emotional turmoil.

"Me and Evie had a great—" Charles managed the first few words before Evie exploded.

"Absolutely awful. In fact, one of the worst days of my life!" Evie spat, not feeling anything but scorn when she saw Charles' smile fade into a mixture of sadness and shock.

"I know you didn't like that girl in the shop but that's a bit dramatic, Evie. We had a lovely lunch in the end—" Charles was out of his depth and clearly signalled to Jason and Maria for some help.

"Sweetie, don't be so dramatic. You girls are always fighting and making up." Maria poured gravy as she spoke, not even fully focused on Evie. Jason didn't even look up from his plate.

"You have literally no idea. At all. If I was Tilly right now, you'd both care!" Evie wouldn't normally have dared to speak to her parents so bluntly. But spending the day with Charles and his brutally honest thoughts had riled her up.

"Evie! Don't speak to your mother like that! Finish your dinner and go up to your room. She can come back when she's going to be a civilised adult and apologise to us all! Speaking to her mother like that, the cheek!" Jason finally contributed to the conversation, he predictably bulldozed in, blamed Evie and then started speaking about her in third person.

"None of you care! Did you become the neighbourhood joke today? Are you *dreading* going to school on Monday? Has anyone posted the worst picture you've ever seen of yourself on Instagram?" Evie was so angry that she was upset. Her voice was shaking and her eyes tearing as she spoke to Charles, the only one who hadn't dismissed her.

She didn't wait for a response. Throwing her knife and fork so they clattered on the plate, she got up and ran from the room. Behind her, there was a pause before Charles spoke. Once she was out of sight, she paused to listen.

"What on Earth is an Instagram?"

"Oh, don't worry, Evie is always crying about something or another. She'll sulk in her room and then sheepishly come back when it's time for her next meal." Maria laughed, and Jason noisily added some mint sauce to his beef, the spoon hitting the side of the dish every time.

"Grandad, make sure you don't forget our anniversary meal is on Monday. I booked the table, and the taxis are arranged. You did get something today, didn't you? I told Evie you needed a nice suit," Maria continued as if Evie hadn't just fled the room. Evie started quietly making her way to the stairs. She could still hear them talking.

"No, I didn't quite manage to find anything suitable. I'll check on her after I've eaten. Maybe take her a cup of tea, Evelyn always needed a comforting hot drink when she was all het up," Charles offered. Evie paused on the stairs to see what response he would get. Neither of her parents responded, Evie imagined Maria's raised eyebrows and ran the rest of the way to her room, slamming her door.

As the slam ricocheted around the room, Evie realised her nail varnish, despite the care and letting them air dry, had smudged.

Chapter 9

"Evie? It's me. Ah! It's Charles, your great-grandfather. Can I join you? I've brought you a cup of tea and some Jaffa Cakes. They sure have changed the recipe since I last had some." Charles was on the landing, knocking on the door with his foot.

Evie was in her room, the lights off and the curtains closed. She had hardly moved since leaving the kitchen earlier. She was all cried out and couldn't muster the energy to be nice to him and pretend that she was okay.

"Evie? I'm coming in." Before she could protest Charles had nudged the door open and took a couple of steps into her room. "I can hardly see you, put a light on for me, will you? Even if you don't want to talk to me you'll want one of my speciality cuppas, and it's no use if I spill it all over the floor because I can't see is it?"

Evie sighed so he knew what an inconvenience he was being before she flicked on her bedside lamp. The dim lighting revealed her swollen eyes and shaking shoulders. She watched as he placed a mug and a plate of biscuits by the lamp. He paused after he stood up straight, waiting.

"Thanks," Evie said in a flat voice.

"This is interesting bedding. Very fancy and frilly," Charles said, after looking around the room.

"I didn't choose it. It's Tilly's old bedding. I get the stuff she discards; it's always been that way," she replied moodily.

"I see. Look, I don't really know what has happened, I don't understand this technology stuff but I'm sorry about the Matalan incident. I realise that fashion has changed and you're not my daughter so if you want to wear a half top then it's not my place to disapprove. If you want we can go back there, and you can have a proper browse. And perhaps I can buy some more of those socks that I liked." Charles bowed his head as Evie took a sip of the tea, while she organised her thoughts.

"Anyway, you're the first person I've made my speciality tea for since right before Everest. I hope it's good?" Charles ventured to break up the growing silence.

Evie looked up suddenly, temporarily forgetting her anger with the unexpected topic shift to Everest. As far as she knew, Charles hadn't discussed it with anyone.

"It's really good. Thanks. Who... who did you last make the tea for?" Evie asked.

"So, I might be a little rusty. I added a little honey, it's my secret ingredient!" Charles evaded the question but was slightly nodding.

"It's very nice, thank you. It might even be the best tea I've ever had!" Evie trailed off. Charles was gazing into Evie's floor as if he could see right through it to the very core of the planet. He didn't speak for a long moment.

"I'm glad. I do feel rather guilty, I don't quite understand what the problem is, but I do recognise that I caused you a problem. I do also hope that you will forgive me and allow us to move on and perhaps pick up where we left off after lunch?" Charles spoke very formally and carefully.

"Look, I appreciate the tea. It's a lovely gesture, and no one has made tea for me before, so it is nice. But you created an awful situation for me, that I wouldn't have had to deal with otherwise. And you overstepped a boundary. It's not okay, and I need some space. My whole school is laughing at me, and that girl you asked for help is one of my enemies and she somehow took a photo of me stuck in that horrible dress. And now everyone has seen it. Do you understand or recognise how awful it will be for me in school now? It is going to be worse than normal, and it's normally pretty crap. You have ruined everything, whether maliciously or not, and despite all the apologies in the world. So," Evie trailed off. She realised Charles was still staring at the floor, and he showed no sign that he had heard her words.

All of a sudden, he sat down on the end of her bed, slumping like a puppet with severed strings. He looked very fragile, without his pride making his shoulders square. Evie took a deep breath and pushed aside her own feelings as she leaned towards him, gingerly putting her hand on his shoulder. Up close, she could see the deep wrinkles on his face and that his eyes were glassy. He didn't acknowledge her hand, but he also didn't shrug her off. She realised he was holding his pocket watch, running his thumb over the top where the duck was engraved.

"I am truly sorry. It will not happen again," Charles murmured at last.

"I forgive you. It's not entirely your fault. It's Isabel and Kendall's fault and my own too. I'm still upset though, even though I accept your apology it doesn't magically erase everything else," Evie replied, her voice gentle. Something about him, and the fact that he'd cared enough to check on her, softened her anger, blunted it until she made an effort to explain to him what had happened.

"I-I wonder if I can ask a favour of you. I don't deserve it, but if you are kind enough to listen I would like to tell you a story about my own Evelyn, and the last time I saw her. If you wouldn't mind terribly," Charles spoke with his head bowed still, his fingers white around the watch as he held it.

"Of course. I would be honoured. Take your time," Evie eventually replied as she overcame her shock.

"There is something that has been weighing heavily on my mind. Perhaps your words just then were a sign to me. You see, I dream of it and wake up in a panic every night without fail. In the dead of the night, it's easy to forget that the sun will eventually rise again. I think if I share it, perhaps the burden will ease a little, and allow me to steal some sleep this evening. This is it. The last thing she said to me. The final words I ever heard from my brilliant daughter were '*Dad, you have ruined everything! I hate you!*' Charles indicated Evelyn's words with air quotes, his voice wavered as he spoke.

"I didn't realise, I didn't mean it. I was being dramatic; you obviously didn't ruin *everything* for me. She probably didn't mean it either, in fact I'm sure she didn't." Evie tripped over her words, horrified by the words she had unwittingly chosen which would hurt Charles the most.

"Don't fret, duck. I know you didn't intend them. It was the morning I was flying out to Nepal; I was furiously packing and had a million things on my mind. You can imagine how much I had to do. I was always a last minute packer, and I always forgot something on the day but I never learnt from it. But that day, I'd argued with Evelyn. She didn't want me to go and the night before she didn't come home. She was at some boy's house," Charles trailed off, lost in his memories. Evie patted his shoulder and leaned back, settling to wait as he wrestled with his mind.

"She'd come home at dawn, boldly knocking on the front door. We rowed until breakfast and then she stormed out. I didn't have time to chase her. She was supposed to come and wave me off, but she didn't, and I had a plane to catch. I never thought she wouldn't come and wave me off. I must've truly upset her. Even if I wanted to, how would I find her? She didn't carry around a mobile telephone, no one did back then. I didn't even know the name of the boy! She was better than that, she could've done anything she put her mind to. But she'd put her mind to fighting me and somehow that correlated to her rebelling and punishing me by staying out and ageing her mother and I ten years from the worry. She was everything I could ask for in a daughter. I just didn't want her getting distracted when she had school exams coming up. She was so intelligent; she could have gone to university. Maybe I was overbearing, that's what my Margaret told me, but I only wanted what was best for her. I loved them both more than anything, but I don't think they knew it." Charles had his head bowed still, but he'd flipped the pocket watch open and his silent tears dripped on to the face of it. Evie spied the engraving on the watch, able to see it properly for the first time. If she wasn't so stunned by the story, she would've been taken aback by the intricate details of the duck. She could not imagine why he would have chosen a duck of all things.

Evie didn't know what to say. She'd heard about Everest; she knew the story of how her nana Evelyn had got pregnant young and raised Maria alone after both her parents passed away. But she had never heard this part of the story. The pause stretched for so long that Evie didn't know if Charles had anything more to say.

"It's my biggest regret. I should've listened to Evelyn, and every second of every day since my heart started beating again it has ached for my wife and daughter. And it hurts, it hurts because the last words I exchanged with my beautiful, smart, kind daughter were unforgivable. I won't repeat them, those words will never cross my lips again. But when I go to sleep every night, in the dark and quiet, I hear myself shouting at her, calling her nasty names and implying terrible things. It is my punishment to relive my worst days, in exchange for this extra time. You may

118

judge me for this, but I told you because I want you to know that one of my flaws is being over protective, and I know it's not my place and I'm working on it. But perhaps you'll view today's events a little differently. And know that I am sincere in my apology, I have learnt the hard way the risk of not making amends and leaving it too late."

By the time he finished, Evie was also crying. Lately, she had cried so much for herself, but now she cried for Evelyn who lost her dad and probably regretted everything she said and did that night too. She cried because it was so unfair, that Charles has a second chance but was cheated out of his reconciliation. They cried together; their thoughts of family members long gone.

Chapter 10

After Charles' confession on Saturday night had struck deep in her heart, she viewed the events in Matalan through a different lens. She had forgiven him but still had to deal with the fallout of his actions.

She had pretended it was no big deal, long after he'd made them both fresh cups of his special tea and they had talked of non-important things and bonded over him sharing his sorrow. She might understand him a little better now, it was easy to lash out at those around you when you're hurting so much. And easier still to push the people around you away when they have everything he didn't have and didn't seem to care. It explained why he hates Jason so much, who has two daughters and consistently fails to shower them in love and support.

Nonetheless, Evie had never dreaded anything more than she dreaded going to school on Monday morning. She had checked the school website and there was nothing about a dress down fundraiser, so she selected a black blazer and wore a light pink blouse with black pants. The sixth-form was supposed to wear work style clothes, and Evie decided she would dress professionally and feign deafness all day. She'd done it before. The only good thing is that after she reported the photo, she'd been emailed to say that it had been taken down shortly after being posted. She wasn't foolish enough to hope no one saw it, but she prayed that the damage was at least limited.

She briefly crossed paths with Charles, who had been

lurking by the front door. Neither of them spoke of last night, but he wished her a good morning and that she'd have a lovely day in school. She'd given him a tight smile before she left the house.

Evie walked to school, each step harder as her feet felt as though they were encased with concrete. Everything was hard, her breath was laboured, and her steps slowed until she had stopped entirely. The world continued to spin, buses and cars passed her, the wind danced through trees, making the newly orange leaves twirl down to the ground and carpet the pavement. Above her, grey clouds gathered, threatening rain.

She stood there, trying to immerse herself in her surroundings to settle her racing heart and mind so she could continue. Evie was taking deep breaths, inhaling the damp scent of mud and exhaust fumes. She breathed slowly until she could regain control of her body and start shuffling towards school, her stop making her dangerously close to being late.

Evie kept her head down and hurried straight to her form room. The only benefit of being late was that most people had already gone into their rooms so mercifully the corridors were quiet. She had walked behind a trio of year eleven girls for the last few minutes of the journey and felt sure they were talking about her. Before they crossed the road to the school, all three had looked back, making eye contact with Evie and whispering to each other. They'd laughed loudly as they walked into school and disappeared to the toilets. Evie knew the worst was yet to come and steeled herself.

When she reached her form room, the door was propped open, which allowed her to slip in and sit at the desk closest to the door. She saw Mr Scott nod in her direction as he read out the daily notices and room changes for the school.

Evie was focusing intently on her planner, not reading

anything on the page but feigning that she was busy. All her actions were charades, as she pretended to be fine, to be unaffected. At this point, she should probably look into pursuing a career in acting. She had one hand on the strap of her bag, ready to dart out of the room at the earliest opportunity and outrun the inevitable nasty comments.

"So, you'll need to think about what our form is going to do for the fundraiser. Not to give you an advantage in this inter-school competition, but apparently there have been a lot of non-uniform days and cake sales suggested. I know we can be a little more creative though. There may be a friendly bet going around the teachers too, so don't let me down. Now, we're a little early so for the last five minutes why don't you guys talk amongst yourselves and share ideas. At the end of the week, I want an idea on paper, including how we can realistically do it." Mr Scott retreated to his desk in the corner of the room and started swigging water as he checked his phone.

Evie doodled circles in her planner as she waited for the bell. She flipped to the back and saw the lists she'd made to keep busy while she was waiting for her family to come home from London. It seemed like so long ago but had only been a matter of weeks. Evie scribbled over her words, trying not to listen but managing to eavesdrop on several conversations going on around her.

In front of Evie were three people. She knew their names but rarely spoke to them as they didn't share any classes.

"It must be true, they're in the country. And we wouldn't be fundraising for a hoax. My only idea is if we have a cake sale. It's classic right? Can't go wrong with some rice crispy cakes, Victoria sponge, brownies. Do you want to go to the shop at break? I really want some brownies now."

"Yes, brownies for lunch! My mum is a nurse and she said if

it is real, they'd be all messed up. I wish we knew who they were. Why are they hiding? It's pretty suspicious if you ask me."

"Okay guys, hear me out, instead of a cake sale, an ice cream sale!"

"And how would the ice cream not melt? That wouldn't work."

One of the girls looked up and made eye contact. The girl looked her up and down until Evie looked away. To her left, though she didn't want to look and betray her interest, was a group of rugby boys including Roman.

"Charity game of rugby. Easy," one of them said and was rewarded with cheering from the rest of the team until their form tutor ordered them to settle down.

"How would it work though? Maybe each team contributes money to play in a tournament, but we'd have to be careful. If they're inexperienced it's a recipe for injury or an accident. The girls only play tag rugby right? So maybe a tag tournament so everyone is included." Even if Evie hadn't recognised the voice, she would have identified Roman from his thoughtful consideration.

Evie glanced at him and saw that he was looking right at her. She flinched and looked away, but not before she saw him smile at her. Evie was starting to slowly uncoil, the tension just slightly less than before. So far, so good. No mention of it.

"So gross!"

"It makes me sick to the stomach honestly!"

Evie fought a shiver as she heard Isabel's voice, closely followed by Kendall's. Without a shadow of a doubt, Evie knew it was all about to come out.

"I couldn't believe it; I wouldn't have believed it unless I saw it with my own eyes – Evie Monroe has a boyfriend and he's like an old man," Kendall spoke again, and most of the class turned to Kendall, eager to hear the juicy gossip.

"You what?" one of the rugby boys asked, earning a frown from Roman.

"You heard. It's totally disgusting. She was eating dinner just her and him, and they were leaning in towards each other. Isabel actually saw them in Matalan, he was buying all this stuff for her and was dictating what she could wear. I'm sure you've all seen what a state she got into in the changing rooms. Lying about our dress size to impress a creepy old man are we, Evie?" By the time Kendall had finished talking, Evie had left the room, as she walked away she could hear the buzzing of conversation as Kendall's speech was discussed, and the sharp tones of the teacher as he tried to control the class. Evie knew it was far too late.

The only good thing was that they were doing practice papers in maths, so apart from some leers and stares, nothing was said to Evie. She had hidden until the start of class where she'd slipped in and sat by the door again, she'd half-heartedly written a few answers down, but spent most of the double lesson watching the clock. She exited quickly as soon as the lesson had ended. Just one more lesson until lunch, she thought with a savage determination as she made her way to her film class.

By the time Evie was on her lunch break, it seemed as though the whole school was whispering about her, making judgments that were the opposite of the truth. But she couldn't put the lies straight, so walked straight past the lunch room, and instead of turning to go into the library where it would at least be quiet, she carried on straight. She walked faster, almost jogging until she reached the office door. Within seconds she'd waltzed through and was out the door before anyone could question her.

She hurried down the road until school was out of sight, where she ducked into a bus stop and collapsed on the seat.

Her tears rolled fast down her cheeks, and she cried because she hadn't been strong enough to endure some silly rumours, and once again she had no power to stand up for herself. She couldn't explain who Charles actually was, even if she wanted to confront Kendall. She had run away, and apart from the fact that she would get into trouble for walking out, she was ashamed when she thought of them all in form, noticing her absence and knowing they had won.

Evie wasn't sure how long she quietly cried in the bus stop, but when she heard a bus approaching, and saw the indicator, she roughly wiped her cheeks and ducked out. She glanced back to see the bus pause, no one had gotten off, and no one was waiting to get on. And after a moment of waiting, the driver pulled away again, as Evie continued her walk home.

"You're home," Charles said, startling Evie as she shrugged her blazer off. He must've heard the key in the lock and hurried into the hall to check who had unexpectedly arrived home early. "Are you okay? You're not sick or anything?" he asked.

"I'm fine, as in I'm in good health. You won't catch anything don't worry." Evie snipped back.

"That's not what I meant, and you know it." Charles discarded the caring tone in a flash. "And even if it was, I do have a right to know if someone in this house has an illness, my immune system has been dormant for almost fifty years, so it is important for me to know if there's an increased risk of me catching anything. Not that you'd know since you spend most of your time sulking upstairs and playing the victim when your dad is on a rampage. There's a lot you don't know," he concluded as he paused to examine Evie.

"I know! I know and I'm sorry *again*! I've had a pretty bad day, can you cut me some slack? They're saying… In fact, it doesn't matter. Just dumb rumours and stuff. I've had worse. It's the girl from the food court, my enemy. And I am actually sorry. You have every right to ask," Evie replied solemnly.

After a day of thinking so loudly that she almost tuned the merciless taunts out, she realised that she couldn't blame Charles for the horrible people Evie went to school with and the nasty stunts they pulled. She knew it was unfair to lash out when he had made an effort to apologise and try to connect with her.

She'd been dealing with problems like this in school for a long time before Charles had taken his first breath. Evie needed to stand up for herself and to do that she'd need some help.

She made a decision and hurried upstairs before she could overthink and talk herself out of it.

"See you soon!" she called over her shoulder to Charles as she took the stairs two at a time.

Chapter 11

Evie changed into some sweats and a t-shirt and splashed cold water on her face.

The cold water felt like scrubbing the rumours and laughter from her skin. Her skin was red raw and tingling by the time she left the bathroom.

She automatically reached for her dressing gown to pull it on but put it back down again. The house was unusually warm. She went downstairs and detoured via the garden to top up Toby C's water and put some more hay and a handful of greens in his hutch.

Then, after a quick drink, when there was no other reason to postpone it any more, she timidly knocked on the living room door. She now thought of it as Charles' room, as the temporary set up had become permanent with no other acceptable options. This was the first time Evie had willingly tried to go into the room, generally, the whole family avoided it, scurrying past as discreetly as they could. The Monroes tended not to spend time in communal rooms in general, until recently, Evie would only see her parents if they accidentally crossed paths in the kitchen or had some sort of mandatory family event. Or when they were telling her off.

Charles didn't reply and Evie panicked and turned to go back up the stairs. He was definitely in there; music was leaking through the cracks around the door and seeping through the thin walls. As Evie reached the upstairs landing, she heard something odd.

"Quack. Quack!"

Evie stopped, foot in the air as she paused midstep and tilted her head towards Charles' room where she suspected the duck sounds originated from. After she considered her options, Evie went back down. This time, faced with the blank oak door and taunted by faint quacks, Evie turned the handle and let herself in.

The living room was unrecognisable. Even the carefully chosen patterned wallpaper was underneath dozens of ironed shirts that hung on the walls, their hangers clinging to the ornamental edging. Since Charles faithfully maintained a wardrobe of bland colours, the wall was a mosaic of beige and pale blues which were more homely than the stark white and black. All the furniture had been pushed into the far left corner, leaving space for the sofa bed which was adjacent to the fireplace. At first glance, Evie didn't see the television as it was now a home for dozens of neatly paired socks to be draped across.

Charles was laying on his back in front of the roaring fire, by his head was an old record player he'd splurged on from an antique shop. Evie averted her eyes, remembering a furious row when Charles informed Maria and Jason that he would not contribute his money towards bills and food and when Jason had almost shouted himself out, Charles coolly informed them that even if he wanted to, he couldn't since the money had already been well spent and that he was to expect a delivery in two to three working days. He had a small fortune coming his way, but he'd forgotten to mention it to anyone but Evie.

Charles caught her eye and gave a mischievous smirk and Evie couldn't help smirking back. She'd heard the cliché that the enemy of my enemy is my friend, but Charles was quickly proving himself as an unlikely ally.

"Quack?" Evie questioned.

"I assumed you would be my haughty grand-daughter or her red-faced buffoon husband so I was pretending to be dead, desperately hoping they would not bother me for a little longer. But when you didn't kick the door or demand my presence in a whiny voice I sent a veiled invitation, that only you would understand. Clearly, it worked, because here you are! Quack indeed!" Charles turned down the music and sat up, looking smug.

"You... your secret word is quack?" Evie summarised, looking faintly bemused.

"I suppose it's our secret word at this point. But always keep in mind that you heard it here first. Ducks are fine creatures, and we should aspire to be like ducks. That's the secret, you ought to appear calm and serene on the surface and be paddling like the devil underneath where no-one can see. I'd be proud if you turned out like a duck, Evelyn!" Charles smiled merrily.

Evie decided not to query the craziness once he'd called her by the wrong name. She was just a plain Evie, but she didn't want to upset Charles over something so small, she was named after Evelyn after all, just more modern.

"More importantly, however, is what you wanted to talk to me about. Go ahead," Charles said.

"I—what? Why do you think I came here to talk to you?" Evie asked.

Charles frowned as Evie spoke, Evie thought she should be the one looking confused; his conversation was all over the place.

"I suppose I assumed, is it purely a social call then?" Charles questioned.

"Yeah, I just thought you might want to chill—hang out I mean, if you were bored or whatever. You don't have to."

"Chill?" repeated Charles, his face suddenly wiped of any expression.

Evie could've kicked herself, of course he wouldn't

understand her slang, chill means cold and of course thinking about being cold would dredge up all sorts of awful memories. Another word she'd have to remember to avoid, at this point, she would need to write them all down, the list was getting so long. Annoyingly, some of the banned topics for the list seem to be added and taken away depending on the whim of Charles that day. Just yesterday, he had kicked up a fuss when they were talking over dinner about where in Europe they wanted to go next summer on their annual holiday. None of them knew which word had caused the problem, and the subject was promptly dropped.

Charles sat up, his back to the fire. His watch was in his hand, closed. He gripped it tightly, and his lips slightly moved as he mouthed something, the movement too small to lip read. Evie suspected that he was talking to his late wife when he did this or saying some sort of prayer. It was definitely words not meant for her ears.

She didn't want to disturb him, so she busied herself in looking through his new record collection. She was taken aback by the wide range of artists. She's expected classics like The Beatles but did a double take when she saw Bob Marley and Dolly Parton. Both brilliant and talented artists with eternally appreciated songs but she could not for the life of her imagine her great-grandfather singing along to *Jolene.*

She looked up and saw Charles watching her. He smiled wryly at her expression, Evie felt like she was missing a joke but was relieved to see him looking more at ease than before. She was very slowly learning how to deal with him.

"Did you have something in mind then, duck? To do while we... chill?" Charles eventually asked.

Evie hadn't considered an activity, usually she meant lounging around and checking social media or watching some TV when she planned to chill out. Clearly, Charles expected some sort of organised activity. It had been years since Evie had spent time with someone else at home, at least since she started high school and stopped playing with her Barbies and dollies. Even though an older Tilly loudly complained about how babyish it was, she always got stuck in and the sisters would spend hours at a time immersing themselves in a world powered by their imagination where Barbies married, fought, and ate Blu Tack feasts before sleeping under blankets made of toilet roll. Evie had loved their pretend games, but once Kendall said that anyone who still played like that were babies who probably wet the bed, Evie had quietly packed up all her toys and left them in the garage. Since then, Evie hadn't really played any games or voluntarily spent any time with her family.

What games did the Monroes even have, she wondered. As far as she could remember, there wasn't any Monopoly boards or Jenga – the concept of a family game night was as foreign of an idea to the family as the idea of climbing a mountain. Evie mentally inventoried all the cupboards in the house she could think of, hoping to remember the location of something she could do with Charles.

"Scrabble? I know we have a Scrabble box around here somewhere; we've had it forever," Evie suggested, thrilled to have thought of something.

Charles didn't answer immediately, he seemed to be mulling it over. Evie wondered if he'd ever played before, or even knew the game. Before she could suggest something else, he agreed to play. She hurried out of his room to the cupboard under the stairs where she had last seen the board games.

Evie had to drag over and stand on a dining room chair, to reach up to the top of the cupboard where all the spare bedding, towels, and blankets lived. On a dusty shelf above it all, were the remains of old board games and various miscellaneous items that had laid undisturbed for over a decade. Evie had no memory of ever playing any of them as a child, it was an accident that she'd even come across them in the first place.

She remembered coughing dust up as she skimmed her hand along the shelf, too short to see herself but frantically looking for her comfort blanket that Jason had 'lost' in the wash.

At the time, she must have been younger than ten years old, she had yet to be dumped by Kendall or to venture into the grown up world of secondary school. She could not sleep without her blanket and had worked herself into a hysterical state after searching everywhere she possibly could and failing to locate it, she'd been shouted at and closed in the dark cupboard by Jason. She couldn't remember now where her mum had been, most likely out, but Evie had never felt so alone and unloved than in that moment, frightened in the dark, without any comfort or love.

The dry, musty smell of the cupboard mingled with a strong cloud of fresh washing detergent brought back the memory. It was something she hadn't thought about in years, but it was the first time she'd consciously thought that her dad didn't like her. Eventually, the blanket had been miraculously found, but only after Evie had worked herself into such a state after two nights of not sleeping that she vomited and then passed out. She'd been branded an attention seeker and accused of hiding her own blanket. Nowadays, though she didn't have it physically in her bed, merely knowing that it was safely hidden and nearby was enough.

Evie shook her head to wipe the memory away and pulled down the Scrabble box. The colour had faded, and the trails of an old spiderweb and dust made the box look a lot older than it was. Evie couldn't recall ever playing it, but she knew the rules, so she must've played at some point. It had probably been Tilly's and surrendered to the storage cupboard when she grew bored of it.

She carefully turned, reaching to brace her hand on the chair so she could climb down without tipping the box up and sending dust in every direction. As she was turning, Evie heard a faint sound behind her. She went to call out to Charles that she'd found it and almost fell right off the chair when Jason was standing right behind her.

"Bloody hell, Dad, you scared me!" Evie exclaimed, lurching forward to get her balance before she tipped. She didn't even know he was in; the house had been silent apart from Charles' music, and his car wasn't in the driveway when she'd arrived home.

"Get. Down. Now," Jason commanded.

"I am, I was just looking for—" Evie started.

"Get off my chair before the whole thing collapses. You are much too big to be clambering around like that. Now!" Jason shouted.

Evie lowered herself into a crouch, carefully placed one foot on the floor and as she was moving her other foot down, Jason grabbed the chair, tugging it towards him and sending Evie crashing towards the ground. She vanished in a murky dust cloud, tiles from the box exploding out and careening off in every direction. Evie landed on her tailbone and let out a yelp upon impact.

At the sound, Charles threw his door open and hurried down the hall. He abruptly stopped as he took in the scene. Jason let go of the chair as if it had burned him and conjured up a vague air of concern.

"Are you fine, Evie? You look fine. Don't be a baby, I did warn you—you weighed too much for the poor little chair." Jason didn't smile at all, but he still managed to convey amusement at the situation.

Charles went to Evie's side. She was wincing as pain shot up her back, radiating from her tailbone where she landed but she still started scooping up tiles. Charles patted her shoulder before he sank to his knees and helped her collect the pieces.

"Are you going to help or not?" Charles barked at Jason.

Jason crossed his arms and looked around, exaggeratedly checking if anyone else was around him.

"Me? It's her mess! It's good parenting to teach her responsibility for her actions. Besides, these jeans are brand new, I'm not getting horrible dust all over them."

Almost all the tiles were back in the box, Charles had been too busy staring Jason down to help much, but it was the intention that counted.

Once Evie had returned all the pieces to the box, she hovered, not wanting to get in between the stare down. Should she tell Charles it's done? But if he looked away then Jason would win. In the end, Evie settled to wait, not quite ready to get up and determine the true extent of her injury yet.

It was Jason who looked away first, his eyes averted and downcast. He knew he had lost the jostle for power. Of course, when he had an equal opponent he would retreat and live to fight another day, and the only thing he could do to make his fragile ego feel better was to turn his attention back on to his youngest daughter.

"Get all this dust hoovered up immediately. You can clean the whole cupboard while you're there. She's a cheeky brat, she thinks I don't know how to tell the time, that I won't realise she's absent from school. Again. And when I come home, and a good job that I did, I find her up to no good, throwing junk around and making a mess. I will not allow it!" Jason spat, infuriated.

"Actually, Evie and I have plans; she is not available to be your cleaner. You're her father, why don't you set the example and teach her responsibility by cleaning your own damn cupboard!" Charles stood up stiffly, pulling Evie along with him, then he guided her down the hallway. She didn't dare look at Jason as they passed him.

They were silent until they were safely in Charles' room and the door was firmly closed. Evie let out a sigh that turned into a sob and realised she was hugging the box to her chest. The hard edge digging into her stomach was nothing compared to the constant throbbing of her tail bone. She fancied that she could feel as blood pooled into a bruise.

Charles stopped the record, and as the sound abruptly cut off, the room plunged into silence, apart from a constant rattling sound and occasional sniffing. Charles looked around the room until he eventually identified the noise to be all the pieces in the box ricocheting around in tandem to Evie's shaking.

Charles had looked on the verge of laughter as he'd closed the door, but his big smile faded into a look of deep concern. He took the box from Evie and set it on the table before he sat down in front of his great-granddaughter.

"Did you really fall?" he asked softly.

Evie squeezed her eyes tightly. She didn't respond for the longest time. Charles didn't ask again, he just sat and waited. When Evie minutely shook her head, his only reaction was a sharp intake of breath.

Evie didn't move until she heard Charles move. He had his back to her and was looking at something she couldn't see. When he turned back, he gave her a small smile, and then asked "how badly are you hurt? Do you need medical attention?"

Evie shook her head, her sobs had subsided, she gingerly touched her back, feeling the sharp pain when her hand gently traced along the skin where the pain radiated from.

"Just a bruise, I think," she replied, in a quiet voice.

Charles sighed deeply and reached for the Scrabble box.

"Evie. I-I'm going to sort this mess out. It's going to be okay. Trust me on this. But in the meantime, do you still fancy a *chill* game? It's been a while, but I used to be pretty sharp at Scrabble. But I know you read and write a lot, so maybe I've finally met my match," he said.

Evie nodded again and sat on the carpet with her legs crossed. Charles slid the box over and gasped when he saw the cover. Now the dust had ended up all over the carpets, basically anywhere but the cover of the box, the image underneath was revealed. The box was khaki green, with a red box and bold white writing announcing the name. Somehow it looked tired, the corners sagging, and the colours muted.

Evie didn't know why Charles had gasped, she watched him curiously, seeing his cheeks lose all the colour. He had become a statue, his hand resting on the box. Evie imagined this was how he had looked on Everest, unmoving and deathly pale. Only the red tint in his hair gave him any colour at all.

"Charles? Grandad? Can I... call you Grandad? I know you're technically my great-grandad. Do you mind?" Evie asked.

"That is... fine," Charles eventually replied. His hand was still on the box.

"Thanks." Evie gave him a big smile. "Are you okay, Grandad? You look kind of shocked."

She watched as he breathed, the movement of his chest the only part of him moving at all. He wasn't even blinking as he stared at the box.

"This was, is, my Evelyn's. I gave it to her for Christmas, the last one I spent with them. We used to play every night," he eventually explained.

Evie looked down at the box, the sentiment and emotion from Charles was almost tangible. The Scrabble represented a link to his lost daughter, a real reminder of their bond and of his previous life. She gently touched the box and wondered if a young Evelyn had ever sat in front of a fire with Charles, the same box between them. The thought of it made goosebumps rise on her arm and a shiver went down her spine.

"I think I understand. This is very special, and if you don't want to play then I completely understand and don't mind at all," Evie told him.

"It's just a surprise. I had almost forgotten about Scrabble, but I am truly delighted that you brought it back into my life. I think I would like to play a game together. It would feel right somehow," he told her.

She waited until he took the lid off and set the game up, allowing him to decide when he was ready. They stopped for a long while when he pulled out the book where the scores and names were recorded. Seeing Evelyn's handwriting, and her doodles as she dutifully noted the game, was another shock wave. As he slowly turned the pages and drank in the writing, he came across a note Evelyn had written. 'Good game with Dad, even if he did cheat. Love you forever Dad'. Upon seeing the note, Evie had excused herself and lurked in the kitchen. Her dread of running into her father was less important than giving Charles some privacy in this unexpected but beautiful moment. When she finally knocked and went back in with two hot chocolates, he seemed normal. She politely ignored his red-ringed eyes.

"Thank you, sweetheart. I hope you've read the dictionary lately," he gamely said as they began to play.

They both heard when the front door closed. Tilly had come in earlier, on the phone as she discarded her shoes and went straight upstairs. When Maria came in, she was like a whirlwind. Before the door had shut she was shouting as she dumped her bags by the door.

"We're leaving at quarter to seven sharp. No one will be late. Everyone will be presentable. Grandad, you will wear a tie and nice shoes. I left an outfit for you behind your door. Thank God for next day delivery. Evie, you better be out of your sulk, you'll be ready, presentable and smiling. I'm going to the bathroom now, no one bother me unless it's an emergency." Maria swept past the door and up the stairs. Even though no one had been in front of her or acknowledged her, she knew they'd all heard and would abide.

They could still hear Maria making her way up the stairs when Jason met her and began talking, his tone indicated that he'd been stewing upstairs and was still in a foul mood. No doubt he was spinning all sorts of lies to Maria.

"Maybe you can stay in here with me for a bit longer, hey? You've still got plenty of time before we're leaving. And I suppose I'll need to investigate this mysterious package from behind my door," Charles added.

Together they opened the package and decided that the shirt, suit jacket and pants were far more extravagant than necessary, but Charles would gamely iron and wear them since he didn't have a matching suit to wear. They chose him a tie and he polished his shoes while Evie kept him company.

After a very intense game of scrabble, when a dictionary and the internet were consulted on almost every round, and their scores and names eternally added in the book from inside the box, Evie stiffly got up. With a hand on her tender back, she announced she'd better go and get ready, lest she face the wrath of Maria for making them late.

Evie left the living room as the sun gently rolled towards the horizon. The rest of the house was still and quiet. Evie realised that she didn't know or care where the rest of the family was, she'd had the loveliest time playing Scrabble with Charles, and he was finally starting to open up to her. Evie was immensely proud to be the confidant and to finally have a family member who loved and stood up for her. It was a novelty she was positive she'd never grow bored of.

She considered grabbing a snack but realised they'd be leaving quite soon for the meal, so she should probably get ready and not spoil her appetite.

When she reached the landing, she was surprised to see light leaking out from around her bedroom door. Evie didn't think she'd left it on since it had been early afternoon when she'd changed her clothes so she wouldn't have needed the light on.

She pushed open the door to find her mother sitting on her bed, surrounded by an array of wrappers. Empty crisp packets, chocolate bar wrappers and plastic covered in slogans of several biscuit brands were all over the bed. Maria had a face of thunder as she perched on the bed, her foot tapping on the floor faster than Evie's heartbeat. An empty glass sat on Evie's bedside table. From the door, she could smell the distinct aroma of vodka. Evie's heart skipped a beat, her mother didn't drink beyond a glass of wine after her evening meal. When she did, it usually ended with disastrous results.

"So," Maria said, her voice loud.

"Hi," Evie replied, eyes averted from the display on her bed.

"So, anything you need to share? You thought I wouldn't find your secret stash? You thought you could stuff your face like a pig under my roof and I wouldn't find out? I'm not blind, Evie, I can see your waistband getting tighter. You are a disgrace. It is

139

disgusting, finding old packets shoved under your bed, in your pockets and in your school bag. Do you want to attract rodents? Do you want to look like a rodent? You're already acting like a snake, trying to set your father against my grandad. Yes, I know all about that, and that you've been bunking off school and making all sorts of messes. What is wrong with you!" Maria was screaming. It was like she'd been angry and stressed about the meal, then Jason had poured oil onto the fire before finding the wrappers had opened the floodgates.

"I just need to clean out, I've hardly been snacking lately with everything going on. Why are you going through my room anyway? You have no right!" Evie retorted, the nasty comments from school, the pain in her tailbone and the unfairness of Maria once again not even listening to her side of the story making her see red.

"I am your mother, although God forbid sometimes I wish I wasn't! If I feel the need to check my seventeen-year-old daughter's room for drugs then I will do so!"

Evie was stunned for a second, she had no idea where Maria had gotten the notion that she may be taking drugs from. It was the last thing she'd expected to be accused of.

"Drugs? Why would you think that? Where would I even get them from? Maybe you're on drugs! You won't care anyway but why don't you ask me how I got hurt today? Who caused me an injury? Why don't you stop for one second and wonder why I couldn't stay in school?" Evie was screaming now too. She couldn't help it as all the hurt and resentment overpowered her mouth and vocalised what she so desperately wanted to say.

Maria's face jerked to the side as if Evie had slapped her face.

She took a step towards her daughter and then halted when

the door opened again.

Charles stepped between them, his face grave.

"Maria, I need you to stop shouting. You are the adult here, and trust me, shouting at teenagers doesn't help much. I sent your cretin of a husband downstairs and Matilda has music on. It's just us three. Everyone needs to calm down and be civil so we can sort this out," he instructed.

"Stay out of this, Grandad. This is nothing to do with you. You clearly don't like any of us, so don't get involved. Go and listen to your dumb records and stay out of it," Maria snapped.

"Now, Maria. That was unfair. I have my fair share of problems to work through, but I have come to develop deep affection for you and for the girls. It may not be my place, but I cannot sit idly by and ignore what's going on. How about I make us all a cup of tea, and then we can sit down and sort this out."

"Yes, tea would be nice," Evie said in a quiet voice.

"Oh my Lord. Shut up about the stupid tea! A hot drink won't fix this. The only way to sort it, is if my greedy, selfish daughter changes her ways and apologises to her family. If she just stopped stuffing her face for a second, I'm not asking for much! She's not normal! Other girls her age don't go to such lengths to secretly eat. She has a problem, and if she stops being a brat, she might realise I'm trying to help her!" Maria started shouting again, every time she referred to Evie, she pointed at her.

"My patience is wearing thin, Maria. Do not mistake my willingness to help as forgiveness for your behaviour. Perhaps you should reflect on why your daughter is comfort eating. If you listened to her and put her needs first, you'd understand that she's having a difficult time. She isn't dangerously unhealthy, and if you truly wanted to help her, then look at yourself! Family meals, cooking healthy food, teaching her about balanced diets and exercise. You are her mother; it is your job to teach her how to be healthy and you have failed. It's not too late though, you still have time to help her," Charles urged her. Sincerity radiated from him as he spoke.

Maria responded by laughing. She laughed until she was red in the face and eventually choked out. "That's hilarious. She's never going to change, and it's no one's fault but her own. I don't have time for this nonsense. If she's so determined to ruin her life by skipping school, burning her bridges with her family and eating herself to death, well good luck to her. Get out of here. Make sure you're ready by half six, we're leaving at quarter to. You will smile through the meal and after that I couldn't care less what you do. You've made your bed, you can lie in it. I'm done trying to help you," Maria said, arms crossed.

"This is her room! I think you're the one who needs to leave. I hope that your mother isn't looking down on you right now, because the Evelyn I knew and loved would be deeply ashamed of your behaviour. Quite frankly, I'm disgusted," Charles told her.

Before she heard her mother's reply, Evie turned and ran out of the room. She couldn't bear to hear any more. The house was a blur as she blindly stumbled down the stairs and through the back door.

Evie was brushing Toby C's fluffy fur when Charles joined her outside. Evie's head was bowed, salty tears were dropping onto the patio, making rivers that flowed all the way down to the overgrown grass. The rabbit squirmed but Evie kept a tight hold on him.

She didn't notice him until he was right next to her, she didn't know how long he'd been watching her quietly crying.

Charles sat down heavily beside her on the patio and

watched the brush for a few minutes before he attempted to talk.

"She didn't mean it. Overwrought emotion and alcohol certainly isn't an ideal combination either. She's just very stressed at the moment. It's a great strain having a family member return from the dead and move in with you I've heard." He chuckled and waited, watching Evie's bowed head. "Look, if you're this upset about your weight and eating habits then use it as motivation to better yourself. You're not terribly overweight, but it'd still be difficult to start with, you'd need to massively increase your exercise and stop snacking so much, or at least switch the chocolate for fruit and healthier alternatives. It's achievable though. If you really want to. I could even help you." He waited for a reaction.

"Of course, I want to! I want nothing more than to lose a bit of weight and maybe Kendall would stop being horrible and everyone else would leave me alone! Do you think I like comparing myself to my perfect sister all the time? That I want to be embarrassed when I'm shopping for clothes? I try! I was dieting before you even arrived, and I do okay at first and lose a few pounds and then I have the worst day and the only thing that I want is some chocolate and I accidentally eat the whole bar and then what's the point?" Evie ended up shouting. She was so angry. She expected Jason to be snide and mean but Maria, when she was paying attention, was usually the more kind and loving one. Her mother's words cut deep, so deep that Evie didn't know if they would ever properly heal.

"Dry your eyes, duckie. Your parents have failed you on this matter. I'm sorry but it's true, me and Margaret would never let our sweet Evelyn be raised this way. But I'm here now. Maybe my second chance was so I could help you and make a difference. Maybe it's just happened for no reason but I'm going to use the rest of my life, however long that is, to help you. With whatever you need. We start tonight at this meal."

"I'm not going," Evie immediately retorted; her voice

143

strained.

"We'll go together. Trust me, I'll be there the whole time. We'll have fun. Besides, you'll be helping me as much as I'll be helping you. I haven't been to a fancy restaurant in almost fifty years!" Charles said.

Face buried in Toby C's back, breathing in his sawdust smell, Evie nodded. She would be expected to attend even after the argument she'd had, Maria had said as much. Maybe this time wouldn't be so bad with Charles there. He'd already proved he was capable of standing up to Jason. Today he had defended her when Maria was on a rampage too.

She put Toby C back in and fetched some fresh veggies for his tea before she wiped her eyes and went to go and get ready.

Evie ended up wearing a burgundy long sleeve top with a sweetheart neckline and a black skirt with black shoes. She braided the front of her hair back and did her signature mascara, eye shadow and eyeliner. She never bothered with lipstick when eating out, it always wiped off unevenly and she couldn't be bothered to go and fix it in the toilets.

By the time the clock got to quarter to seven, the family had assembled by the front door. Evie was last to go downstairs, she'd heard Charles and Jason arguing, and decided to stay out of the way until the last possible minute. Usually, Maria would have been shouting her, but it seemed as though she wasn't speaking to Evie at the moment.

Evie stayed on the landing, bathed in darkness as she waited. She caught the end of the argument Jason and Charles were having.

"I don't care. It's my house, I pay the bills and I say you don't touch the thermostat. I don't put it on in autumn, and I decide when it's cold enough in the winter. If you're cold put a jumper on. My house, my rules, do you understand?" Jason asked, the patronising tone obvious.

"I know that. I don't think you understand, I will not be cold. I will not live in a cold house. If this is a problem, you can take it up with my friends on Mr Dexter's team. They would be very interested if they heard you were actively causing me further discomfort," Charles retorted.

The lights which marked the first taxi's arrival broke up the argument. Jason and Tilly climbed in, followed by Maria after she warned Charles to be on his best behaviour and not to be late. Evie had been peering down the stairs, spying on her family.

Maria hadn't looked for Evie or made any effort to find out where she was or if she was okay. She'd been too busy fussing and checking the time for the taxi, and then loudly complimented Tilly on her outfit. Jason had been standing in a cloud of too strong aftershave and glowering. Tilly had been waiting outside, on her phone as usual. The invisible tension in the house dramatically decreased as the three of them left.

Once the coast was clear, Evie hurried down the stairs and nodded to Charles. They moved to the street to wait for the taxi, locking the front door as they went. The back of the first taxi was receding into the distance until all they could see was the red lights before it turned the corner.

"It seems such a shame to get two taxis, couldn't we fit in a bigger one? I've been in one that was a mini-van, it was big enough to fit a small sports team in," Charles said.

"Oh, you can get those, but Mum prefers the smaller, fancier cars. She doesn't care about spending extra money if other people can see it. She cares a lot about the *family image,*" Evie explained.

Charles merely nodded, and soon after the other taxi arrived. Neither talked much on the short journey.

The group entering the restaurant that evening was a sight to behold, Maria and Jason were at the front, glammed up as much as they possibly could. Maria was wearing a cocktail dress, with diamonds encircling her ring finger, around her wrist and holding up her fancy hairstyle. She looked like she was attending a tea party with a princess. Jason was stomping along beside her in a three-piece designer suit, his shoes had been recently cleaned and shined. They could've passed for a celebrity couple, if not for the ugly expression on Jason's face and the dark circles under Maria's eyes.

Behind them, Tilly strode along. She was on the phone, upset that she was missing a party or something. Evie overheard her promising she'd be there as soon as she could escape.

Unfortunately for the sisters, their parents always insisted on full family attendance at social events such as birthdays or anniversaries. She begrudgingly knew to not even ask permission to miss it, and had also put a lot of effort in. People's heads were turning to keep watching Tilly as she went past. She was wearing a short burgundy wrap around dress, with matching lipstick and black heels. It wasn't a crazy expensive outfit or anything, she just managed to look effortlessly lovely in the simplest of clothes.

Quite a distance behind them walked Evie and Charles. Evie was holding Charles to his promise to stay by her side the entire night. Charles had already clashed with Jason as they'd assembled in the hall to drive over, the night wasn't off to a smooth start. Jason was deeply offended that Charles had opinions on the running of the house, and from his expression, he was still thinking about it. Charles had kept his cool, and dismissed Jason, further provoking his fury. But at least it meant that Evie escaped notice, she thought her parents were ignoring her but wasn't sure. Sometimes they just didn't speak to her anyway.

Now they had arrived, they were far enough apart that they wouldn't even be acknowledged as a group. Jason and Maria had switched on the fake charm and were pretending their family life was perfect as they always did in front of other people, at least if it would reflect on them. They didn't care so much when they were dragging Evie out of dessert parlours. Evie knew from past meals that her parents would want to be seen interacting as a happy family and keep any of their true thoughts quiet until no one was around.

When Evie and Charles finally reached the door, her parents and Tilly had settled into plush chairs by the bar and were already ordering drinks.

"Charles, what are you having to drink, mate?" Jason asked, gritting his teeth into a mock grin for the benefit of the bored waiter.

Charles looked quite startled. Evie almost snorted, she'd forgotten to warn him about this act they put on amongst all of the earlier drama. He seemed to be quite quickly forging his own conclusions though.

"I'll take a glass of champagne, young sir, whatever you have open! I believe we have some celebrating to do!" Charles replied smoothly. He wouldn't know, but Jason always drank several pints too many considering that he was usually the designated driver, and Maria was notorious for drinking cocktails with Tilly. Many posts had been made on social media of the glamorous mother-daughter duo with their matching drinks in a fancy restaurant.

"Yep, and for you?" the boy asked Evie, barely glancing up from the tablet where he was entering their orders.

"Coke, please. Or Pepsi? Whichever," Evie answered.

Evie chose to sit in the chair furthest away from Jason,

preparing for the fakeness of the night with some time away from him while she could. She turned to Charles, about to ask him why he chose champagne when she realised he had gone. She slowly scanned the room before spotting him by the bar, talking to the nodding waiter.

He strolled back over and sat down next to Evie.

"If you're serious about this health kick thing, we start now. I need you to make the effort though, I can try to help but you have to meet me halfway. It's got to come from you. Agree?" he said.

"Yes, agree. I said earlier, I'm deadly serious," Evie immediately replied.

"Good, I'm telling you, kid, you'll be stronger, sleeping better, feeling better. Are you happy for me to perhaps help you order? You already admitted you go straight to the comfort food. No longer!" Charles declared.

Before Evie could agree again, their waiter returned, with a man in a suit.

"Many congratulations! Allow us to offer you each a free dessert, in light of your happy day. And of course, here is your champagne!" the man said as the waiter deposited a bucket of ice on the table that held an entire unopened bottle of champagne. Four glasses followed. "I am the manager here, please ask for me if you need anything, I want you go have the best night! Enjoy." He bowed and then turned to leave.

Maria and Jason were visibly shocked. His vein was pulsing in his head and her mouth was ajar.

"Thank you!" Maria managed to say to the waiter when he returned with the rest of the drinks. He gave Evie hers last. "Diet Coke, enjoy." Before leaving once again.

"Diet?" Evie repeated. Frowning as she tried to recall if

she'd asked for diet.

"An *entire* bottle?" Jason hissed at the same time.

"It's a joyous occasion! We all made such a huge effort to come out, I thought it was only right we get something fancy to drink. Is there a problem, *grandson in law*?" Charles had very quickly worked out how to counter Jason.

"You are a very thoughtful man!" Jason's malice switched to a beaming smile as he spoke, the effortless transition for the manager who had come back over.

"If you'd like to follow me? Your table is ready."

They got up, every person looking distinctly uncomfortable about the turn of events, except Charles who was already following the manager.

The table was in its own nook, with candles and flower petals artfully arranged as the centrepiece on a crisp white cloth. Charles paused, it was a rectangle table, with six chairs on each side, no chairs were at the head of the table.

He chose a seat right in the middle and gestured for Evie to go on the other side of him which left Maria directly to his left and Jason and Tilly sitting on the opposite side. Evie couldn't believe how smoothly he was guiding them all and keeping his promise. One of them wouldn't have someone opposite and Evie was lucky enough to be that person.

"Brilliant!" Evie whispered.

Charles smiled and reached for the champagne, neatly twisting the cork out and pouring himself a glass.

"Care for a glass, Maria?" Charles offered.

"*No*, thank you. I always have cocktails. I don't know why you got the whole bottle, Grandad. But I suppose it doesn't matter. Just don't waste it. Actually, waste it if it means you're not a drunk mess. Just do not embarrass me. Also, exactly what occasion did you tell them we were celebrating?" Maria replied.

Charles only shrugged and filled up half a flute for Evie. He paused and then did the same for Tilly.

Tilly raised an eyebrow but gracefully accepted the glass and took a small sip.

Before anyone else could speak, the manager returned.

"Are you all ready to order?" he asked.

"Ah, another minute, pal?" Jason said, the menu before him was still closed. Once the manager had left, Jason shot daggers at Charles and then opened the menu.

"Starter, darling?" he asked Maria, opting to ignore the rest of them.

Tilly had her phone low down, texting away and occasionally sipping her drink. Jason didn't care when Tilly was blatantly on her phone.

Charles turned to Evie, laying the open menu on the table between them. For a few moments, he just looked at Evie, thinking intently.

"The first thing I'll tell you is not to skip meals or starve yourself. I want you to eat healthy, decently sized portions at each meal. We can work out some healthy snacks if you're peckish in between. And once a week or so you can have a day off. I learned all about eating healthy when I was in the hospital. If you want, today can be that day and you can order anything you like. Tomorrow we'll sit down and sort an exercise and healthy eating plan. How about that?" Charles spoke quietly so no one else heard him.

Evie nodded her agreement.

"Oh, like a cheat day?" Evie asked.

"Yes, if that's what you call it," Charles replied.

The manager returned once more, quickly cementing his place as the most attentive waiter. His eyes darted to the glass of champagne that was bubbling away in front of Evie, but he did not comment.

They all ordered steak and chose dressing for their lettuce. Jason and Maria ordered a sharing starter to eat together.

Charles asked the manager to linger for a second, as he checked the menu and ordered another sharer starter, "For myself and the girls, and a pint of full fat Coke please sir," he said with a smile. When Evie sent him a questioning look, he merely said: "Well, I'm not paying so why not!"

Charles skilfully steered the conversation, directing them around potentially dangerous waters with flair. As it happened, Maria was ignoring Evie, but disguising it by constantly chatting so no one realised Evie was being excluded. Tilly had one eye on her phone as she texted non-stop, and the other on the table as she managed two conversations. Anytime the conversation drifted towards any form of conflict, Charles was on hand. He asked endless questions.

Maria painstakingly explained why she was taking photos of her food for social media and tried to make Charles care about followers and likes in vain. While her mother droned on, Evie mused that although Charles was talking a lot, it was all nonsense, nothing of any importance was being said. None of them knew anything about him. She made a mental note to ask to hear some stories from his past when they were alone, he certainly wouldn't appreciate her asking in front of everyone.

He carried on in a similar fashion throughout the meal. He asked about advancements in space, the pros and cons of YouTube and had an intense debate about the disadvantages of being contactable twenty-four seven. Evie remained carefully neutral, although she was delighted by Charles controlling the conversation. The only time he paused was when he was examining the menu for dessert. They all studied the options, the quiet only disturbed when the manager returned to clear their plates and determine what everyone wanted to order next.

Evie already knew she wanted the giant chocolate fudge cake they offered, and when her gaze drifted from the menu she had scanned to double check, she saw Maria staring directly at her.

"Evie, don't you think dessert will be too much? Sweetie," Maria said through a fake smile.

Evie recognised the warning tone in her mother's voice, and feeling brave with Charles by her side, she dared to disobey.

"But, Mum, it's a special occasion. We're getting complimentary dessert; it would be so rude of me to decline it." Evie smiled and narrowed her eyes at her mother. The first communication they'd had since the big fight, and she was hounding her about her food.

"Greedy!" Jason huffed.

"For. God's. Sake. Evie." Maria hissed through her teeth. "Do you really want to do this now?"

"I'll give you a moment to think about it." The manager bowed away.

"Evie! Now you've done it! Everyone finish your drinks. We're leaving," Maria told them.

"The bill please?" Maria called to the manager and smiled with all her teeth as she left a generous tip and thanked all the staff. They each played their part, smiling or in Evie's case grimacing as they maintained the charade of happy family just a little longer. Evie was having heart palpitations; she knew she had crossed a line. They had never left early, certainly not before dessert and coffee.

Maria herded everyone out, and only once they had left the restaurant, and walked further down the street until the light from the window didn't reach them, did she let out the rage that had been simmering under the surface.

"Let's all take a deep breath. I think enough shouting has been done tonight. Everyone is quite emotional, and we've all had alcohol. Some things are better said after some time has passed and we can think a little more rationally. Let's order taxis, go home and everyone sleep on it. How about that?" Charles dived in to get the first word, as brave as a bomb diffusor trying to avert a crisis at great personal risk.

"Shut it, old man, you've done enough tonight. You have drained my hospitality and are running on reserves. Don't go interfering. This is between my wife and her," Jason interjected. His eyes were lit up in anticipation of the brewing fight.

Before anyone else could speak, Maria let loose a torrent of anger upon Evie. Looking at her not with love for her youngest daughter, but with thinly veiled contempt and hatred.

"Evie, you can wipe that dumb look off your face. I am sick of you. I don't even recognise you anymore! You embarrassed us all tonight and ruined our anniversary. God, I wish we didn't have to take you anywhere with us. You are bitter and jealous and attention-seeking, and you are seventeen years old! What is wrong with you? Why can't you slap a smile on your face and sit through a dinner once in a blue moon? Like it not, you are part of this family and you will act like it!" Maria shouted every word.

"I hate you, I hate both of you! You drag me to these stupid things and parade us around like a perfect family as if anyone cares, which, newsflash, they don't! Just let me stay at home and everyone will be happier. You don't shout at Tilly for being on her phone or ordering dessert, do you? You don't dictate her life or constantly compare her to anyone! You said yourself you don't want me around, well great! I don't want to be around, the second I can, I'll be out of your lives for good. I'll count down every second until then," Evie challenged her mother, asking her the questions which kept her up at night and made her detest her sister just for existing and being the preferred child. She ignored Charles when he shook his head at her.

"There you go again, whinging about your sister. Blaming

153

her because she's everything you aren't. So what—you think she's prettier and more popular. She's in better shape, and guess what? *Newsflash,* it's your fault that you're like this. Stop blaming us and making our lives hell because you never stop eating, have no friends and hardly leave the house. This is on you! It's clearly not our fault, seeing as Tilly doesn't have any of the problems you have. We should've stuck with one child. You were a mistake, this is why we only wanted one child." Maria burst into tears as soon as she finished speaking.

Evie was stunned into silence.

She distantly heard Charles furiously shouting at Maria and Jason. Like a firework, he exploded, and Evie couldn't see past the tears that filled her eyes. But she could hear, and the word 'mistake' was on repeat in her brain. She was an unwanted mistake.

She distantly heard a car door slam, the shouting subdued and then Charles was in front of her, he wrapped his arms around her shoulders and held her. He stroked her hair and murmured meaningless, comforting words.

Then she was stumbling into her room, the door firmly closed behind her and it took all her effort to pull her shoes off before she collapsed on top of the covers. She didn't recall the journey or where Charles had gone. She couldn't bring herself to care.

The last thing she thought before she tumbled into unconsciousness was 'mistake'.

Chapter 12

After barely managing a few hours of sleep, Evie eventually dragged herself out of bed. She'd heard everyone else moving around already, and the last thing she wanted to do was to go downstairs and fight some more so she'd prolonged the inevitable as long as she could bear her stomach rumbling.

She always felt like rubbish after a family meal, never mind one so turbulent. She stomped down the stairs to the kitchen, risking further family conflict to satisfy her craving for something chocolatey to make the day a little brighter.

The mood in the kitchen was subdued this morning. They were all up earlier than usual and getting ready at the same time for a change. No one knew how to act after the big fight, and they'd never been particularly polite or cheery so early. Evie avoided every eye in the room but was painfully aware of all of her family member's movements as they went about their morning routines. The tension was like static energy in the room.

Jason was ignoring everyone, and ironically behaved the most normal seeing as silently glowering was his standard setting. He collected an energy drink from the fridge and loudly slammed the doors as he got ready for the day. The huge bang as he yanked the kitchen door closed echoed around the house, like dozens of tiny slams.

Through the ajar kitchen window, Evie could hear her rabbit thumping in displeasure. She detoured on her way to the cupboard to present Toby C with some apple slices she'd chopped up the day before. He begrudgingly accepted the treat but turned his back when she tried to stroke him. With a sigh, Evie returned to the kitchen. She paused in the doorway and checked her family members to gauge the mood of the room before anyone saw her.

Maria was rubbing her temples and looked distinctly irritated. A full mug of creamy coffee sat in front of her, but no steam escaped so it must've been sitting there for a while. Maria was a notorious coffee drinker, so it was a red flag that she'd wasted a cup.

Evie scanned the rest of the room and suddenly noticed that Charles was waiting to catch her eye. He gave her a big smile and nodded towards Maria, silently urging her on. She knew he would want her to smooth things over, or at least make an effort to. Now was as good a time as any, with Charles in her corner and Jason somewhere else.

"Mum? Are you okay? Shall I put the kettle on again?" Evie asked, eyes still on the ice cold drink in front of her mum. She was tentative in tone, ready to recoil as soon as her mum indicated just how angry she still was.

"Bloody hell, Evie!" Maria exploded, making them all jump as she interrupted the silence "Can't you shut up for a minute? I feel like death, I've got a really important meeting with the regional boss in less than two hours and you're already pestering me! Don't you think you said enough last night? Go to school!"

Evie didn't even bother responding, her mother would be in the worst mood all day with the migraine, and probably tomorrow since she had to work and couldn't medicate and sleep it off. They'd never had a fight like last night, and in the early hours, Evie knew she wasn't the only one lying awake. They were all tired and angry still, not a good combination. Usually, when she fought with Jason she'd go to school early and read. Then after school, go to the cinema, library, or her favourite dessert place to avoid her father as much as she could.

Jason would typically act passive aggressively for several days, referring to her only in third person and punishing her until he stopped caring or forgot he was in a mood and then the cycle would be reset. Evie didn't know how her mum would treat her, and it saddened her that she was about to find out. The only silver lining was that Charles was there, a steady pillar of support. At least one person had been kind to her this morning.

Charles had produced a newspaper and was holding it in the air in front of him to read. No sign of food or drink in front of him. His eyes, which were the only part of him Evie could see over the huge paper, weren't moving on the page. For a second Evie wondered where he'd got a newspaper from, she thought everyone just used the news apps on their phones or iPad. But then she realised who Charles was, and of course, he managed to find a paper copy to read as he leisurely passed the morning.

Tilly was being uncharacteristically quiet, but that was probably because she was hungover. Her eyes were almost closed as she slowly sipped cranberry juice. She would most likely disappear up to bed for the day and only appear once she'd fully recovered and applied a fresh face of make up for whatever social engagement she was gracing her presence upon that night.

She left her post at the back door and made straight for the sweet cupboard. As she reached for the pop tarts, she hesitated, her hand frozen in mid-air, fingers outstretched. She finally turned to look at Charles, she could feel the weight of his stare as he watched her. He shrugged when he saw her looking and returned to his paper.

Evie defiantly let her hand drift closer to the pop tart, finally picking it up and inhaling the beautiful scent. She could almost taste the soft chocolate, already anticipating the calm that only food could give her. It was an overwhelming desire to adhere to her morning routine and embrace the comfort of her food, she'd never thought twice about it. Without turning, Evie knew Charles would be waiting for her next move, he wouldn't say anything but rather will her to be strong enough to reject the routine.

Evie closed her eyes, she thought of Jason smirking, and Tilly's horror that she was related to her in the Matalan incident. She recalled Maria's cruel words last night, each forever etched into her mind. And Charles. He smiled at her, *quacked* and looked around as if to see where the noise had come from. Charles who held his only physical link to his old life and his family, the pocket watch, so tightly that it left raw imprints in his skin and still he took strength from that to carry on and face his new reality.

Without opening her eyes, she dropped the pop tart onto the counter, like it had scalded her. It was oats that Evie instead reached for when she opened her eyes and turned away from the cupboard. Charles believed in her, she could exchange the stupidly delicious and unhealthy breakfasts for something better.

Holding a single serving of oats in a slim packet, Evie shook it, doubtful that there would be more than a handful of porridge in there. Certainly, there wasn't enough to fill her up, when she was used to eating so much of a morning. She carefully opened the packet, peering in. It looked very dry, not at all what she imagined porridge to be like. Someone else must eat it in the house, they had several boxes worth in the pantry, but since they rarely shared the dinner table, Evie hadn't actually seen porridge up close.

She had to read the packet, she wasn't even sure if it was

water or milk or something else entirely used to make the dry oats turn into porridge. She double-checked the instructions and measured out the milk that was out on the counter by the kettle. When it was ready, she took the beige sludge to the table, pulling the long sleeves of her black top over her hands to cradle the hot bowl.

Charles had won the fight about sitting at the head of the table, mainly since Jason avoided the kitchen as much as possible, and Evie settled into her usual seat to his right.

As she glumly picked up the bowl and sniffed the porridge, Charles leaned closer to her and peered into the bowl.

"Well done, duck, I'm proud of you." He murmured before he folded the paper, leaving it on the table in his place as he drifted out of the room. It was so quiet that neither Tilly nor Maria noticed the exchange or his exit.

Evie's heart swelled with joy. No one had actually been proud of her as far as she could remember. She forgot about her trepidation about the porridge and scooped up a spoonful. It didn't even taste of anything in particular, it was just hot. Charles saying those few words did more than every single snide comment Jason had ever made. Suddenly, Evie wanted to do something else good and for Charles to be pleased with her, it was exactly what she wanted her great-grandad to be like.

She polished off the bowl, for the first time in a very long while she felt proud of herself too. Charles inspired her.

Evie, feeling a little bit more positive than she had all morning, was rinsing her bowl out when Jason stalked back into the kitchen. The door slamming into the wall set off Toby C again and rattled all the windows in the house.

"Maria, where are my black shoes? The shiny ones? They were by the door. I need them immediately, I'm late and sick of you tidying my stuff away!" Jason was softer when he spoke to his wife, though still short and clearly irritated.

Evie put her bowl in the dishwasher and caught her great-grandad's eye from where he stood in the hallway. He was smiling faintly and hovering near a pile of boxes he had left out there to be broken down and recycled. He'd had so many deliveries that they needed to wait until the recycling bin had been collected and emptied before he could fill it up again. Charles had reluctantly ventured into the online shopping world with a lot of assistance and grumbling. Though he liked the convenience, he resented the process. Suddenly, Evie, without a shadow of a doubt, knew where the missing shoes had gone. She suppressed a smile of her own and turned away from Charles as he reached into the top box. Evie shook her head at him with a small smile and opened the fridge.

A glass bottle of oat milk, which must have been precariously balancing in the door, cartwheeled right out of the fridge. Evie saw it go and lunged to catch it, but missed entirely and was leaning forward, arms outstretched when the bottle hit the floor.

A tidal wave of milk rolled in every direction across the kitchen tiles. It was unfortunate that it had been unopened, which meant so much milk was wasted. Evie froze, the milk already soaked through her socks. If she moved, she'd be splashing it all around the kitchen, and potentially hurt her feet in the glass that had shattered into tiny glittering shards.

Jason turned from Maria and took in the scene in silence.

"Sorry – it was on the edge, I'll clean it," Evie said into the frozen room.

"EVIE! Do you ever think? At all? Why are you just standing there? Start cleaning! I swear if she's standing there with that dumb expression for one more second..." Jason trailed off and stormed out of the room.

"I said I'd clean it," Evie muttered, carefully peeling one sock off and taking a big step back, out of the mess. She took off her other sock and surveyed the puddle. She couldn't see the glass under the milk, so she'd need to carefully clean that up first. After placing several sheets of kitchen roll on top of the milk and absorbing the worst of it, Evie used a dust pan and brush from under the sink to brush up the shards.

"You need a separate bag. Glass doesn't go in the regular bin. Obviously," Maria said without looking up from where her head rested in her hands.

"Oh, right. Thanks. It was an accident honestly. I don't know why it was leaning on the edge, it would've fallen out no matter who opened the door. I used the milk that's over there by the kettle, I've never even had oat milk! It wasn't me I swear!" Evie was suddenly desperate for her mum to know it wasn't her fault. She didn't see it happen and had just accepted it was Evie being clumsy as usual.

Maria didn't respond, but Tilly opened one eye.

"Can you be quiet? No one cares. You spilt it, you clean it. Get over yourself," Tilly said in a monotone voice.

Jason came back into the kitchen. Since he'd gone, Charles had drifted back in and picked his paper back up. Evie spotted a pair of black shoes by the back door which hadn't been there before when she took the bin bag of glass outside. He could move as silently as a ghost sometimes and escaped notice as he got up to all sorts of mischief. Only a few minutes had passed, while Evie had been cleaning and Jason boiling, Charles had been on the move. Evie returned to her seat by Charles since she was still too early for school.

Jason barrelled over to the kettle, flicking the switch and setting up a mug with coffee in. Despite being all wound up about being late, he didn't seem too concerned any more.

"Stupid girl! Pouring money down the drain she is, what a waste," Jason was muttering into his coffee.

"Jason, are those your missing shoes by any chance?" Charles interjected, cutting off Jason's passive aggressive ranting. Jason almost cricked his neck turning so fast, and he hurried over to the shoes. Evie noticed smeared mud all over them and thought it served him right for always being horrible.

"When I said leave them by the door, Maria, I meant the *front* door obviously. And I thought I told you to clean them up?" Jason demanded.

While Maria looked at the dirty shoes and they started bickering, Evie indicated to Charles that she was going into the garden.

"No use crying over spilt milk, little duck. If you need me, I'm going for a sit down in the other room," Charles murmured as she passed him.

It was nice, Evie thought, having someone on her side for once. It took the edge off all the bad stuff when Charles was there to call her duck and divert attention away from her.

Evie decided to try harder to avoid both her mother and father for the rest of the morning. Thankfully, they all had somewhere to be, so it wouldn't be too long. She took herself outside into the brisk October morning and checked on her rabbit again, he'd been thumping so much lately. With everything going on lately, she hadn't spent as much time with him, he probably wondered where she'd been. He had a rare personality as he didn't thrive amongst other rabbits, so he didn't even have a friend to keep him company when Evie wasn't home. She used

162

to come out and chat to him for hours every evening, he was the only family member who didn't mind her presence, which made sense since she fed him and loved him. He had actually been a gift for Tilly, who took a bunch of photos with him and then lost interest so Evie quietly took over his care. He was the closest thing she had to a friend. She was handfeeding Toby C pellets when she heard the phone ringing through the open window.

The family didn't usually receive calls in the morning, when all members of the household were normally rushing around and cursing each other in a whirlwind of lateness and aggression. Evie felt a jolt of panic as she suddenly thought it might've been much later and she'd missed school, or maybe her premature departure yesterday was noticed and being formally chased up. She looked up at the sky as if she'd be able to figure out the exact time from the position of the sun.

Jason was shouting for someone to answer but Evie gleefully ignored him and told Toby C that he was the most gorgeous bunny in the whole wide world. She was outside, so of course she couldn't hear the phone ringing and Jason shouting if he blamed her for failing to pick it up. There were four other adults in the house, all of them were capable of taking a call.

Right when Evie thought no one was actually going to get the phone, and she'd fastened the locks across the rabbit's hutch and started heading indoors, she heard the ringing stop, and Jason answer in his phone voice. He said 'yes' a couple of times and was listening.

For the second time that morning, Evie found herself hovering by the back door to observe and listen to her family before they noticed her. She had no idea who would be phoning, if it was a telemarketer call, Jason would've told them off and hung up by now.

"Leave us alone. No comment! I'll not have you journalists hounding my family! Do not ring this number again and tell your writer friends! I know a very good lawyer!" Jason's suddenly loud tone made Evie jump out of her skin.

"Yes, I am very much up to date with current affairs. No. How dare you! You have the wrong number, it's nothing to do with us, and you need to delete this number and never contact us again, do you hear me?" Jason slammed the phone into its charging cradle. He shouted each member of the household by name and ordered a family meeting before he stalked into Charles' room, not even knocking before he burst in.

Evie had to double check the hutch and tidy up before she could find out what had happened. By the time she shuffled into Charles' room and sat on the edge of the sofa bed next to him, Maria and Tilly has materialised and were conferring with each other. The phone's annoying ringing had immediately started again, seemingly louder than before as no one moved to answer it. The sudden silence as Jason yanked the plug from the wall was a blessing. It hadn't been that long, yet phantom echoes of the ring tone were already settling in the house.

"Jason, darling, who were you talking to on the phone? Not one of these telemarketers again? Isn't our number private?" Maria asked, her soft voice the only sound. "Only, I have the most horrendous migraine and the ringing really didn't help."

"Shut it, Maria, I don't have time for your silly headaches today. They've bloody found us! That was some journalist asking about *him*. Brilliant, I knew we shouldn't have taken him in, they're hounding me! I won't have any peace again! It's a nightmare! I don't know how celebrities deal with all this; the stress is too much. I can't go to work, in fact, none of us can go out. We all have to lay low, it's the only way." Jason strode over to the window and discreetly looked out.

"Oh no! What do we do? I'll ring Dexter – they'll tell us

what to do. Their job is to help us sort situations like this. If it's happened to us it must've happened to the others wherever they are—" Maria started.

"It's only myself and two others, the rest are false leads. We don't know how they got our names and numbers, but somehow they have. I am very unhappy that this has happened and the effect it'll undoubtedly have on all of us, but I have been expecting something like this to happen for quite some time. I understand that there aren't really secrets with all this technology. It was a matter of time." Charles declared from the corner, where he was calmly sitting on the sofa bed. As one, everyone turned to him, not expecting him to have contributed.

"You… know… the others?" Jason spat, his face vaguely purple.

Evie was startled, but after a second realised that of course he'd have reached out to the only seven others who are in the same position. They were the only ones who would truly understand. As she reached that conclusion she shrugged and smiled at Charles.

"That's nice! It's a great idea, you should all get together and support each other, after all, you're the only people alive that share the experience. What are they like?" Evie asked.

"Is that a joke? How did you even get in contact with them? You're out of order! You're bringing all this trouble onto my family and I am not having it! How do they even have our number? They'll be camped outside next. I want you out…" Jason said, uncharacteristically trailing off.

Evie smiled at Charles again, he'd gotten off lightly. Until Jason swung around to point at Evie.

"You—you've been bragging in school and you're always on your phone desperately trying to make friends and copy your sister. You told someone, didn't you? You're the leak and now they have our phone number, they'll find our address next. It's her fault, she's so stupid!" Jason continued, spitting as he talked. It seemed like his rage was almost choking him, forcing him to spit his words out.

For the first time, Evie felt like her father's anger would surpass a verbal attack and turn physical. She took a step back, shook by Jason's fury.

"But I—I haven't. I didn't tell anyone!" Evie protested.

"How could you, Evie? You knew how important this was. I thought over these past few weeks, last night excluded of course, that you were finally starting to take some responsibility but clearly not. I can't even bear to look at you right now. Get out. Stay away from me," Maria said.

"Mum," Evie said once.

"Why don't you run upstairs, Evelyn, you too, Matilda. I need to talk to your parents. I'll come upstairs and see you soon, okay?" Charles looked calm on the surface but there was fury blazing behind his brown eyes.

As Evie ran from the room, she exchanged a look with her sister. Tilly looked glum, her eyes ringed with shadows and the normal sparkling blue seemed dull. Evie realised with a start that she hadn't seen her sister without make up on for years.

They both stopped to survey each other at the bottom of the stairs.

Surprising herself, Evie whispered, "They both hate me. They wish I wasn't born. They mean it too. Even Mum—" she broke off with a sob.

"It'll be okay, Evie. Try not to worry. Mum doesn't hate you, and me and Grandad definitely don't hate you. And Dad… we both know better than to listen to what he says when he's kicking off," Tilly said to Evie as she gave her a one-armed hug before she ran up the stairs.

Evie was in her room with the light off, her curtains drawn tightly, and the door firmly closed. She hadn't had such a severe fight with her parents in quite a while, and she was angry that they could devastate her like this. It had been hours and Charles hadn't come up to see her like he'd promised. She'd cried for a while until she had no more tears and then she'd just been waiting.

From downstairs she heard a door slam and a car engine but couldn't be bothered to go to the window to see who was leaving.

Without warning, there was a brief knock on her door, and it was thrown open before she had the chance to respond. Charles crossed the threshold with a bowl of popcorn and a mug.

"I hate that this is becoming a regular thing, duck. But at least you get another one of my speciality drinks. Are you okay?" Charles asked, sitting on her bed and setting the popcorn in between them. "Popcorn is relatively healthy, have as much as you want," he added.

"Thanks, I'm fine. I should be used to it. It's just been going well lately, and I've been kind of… happy so it's more of a shock I guess. I never normally fight with my mum, not like this. And Jason, I always annoy him but neither of them has looked at me like that before. Like they don't love me," Evie explained, her voice shaking but she had no more tears left.

"I've had a stern word with them, more than a few words actually. And… I have something to tell you. Or to ask you even—" Charles paused, as if weighing every word. "I have been looking into it for a while, but I didn't want to mention it until it was set in stone. But in light of what happened last night and today, well even if this one doesn't work out, I'll find something else and what I'm trying to say is regardless, this will happen. I just don't have details yet."

"What is it? What's happening?" Evie asked.

"I'm moving out. Getting my own place, I butt heads with Jason, and I hate relying on his hospitality and he reminds me constantly that it's his house and, to be honest, I've gotten used to life a lot more and settled in to my new life. So, it's about time really, it was only supposed to be a short term thing anyway. I can't camp in the living room of my granddaughter's house forever and—why are you crying?" Charles asked, frowning.

"I'm sorry. I'm trying to be happy but all I can think of is how horrible it'll be living here without you!" Evie realised she did, in fact have tears in reserve to use.

"Evie. Honey no. No, no, no! You misunderstood, I'll be taking you with me. That is, if you want to come," Charles explained, wrapping Evie up into a huge hug. "I'm sorry, I thought that was obvious, that's why I didn't mention it straight away."

"Really? It's not a joke or you just saying it?" Evie could hardly breathe, and her words were coming out in gasps.

"Evie, I promise. You deserve better. I'm not saying everything will be perfect and easy, I daresay we'll disagree and bicker but there will always be love behind it. You are one of the best parts of my life, and this is the last time you'll cry in this room. I will not stand by while my great-granddaughters are so desperately unhappy."

"What did my mum and dad say about it?" Evie questioned after a lengthy pause.

"I'm not going to lie to you, but I'm also not going to recreate the argument I just had with them. Basically, they've agreed to let you come with me. That's the bottom line and what matters. You don't need to worry about anything else. I also think you may have a better relationship with them when you've got some distance," Charles continued.

"Now, this won't be instant. There'll be a lot of planning and paperwork and some mandatory therapy sessions ahead, but the process has started, and I have a lot of people helping me. I will keep you updated, and we'll stay out the way of your parents for the time being but now you know there's an end in sight. You can start thinking about what colour we're going to paint your room. One of the top priorities will be you choosing your new bedding, you can have anything you like, brand new and all yours. You'll need to toilet train that rabbit too, if it'll be living in my house. Our house," Charles grinned at Evie. "Why don't you grab some popcorn and I'll answer your question."

"Oh, Grandad! Thank you, thank you, thank you! And which question?" Evie asked, as she scooped up a handful of popcorn.

"You asked me what the other seven Everest people are like, didn't you? And I know for a fact you haven't said a single word about me to anyone, so I'm not worried about telling you all this highly confidential information," he said with an exaggerated wink.

"Thank you, Grandad. Truly. For everything," Evie said seriously.

"You are very welcome, duck. Now, I know I joked about it just a second ago, but what I'm about to tell you... I'll be breaking the law, but I trust you and to be honest I'd like to discuss it with someone. While I totally trust you, I need you to understand how imperative it is that you don't discuss it with anyone or write it anywhere. Not your online blog or diary or anywhere. We would both get into a lot of trouble. I'm sure you won't but I have to say it." Charles took a deep breath before he continued, "One of us, there's a lady, and I don't know how much you understand about what happened. But I've had to report weekly about if and how much my hair has grown and any changes. It's unchartered territory and they weren't sure if my body would grow and change as it should. Now it seems like my hair hasn't grown a millimetre since the day they picked me up from the side of Everest. I think my molecules have stayed frozen and are damaged beyond repair. But I can cry like anyone else, and they're pretty sure I'll age like I would've. So, some things are fine, and others like my hair, will never change. So, it's a good job I've got nice hair hey? Anyway, so one of the ladies, her name is Rose and she's actually an identical twin but that's beside the point. She was waiting for her menstruation to pick up, and basically, it wasn't all working as it should be and it turns out she's p—" Charles abruptly broke off as the door banged open.

"Your phone has been ringing non-stop. I can't open the stupid thing since you put a password on and it's making Maria's headache worse. It's called a mobile phone for a reason old man. You're supposed to take it with you. Next time answer it yourself because I'm not your personal assistant. If you leave it lying around and it disturbs me again, you'll be fishing it out of the bin." Jason spat and launched the phone towards Charles like a rugby ball before he stomped away.

Charles energetically pushed off the bed and lunged to catch it. He looked at the display and faintly smiled when he saw the name on the screen.

"I need to take this; I've been expecting an important call. I'll tell you about that other thing another time. Chin up, duck. I'll come back once I'm off the phone," Charles said before he hurried out.

After he left, Evie teared up again as she realised exactly what Charles had done. He'd stood up for her, put her first and was taking her with him when he moved. She couldn't think of a time when she'd ever felt more optimistic for the future.

She didn't want to let her mind visualise what it would be like moving out. She couldn't let herself get too excited until it was properly planned. But for the first time in a while, she breathed a little easier, as if an invisible weight was off her. There was an end in sight, finally.

Chapter 13

Evie stayed in her room for most of the day. Eventually, Charles came back, this time bringing two bowls of tomato soup. They ate together, discussing their favourite and least favourite meals and then played Scrabble again. Knowing it belonged to Evelyn made it special, so Evie handled the box with great care, and on the score sheets she wrote in her neatest handwriting. There was something magical about the fact that the scores from her game with her great-grandad were directly next to sheets from the past where Evelyn was the one keeping score as she played on Christmas day with Charles. She briefly wondered if one day it would be passed on and played with a younger generation, with Evie taking the role as wise protector to her imaginary children and grand-children.

They heard Tilly come home from wherever she'd been and heard when Maria and Jason met in the kitchen for their own dinner and started bickering. The words were too low to hear but the sound of their annoyance drifted through cracks in the floorboards and reminded Evie and Charles of the storm that continued to brew below.

Right before tea time, Charles' mobile rang again. He'd been awkwardly carrying it in his hand as he went between rooms of the house. Not quite used to taking it everywhere with him and he was vehemently against putting it in his pocket. It was remarkable progress Evie thought, as she remembered trying to show him how to use his shiny new iPhone, courtesy of Dexter.

Even now, he only used it for phone calls. She'd never seen him send a text or download an app. He had taken a few photos, but all of them were blurred and zoomed in.

Charles announced that it was Dexter calling, whisking Evie out of her memories. Since the volume was turned all the way up, Evie overheard every word.

Dexter had called Charles to apologise for however Charles' name had been released. He'd solemnly vowed to find out who did it and sue them for the breach of their NDA. Evie listened carefully as they talked legal terms, trying to memorise them so she could search them later and explain them to Charles. Although he didn't admit it, the deep crease between his eyebrows was a telling sign that Charles was confused but too proud to question it, wrongly assuming it's stuff he should know.

After a long chat about the legal system and code names, Dexter suggested that he speak to everyone together. The whole family were called to the kitchen where they met in a temporary truce to listen to the conversation unfold. The phone was to be put on speaker so they could all be told at the same time. After several failed attempts by Charles, Tilly had plucked it from his hands and pressed one button before placing it on the table between them.

"Hi, everyone. Am I on speaker now? You can all hear me? Okay good, hope you're all well, I'll get straight to business. I'm sure you're already aware, that the whole world is once again captivated. As far as we know, Charles and two others have had their names leaked. After the media had lost the trail with vague tip-offs that the Eight were in the UK, by some public relations miracle the interest had died down when nothing new was brought up. Many people wrote it off as a hoax and thought they were right when no further details were released. We were more than happy to let them believe that. There was a lot of chatter on social media, and several memes were made with generic images but that was it. All manageable and better than we'd dared to hope for. I know we've already told you, but you need to avoid the media at all costs. Don't give them anything, usually they move on to the next big drama quite quickly, but given our unusual situation, we expect them to hang on as long as it takes for them to get the story. We can send security to make sure no one trespasses on your property; we can also send people to train you in what you can say for when the time is right to release a statement. The important thing now is to stay positive and not get too worried. You are safe, and we are with you every step of the way. The media is pushing for interviews and for Charles to feature on just about every television, radio show, podcast etc. that there is. We have put this off so far, but the public are desperate to know more since we have been withholding information since day one. I already know your thoughts on this, Charles, and I will not force you into the media circus just yet, but sooner or later you'll have to say something. In the meantime, keep your heads down. And remember, there will always be someone with a phone camera or someone listening, so I suggest for you all to be on your best behaviour until the frenzy calms down. Charles, I'll speak to you tomorrow at the normal time. Everyone else, thank you for your patience and understanding. Call us if you need any help. Take care, bye. Bye, bye."

After Dexter had rung off, no one spoke for a long moment.

Eventually, the silence grew so long, it seemed as though no sound would ever break it. When the heating came on, sending pipes rattling through the house, they were all startled out of their thoughts.

"The way I see it, is the scrutiny of the world is upon us. All five of us here will feel an effect from the media learning my name. I didn't ask for it, and I know for a fact none of you caused it. So, there's no use playing the blame game. If we have any hope of surviving the warzone that is the modern day media, we need to stop these ridiculous fights. We are a family, and we will remain as a unit until we can quietly separate once the attention dies down. I want all of this nonsense laid to rest, and I do not expect to hear anything about it after today. No. More. Fighting. Now, Maria, Jason, I think there was something you both wanted to say to your daughters before we move on?" Charles' tone brooked no argument.

Neither of them spoke. Maria sighed and rubbed her temples, and Jason glared at the ceiling.

"Do you need a reminder of our conversation? I can ask the girls to wait outside if you have forgotten our agreement?" Charles' voice was braided with power. He spoke like a monarch addressing the people, proud and fearless and offering no opportunity for argument.

"My head is killing; we need to wrap this up. But fine, girls I love you both the same. Nothing you can do, no matter how selfish or dumb, can change that. Evie, I'm sorry about yesterday. I'm under a lot of pressure at the moment but I shouldn't have lost my temper with you. You are both my daughters, and I wouldn't swap you for anything," Maria spoke quietly but with sincerity.

Evie looked at Charles, in awe again of what a difference he has made in her life.

"Yeah, what she said," Jason muttered, in a voice that sounded dangerously close to being flippant. Charles made a sound of annoyance but didn't press the matter.

"If that's everything, I was in the middle of an online

meeting for work. Fat chance they'll believe I have a virus when they see our faces splashed all over the news. You all better hope I can continue working otherwise we'll be having these *lovely* family meetings outside on the streets once we lose the house. Someone around here has to work hard and pay the bills." And with that, Jason stomped back up the stairs and slammed his bedroom door.

Maria winced at the slam and got up as well. She dragged a blanket outside and climbed into the hammock. It was clear she did not want to be disturbed.

The rest of them stayed around the table.

"How was that? For all I call your dad bossy, I sure did sound like him when I was commanding them to apologise didn't I?" Charles asked.

"Awesome," Tilly replied, as she stabbed her phone screen and typed away.

"It was so cool-great! I can't believe they did that. Thank you! All I do is thank you, but I mean it. I really—" Evie's gushing was interrupted by Tilly's gasp.

"Matilda? Are you all right?" Charles questioned as he leaned towards her.

"The news, he's saying—put the news on," Tilly whispered.

With a grim expression, Charles led them into his room, where he swept his socks into a pile on the floor and stabbed the remote until he found the right channel.

The weather forecast had just wrapped up before cycling straight back to Andrea Cabot, she was joined by a man who looked nothing like Jason, but strongly reminded Evie of him.

"Good evening, I am joined by Mr Kane Winters who is a special guest today to share his opinion on the current situation. Mr Winters has been protesting outside parliament every single day since the news broke about the Everest Eight. He is a former journalist and has an intriguing perspective. We come to you now, with the next *peak* in our extraordinary tale as three of the Everest Eight have been named. I can exclusively reveal that our real life returned from the dead citizens are Mr Charles Hartley, Mr Frank Hillferd and Ms Dorothy Watts—" Cabot paused after she said the names, safe in the knowledge that every person watching would be leaning closer to their screens.

"Freaks! Three freaks named, five to go. We need to act—" Winters seized the silence to start speaking. His microphone was abruptly cut off, he was still ranting, arms flailing around but no sound was allowed to pass.

As soon as they heard the word 'freaks', Evie exchanged a grim look with Tilly. Charles just intently stared at the screen.

"Thank you for that insight. Anyway, our sources have yet to track down their locations so we can get some of our questions answered and their unbelievable stories shared. We have been a little more successful in using public records to trace family members. So far none of the families have had a comment, but as always, you'll all be the first to know when I get any fresh information. Now, I'm also joined today by some scientists who are specialists in their fields and who have dedicated their lives to genetics, who have kindly agreed to answer our questions. Doctor, do you believe these people can safely live amongst us after…" The TV was turned off mid-sentence, none of them cared what scientist or person was offering their opinion today.

Evie didn't know what to say. Everything had changed now. Three of the Eight had been identified publicly and though Dexter was on a war path to identify the leak, it had still happened and could never be taken back. Although their addresses and personal information was so far being kept out of mainstream news, it was only a matter of time. The call Jason had answered earlier was surely only the start.

Evie had been following the E8Updates page online, but

177

lately she had been far too wrapped up in her life and the constant drama, and it had upset her so much that she'd vowed to avoid it. She hadn't seen their latest predicament coming round so soon, thinking as Dexter did, that most people had moved on when the story went stale. Dexter and his friends in the public relations department had ordered them to avoid the media, which hadn't been hard for her since she'd deleted Instagram. They weren't to give statements, post online or even pose for photos, but they couldn't stop her from looking online anonymously.

Evie knew how nasty people were to each other's face and that it increased ten-fold when coming from an anonymous nickname. People were like sheep. A prime example being the whole school avoiding Evie based off one idiot's opinion. After today though, she needed to know what people were thinking.

She hugged Charles tight and was the last to leave, heading straight to her room. She realised her parents were once again in the kitchen and talking about Charles, but she didn't care to listen. While her laptop loaded up, she took deep breaths, preparing herself for the worst. Evie went on to Twitter and immediately saw the number one trending hashtag. As soon as the hashtag loaded, it became alarmingly apparent that a lot of people were suspicious and didn't support the Eight.

#EverestFreaks

MareverlyNotts0115: These ppl r unnatural and should die! #EverestFreaks

PrincessLou244: Omg #EverestFreaks this is wild! Can my grandma come back to life? Will she be a skeleton? Glad we didn't cremate her!

Reelslim_shady206: Yo peeps is anyone else wondering where they are? Might walk past one of these freaks in the Asda and not even know :o #EverestFreaks

Freedomhunter12345: #EverestFreaks PUT THEM IN PRISON. PUT THEM IN PRISON. PUT THEM IN PRISON. #BeforeItsTooLate

HolyRoeJ11: Daniel 12:2. Isaiah 26:19. It was foretold! #EverestFreaks

VigilanteSwedeNO1: Let's go hunt us some freaks. I bet my life they're in London. Now we have names to go off! Who's in? Retweet to join. We can fix this #EverestFreaks

WoolyBack5: Has no one else noticed that we haven't seen faces of the #EverestFreaks? Why aren't their pictures out there, what are they hiding?

TweetyPie1956: The government are hiding stuff from us they are tracking us don't trust them we can't run knowledge is power retweet #EverestFreaks

SkullTwins04: 4 real tho, how did they do it? Who else wants to live 4ever? #EverestFreaks

Bigbadbill35: IF U ARE HIDING ONE OF THE FREAKS YOU ARE AS BAD AS THEM. U WILL BE EXPOSED. UR ALL FREAKS IN MY BOOK #EverestFreaks

Scouse_Heart : DEATH TO THE FREAKS #EverestFreaks

RabbitMama1: THEY ARE THE #EVERESTEIGHT NOT THE #EVERESTFREAKS. HAVE SOME COMPASSION! XO

Evie slammed down the lid of her laptop and ran as fast as she could into the bathroom. Kane Winters had riled up the haters. All those people out there who hate Charles and think he's a freak and unnatural and some of them are now planning to hunt them down and kill them. Actual people were making threats to her family and now the news had revealed his name, it was only a matter of time before his relationship to the Monroes was discovered. Soon enough, she'd be a pariah in school, even more

179

than usual. She lunged to the toilet and noisily emptied her stomach. Her hands shook as she sank onto the cold floor, gently rocking as she fought a growing panic.

Evie stayed in the bathroom all night. The cool tiles caressed her face as she lay on the tiled floor. From her vantage point, she found a forgotten toothbrush, lost in a cloud of cobwebs and dust under the bathroom cupboard. Evie didn't care enough about the evidence of spiders to move. Even the dull pain from her bruised tail bone wasn't enough to persuade her to move to her bed.

She varied between retching over the toilet bowl and trying to think of nothing at all as she willed the unconsciousness of sleep to steal her away and provide a little relief. It was not granted though, so she lay there and waited. When the frosted window allowed a little more light to seep through, she sat up. Evie knew that she wasn't ill. No bout of food poisoning or virus plagued her, rather her heart and soul were sickened by what she'd seen online. The wave of panic and fear was enough to upset the contents of her stomach.

She was still sitting there and thinking about throwing up again when she heard an argument explode from downstairs. Evie hauled herself off the floor, splashed some cold water on her face and staggered out the bathroom, leaving a trail of droplets as she slowly went down the stairs to see what was going on. She stopped in the doorway to the kitchen, her parents too involved in their discussion to notice her.

As time inevitably had been pushing forward, Evie had emerged from the long night and somehow the early morning had slipped by. The clock showed eleven thirty, and the remnants of breakfast lingered in the room. The aroma of bacon stubbornly remained, and dishes piled high in the sink. The smell alone threatened to turn Evie's stomach. Only the focus on the air as her lungs inflated and deflated kept her from fleeing back to the bathroom.

"He is dangerous! People want to kill him! It's all over social media and it's putting us at risk!" Jason cried out. It seemed like they'd all ventured into the online world to assess the damage. While the comments made Evie sick, they made her father furious.

"But it's my grandad, there isn't anyone else to take him in. I don't know what you want me to do!" Maria replied, raking her hands through her hair.

"Do something. Anything. Speak to those government guys. See if they can take him off our hands. If they can't... see what else they can do. In fact, why don't you see if they'll compensate us for the trouble," Jason snapped, and then he laughed at the same time that Evie gasped.

"Jason! We're being scrutinised from every angle, and you think trying to squeeze money out of them is the best thing to do right now? We need their help, we have to play nice, okay?" Maria answered, her tone steel.

"Are you for real? You want money for taking him in? Even though he's Mum's grandad and has no other family? How selfish are you?" Evie demanded, emboldened in her outrage. Neither parent showed any sign of surprise that she was there or offered her anything other than dismissive glares.

"This is pathetic. Just for a second imagine that it was you on Everest, and how it would feel. He doesn't need his own family turning on him, using him for their own gain. It makes me sick, sicker than any of the comments online!" Evie's voice rose to shouting levels.

"There you go again, running your mouth. Give it a rest, Evie, you're making my migraine so much worse. It's your own fault we're in this current situation. Just do everyone a favour and get lost." Maria barely glanced at her before she pushed past and stomped up the stairs.

Evie was a statue. Frozen in place, her surface smooth and never changing. She had agreed with her mother and argued for what was morally right and it was crystal clear that her mother would rather have no help than Evie's help. Despite the apology that Charles had coerced from them, they clearly said what he made them say, and it wasn't a true reflection of their feelings. Evie just remained there, with the taste of vomit on her lips and a crushing hopelessness in her heart.

"Why are you not ready yet?" Jason startled Evie from her thoughts when he suddenly turned to address her.

"Er, ready... for what?" Evie replied.

"For school dummy! It's a weekday? You've been skiving off and we're not having it any more. Your attendance is appalling this year. Hope you've done your homework," he continued, smirking.

Evie felt like a rug had been yanked out from under her. She knew they were in the middle of an unbelievable situation, but when they'd first had the call yesterday morning from the reporter and after being told to lay low by Dexter, they'd planned to camp in and avoid everyone. Her parents hadn't been to work, even Tilly had paused her chaotic social life. The last thing she thought of was going to school and facing so many people.

"But, Dad. You can't be serious. I know our names aren't in the news yet, but it's only a matter of time before someone figures it out. Then I'll be hounded! I already know Kendall will call the papers and they'll take photos of me and follow me home and everyone will want to kill me on Twitter too! We have to stay at home, Dexter said!" Fear laced Evie's words, after what she'd read online, she knew there was a real danger. Some of the talk online was merely talk, but Evie had no doubts that there were people in the world who would not hesitate to act upon their hatred.

"It isn't safe, did you not see the death threats online? Do you not care? I can catch up on my school work from home. You and Mum are working from home!" Evie beseeched.

"We leave in fifteen, I'm driving you myself so I can make sure you go in. If you hurry, you'll get there in time for lunch. Your favourite time," Jason retorted, his lips quirked up in the corners.

"I can't believe you." Evie spat as she turned and started towards Charles' door.

"That rabbit of yours has been very noisy. And it stinks. It's not really yours though, is it? It was bought for your sister, and she is far too busy to care for it. Maybe the kindest thing to do would be to… rehome it. Let it go. Give it to someone who is smart enough and not too emotional to care for it," Jason's voice was even, his cold eyes promised the words he didn't explicitly say.

Evie stopped, a statue again. She believed he'd do it. If he treated his own daughter so poorly, he would have no reserves about the rabbit. She was at a very tricky crossroads. If she dared deceive her father, if she argued or went to Charles as she so wanted to, then she would be responsible for anything happening to Toby C. But in obeying she would gift her father with power to control her, to push her around even further with the knowledge she wouldn't dare fight back at the risk to her beloved rabbit.

Then Evie remembered what Charles had said, had promised. Soon, as soon as they could, Evie and Charles would be out of this house and they would whisk Toby C to safety with them. She just had to play the game for a little longer. She should be grateful Jason had never thought of this threat before. Withholding food and grounding her, confiscating her possessions and parading her around at social events, were all tolerable. Losing Toby C was not.

With that thought, Evie gave the briefest of nods and backed away until she reached the stairs. She darted up to her room and raced to get ready as quickly as she could.

In twelve minutes, Evie was breathless but by the door, school bag in hand.

The drive to school was silent, Evie remembered the last time it was just her and her father in the car, when he'd made a holy show in the dessert parlour. She sighed as she compared the two drives. Even when everything has changed, some things remain the same.

"Have a *great* day!" Jason finally said, with a snake's smile. He watched until she'd gone through the office door and the receptionist had called her over.

Evie signed the late book and shuffled into the main school. As Jason had predicted, she'd arrived just as lunch had started. With no appetite, Evie made a beeline for the library.

Most people were probably in the canteen or sprawled in small groups at various places in the school. As she scanned the room, she was relieved to not recognise any faces. She picked her way across the room, and most people didn't look twice at her. They might not know yet, might not have jumped to the conclusion, especially since Evie, Tilly, and Maria all had Jason's surname, so it wasn't the same as Charles'. They'd eventually realise, but for today Evie had gotten away with it.

"That's her. Apparently, she's not ashamed like at all. It's so gross; her boyfriend is older than my Dad!" A girl from year ten didn't bother whispering as she gossiped to her friend, who gaped at Evie, mouth hanging open.

Evie looked away, feeling blood rush to her cheeks and to the back of her neck. She walked faster, knocking into a table and hitting her knee hard enough she expected to find a bruise later. Serenaded by laughter and clapping, Evie dived into the corner seat in the computer section of the library.

She kept her head down as she wasted time on the computer. After having to re-read the same opening paragraph on IMDb about the new '*Joker*' film, she gave up. Occasionally she opened a document or scrolled on the page so none of the students who had come in after a quick lunch could demand her computer. But while pretending to be busy, she thought.

Evie had been so wrapped up in the fact that Charles had been on the news, that she had forgotten the silly rumours. She had walked out halfway through the day to avoid it and all the feelings rushed back to her as she remembered.

"You finished?" a boy asked, and Evie quickly opened her school email.

"Sorry, no," she replied, and then made an effort to actually read her emails until he left her alone.

It was mostly junk, notices about upcoming bake sales and carnival activities which were being arranged at break times to fundraise for the Everest Eight. Evie deleted them all, and then came across a message from her film teacher. It was a short but friendly email asking her to catch up on a film they'd started discussing and reminding her of the homework she owed him. Evie couldn't even recall what the homework was on and knew she would be in for a lecture this afternoon when she had double film.

"Hey—" someone said, from directly behind Evie.

"I am busy. Can't you see that I. Oh, hi, Roman—" Evie broke off awkwardly as she realised who was standing behind her.

"I'll leave you to it if you're busy." Roman smiled but it didn't reach his eyes.

"No. You don't need to go. I thought you were this kid who wanted my computer before. I was just checking some emails, apparently I have homework due in. I always forget to check my school email," Evie quickly explained.

"Mine is synced with my personal email account so I get notifications for both. You should do it too! Anyway, I was just going to say hi. I didn't see you this morning in form."

"That would be so much easier, can you show me how to do it?" Evie replied.

"Sure. Pass me your phone." As Roman tapped on her phone, he tried again. Either oblivious to the fact she'd deliberately dodged the question or relentlessly wanting to know the answer. "So, did you just come in? I was going to text you and see how you were doing after what Kendall said, but I don't have your number."

"It's a dumb rumour. You do know that right? I'm not dating anyone, never mind an old man. It's just Kendall being a b—"

"Speak of the devil," Roman interrupted as Kendall swanned into the library, entourage in tow.

Evie felt the weight of the glares as they swept across her. From the corner of her eye, she could see Kendall, arms crossed, watching.

"This should do it. It'll save you from missing any important emails. Anyway, I better go, I want to grab a drink before form. See you later, Evie!" he called as he strolled away. She didn't miss the polite wave in Kendall's direction, but he didn't stop and chat to them.

Evie smiled a little as she logged out of her email and started gathering her belongings. The day had certainly taken a turn she thought, as she turned the computer off. The ridiculous rumours would be set straight when Charles' identity was connected to her. Then she'd be in a totally different type of hot water, but maybe it wouldn't be so bad. If Roman was by her side, her classmates wouldn't risk falling out with him by upsetting her. Even Kendall might permanently back off. Evie sighed as she banished the thought away.

Evie didn't even flinch as she left the library to sniggers and hissing.

"Gross."

"Dirty."

"Stay away from him!" whoever hissed this was particularly venomous, but Evie didn't deign to look and give them any satisfaction.

She drifted to class to get her afternoon attendance mark, and on to film where she apologised sincerely and promised to catch up next lesson. Film was usually her favourite lesson, since she typically had good grades and turned in homework on time, the teacher gave her an extension and advised her to make sure it doesn't happen again.

By the time the bell had rung marking the end of the school day, Evie had gotten very good at tuning out hateful comments. Every time she heard one, she'd think *you'll see*. Soon enough you'll see the bigger picture. And I'll remember who you are and what you said when you come crawling over with eager questions. As Evie thought this, she imagined pulling on a coat, like invisible armour and she imagined the words bouncing off her harmlessly. She had thick skin, so strangers jumping on the gossip wagon and judging was no big deal.

She walked past a group of sixth-formers who gathered by the gate. Kendall's lot mixed with the rugby boys. The snide comments again fell on deaf ears. Kendall, who took the top spot for most hostile, wasn't there yet so all the words ricocheted off her imagined armour. She glanced at Roman and returned the smile he offered. Before she could draw any more attention she hurried past, head held high.

Evie was walking home when her phone vibrated with an incoming email. It was from her school account, which had now merged with her own emails. The first line of the email popped up, along with the name.

Her heart skipped a beat as she read and re-read it. It was from Roman.

Roman: *Hey, Evie. I didn't get the chance to talk to you properly earlier. Shall we video call later and catch up? I don't have data until I get home, so I can't reply. But I'll be ready at five and praying you feel the same way as me. R x*

Evie was practically skipping as she arrived home. She analysed their lunchtime conversation through a new lens. He had said he didn't have her number to text her, and he would have seen her email address when he helped sort her phone out. And he had said 'see you later' when they had parted ways. He must've been planning it and maybe, like her, he was shy.

As the invitation sank in, a flutter slowly flared up in Evie's stomach. A video call with Roman. She couldn't decide if she felt like she needed to be sick or like she'd won the lottery. She'd dreamt of something like this happening, but now it actually had, it was too good to be true. She'd never had a video call before, but she knew she needed to look nice. Tilly was always hurrying upstairs to take calls and was the closest person Evie had to an expert on the matter. Evie knew she should ask her sister; the internet could only help so much, and time was wasting.

After she picked out a black top with ruffled sleeves which would be perfect since the camera only covered her face and shoulders, Evie gathered her courage and slowly crossed the landing. Seven small, slow steps brought her to the door.

It had been years since she'd voluntarily gone to see Tilly in her room. In the hallway, Evie dithered over whether she should knock or go right in. Before she could talk herself out of it she timidly rapped on the wooden door, right on one of the glittery golden stars her sister had etched into the whitewashed wood years earlier.

"Yeah?" Tilly called.

Evie opened the door and poked her head in. Tilly was applying fake eyelashes in the mirror and her eyes widened when she spotted her sister on the threshold.

"Oh, Evie! Hi, what's wrong?"

"Hey, nothing. Why would something be wrong?" Evie felt herself getting defensive. The whole family wrote her off, stupid Evie always messing up. Most sisters should be able to have a conversation without conflict, but they weren't like most sisters.

"It's just—you hardly ever come here that's all. Come in. If nothing's wrong then what's up? Ooh do you think these lashes are too much?"

Evie took a few steps into the room and peered at the lashes which made Tilly's sparkling blue eyes huge and had no idea what would be counted as too much. They were thick black extensions, but Tilly notoriously could pull off any look.

"They're fine? But I need, well I was wondering if I could borrow some hair stuff?"

189

Tilly finished adding extra glue to her eyelashes and turned so she was properly facing Evie.

"Are you feeling okay, Evie?" Tilly asked.

Heat flared in Evie's cheeks. She started backing away, but accidentally kicked a plastic bin across the floor and sent lipstick stained tissues and empty packets of chewing gum across the floor. "Whatever. Just forget I asked. Bye," she said to the messy floor.

"Bloody hell, stop. You're being so weird! But yes, what do you need?" Tilly sighed but she was still looking right at Evie, the fact that she hadn't dismissed her and resumed applying her make up made Evie's heart flutter.

"Er, I want it to be like, smooth and flat and down. Like straight down? But I only have my brush and it's all…" Evie hadn't planned on getting this far along and hadn't considered what she was actually asking for.

Tilly's eyes were rolled so far back in her head she could probably see her brain.

"It's dumb. He probably won't notice anyway. I'll just put it in a bun. Thanks anyway. Have a great night doing whatever you're doing. Okay, Bye." Evie should've known better than to expect Tilly to not act superior and patronising. She'd never normally bother but she was wound up about Roman. Feeling nervous and desperate to not mess it up drove her to make extreme choices. Evie scooped the rubbish she'd spilt back into the bin.

"Evie! Shut up and sit down right now," Tilly gestured to her seat as she stood up and began rooting through her drawers.

Evie perched on the edge of the seat and looked around Tilly's room. She hadn't been in there in years. The old pink walls and princess theme had transitioned into a mature grey themed room. A fluffy rug matched the lampshades and curtains. The double bed dominated the floor space. The dresser had a huge wooden mirror on top and eight drawers, it matched the double-length wardrobe. Evie didn't care as much about clothes and brands as Tilly, but she rarely saw her in the same outfit. Her sister had a knack for adding a chunky belt or switching low top converse for thigh-high boots and looking like a model. There wasn't much else in there in terms of decoration, a lavender candle sat on her bedside table next to a phone dock but nothing else was out on display.

"Okay, nosey. I'll straighten it for you. Move back a bit. Okay, yep, stay there." Tilly had lined up several contraptions and sprays and accessories. Evie jumped as a sudden cloud of sweetly scented mist billowed around her face, stinging her eyes.

"Close your eyes and mouth Jeez. Stop wriggling, do you want heat protection or not? You can't use heat on your hair if you're not going to use the right defence! When was the last time you had your hair done? You have *sooo* many split ends and it's all dry. You know, Evie, you really could help yourself if you made a bit more of an effort," Tilly lectured as she pulled the straighteners down. "Katie says Kendall told her you're always such a loner. You're always creeping off to the library at every opportunity and acting all aloof. You don't help yourself! Make a bit of effort for a change, try not to frown at people. Be confident, Evie. Why don't you ever wear any of your nice clothes? You always wear old, oversized jumpers. You're naturally pretty, Evie, and I know how kind you are but no one else does. Apparently you're always on your phone, why don't you try and join in with the conversation?"

Evie glared at her sister's reflection. Does she not know that nothing she could do will help? She's been branded a freak by

Kendall, everyone avoids her, the best she could hope for is to be invisible and hope no one starts on her. There's no point saying it to her sister though, people flocked to Tilly because she was pretty and charismatic, and she'd never known anything different. She was trying to think of a witty come back when she looked at her hair.

Silky brown strands floated down her back. Her hair was longer than she'd ever seen it and seemed to shimmer in the light. The transition had happened so quickly.

"Oh! It's beautiful!" Evie cried out.

"Ten mins tops sis, no big deal. See how easy it is? And the hairspray has glitter in that catches the light when you move. Cute right? Anyways, who is this mysterious boy then? And I'm telling you now, he'll notice this hair." Tilly briskly sprayed and then moved on to the final section.

"It's no one really. Just this guy in my form group. I've known him since pre-school and he's so sweet and we've been chatting in the library lately. It's only a video call. So." Evie had the urge to confide in her sister, but she knew she couldn't trust her. And Roman was too special for Tilly to judge and dismiss as she always does.

"And? Who is it? Does he have any brothers or sisters in my year? Spill!" Tilly flicked off the straighteners, setting them onto a heatproof mat. Her hand drew circles in the air for a moment before selecting a pair of false eyelashes.

"Close your eyes, and don't move. Then you have to stay still until the glue dries," Tilly commanded.

Evie couldn't repress a shiver of disgust. Hair products were one thing, but spider leg lashes were quite another and she was absolutely sure that she did not want any fancy make-up or false eyelashes on her face.

"Thank you so much, Tilly. But I've got to go! I need to finish getting ready!"

"Whatevs, loser," Tilly replied, already focused on herself again, ruffling her hair and posing with pouted lips in the mirror.

Evie bounded across the landing, feeling as if her feet were barely touching the plush carpet. She couldn't believe her luck. Everything would get better now; she could sit with Roman at break times and Kendall would have to back off knowing she had a friend – and not just anyone but one of the most popular guys. Suddenly the thought of facing school when news about Charles breaks was less intimidating when she had a friend by her side. And she might've just bonded with her sister for the first time in years.

Back in her own room, Evie threw open her curtains, allowing some golden light from the setting sun to gently bathe the room. She sat down, back against her headboard and turned on the camera, just to see if she looked okay. Her eyes swept over her familiar features, always coming back to her lovely, shimmering hair. The straps of her top just visible in the shot were cute and then she looked closely at her face. Her lips were badly chapped.

Evie leapt from the bed and hurried over to her drawers. She pulled the middle drawer sharply open and began rummaging around. All of her make-up and hair stuff fit into one drawer and she was sending mascara rolling onto the floor and upending a box of bobby pins before she located a pot of red-tinted Vaseline. That one was taken and thrown on the bed as a backup, but she really wanted the classic blue one. How do things just disappear like that? She realised that she had been searching for almost ten minutes and slammed the drawer with an irritated sigh and picked up the red one.

Once her lips were tinted ruby red, she sat back again and

checked the camera. It was noticeable that her lips looked fuller and glistened, but the overall effect was quite nice. Her cheeks were also rather pink, the exertion and frustration of looking through the drawer had Evie catching her breath. She didn't want Roman to think she was blushing or something. As soon as the thought occurred to her, she was up and on her way to the kitchen.

She could hear Tilly singing along to her music and instead of finding it irritating, Evie wondered if she had time to put some music on. It was almost quarter to, so she had to hurry. This is one occasion where she was determined to be exactly on time. Unless he was early, and then she would be ready early too.

Evie skipped right into the kitchen, skidding to a stop when she saw Charles sitting at the table. There was no light apart from the ever-fading glow from the sun, and he had nothing in front of him. He was just silently sitting with his thoughts. Evie hadn't spoken to him since the news had broken, she'd been forced to go to school, and she'd been in such a rush to get ready once she arrived home that she'd not spared a thought about checking on him.

"Hi, I'm just grabbing a drink. I have a call in a minute. With a friend. Anyway, hope you're okay and had a nice day. Maybe I can come and play Scrabble after I finish on the call?" Evie asked, trying to relieve the guilt of neglecting her great-grandfather right after the media had found them.

"Sure thing, if it's not too late when you finish come down and find me. Have fun, kiddo." Charles didn't sound particularly upset, so she brushed her guilt away and snagged a can of Coke from the fridge.

"I only have one can per day, it's my daily treat. So, don't worry or anything," Evie told Charles, though he hadn't asked or given her a pointed look.

With a quick check of her phone, she hurried back out of the kitchen. On the landing, she thought for a second. There was no danger of either of her parents disturbing her, or Charles since she'd spoken to him. But her sister was home and likely curious.

She hammered on Tilly's door and threw it open as soon as she heard her sister call out.

"Hi. Again. Thanks again for the hair. Er—I know you don't normally come to my room, but if you wanted to today, please knock. Or wait until I'm off the phone," Evie pleaded.

"He's important to you isn't he?" Tilly asked.

Evie nodded once.

"I promise, I'll make sure you're not disturbed. Have fun, Evie, and tell me all about it when you're done yeah?" Tilly's smile was full of warmth.

Evie smiled back and then yelped when she caught sight of the time.

"Got to go! Thanks, Till!" Evie said as she darted back to her room and closed the door.

She sat on her bed, sitting up straight and testing how she looked on camera before she felt comfortable. She turned her light on, and then closed the curtains and sat back down. Before she could message to say she was ready, she became aware of how dry her throat suddenly was. Evie picked up the can she had retrieved earlier. With a hiss the can opened, and Evie took a sip, it tasted so good that sip turned to a gulp and within a few seconds half the can was gone. Evie burped and then redid the Vaseline on her lips.

A bead of sweat ran down Evie's neck, she had no idea how people video called every day, and how their hearts could stand it.

At last, Evie was as ready as she could be and had compiled

a mental list of fool-proof topics she could talk about. She had considered sharing her secret about Charles but ultimately decided she should speak to her great-grandad first and they could decide what to say together. If he was even happy for her to share.

Evie wasn't quite sure what the protocol was. She had deleted Instagram and barely used Facebook. She didn't have his number, so she'd email him. She quickly typed an email and sent it before she could second guess her every word. It was simple and casual.

Evie: *Hey Roman, I'm ready when you are. Let me know the plan!* She'd signed off with her phone number, name and a tentative 'x'.

Fifteen minutes crawled by, while Evie fussed over her hair, arranging it behind her, and then she pulled it forward and then back again. She settled with it forward, trusting Tilly's magic that made it look good. She drained the can of coke and reapplied her Vaseline again. She took a few selfies, her lovely hair captured forever on her camera roll.

Still no sign. Her email had sent, but she couldn't see if it had been read. She kept on reading the email he'd sent earlier, checking the date and time on her phone to make sure it was the right day.

Evie debated with herself, she didn't know if she should message again, or if she'd annoy him by repeatedly messaging. It just didn't make sense, why would he set up the call and then ignore her? She hadn't done anything wrong... had she? Maybe there was an unsaid rule she had ignorantly failed to abide by. She tried to think rationally, anything could have happened, an unexpected visit from a relative he rarely saw, his dog taken sick and being rushed to the pet hospital, maybe an emergency.

Maybe he had a better offer. He couldn't have forgotten, not when he'd arranged it only a few hours earlier. The best case scenario would be if something had suddenly come up or he was asleep or something. She tried not to imagine the worst case, which involved Roman and Kendall together.

Evie didn't do anything for an hour, except refresh her emails and repeatedly check her phone was on and working. She didn't dare put a film on, lest she miss Roman if he tried to call. She also felt as though her doing something else would tempt fate into separating her and Roman. If she gave up, maybe he would give up.

Another hour dragged by, as fast as a snail going backwards. She knew in her heart he wasn't going to call. She had thought it two hours ago but refused to entertain the idea. She felt so foolish, he and all his rugby friends would be laughing their heads off as Evie sat there, with her hair done fancy and so much effort put in. She was at least thankful that she was in the sanctuary of her bedroom. No photos of her, shoulders hunched, and lips compressed into a straight line, eyes shining with unshed tears, would make it online tonight.

Evie let out a bitter laugh at herself, for believing it. For getting her hopes up and thinking things were looking up. She should have known when any semblance of good happens in her life, it is swiftly followed by a flood of bad.

She didn't know how she would face him tomorrow. Her only friend, or as close to one as she'd had in quite some time, and even he had turned on her. Now she had to deal with her reputation, the rumours, and the relation to Charles as well as a rift with Roman, the star and sweetheart of the whole school.

Eventually, the hollow in her stomach forced her to get up, tug her dressing gown on and go downstairs in search of food. As she passed Charles' bedroom door, she softened her steps. Not able to face him and smile and play Scrabble when her heart was so heavy. She didn't know how he'd react to her tearing up over a boy, and she didn't want to find out whatever old fashioned views he had.

At almost eight p.m., she expected most of her family to have eaten by now. They tended to eat earlier. At least she would be spared the hassle of having to speak to them. She couldn't stand to see Jason's delight at how miserable she was, he would expect it to be merely from her attending school and taken full credit.

As she grated cheese over a half dozen of crackers, Tilly strolled in and collected a bottle of water from the fridge. She started speaking before she turned to face her sister.

"Spill the tea, Evie! Are you going back on in a minute? Is he cute? What did you talk about?" Tilly demanded.

When Evie didn't immediately reply, Tilly finally looked at her younger sister. Evie's whole face resembled a tomato, and the tears she'd been fiercely holding in place had at last burst through the dam and now flowed freely.

"Oh, Evie. Did it not go well? Did he break up with you?" Tilly asked, as she moved to her sister and began stroking her hair.

"No. Worse." Evie gulped through her sobs.

"Worse?" Tilly repeated, with a sharp intake of breath.

"He—he—" Evie tried, before she broke off.

"What did he do?" Both of them jumped, having not noticed that Charles had materialised in the doorway. He looked like a boxer, surveying an opponent, planning his next move.

"He didn't call. He ignored me when I messaged him, and I didn't want to be annoying and I waited for two and a half hours! He's ghosting me!" Evie finally managed to say.

"Oh, Evie," Tilly murmured.

"That young man has made a grave mistake, duck. It is truly his loss. He is not worth your precious time. What's this about a ghost? He is… pretending to be dead?" Charles took her silence as a yes and moved further into the kitchen.

He pulled tea bags, honey and milk from the cupboards and fridge and was silent as he made them all a drink.

They fussed over her, pressing warm mugs into her hands and re-making the drinks every so often when they went cold. They offered a lot of advice, getting more and more hostile towards Roman. They didn't know his name or anything about him apart from the fact that he'd humiliated and upset Evie. That was enough for Charles to judge him and brandish him no good.

Evie was torn, she felt so let down and fed up, but still clung to a tiny shred of hope that there was a logical explanation. Surely, her Roman, who had been the kindest person to her in the whole school, surely, he wouldn't have been so cruel.

Chapter 14

Another sleepless night. After hours of crying and listening to her sister and great-grandad try to console her, she'd eventually left the kitchen, feeling hollow and empty. Evie had gotten into bed and lay there awake most of the night. Her bloodshot and dry eyes were a souvenir of one of the worst nights she'd endured. She'd heard Tilly and Charles as they debated whether to check on her, but they had decided to give her some space. She'd closed her door over, and mercifully been left alone all night.

After trying not to think about it at all, but it being the only thing on her mind, Evie had reached the conclusion that she should be less trusting, and that although that she didn't want to believe it, she couldn't imagine what could have happened that meant he couldn't have sent a single message. Roman knowing that she was waiting was unforgivable. She deserved better and would tolerate nothing else.

Evie dragged herself out of her toasty bed when she heard the crowd. Her brain had labelled the noise, a cacophony of different tones and voices, blended with laughter and shouts. For a while, she ignored it, unable to bring herself to care. But when it got too much, and a kernel of interest flickered in her dark enveloping sadness, she looked.

At the exact point where the Monroe's driveway met the pavement, a group of people stood there. Cameras with huge lenses aimed at her window, Evie immediately leaned back, waited for the curtains to settle into stillness before she created a tiny gap to press her eye against. Dozens of people gathered, some clearly reporters or photographers or a combination, while some were neighbours, following the scent of drama to the Monroes' door. Evie decided in that moment that she would hate being famous, never having privacy and untold amounts of people judging her from afar. Her vertical blinds were now bars to her cage.

The only glimmer of positivity from the situation, was that the crisis meant her feelings for Roman seemed insignificant. She would have to push her anguish aside to get through the next few days. Evie had no doubt that they may be the hardest yet, as her family were suddenly fish in a clear tank, with no plants or ornaments to hide themselves from sight.

Evie threw some clothes on, did her hair and swiped on some eyeliner and mascara before leaving her room. The only time she usually got ready that quickly was if it was the early hours and she was going on holiday. Instead of the thrill of pulling on the clothes she would always set out the night before and furiously packing last minute, she was getting ready so no unflattering photos of her in her old dressing gown with her hair in a nest would be taken. Again, she thought of famous people, and just how much effort they had to put in to do the most basic tasks. Evie then snorted as she considered their mansions and acres of land, protected by high walls and sometimes security which afforded them privacy the Monroe's did not have the funding for.

Once she was ready, Evie went downstairs. In the kitchen, Charles and Tilly were sitting together, each nursing a hot drink as they murmured to each other. Tilly had been gesturing at a piece of paper covered in names and numbers. Upon Evie's arrival, the paper she had glimpsed was quickly and casually moved.

"The secret is out then; did you see all those people outside?" she said as she entered the kitchen.

Evie had expected them to be concerned after last night, but what she saw, the guilt on their faces, was something else entirely. Charles took a sip of his drink but didn't meet her eyes. Tilly, on the other hand, was the image of deceit. She was fidgeting with her mug, eyes downcast. Her face was pale with a shimmer of sweat above her shaped eyebrows. Something was clearly brewing.

"What?" Evie asked, she finally looked away from her sister, and instead watched the table where the paper was moments before.

The fridge groaning and the pipes moaning were the only sounds. Charles and Tilly exchanged a look, but nothing was said.

"What?" Evie repeated. "Can't I know this secret? Do you have to hide that paper from me? From *me*?"

"It's… complicated. Matilda and I—" Charles broke off into uncomfortable silence.

When it was apparent that he wasn't willing to continue in his explanation, Evie briskly rubbed her hands in a washing motion.

"Whatever. I don't care anyway. I was just being polite. Anyway, good talk," Evie muttered as she ducked into the garden.

She flushed her sister's and great-grandfather's scheming out of her mind as she let the sawdust smell of Toby C's hutch wash over her. The rabbit himself was already biting on the latch to open the door, eager to greet his mum.

Evie scooped him up and buried her head in his neck for a moment. Toby C returned the favour, content to be held by Evie.

She ran her hand from his ears to fluffy tail, over and over. When she heard clicking, Evie paused. She lifted Toby C to eye height and put her ear to his stomach. There was no sound.

Evie glanced around, but none of her family had joined her outside. No other animals were nearby. She mused that it was strange and resumed cuddling her rabbit. He licked her chin a few times and relaxed into her arms. She had just set him down for a breakfast of fresh grass and Jason's mint plants when she heard it again.

Head tilted to one side, Evie listened and focused on the noise. When she realised where it was coming from, she gasped. After retrieving Toby C and safely putting him back in his hutch with a wad of mint leaves, Evie darted back into the house.

Charles and Tilly still sat together and had been looking at something on Tilly's phone. Both had furrowed eyebrows and solemn expressions. They both looked up as Evie hurried in, though Charles stole several more glances at the screen.

Evie also realised her parents were there. Jason was making something at the counter and Maria was at the table, strangely she had huge sunglasses on.

"There's a photographer, he's climbed the fence and was taking photos of Toby C and me – in the garden!" Evie exclaimed breathlessly.

"Nice one, she's pointed out the obvious. What a genius. As if we all haven't seen the vultures circling. If she wasn't messing around out there and no doubt uprooting my herb garden, she would've been here ten minutes ago when we'd all been discussing it," Jason said with venom.

Evie merely shrugged and pulled a bowl from the cupboard. She didn't have the energy to fight with him so early, when her whole body ached, and her heart mourned for Roman. As she reached for a chopping board, she decided that next time she simply wouldn't bother sharing with them. The room dissolved into an uneasy silence once again.

Evie had sat down and was eating porridge with chopped banana when the next argument erupted. They were all still in the kitchen, which had fast become one of two places where they had family meetings or arguments these days. Now they apparently couldn't even go in the garden without seeing a camera over the fence, and with all the curtains closed and phone off the hook, the house was feeling more and more like a claustrophobic jail.

Evie felt the strain from how much time she was being forced to spend with her family. Many other family units would bond and emerge from the other side stronger than before, but it seemed like the opposite of the case in this house for this family. The more they were forced into each other's company, the greater the friction that inevitably would develop into a raging and uncontrollable fire. Time would tell if Evie survived with some burns or got consumed entirely in the flames.

"Right, I've decided. Here's what is going to happen. You will go out there and address the press. Give them a statement, ask them to respect our privacy. Tell them there's an under eighteen-year-old kid, you have PTSD, you're sick, confused, whatever. Say whatever it takes to get rid of them," Jason commanded, pointing at Charles.

"Nope, not happening," Charles replied.

"I swear to God. You are skating on very thin ice. We are getting quite sick of all this. They're on the pavement which is public property so we can't legally get them moved. They can stand there and use their cameras to zoom in, they can follow us when we leave and record anything and everything we say. All of our lives are on pause. I knew this would happen, and it has, and your science friends aren't helping. It's your problem, you fix it!" Jason retorted.

"Admittedly, we wouldn't have had this problem back in my day, it wasn't so easy to share information and find people. But I have already taken advice on how to appropriately act, and myself and the other seven will be keeping a low profile so to speak until we receive further instructions. Mr Dexter is sending a security team to us this morning to prevent any trespassing or over-excited reporters from pouncing at their earliest opportunity. I have been advised to lay low and not make any formal *or* informal statements yet. So that is what I'll be doing. There's nothing you can do to change my mind. Nothing. And to be honest, *son*, I'm not in the mood to play silly games and bicker. Go bother someone else for a while," Charles told him.

"You. Owe. Us," Jason said, quietly.

"I owe you. You think I owe you? How do you figure that genius?"

"I welcomed you into my home. Put the clothes on your back and sacrificed my living room. All of a sudden I can't have people round to my own house and have to watch what I say because you turned up and now I can't leave my property without my privacy being violated. They take photos and shout at me when I get something out of my car. They called the house so much that I had to unplug the phone. I'm sure they're upsetting all the neighbours by blocking the road. I can't even go to work! All because of you! At every step, you've been bitter and sulking and now you're being unreasonable and selfish. You've decided to try and ruin our family. You're poisoning my kids with dumb ideas and trying to create a rift in my family. The sooner he listens to me and sorts out this disaster, the better. He's unwanted and very lucky to still be here. The sooner he goes the better." Jason was in a rage, roaring as he let out a torrent of complaints.

"You must be joking. Welcome? I'd have been more welcome in the home of one of these conspiracists who think I'm an abomination. And rest assured, *son*, I will be leaving at the earliest opportunity and never once looking back, and I'll be taking the girls with me. Assuming they both want to come of course. I have done nothing except love them and support them. Don't you dare say I have poisoned them," Charles said through gritted teeth.

"You—" Jason started, but Charles interrupted before he'd fully formed the first word.

"No, Jason. You—you have taken every opportunity to create conflict and don't even get me started on money. Don't even go there, I don't think you'll like it if we do. You say I'm sulking; well I say you are a terrible human. You have distorted every good thing about this family and it's a miracle the girls aren't like you. You need to remove yourself from this room and calm down before I say something I won't take back." Charles' voice was even and hadn't gotten louder but his cold anger chilled the room. Evie had goosebumps as she helplessly looked between the two men.

"You are nothing without us old man. I will not let you speak to me like that. I will not be told to leave my own kitchen. If I kick you out, you're done. I have half a mind to kick you out and onto the streets right now. With any luck, you'd freeze again, and we can wash our hands of you!" Jason hissed.

"You bloody fool! You stupid, delusional idiot! Do you think, in your tiny brain, that I want to be here? If I could trade all the money and the lives of everyone just to see my wife and daughter one more time, I'd do it in a heartbeat. I'd do it a million times over and never look back. I would choose them over you every single time. This house is a prison and I hate it here! What a rotten deal, coming back to life and being stuck with all of you!" Charles shouted, and they'd never heard him shout before. Even Jason flinched at the intensity.

Before anyone could react, Charles stormed out of the room. He didn't look at any of them on his way out, and no one said anything until the living room door slammed.

Evie knew what was about to happen. She launched herself up and ran from the room, even as Jason turned and started screaming and hurling blame at her. She didn't stop until she was halfway up the stairs out of sight.

Her heart was pounding as if it was about to explode through her chest. Evie closed her eyes and found the pulse in her wrist, counting and not allowing her mind to think of anything else. When a few minutes had passed without either of her parents chasing her, and her heart had marginally calmed down, she stood up. Moving silently, like a ghost whose feet wouldn't disturb dust on the floor, Evie went right up to the living room door. She knocked quietly and said *'quack'* a few times towards the narrow gap where the door didn't reach the floor.

She couldn't hear anything from in the room. In the kitchen, Jason was still grumbling, but not as loud as before. Right as she was going to knock again, she heard a metallic click. Evie immediately recognised the sound of a lock clicking into place and knew she wasn't wanted or welcome.

Once she was in her room, her own door locked, Evie heard music and knew Charles was listening to his records. He had shut her out and found solace in his music, the message was undeniably clear.

Evie knew he was angry. He desperately missed his family and old life. He had to put up with all this scrutiny and judgement in ways he couldn't have imagined in the 1970s. Evie knew she should understand and comfort her great-grandad, but instead she felt like her throat had closed and she could hardly breathe, and she thought that somehow she was making a difference and Charles loved her but apparently not. Not as much as he loved his actual family, his wife and daughter. He'd lumped her in with the rest of them and had swept out of the room without even looking at her. Every time she had a problem, another one that was undeniably bigger and more horrible would surpass it. This morning she had been devastated over Roman getting her hopes up and then cruelly ignoring her. Now she had been stabbed in the heart by Charles' words and reporters were surrounding the house, watching their every move. Altogether, Evie hated her life too.

A glutton for punishment, Evie logged on to the internet, to see how bad the damage was now the Monroes had been identified. Evie expected the worst, photos of her and Toby C, perhaps one of her peeking from the window this morning. She was cringing in anticipation of the comments she was about to read. She imagined an iron shield clicking into place around her stomach, willing herself to keep her breakfast down as she looked.

She loaded up the familiar E8Updates page. On the home page was a video from this morning's news with Andrea Cabot updating the nation, and underneath a torrent of comments went on for as far as Evie could see. With dread replacing the blood in her veins, she started the video.

"Good morning all, I come to you this morning live from the studio. We have a very special show for you all today, the first photograph of one of the Everest Eight, who we have recently formally identified to be Charles Hartley who was the eighth person to be rescued from Everest last month. We have on good authority the locations of a few of our missing mountaineers. First of all, in Cheshire, is Charles. We cut live to his home where our correspondent is waiting for any movement or statement from the occupants. We have had official confirmation from an inside source Charles is staying with his granddaughter, her husband and their two children in this modest two-storey home. The government department who have been linked to the Everest Eight since day one, has for the first time offered us some information along with a stern but polite request to leave the families out of the programme. One of Charles' great-granddaughters is under eighteen so we will not be featuring her. However, our exclusive source has provided a lot of fascinating information which we will divulge, discuss and analyse later on today. We have been told where Charles shops and what he orders when eating out and much more! Join us at four p.m. to learn more! We also have two more names of the Everest Eight and are expecting photographs and statements any time. As soon as we get any footage, you will be the first to see it. At last, we get to see the Eight who defied death and then disappeared. The story still gives me goosebumps! In the meantime, let's take a look at Charles. Charles was climbing Everest in 1974..."

Evie paused the video, not wanting to hear the history lesson. She scrolled down to the comments.

Asdfgh123: Hahahahah there's no hiding now #EverestFreaks

Urfavedrinkingbuddy01: I haven't seen any social media pages for the #EverestFreaks. Who doesn't have Facebook these days? Can't find the family either...

Roxie.cat19: Omg I think I saw him in Chester in the food court last week and his granddaughter goes to my school! :o #EverestFreaks

SuperNova04: @**roxie.cat19** When? Where? Who is the granddaughter? Dm me #EverestFreaks

KeisMill99: @**roxie.cat19** I go to uni in Chester where is the #EverestFreaks? I might know her!

HatchetGamer13: Hi this is my first tweet did someone really come back to life #EverestFreaks

Sweetboi21: @**roxie.cat19** Hi what do the #EverestFreaks look like?

DothewormJoe0803: Everyone is being so mean, we shouldn't judge unless we've walked in their shoes. Be kind, be humble, keep your minds open #EverestFreaks

Anon11111: Trending now: #EverestFreaks #Unholy #Abominations #Devil #Zombies #Sinners #Cursed #Everest #AndreaCabot #KaneWinters #CharlesHartley

ChickenLegend28: Me and @**Queencastaway25** have been in the food court all day and no sign of Charles! Does anyone know where they live? We want to meet him! #EverestFreaks

Heyfield208: Who is coming to Chester to help me right the world? #EverestFreaks

RabbitMama1: These people deserve privacy. They are no different to you or I. Move on with your boring lives and LEAVE THE SO CALLED #EVERESTFREAKS ALONE!

Chapter 15

Evie lay on her back on the carpet of her room, her legs in the air. She couldn't decide what to do. After her breakfast had gone down and stayed down, she considered her options.

She had been planning to stay off school, now Jason had bigger problems to deal with she was flying under his radar and for once she didn't have a bullseye on her back. Maria hadn't spoken to her directly in days, so she could've plausibly hidden in her room, undisturbed. They'd been advised to lay low, and though she hadn't had explicit instructions since the latest development, she knew the sentiment would only be strengthened.

She was also so full of embarrassment that she could explode after Roman had ignored her and clearly changed his mind. The thought of facing him had her cringing. She would probably cry if he laughed in her face.

But on the other hand, now the reporters were camping out in their driveway and photos of her family peeping out from the curtains taken with extra-long camera lenses were trending online. Now everyone would know she was related to one of the Everest Eight. There was no point trying to hide it, she had all but been described and the front of her house was on the news. She was dangerously close to wanting to never go back but even school was more appealing than being stuck in the house.

Now Charles had made it exceptionally clear that he didn't want her around, it was preferable to deal with the whispers and rumours in school than it would be to hide away in her room while she waited for one of her family members to pick a fight with her. Evie also knew that the longer she put it off, the worse it would be to go back.

She carefully re-did her make-up, straightened her hair and picked out her reliable black skinny jeans and a grey jumper to wear. If everyone would be staring, then she wouldn't give them any extra ammunition to gossip if she looked all right. She already had a game plan to look as nice as she could around any cameras, and she'd be applying that philosophy to all aspects of her life.

When she was ready and figured it was as good a time as any to leave, Evie crept down the stairs, slipped through the front door and closed it quietly behind her. She didn't alert anyone to the fact that she was going to school. As soon as she turned, Evie realised that in her haste to silently leave, she'd miscalculated one thing – the camped out reporters.

She was torn between diving back into the house or braving the throng of adults who were at the end of the driveway and all watching her. In a split second, she decided to tough it out, knowing she would be out the house and free from the fighting for at least a few hours.

As she walked down the driveway, Evie felt like what she imagined a runway model must feel like. How odd to be watched by an audience when she was merely walking along. As she neared the end of the drive, metres away from the waiting reporters, a few clicks indicated photos were taken, and Evie suddenly forgot how to walk. She stopped dead, trying to remember if her foot goes directly in front of her or more to the left.

She looked back up and at her audience. One man had sat back in his camping chair and was scrolling on his phone. Evie had associated reporters like vultures, relentlessly circling their prey and poised to strike.

But they were just adults, doing their job and jostling to get the best photo or write the fastest report. She wrote reports and waited outside cinemas for films. They weren't that different in reality.

"Good morning," Evie said, surprising herself. She'd been debating speaking to them and had spoken before she could scare herself out of it.

A couple of them smiled, the one sitting down nodded and the rest were an array of 'morning', 'all right kid' and one 'are you related to one of the Eight?'

"I'm actually just on the way to school, but I'd really appreciate it if you guys don't take photos of me right now, I get enough hassle as it is, never mind when unflattering photos are posted online." Before they could reply Evie hurried away, realising that she did know how to walk just fine as a new worry overtook her mind – she'd just spoken to the reporters and told them she got hassle in school. Dexter had warned her many times that the media can twist and turn words to force them into a story. She'd just handed them an easy scoop; she could already imagine the headline 'Everest Eight Relative an Outcast in School'. She'd never live it down.

The one saving grace was that no one had known she was leaving the house, so no one would know she'd been so dumb and volunteered information so naively.

Evie walked to school in a daze, refreshing her news feeds constantly to check for anything about her. It was only once she crossed into the school gates that she put her phone away and accepted she'd have to wait and see. No doubt Tilly would message if Evie did anything that negatively affected her.

Evie naturally looked down as she entered the school like

she always did, gazing at the sticky blue floor and avoiding eye contact. As she walked to her registration class, she thought about the fact that her great-grandad is now famous, and loath as she was to admit it, if she was a girl like Tilly, or Kendall or Isabel, she'd be so popular and wielding that power to her advantage and never in a million years would she be ashamed by it. In a roundabout sort of way, she was slightly famous. She was proud to have kept such a secret for so long and even if Charles didn't like them much, his candour and willpower was something she should embody.

As though it had never occurred to her body to straighten up before, Evie stiffly squared her shoulders and looked ahead, and nothing happened. No one even looked twice or cared. Evie smiled, shocked that she hadn't realised this before. Some random kid smiled back at her and a girl behind him looked Evie up and down but didn't say anything as she passed. The bell rang and Evie didn't hurry, she walked along, looking at the posters she normally didn't see and thinking about what Charles had said.

Evie reached the door to her classroom, pleased that she'd beat her teacher in and wouldn't be marked as late. As soon as she stepped into the room, the babble of chatter ceased. Most of her classmates looked awkward, after clearly talking about her. Some looked away with pink cheeks, and right at the back of the room, sat Kendall and her posse. They had also gone silent, but studied her, eyes calculating.

Evie shuffled down the aisles to her usual chair, head held high and ignoring Kendall. Once she sat down, she pulled her notebook out her bag and faced the front, wondering why her form tutor wasn't in yet. A few curious people turned around to look at her, when they realised she was looking straight at them, they muttered greetings or nodded and turned back around. Evie could've laughed, for the first time she wasn't afraid of what people were thinking when they looked at her, and it had taken years of excruciating social anxiety to realise it.

While pondering her revelation, Evie blinked as a small white ball dropped in front of her and looked up in time to see a handful of screwed up paper balls rain over her desk.

"It's snowing! Snow for Evie and her Everest Freak Grandad!" Kendall crowed, delighted with herself.

Without even turning, Eve brushed the paper off her desk and tried to convince herself that she was confident and no one else had a story like hers to tell so she should own it. None of these had spoken to reporters on their way to school or seen their great-grandad on the news this morning. It was a lot harder to own it when people were throwing paper balls at her though. But ignoring it, in this case, wouldn't give them the reaction they were fishing for.

"How's it going, Evie?" She jumped as she realised Roman had arrived after her and chose to sit to her right. She was so determined to ignore the girls behind her that she hadn't even noticed him in her peripheral vision.

"Roman, come and sit with us!" Kendall called. "You don't need to sit on the loser table, there's plenty of room up here!"

Roman must have heard because Evie had heard it. Neither acknowledged it though.

"Roman, hi," Evie trailed off. She'd been too preoccupied to decide what to do. She was in a confrontational mood, enjoying how it felt to square her shoulders and look people in the eye. But it was Roman, and he had sat next to her. She had no idea what was best, Tilly would probably tell him off and have nothing to do with him. Kendall would probably kick off and then make up the same day, revelling in the attention. Evie just wanted to have a minute without shouting or drama. The taunts and stares were preferable than the abuse and cool fury that was contained in her house. She decided at that moment that she simply couldn't be bothered to fight. She also didn't need videos of her crying and arguing with him to be posted online and picked up by the news. She could do with making sure she didn't add any more fuel to the fire she may have accidentally kindled this morning.

Roman was patiently waiting for her response as she thought it through.

"It's weird, my front garden is on the news. I'm sure you've seen it already. But yeah. How are you?" Evie replied, suddenly unsure what to say.

"Not bad, my garden isn't on the news so there's that at least. Hey, why is there paper all over?" he asked.

"Oh, the idiots at the back are throwing stuff. Where is Mr Scott by the way? He is so late," Evie replied.

Roman didn't reply, he was looking over his shoulder with narrowed eyes, and then brushed a strand of Evie's straight hair back, dislodging a piece of paper.

"They're so immature, Evie. Just ignore them yeah?" Roman looked genuinely pained, and Evie nodded to reassure him. "Anyway, have you seen any good films lately? I need a recommendation."

"Roman, you don't have to trouble yourself. If you don't want to talk to me, just don't. I'm fine by myself anyway. But do me a favour, don't mess me around again. I didn't appreciate my time being wasted last night," Evie told him, her voice weary.

"What are you talking about? I came to see how you're doing, because I thought we were friends. Is this because I didn't invite you last night? It was supposed to be just the rugby boys and then some others overheard us discussing it and it turned into

216

a group thing. If it bothered you then I'll make sure to invite you next time, okay? Is that what that sarcastic email this morning was about?" Roman retorted, a little defensive.

"Why are you playing dumb right now? It's not because you all went out, which I'm sure you do every week anyway. It's because *you* emailed *me* and wanted to video call and I waited and waited and messaged you and you just ignored me!" Evie snapped as she let some of her built up anger spill but made sure to keep her voice low. This was a private matter after all.

"Evie, I literally have no idea what you're talking about. I didn't email you. I don't think I have ever emailed you. Why would I arrange to call you when I knew I was out with the rugby boys where we have a no phones rule? First one to cave has to pay so obviously I wasn't going to be on my phone. Are you listening? Whatever mix up happened, it wasn't me deliberately ignoring you or hurting you okay?" he said, breathing heavily as if he had just done ten laps of the rugby pitch.

"You... didn't... email me?" Evie asked, her voice strangled.

"No! That's what I'm telling you. The last time I was on my emails was at the end of the day yesterday when I logged in at school. I have notifications off outside of school hours and didn't check until this morning. Do you believe me now? And if I wanted to call you, I'd do this," he continued as he held out a hand for her phone. Evie, her eyes wide in surprise, handed it over silently. She watched as he opened her contacts, with pathetically few numbers saved. But he didn't comment as he added his number and name and called his own phone for a few seconds before hanging up.

"Now you have my number too. I'm sorry that this happened, maybe I left my email logged in on the library computer and someone played a prank. I am sorry, Evie. Can we move on and pretend it didn't happen? Next time I want to call you I have your number now, so you know it's really me. I would never ignore you on purpose." His eyes shone with sincerity.

Evie paused again to consider his words, to do some maths and reach the conclusion she had suspected as soon as she saw how confused Roman was. Another practical joke at Evie's expense. It wasn't difficult to hazard a guess at who it could have been. She finally nodded and noted the slump of relief in his shoulders.

"If you still wanted a film recommendation… I haven't had a lot of time recently to watch any films, obviously with all this going on. So, I'll have to get back to you on that one. And I appreciate you not asking by the way, that's cool that you're just talking to me normally. That you haven't bombarded me with questions about him. I wasn't sure if I should come in today, but I'd rather be here than at home right now." Evie laughed and then stopped talking, aware that she was nervously babbling.

As she stopped talking, she realised Kendall had stood up, and was addressing the people sitting around her.

"Every other form is doing stupid bake sales, fancy dress, sponsored walk *blah blah blah*. We have to do so much better! It's extra important now, and that's why we have to do a dance, because all the money we raised is going to people who really need it, who are worse off than all of us and deserve our charity. Like Evie Monroe's family. I mean look at the state of her, she clearly needs some new clothes, that grey jumper is tatty, and those tragically faded jeans have clearly been through the washing machine one too many times. Although no one can argue that she needs any food." Kendall smirked, and a few people outright laughed at Evie. Most of the class were uncertain, waiting to see what would unfold before they considered getting involved.

"What does she mean, Evie's family?" someone asked in the background. She almost smiled as she realised the majority of them didn't understand what Kendall was truly saying.

She saw Roman turn and start to stand up. Evie put her hand on his shoulder as she passed him, heading straight to where Kendall was standing. The anger she had been holding had barely leaked out of her during her conversation with Roman. She'd contained it all night, letting it build and burn like lava in an erupting volcano. Kendall's speech was the final earthquake that triggered the eruption. She hadn't seen her family since the breakfast fight, hadn't had the chance to calm down. All that emotion rose to the surface, too fast for Evie to contain. The laughter trailed off as she turned to face the class, the expression on her face promising consequences.

"Wow, as much as I appreciate you all wanting to raise money for those poor people who literally came back to life to find out their entire family has gone, all their possessions passed on, their life as they know was frozen in 1974 and now they're in the future and they don't recognise anything. That's great, because they do need help so by all means raise money with a dumb dance. And they're getting crucified by the media and hounded by photographers and journalists and imagine how confused they must be. And scared. And lonely and sad. And you're all here judging them on Twitter and treating it as a joke. Well, my great-grandad doesn't tolerate any nonsense, and I finally realised today that I have to stand up for myself and be proud of who I am because no one else is or will be. And, Kendall, you know what they say about the biggest bitch…" Evie said.

219

Kendall looked comically confused, her eyebrows arched and slightly shaking her head. A floating question mark above her head wouldn't have looked amiss. She hadn't prepared for Evie to retaliate, usually Evie would shy away, not square up to her. Her brain hadn't caught up, and Evie could almost hear her repeating the words in her head, trying to quickly figure out what Evie had said.

When Evie slapped her, she wiped the expression off Kendall's face and knocked the words right out of her mouth.

A sharp crack accompanied Kendall's head as it snapped to the side. The world was frozen, time itself had stopped as Evie felt shock and the thrill of power course through her body with not even a hint of regret. Evie fought a smile, as time carried on and she heard gasps and whistling, and her classmates reacted to what may be the sixth-form's biggest drama ever.

Verbal arguments were common in the group of seventeen to eighteen-year-olds. Physical fights, on the other hand, were few and far between. Most of the class appeared delighted by the turn of events, a few started to applaud and congratulate Evie.

"Evie! Kendall! Straight to Mr Loche's office!" Their form tutor finally made an appearance, typically in time to see the slap and send both girls out of the room.

Evie strode over to her seat to grab her bag and turned on her heel and stalked out of the room. She knocked chairs as she pushed past, and she knew she was failing to disguise her smirk again. She'd never gotten into trouble in school before, always getting good grades and keeping her head down. It was something of a novelty, and after all the frustration and turmoil of her life, it felt great to be reckless and not worry.

Her swift exit had her arriving at the school office quickly, and there was a delay in Kendall leaving the classroom behind her. If Evie knew her arch-nemesis, she knew she'd be kicking up a huge fuss and claiming injury far more serious than a red mark on her cheek and a wounded ego.

She was made to sit in an uncomfortable chair in one of the spare offices and had no idea if Kendall was nearby too. Evie felt justified in what she did, but she was sure the school wouldn't appreciate that she was provoked and has been getting harassed by this bully for years.

Evie still felt pride and power surging through her body, and then realised it was adrenaline and that was why she was now shaking.

It was easier to pretend to be brave and leave the room with her chin up, but now she was sitting alone, waiting and wondering what her punishment would be, she started to worry.

What would she do if she got expelled? Could she make it as a successful review writer without completing her A-levels? And she'd been neglecting her blog lately. She knew what little momentum she had scraped together had entirely disappeared when she was grounded when Charles first joined them, and she'd missed a bunch of new films. She knew that the same people who would comment and debate with her every week would have quickly found someone new to follow.

She'd seen a really successful blogger with thousands of followers lose hundreds of them after posting a day late and all the keyboard warriors punished her before they moved on.

She'd have to find work elsewhere, so she wouldn't be stuck at home with her family. The one thing she has to do is make sure she doesn't end up at home all day every day. Anything but that. She'd be driven to despair if she was trapped in such close proximity with her family, and with scrutiny from the media already on them... it would be unbearable.

Evie was spiralling and she knew it. She was actually terrible at breaking the rules, she could act rashly and boldly but when the time for repercussions came around, she was a wreck.

When one of the ladies from the school office silently approached and announced that she could go, Evie jumped out of her skin and was too surprised to question why she hadn't had to explain herself or receive a telling off.

She got up and followed the lady to the main reception. She was being escorted out of the school. She was leaving and she hadn't been told off so maybe they were skipping all that and making her leave.

"Excuse me – please, I need to speak to the head of sixth-form or the headteacher or something. There's more to the story I promise, I don't usually hit people! In fact, this is the first time that I've ever hit someone, and it won't happen again if I can stay. I swear it," Evie was talking as she walked, and the lady only responded once they got to the door that separated the reception from the main school.

The lady opened the door before she said "Ms Monroe. Do not panic, we'll see you on Monday. You can go home with your guardian. The school has authorised for you to take the rest of the week off in these special circumstances."

Evie almost cried, the emotional day had exhausted her, all she wanted to do was go home and sleep. That feeling evaporated when she went through the door and saw Charles waiting for her, his face expressionless as he gestured for her to go first through the main door that led to the car park.

She quietly followed him to a waiting taxi and slid into the back beside him. He didn't say anything, merely nodded to the driver to smoothly begin driving. He must've discussed the return with the driver on his way to the school.

He still didn't speak, so neither did Evie. She studied the floor mats of the taxi, cringing in anticipation of the lecture that was brewing. She knew Charles would still be angry at her, his silence spoke volumes. But Evie had dodged a bullet, it would have been drastically worse if Jason had shown up to collect her instead. Evie could vividly imagine the scene now – lots of talking in third person, spit spraying from her father's mouth as he ranted, and the episode mercilessly repeated and re-enacted by her peers. Perhaps the media would have been there, capturing every word and expression to build the drama.

As the thought of the media occurred to Evie, she craned her neck to peer through the back windscreen, unable to spot any cars following or lenses aimed at her, but suddenly certain they'd be there. They wanted Charles, to speak to him, photograph him, to interact with one of the Everest Eight. Dexter had been on the phone with Charles for hours every day. Evie only knew because when she walked past his room, she'd heard him vehemently reject the idea of sharing his life. He insisted that there was no privacy these days, Evie and Tilly had had a similar argument with him days earlier, when he'd been caught reading through the full terms and conditions online and was outraged that they so freely agreed to such things. For someone like Charles, there was nothing worse.

"There's no one following us. I burned rubber and got away," Charles explained when he noted her scanning the roads.

They pulled up on a familiar street, and Evie turned to Charles. She found a small smile on his face. They were in town, not on the road of sprawling semis and fancy gardens that they called home.

"After you," he said.

Evie walked straight into the dessert parlour that had been

223

her safe haven for so long and looked around as if she'd never seen it before. Charles glanced around before he asked where they should sit.

Evie led the way to her normal booth and realised that this was the first time she'd come here with someone. She didn't include the time Jason made a huge scene and dragged her out. It felt like only yesterday but also like a distant memory from many years ago. Everything had changed since then, she now had a great-grandad, and she'd been in a fist fight, albeit a brief one. She had changed somehow, and the enticing smell of cookies and pancakes didn't settle her fluttering nerves or cause her a desperate desire to eat and forget.

Charles was studying the menu with a finger sliding along the line as he read what each dessert was made up of. Evie was so thrown by the situation, of her old and new world colliding, that she didn't know what to say or how to act.

"Evie! Sweetie it's been ages, how the hell are you?" Oline smiled broadly as she perched on the edge of the seat by Evie. Before Evie finished smiling, Oline had turned to Charles. "Good morning sir, I am Oline, your waitress and friend of Evie. Can I get you a drink to start with? Your first one is on the house. Anyone special enough for Evie to share this place with is someone I know I'm going to like."

Charles studied Oline for a moment, his eyes flicked towards Evie and as if he had reached an inner conclusion, he smiled at Oline and introduced himself.

"Good morning, I would absolutely love a cup of tea, and I insist on paying for it. I am Evie's grandfather, it's a pleasure to meet you. And for you, Evie?" Charles asked.

"Just water please, Oline," Evie said.

As Oline hurried towards the hot drinks machine, Charles

leaned back in his seat.

"I can see why you like her, and why you like coming here. And I will not judge you if you want to indulge. I've said it before, even when eating healthily it is important to have a day off here and there. We've eaten vegetables every evening this week and I noticed that you have switched crisps for fruit in your lunches. You're doing very well. But on occasion you shouldn't feel guilty about enjoying yourself. If there was ever a time to do so it would be now, with the turmoil of your last few days," Charles sincerely said.

"I know. I just don't fancy anything crazy. I don't feel very hungry right now," Evie replied quietly.

"*Hmm*," was all Charles said.

When Oline placed a pot of tea, a jug of milk and some sugar sachets on the table, Charles ordered some more.

"Could I trouble you for a Coca-Cola please? And I would love a banana split please, with all the works. Evie, is there anything that tempts you? It's my treat."

"I suppose I could get something little. Maybe I can finally try the cookie dough platter. Will you share it with me, Grandad?" Evie finally said.

"I would love to," he replied immediately.

As Oline left to put their order through, Evie leaned forward so she could speak to Charles with no one nearby able to overhear. She was paranoid of people listening and tipping off the media, thanks to Dexter's fraught warnings.

"Last time I came here, it was the day we found out about you, but we didn't know if you were actually our grandad yet. I had a huge fight with my dad because they paid for me to go to some self-defence classes and I hated it and came here instead. So, I've never actually tried the cookie dough before. It's kind of funny that I'm here with you now, and instead I've been in trouble in school."

"Woah, slow down a second. What's this about self-defence? We'll discuss the trouble in school later."

"Another failed attempt at bettering myself. It seemed like a good idea, learning useful real life skills that might make a difference in my safety one day, and I thought it would make me braver, knowing I can fight back. But in reality, the class was horrible. I'm pretty sure I still have another couple of classes left in the package I pre-paid for. Not that I'm ever going to step foot in that place again." Evie looked up as Oline deposited a huge glass of Coke in front of her. The glass had condensation on the side and was fizzing away.

"Go ahead, I got it in case you changed your mind. But if you don't fancy it, it won't go to waste. I will drink it after my tea." Charles told her as he poured his tea.

She rolled her eyes a little but still took a deep gulp from the glass. It might have been the most refreshing drink she'd ever had.

"If you ask me, it was a big step to even sign up and go to the class. Certainly, a step in the right direction. Now, the thing that gets me, is that it was something you sounded like you believed in and wanted to do. Until you faced one obstacle and immediately gave up. You can't do that, kiddo. Did you look and see if there were any other classes? Did you speak to them about what you didn't like, or see about getting your money back? I know you're young, but you need to be resilient, and not be afraid to question. You'll learn that as you grow and experience the world, I'm just trying to give you a head start. When I was your age, I know I didn't do any of that sort of stuff, but by the time I got to Everest, I was a pro at working around problems."

"My mum used to say, that you were the most competitive person," Evie said.

"She wasn't wrong. I used to be competitive in everything. Once I achieved one goal, I'd immediately set my sights on something bigger and better. It's why I ended up on Everest. I joined a hiking club. I'd drive into Wales on the weekend and walk with a group. A few of them started travelling to Europe and properly climbing mountains and it ignited my desire to compete and win. They are probably still alive and walking in their retirement while I'm here. I try not to be like that any more," he explained, stirring milk into his tea.

Evie sipped her drink as she considered his words.

"In moderation, like when we play Scrabble, it's okay—" Evie paused, thinking. Then "I need to ask you something. Are you still angry at me?"

"Angry? About you fighting in school?" Charles asked.

"No. When you said you hated living with us, and that you were stuck with us," she whispered back.

"Oh, Evelyn. No, that was to your dad. It was all to your dad. I didn't think you'd think any of it was aimed at you. I've told you before, you and your sister are the best parts of my second life. I'm sorry. I feel awful."

"Thank goodness. I could barely sleep. I was so upset when I thought—thank you, Oline! It looks great." Evie switched halfway as the desserts arrived.

A long rectangular plate with cookie dough, balls of ice cream and all sorts of chocolates and sauces was placed between them. Then two banana splits, much larger than their normal portion size, were deposited on the table.

"Oline!" Evie gasped as she looked at the food.

"Shush now. I haven't seen you in a while, think of it as a

227

welcome back gift." Oline laughed as she drifted over to another customer.

Eating the dessert with Charles was a million miles away from where she'd been that morning. Roman had a genuine explanation, smoothing over her embarrassment. She'd been dreading this day for so long, the day everyone found out about Charles, and she'd slapped Kendall and got a week off for it. Charles didn't hate her, and their relationship was stronger than ever as they alternated dishes and ate until only smears of sauce were left on the plate.

In no rush, they said goodbye to Oline and strolled through town. Since it was still mid-afternoon, all the school kids had yet to arrive, so it was mainly young parents with babies in prams and elderly people strolling down the high street. Evie and Charles fit right in as they walked a few short steps to the bus stop.

They alighted the bus with memories of the last time they'd boarded at this stop with bags and angry silence. This time it was more of a thoughtful silence as they settled in seats on the top deck.

"What about your driving then? Where are you up to?" Charles asked.

"Nothing. I failed three times, and no one expected me to pass anyway. I'm not Tilly who can do anything perfectly. I can drive when I'm practising, it just goes wrong in my test. Can you drive? You can't judge me when you're sitting on the bus next to me." Evie's voice got louder, fuelled by the simmering anger that had been pushing her into conflict all day.

"I didn't ask about Matilda. Or bring up her name. This isn't a competition or comparison. And to answer your question, I used to drive. My car didn't have seatbelts in the back, and the rare occasion when I took the bus, well where we sit now upstairs would have a roof of smoke. I will need to pass an examination as you will before I will be granted freedom behind the wheel. But there are some other problems, in regard to my health and it's a situation where the powers that be have yet to decide if myself and the seven others will be allowed to operate vehicles at all. I'd be lucky if any car insurance provider would be willing to insure me, and even more so if it didn't cost a small fortune. But what I can do is help you study for your test, and maybe next time you give a bully a taste of their own medicine, you can drive us both to the dessert place, how about that?" Charles asked.

"Next time?" Evie smirked.

"Well, any grandchild of mine will not tolerate any form of bullying or allow anyone to treat them poorly. I don't approve of fighting, but I do understand certain situations require more extreme action to be taken. I have no doubt there will be a next time, but perhaps we don't resort to violence or get in trouble in school over it," he added.

She thought, as the bus weaved through the streets and gradually brought them closer to home, that she might try again at a couple of things. She pulled her phone from her pocket and sent a short text to her driving instructor, letting her know she was ready to resume her lessons. In three messages, a weekly schedule was agreed, and she'd be able to have the lessons during her free periods in school. She decided in that moment, to not tell Charles. She'd accept his help, and perhaps try and persuade Tilly to help her master parking, and then when she persevered and finally passed, Charles would be so proud.

Evie looked at him as they neared their stop. He was watching the world roll by, and when he felt her looking, he turned and gave her the warmest smile. She would enjoy surprising him with this.

They walked the final leg of the journey home in a companionable silence.

Before they rounded the final corner, Charles stopped in his tracks.

"Oops, I forgot! I may have climbed over a fence or two earlier. They will be very surprised if we stroll over. We would be torn apart. How do you feel about some climbing and sneaking?"

Evie laughed a little, unsure if he was joking. She followed him as they looped around the back of their road. She soon realised that he had not been joking.

"I can't climb a fence! It'll probably collapse on me. Or I'll get splinters. I'll just go round the front," she told him.

"Come along, I'll give you a boost up. If we go through here, they won't see us entering the alley and we can go through the back gate. I have the key in my pocket from when I left earlier." Charles linked his hands and offered them as a sort of hand-made step.

"Whose house is this? What if they see us running through their garden? I can't do it. I'll meet you in the kitchen in ten minutes, okay?" Evie started walking as she finished speaking.

She glanced back when she rounded the corner, in time to see the top of his head vanish over a six foot fence. She shouldn't be surprised, he'd climbed Everest and was clearly in good shape.

In a matter of minutes, she'd circled round and joined the throng of people waiting in her driveway. At first, they didn't recognise her. She was just another face. Only as she squeezed through the tripods and camp chairs did they realise she was moving with purpose towards the house.

"It's the younger daughter I think," one said and gave her a friendly smile as she shimmied past.

"How's your grandpa? Is he home now? Tell him we can't

wait to hear his story!" another added.

"Excuse me, sorry if I could just squeeze through. Thank you. Thank you all, have a nice night. Don't get too cold," Evie said as she retreated down the driveway. She didn't look back when she got to the door and slipped inside.

She rendezvoused with Charles inside. He sat at the table, reading a newspaper and sipping tea. If she didn't know better, she'd assume he'd been there for hours. He gestured to another mug that waited for her. As they both sipped their drinks, they looked over the top of their mugs at each other and shared a mischievous smile.

Chapter 16

Evie woke up early on Monday morning. She was thinking a lot about school, about whether Kendall would retaliate and how she'd be treated. She'd had a wonderful few days with Charles where they'd been so busy that she'd had no time to worry. She was like glue to Charles' side, which meant her parents had avoided them like the plague. Aside from the smell of the food they made lingering in the kitchen and their heavy footsteps on the stairs, it was like they weren't in the same house.

Charles and Evie camped out for days, the only contact with the outside world was when Evie donned her winter coat and boots to clean Toby C's cage and brought him in for long afternoons of exploring Charles' room. He particularly enjoyed the spot under the radiator, which was permanently switched to its highest setting, and for some reason, he loved Charles and was forever trying to force his affection upon the reluctant man. They'd also ducked outside to wave sparklers around to mark Bonfire Night before bringing Toby C indoors away from the fireworks and eating their weight in hot dogs and s'mores. But neither stepped so much as a foot out the front door, and enjoyed every moment staying indoors. Even Charles' medical appointments and regular conversations with Dexter were postponed in light of the recent chaos.

As well as that, they baked carrot cake, which was a secret speciality of Charles' once he remembered the recipe. They played Scrabble, and he tested Evie on the highway code. Though she'd passed her theory test, knowing the rules of the road inside out would only be beneficial. Every evening, Charles cooked a healthy meal and would play the role of DJ with his records while she did abdominal exercises. He counted for her, having done his own sets as soon as he woke up in the morning before he showered. Occasionally, Tilly would join them, and they'd sit and chat for hours. They told him all about their childhood, the good and the not so good. He listened and in return shared stories about his own life, from when he was a boy to having his own family.

Evie couldn't believe it when he told her that he was the youngest of seven children. It had led to one of the only disagreements they'd had, a war of old school versus new, technology against privacy and simplicity. Charles admitted that he'd been trying to track down his siblings, but it was proving difficult as he had one brother who had moved from the area, and the other five siblings were sisters who had married, and he didn't know their new surnames. Or if they still lived.

"Margaret used to send the Christmas cards every year, it wasn't my department. By the time our parents passed on, we all had our own families and traditions. None of us knew our parent's siblings or their families. It's just how it was back then. It was a great deal of effort to communicate in letters and the occasional phone call. Perhaps they'll be able to track me down now my name has been released, it'll be one of the only good things to come from this media circus."

Tilly had been even more shocked when Charles had explained phones to her. She'd sat there, mouth open, and not spoken for several minutes.

"Your nana, she lived on the other side of the water in Liverpool. I met her when I went out with my brother's buddies in town and she was there with her girlfriends. We danced together all night and arranged to meet at the same place, one week later. Eventually, we started courting, and her family shared a phone with their next-door neighbours, but we didn't have one. I had to use a public phone box to call her, and kindly ask whoever answered to get her quickly, seeing as I was fast using my change to pay for it," Charles had explained. "I admit, this new thing of calling on video to someone in the world and it being instant, that is a pretty nifty trick. But you girls don't know what it's like to not be in constant communication. I sometimes hear your mobile device in the night, Matilda. You can bet that I was never disturbed so late at night by such things. How are you comfortable with being contacted twenty-four seven? You can never truly have peace."

By the time Tilly had gotten over the idea of not having a phone in the house, they'd moved on to other household appliances.

"Okay, sometimes it gets annoying when the group chat is going off at three in the morning and it's just drunk nonsense. But I can just put it on do not disturb. Easy. And I know you won't argue about the internet. I search things constantly, I can shop, find out information, pull up a live map and directions. That's just a few examples. Always having the option of people contacting me is a very minor price to pay, and one which can be resolved if I was bothered," Tilly had argued.

"Ah, but you're forgetting the sacrifice and burden of being reachable. Of what you search being documented and collected as data. It astounds me how little regard you girls have. These microphones and cameras are on you all the time. You can't deny it, I saw it when you spoke to the device and it answered questions for you. It must always be waiting in case you address it. I happen to like my conversations private." He nodded when he finished speaking as if saying point won.

"I guess we take it for granted. As far back as I remember, I've known how to use a computer. I never learned how to use a smartphone. I sometimes forget exactly how different the world is for you. Is there anything in this house that is really different than what you were used to before?" Evie interjected, to side track the conversation before they got drawn into a fierce technology debate.

"Just about everything. The washing machine and dryer for one, I used to either go to a laundrette or we had a twin tub your nana would use. None of this wash and dry and back in your wardrobe in a couple of hours. There are also automated dishwashers now. No more rubber gloves and boiling our own water and leaving dishes on a rack to dry. That cordless hoover your mum is always shouting at us about because we forget to put it back on charge. The full size freezer, we had a cool box in the corner of the fridge, we certainly couldn't fit a big tub of ice cream in it. Every day, something so mundane astounds me, and I turn to one of you to marvel at the wonders of technology and you don't even blink. I often wonder what my Margaret would make of all this. She was far more modern than me, she would have taken to it like a duck to water," Charles smiled sadly, as he said the last few words.

Evie smiled as she remembered the conversation and tried not to think about what her day had in store.

She longed to stay at home and live in the happy bubble she'd spent days in. She knew Charles would understand if she stayed off another day, but Evie knew he'd be prouder if she went in. She had the good grace and understanding of her teachers so far, but there was only so much making up assignments and catching up she could do before they grew tired of her absences. She had university to think of, those UCAS points didn't earn themselves. A-levels were already like treading water in the middle of a storm in the ocean, she would drown if she didn't act now.

She smiled as she thought about her happiness over the last

few days and got out of bed with a smile on her face. She did her make-up carefully, dressed in a black and white polka dot top and black skinny jeans. To complete the look, she wore a matching polka dot hairband. When she was happy with her reflection, she went downstairs to make some lunch.

In the kitchen was Charles, who was at the cooker making pancakes. Evie suddenly realised that they'd missed their monthly pancake breakfast this month. It was probably when they were all fighting.

Surprisingly, Jason and Maria were seated at the table. Maria had a pancake in front of her which she had cut into tiny pieces and she was slowly eating it.

"Good morning, sunshine. Your pancake will be ready any second. Get yourself a drink, the syrup is already on the table," Charles cheerily greeted her.

"Wow, thank you! This is a lovely surprise, it's not the start of the month though, what's the occasion?" she asked as she poured herself half a pint of orange juice.

"I can't send you back to school without a decent breakfast. I made you some lunch too, it's the bag in the fridge. We'll start the day off right and begin as we mean to go on," he replied while he flipped the pancake expertly. It spun three times and landed in the centre of the frying pan. He deposited it in front of Evie and scooped a generous helping of lard into the frying pan.

Jason, who had been glaring at the lard, suddenly spoke. "No, I didn't say she could go to school. We are laying low you idiots, not letting her go off galivanting and threatening our safety. I won't have it. I'll report her. To the science lot," he announced triumphantly.

"Good luck, *son*. I think you've forgotten the law that under eighteens have to be in education or an apprenticeship. I am very clear on these things, and I've personally spoken to the school, who are expecting Evie back today. If you had tried to use your one brain cell, you might have contacted the school yourself. I knew you wouldn't and stepped in, and luckily I did too. Eat up, duck, it'll go cold," Charles spoke calmly, and added the last bit to Evie.

From Jason's nasty expression, it was clear that he knew he had been caught out. He noisily got up, going out of his way to bump the table.

"Have a great day, I hope she doesn't get attacked by any of those nutters that have been sending the death threats. That would be terrible. If we're no longer laying low, then I'll take my meetings at the office. Don't wait up for me, Maria, after work I'm going to play some golf," he announced as he strode out of the room.

Maria ate another small piece of pancake. She swallowed and sipped her drink before she spoke.

"Have a great day darling!" she called after Jason, and to the kitchen, she said, "Well, I think I'll cancel my morning meetings and get my hair done in town. If we're going out and about I'd better look nice. Thanks for breakfast."

Maria also left the room, without any further conversation.

"That's better. Another pancake?" Charles offered.

Once she'd finished her pancakes, she brushed her teeth and put her mystery lunch in her school bag. She darted outside to deposit some leafy greens into Toby C's bowl and promised him she'd get him out when she was home later. Charles was waiting by the front door to see her off. He spoke to her as she pulled on her winter coat, hat and gloves.

"See you tonight, duck. Remember to keep your head high. I don't think these journalists will bother you, just be polite and courteous but firm as you walk past. You look really lovely in

237

polka dots, just like my Evelyn. She had a 1950s type tea dress in the same pattern and some ribbon she'd tie in her hair. She looked a picture, and so do you. I wonder…" He trailed off. He looked as though he was thinking intently.

"To be honest, they aren't too bad. They ask questions but let me pass through. Oh, my nana really had a dress like this? I love that! What are you wondering?" she asked.

"It's silly. I wouldn't know how to do it anyway. You have a good day, you hear? You can always phone me on my mobile telephone if you have any trouble. I can always sneak out and come into the school, it's no trouble at all."

"Now you've got to tell me! What is it? I won't think it's silly I promise," Evie said seriously.

"If you insist on knowing, I had a thought that I wish I could capture this memory. I was going to see if I could take a photograph, but you know I'm no good on the phone doing the camera. You probably wouldn't want to anyway." He looked very uncomfortable, shuffling his feet and his eyes looking anywhere except at Evie.

"I don't mind. Here, if you hold your hand as still as you can, and press the white button, and that's it! Let me put my bag down and take the coat off. Okay, I'm ready." Evie smiled and put one hand on her hip to pose.

He frowned at the screen and pressed the screen a dozen times. She stayed still and when he looked over the phone at her, she went over and showed him how to open the gallery. She swiped through them, showing him what to do.

"There, you did a great job! You're really getting the hang of your phone now. That photo, it's actually not bad. I look smaller and nicer than normal somehow. Huh." Evie was the one who trailed off now.

"That's exactly what you look like, duck, and you do seem to have lost some weight. All that porridge and all those sit-ups have started to pay off. You're making me so proud." He hugged her and then opened the door for her to leave.

She zipped up her coat after she put it on, and when she got to the people at the end of her driveway, they made a corridor for her to pass through. They exchanged pleasantries and in a matter of seconds, she was on her way to school.

She arrived faster than normal and went straight to her form room. In her big coat and hat, she blended in with the other early birds who were equally as wrapped up. No one recognised her and she didn't see anyone she was warily keeping an eye out for. Luckily, when she got to her form room, Mr Scott was already there and was happy for her to come in early.

Evie took her old window seat and tapped her finger on the desk as she waited for the trickle of students to start coming in. This was where the true test began. The reporters and walking through school was a warm up to the fast approaching main event.

"Evie? How are you? Listen, we teachers have been informed of everything going on, and if you need anything, or if anyone is bothering you, please do come to us okay? I know what happened last week was very out of character, and I argued that to Mr Loche. In the end, they decided to give you the benefit of the doubt and give you the week off, just don't make me regret defending you, okay?"

Evie blinked as several jigsaw pieces connected in her mind. Last week's events made a lot more sense now. She nodded in agreement; she had no desire on being in any more fights any time soon.

"One more thing, you should know that there was an

assembly. You weren't named, but it was basically telling everyone to be kind and mindful. Rumours were flying since Mr Hartley was on the news. Your fellow sixth-formers know of your relation, but the rest of the school only know gossip. Don't look so worried, as I said before, all of us teachers are going to be looking out for any anti-social behaviour. You'll be okay." Just as he finished speaking, the door opened and a few of the rugby team, including Roman, came in.

The rugby boys went silent and stared at Evie as they took their seats. Roman said something under his breath to them and as one, the whole team turned to face the front.

Roman made his way over to her. More and more people were coming into the room, but she ignored them, ignored the stares and whispers as Roman dropped into the seat next to her.

"Hey, Evie. How are you? You look really cute in the polka dots!" Roman told her.

"Morning. And, thank you?" Evie replied.

"Evie. Listen, about what happened last week, I'm really sorry, I should've—" Roman started, and as he talked, Evie realised she wasn't awkward and painfully shy like she used to be. She didn't have time to care if Roman was apologising, she didn't even know what he was apologising for. They'd agreed to move on past the whole email thing. She had far more important things to be concerned about, like the fact that she'd been basically suspended and since she'd arrived at school this morning, she hadn't yet bumped into Kendall and co, so was looking around every corner, literally on the edge of her seat waiting for the inevitable confrontation.

"Whatever, it's fine, Roman. I honestly haven't thought about it, the fight pretty much eclipsed the stupid email prank." Evie cut him off to stop the apology.

"That's what I mean, Evie, I am still sorry about the email misunderstanding. But during the fight, I should've stepped in or backed you up or something. I felt so bad, and when you didn't come in the next day I was so worried. I didn't know if I should text, but I thought you had enough going on and it's probably better talking to you in person anyway."

"I think I dealt with it quite well at the time, I didn't need you or anyone to save me. I'm over it now," she told him but couldn't prevent the smirk that flashed across her face.

"Evie, it was bad ass. It was so cool! You should've seen the chaos after, it's all anyone is talking about. Well, the same amount about the Everest thing. But people keep saying that it's about time someone stood up to Kendall. She was being a real bitch and was out of order," Roman said.

"I know, she has been for years now. I'm just sick of her, I have way more important things to focus on in my life than her. She's lucky it was just a slap," Evie boldly said, feeling very brave and proud.

"For a second, when you stopped in front of her, you kind of stepped back and raised your hands by your face and I thought you had turned into like a professional boxer and I swear she went pale under all her make up. I thought she was going to cry," Roman continued.

"Funny you should say I looked like a professional boxer. I have a story about that but it's quite long and embarrassing."

"You have to tell me now, Evie!"

"Well, you know in town there's that gym where they have classes? It's like a martial arts place? Well, I signed up for some classes a couple of months ago, to you know, get fit and learn some important skills – and it's not the main point but don't you think everyone should be taught basic self-defence, it's literally life-saving and it's like first aid and tax stuff that would be better taught in school than advanced algebra right?" Evie started to explain, getting side tracked as she did but not caring because Roman didn't seem to care that she was going off the point.

"No, totally, when am I going to use Pythagoras in the real world? I can use the Pythagoras theory to find the angle in a right angled-triangle, but I have no idea how to change the oil in a car or what to do if someone is choking. In fact, remind me to look both of those things up after practice later, I feel like that's stuff I should know. But anyway, the martial arts place?" Roman prompted.

"So yeah, anyway, don't go to this place in town. It was all these middle-aged men, and they were shouting in each other's faces and slamming each other into the ground so hard that it was like the floor shook. And then I joined in the stretching, I just went on the end of the line, and I was copying them, and they had their legs so high. Their leg was like higher than the height of my head." As Evie wove the story, she emphasised and embellished it until she reached the part about Jason tracking her to the dessert parlour.

Roman howled, he even slapped the desk in front of him as he gasped and tried to stop long enough to speak. Every time he seemed to stop and open his mouth to talk, he would start all over.

Their other classmates looked over, one of the rugby boys asked Evie to repeat the story that had Roman so amused. She let Roman tell them and smiled along. A few raised their eyebrows and looked away, not bothered. Evie saw Kendall, who had appeared at the back when she had been talking to Roman. So far, she'd escaped Evie's notice by keeping her head down and staying at the other end of the room. But as soon as Evie noticed her, Kendall got up and strutted down the side of the room, she flicked her hair and ducked out of the room. Her clones copied her and filed out.

Once her enemy left the room, Evie felt a slight air of relief and was able to relax a little. Roman's eyes flicked to her shoulders which were not held so stiffly, and her eyes which had stopped darting in every direction. She knew the tension was undoubtedly still brewing, but for the rest of form, she wouldn't have to be so vigilant.

"Evie, I am truly sorry. I know we used to be good friends when we were younger, but even over the past few years, I've always considered you a friend and I should've said something when Kendall has been so awful to you. I was so upset last week, although the slap was the highlight of my entire year. But yeah, I'm sorry. And that dessert parlour sounds really cool, I'll have to go there sometime, not after a crazy self-defence class though." Roman had apologised two times already since Evie had arrived at school, and she was running out of things to say.

"Roman, I swear you'll be getting a slap if you say you're sorry one more time. I told you the first time, it's fine. I appreciate it, but let's forget about it. Apart from the slap, you can remember that," Evie said, exasperated.

Roman agreed, and they discussed homework and swapped gossip until they separated to go to their first lessons.

Evie felt a shift in the school, the whispers that had swirled around her last week had muted, at least in her hearing. She did catch the words 'slap' and 'suspended' floating around and decided she would use them if it made people leave her alone and not harass her for information about Charles. By the time she reached her form room to get her afternoon mark, she was actually late. In the afternoon, they had a five minute window to swing by and greet their tutor and be marked present before they could disperse to their classes.

At lunchtime, she'd ended up sitting outside, which was eerily abandoned as the rest of the students chose to stay inside, away from the bitter cold. Evie had been wondering what was in her lunch and was pleasantly surprised to see a can of Coke, a tub of pasta and a slice of carrot cake. The best part, however, was a note from Charles. She read the words until she'd memorised them and recited them as she walked to her form. *'Enjoy your lunch, duck, I'll be waiting to hear all about your day. I love you and I'm so proud of you.'*

Evie realised she walked slower when she actually looked around and didn't speed walk around the place. Only a few people lingered, Kendall's friend Isabel lounged on a desk at the back as she carefully applied lip gloss to her already glossy lips. A group of rugby boys not including Roman were play-fighting and everyone else quietly worked or scrolled on their phone. Evie checked again to make sure Kendall wasn't at the back of the room. She rolled her eyes when she saw Isabel as she coated her already thick, dark eyelashes with more mascara. Isabel stuck her tongue out, but no words were exchanged.

Evie put her bag on the desk where she'd sat in the morning as she waited for Mr Scott to finish talking to someone else. She glanced idly around before she noticed the note on the desk. Her name was scrawled on the folded in half piece of paper.

Evie opened it, her heart pounded as she read the words, and re-read them.

Evie – I can't stop thinking about you. You're so beautiful and funny and great. I want to go out with you. Tonight. Cinema @ seven p.m. You always choose films for me, so now let me choose one for you. No excuses, I'll be wearing a shirt and tie. Coming straight from training so I can't speak to you before, but I'll meet you there. I can't wait – R xxx

She re-folded the note and slid it into her pocket, and when Mr Scott called her name and said she was marked in, she beamed at him. Evie floated through the rest of the day, hoping to see Roman and hoping she didn't see him.

She had a crush on him when they were younger. A lot of the girls did, even Kendall. He was good-looking and always getting awards for his skill and dedication to rugby. Evie knew it was as cliché as it sounded, she'd seen it a hundred times over in films, but more often than not it was a football star instead. But to Evie, who despised sports, it was more important that even though he was popular and always training with his tight circle of rugby friends, he was kind to everyone.

Evie had never been on a date, had never been close to being asked. And the fact that it was Roman, was perfect. It was like it was meant to be, fate had led them both on this path and for once things were going right for Evie.

But then Evie remembered what happened last time when she had gotten ready and been stood up. She knew it wasn't Roman's fault. Although she didn't want to talk to him after out of embarrassment and misplaced anger, she had understood that he was oblivious that his name had been used in the horrible trick. He'd certainly apologised enough. But what he'd said today echoed in her mind. He thought she was cute, and although he could have texted her, he had hesitated and chose to speak to her in person. Maybe he was shy and wrote it instead, he'd specifically talked about them sharing film recommendations, which she doubted anyone else knew about. And Kendall wasn't even in the room, it would be a pretty elaborate set-up, and Roman would have had to be involved for the level of detail. She was just so afraid of being hurt again that her instinct was to push it all away. She barely recognised when something nice happened.

Evie internally argued with herself for the remaining lessons of the day and for the entire journey home. She changed her mind a dozen times before she'd put her key in the door. She didn't know how Tilly maintained such a busy social life, she had been asked on one single date and panicked.

She only stopped her chaotic mind when she reached the reporters.

"Afternoon everyone. Can I grab anyone a hot drink or fill your water bottles?" she offered. After no quotes or photos of her were posted, her estimation of the reporters improved a little. She always tried to make an effort to be kind to any and every person, but she was far more inclined to go out of her way for decent people.

When she emerged from the house five minutes later, she returned two water bottles and gave the group a packet of biscuits, the nice digestives Jason had picked up the day before.

"See you all later, stay warm!" Evie said to them as she went back up her path.

She was followed by several well wishes.

"You have a nice night, Evie," one lady told her.

"Thanks a lot kiddo, see you tomorrow."

"Bye for now!"

After letting herself in once again, she sneaked up the stairs, listening for any indication of who was home. From Charles' room, she heard voices. It sounded like he was having an intense conversation with a girl who sounded a lot like Tilly. She couldn't make out the words, but they were speaking fast and low. Evie paused outside her sister's door. She heard the radio on and thought about knocking for a second but thought better of it and stole across the hall to her own room before anyone caught her.

She had a choice to make and interacting with her family right now would only distract her and cause further conflict.

Chapter 17

Evie took out her hairband and brushed her hair. She kept on brushing even after it was smooth and shiny. The repetitive motion soothed her as she gazed into the mirror, scrutinising her face. She pouted her lips until she could see her cheekbones, and then smiled at herself.

She wasn't going to do any fancy make up or let Tilly glue false eyelashes on her. Roman knew what she looked like, and he liked her when she was in school with her hair scraped back into a ponytail and bare-faced so he wouldn't care what she looked like.

The hardest decision was what she should wear. She always thought cinemas were cold, and usually wore comfy clothes so she could give the film her full attention. But somehow wearing joggers and a hoodie didn't feel right.

Evie opened her wardrobe and let out a groan. She didn't want to ask Tilly for fashion advice and have her sister learn about the sort of date. Evie had learnt a long time ago that her business was best kept private. But that didn't help in her clothing predicament. Surely, she couldn't wear her nice polka dot top, date clothes didn't double as school clothes. What should she do?

The knock on her door was like a sign, a decision taken out of her hands. When Charles popped his head in, Evie knew he would keep her date a secret without her even needing to ask him to.

"Hi, sweetheart. I didn't hear you come in! How was your school day?" he asked.

247

"Well, I didn't have any fights. A few people were staring and whispering but I ignored it all. Kendall steered clear. I took some biscuits out to the people outside too, since they kindly don't write about me or take photos. And then, in the middle of all that, Roman asked me to the cinema," Evie answered, excitement laced in her voice at the end.

"That's something. No fighting and a new admirer! People like this Kendall, they say hateful things usually because their own lives are sad or angry or sometimes boring. They get a kick out of lashing out, and it isn't fair, but I try to feel sorry for them since they have to take out their negative feelings on other people," Charles told her.

"I don't know if she's sad or angry. If she is, she's been this way for years and years. But I'm very good at ignoring her. Apart from last week when I called her out and I also called Roman out at the same time. It turned out that it was Kendall who sent me the email from Roman's account and Roman had no idea I was waiting so it wasn't really his fault. It all makes sense now. And today he was so sweet, and he invited me to the cinema," Evie trailed off as she noticed Charles' frown.

"That's... nice. I'm glad you feel better about it," Charles slowly replied.

Evie silently nodded. He continued to frown.

"What? Why are you doing that face?" Evie demanded.

"I just don't want to see you upset again," Charles answered.

"I won't be. This is Roman. I already told you it wasn't his fault last time. You don't get to dictate my life! I want to go. I've liked him forever," Evie declared.

"I don't follow. You liked him? I thought he was your friend, I always assumed you liked the chap, or why would you be friends with him?"

"What? Oh. No, there's liked which you're referring to, and then there's *liked* which is what I'm saying and that's when you like someone as more than a friend. And I *like* Roman," she explained.

"Ah, okay then. It's your choice. I won't say another word on the matter. I've made that mistake once before with my Evelyn and I will not do it again—" Charles paused. "Well, what are you going to wear then?"

"I don't know!" she wailed.

Then she learnt that despite his old fashioned sense of style, he had a lot of opinions. Somehow it was reassuring when he'd give the nod to her options. Finally, she settled on a black long sleeve top with glittery spots and black jeans with stud earrings and a necklace. She was perplexed to find her jeans settled a little lower than usual. She swiped a belt from the back of her door to secure them. Maybe this eating healthy and exercise thing really was working.

Once she had returned from the bathroom where she'd gotten dressed and brushed her teeth, a wave of fear hit Evie and she stopped dead in the room, in line with her mirror.

"You look lovely," Charles told her with a small smile.

Evie smiled back at her reflection, staring until the mirror image was distorted. Then her smile faded, and the room blurred until she could only see glitter and black in front of her.

"You look lovely," Charles repeated. Then more softly "What is it? You look really torn."

"I shouldn't go. The news people are everywhere. What would it look like if I'm going on dates and having fun when all this is happening? They leave me alone when I'm going to school, but this is different. It isn't right. I'll just stay here."

"Duck, what is life if not for living? I don't care a dot if you want to go out and enjoy yourself. If you ask me, you haven't had enough of that, and I'll support anything and anyone who changes that. Including this boy, if you like him and he's obviously smart enough to know how brilliant you are. Even your father is out having fun. Your mother is still not back from her 'Freedom Day'. I also happen to know Matilda is going out this evening too. So yes, why not?" Charles asked.

Evie nodded slowly.

"Have fun, duck, and don't you overthink or worry one bit. If you want, I'll open the curtains to distract the cameras and you can run out the back. I think there are only a few hardcore people camping out now. Half of them got bored and went home now they know I'm not playing ball."

Evie shook off the worry that sat low in her stomach as she hurried through the back door and through the usually locked gate. Charles would lock it behind her once he'd stalled the cameras after she had enough time to cut through the alley to the bus stop. She'd donned her winter wear seeing as it had made such an effective disguise earlier.

She put her earphones in and barely noted the bus journey to the cinema as she wondered what the night would bring. She didn't even know what film they were seeing, but Roman knew her well enough to pick a good one. She had already decided that if he paid for the tickets then she would buy popcorn and drinks in there. She wondered if they might kiss goodnight at the end of the date, and a pack of butterflies started flying around her stomach.

Evie arrived fifteen minutes early and scanned the area, not spotting any familiar faces. She texted him to let him know that she was waiting by the front door. He'd said he was coming straight from training so he might not see his phone yet, but when he looked it'd be there to direct him.

She shuffled her feet and looked up what films were on as she waited. Then she read plot summaries and reviews on the three she'd narrowed the potential list down to. Seven p.m. rolled around and no sign of Roman.

She thought he might run a little late, sometimes training went on longer than expected, and with traffic, it wasn't a huge surprise. She did send another quick text and walked to the end of the road and back, her eyes darted in every direction as she walked. She had to take her hat off because she was sweating from all the walking.

Evie saw the messages hadn't been read and she walked back towards the bus stop. She waited until the bus arrived, one she had taken herself many times before on the journey from the school straight to the cinema. She scanned the face of everyone who alighted, and only when the bus door groaned closed and the bus chugged away did she start walking again.

Evie fished out the crumpled note, that she's memorised hours earlier but she still checked the time on there. She began to doubt if she was in the right place. She tried to call him, but when she heard the automatic voicemail message, she wanted to launch her phone away from her and scream out loud.

The worry in her stomach had been silently growing, snowballing into panic. Evie desperately looked around, couples and families walked into the cinema, several people walked past, heads buried in their phones. Across the road a phone pointed at her, it caused her heart to falter as she considered the headline with the photo of her hitting the papers. She froze for a few seconds and stared into the camera. Vomit threatened to come up her throat as she thought about what the girl must see. Then the girl turned and walked away, not looking back once. Evie considered that she might be paranoid, but anyone could be a reporter or sell photos to one. She didn't expect to have spent over an hour loitering outside the cinema.

Evie stumbled on stiff legs into the foyer and ducked into the café where she leaned against the wall and lifted her phone again.

The smell of coffee calmed her pounding heart for a second, and at this time of day, it was almost empty. She breathed deeply and brought up her texts to Roman.

She messaged again, watching the one-sided conversation grow longer. Evie knew sending more messages wouldn't make him reply any sooner, but she couldn't just stand there doing nothing.

She called again, as a nearby clock chimed eight times, and this time Roman picked up, sounding out of breath.

"Evie. What happened?" he gasped.

"Romaaan? Where are you?" Evie cried.

"I'm at practice. Coach did a fitness test, so I've been running. I just saw like a million messages. Are you okay? What happened?" Roman asked again.

"Nothing. It's fine," Evie said before she hung up and turned her phone off even as Roman's name flashed up with an incoming call. Although she knew once again that Roman was being used against her, and he probably wasn't to blame, she couldn't bear to explain to him what had happened again. And how much it affected her.

She suddenly remembered where she was, and briefly considered going to watch something anyway, but after only a moment of consideration, Evie knew her heart wasn't in it. She instead turned and trudged towards the bus stop.

Fortunately, the bus was quiet. She had no one sitting next to her for the whole way home. As she walked down her road, she spotted the reporters who camped out all day. None of them even raised their cameras, but a few murmured greetings as she got to them. With a tired smile, Evie politely replied and went up the drive.

When she got to the front door, Evie moved as slowly as she could, almost silent as she turned her key in the lock. For the second time that day, she climbed the stairs on tiptoe and closed her door so slowly it didn't click as the latch was triggered. Evie knew the phrase fool me once, and she was too emotionally exhausted to feel anything but empty as she was once again let down.

She sat on her bed and stared at the flickering light as a tree swayed in front of the streetlight outside her window. Eventually, thick grey clouds joined together and unleashed a torrent of rain which dimmed the natural moonlight. For a long time, she didn't move, she just waited and tried to not think of anything.

Time passed, Evie realised that she couldn't make out the handle on her door, or the clutter on her desk. She should've closed the curtains and put her light on, but she couldn't muster the energy.

She was still sitting there when there was a brief knock on her door, and it opened a crack for Tilly to peer in.

"Hi. I wasn't sure if you were in. Are—are you okay?" Tilly asked tentatively.

When Evie didn't reply, her sister eased into the room and quietly shut the door. Tilly crossed the dark room in three steps and lowered herself onto the bed where she wrapped her arms around her little sister.

Evie couldn't bring herself to explain, to retell the whole sorry story. The strength of Tilly's arms, secure around her shoulders, one hand idly stroking her hair, was what released her emotions. As if bursting through a dam, tears poured down Evie's face.

"I know. Shh, you'll be okay. He isn't worth it. Or maybe he is, he seemed surprised and furious when he realised what had happened. Never mind that now, you're home and you're okay," Tilly murmured, seemingly speaking to herself.

When the tears had slowed to a trickle, Evie spoke. Her voice was gravelly and raw as if she'd been screaming all day and all night and only a broken rasp remained.

"How?" was the only word she said.

Tilly shuffled her feet and paused for a while with a thoughtful expression on her face before she finally said, "There is—there was another video. It's gone now. Your friend Roman kicked off, and Katie and I reported it and I think her actual account has been banned now."

She didn't need to explicitly say who the 'her' in question was. Evie waited for red hot embarrassment and sorrow to set in but there was nothing. No feeling painted her blank façade.

"Do you... want me to tell you about it? So you know?" Tilly asked.

Evie merely shrugged.

"Clearly they left the note, and they took a photo of you holding it in your form room, but you were smiling and looked nice. Your top was so pretty, and you were smiling so it was fine. And then it jumps to you outside the cinema but it's a time-lapse of you waiting and then you go into the cinema and then there's a shot of you running out looking quite upset. I mean, it's not so bad. You have a cute outfit on and you're not doing anything awful, just waiting around. The worst thing is probably the title but as I said, it's gone now, and she's been banned so this won't happen again. I've already spoken to Katie and I'm going to—"

"What is it?" Evie interrupted.

"What's what?"

"The title?"

"It's dumb, you don't need to hear it." Tilly tried.

"Title," Evie growled.

"Losers never learn. And there was a hashtag too, hashtag freak," Tilly said quietly.

Evie didn't respond. She just sat in the dark with her sister stroking her hair. She didn't know how much time had passed before Tilly suggested they get some food. They got up together and went downstairs.

"Junk food?" Tilly offered, and she gestured towards the crisps and biscuit cupboard.

"Something healthy. Maybe a bowl of granola or something," Evie replied. The thought of chocolate biscuits turned her stomach.

Before they decided what to eat, Charles shuffled in to join them. Evie suddenly remembered what he'd said and his reservations about the date that she had harshly shut down. She couldn't explain the situation to him. Before he spoke, she looked at Tilly, trying to convey a message of silence. Tilly shrugged ever so slightly.

"All right girls. Did you both have good nights with the people you *like*?" he asked them. But before she could think of a reply, he addressed Tilly. "I need some help if you don't mind, Matilda. Can you spare some of your evening to assist me, I was thinking right now if you weren't busy?" he asked.

"Of course," was all Tilly said. She snagged a water bottle from the fridge and sauntered from the kitchen straight into Charles' room.

Evie blinked at her great-grandad.

"Enjoy your meal. See you later," he said as he turned to leave.

"I didn't have a good night actually," Evie said to his back.

Charles' shoulders stiffened but other than that he showed no other sign of hearing her. A minute later he was gone, and his door firmly closed behind him.

For Evie, it was the last straw. She yanked open the freezer door and pulled the entire tub of ice cream from the bottom drawer. Instead of reaching for a bowl, Evie grabbed a spoon and a handful of kale as she took herself outside. She made plenty of noise and left the door cracked open to signpost her location to anyone looking.

She collapsed in front of Toby C's hutch, opened the top so he could lean out and dumped the kale unceremoniously in a heap. He dived in and both of them ate, the only sound was the nature around them, owls hooting, cars rumbling past and further away, a dog barked, and a plane soared over.

When the ice cream froze her empty mind and solidified her churning stomach, she put her hand in to Toby C. He licked her hand as she gently traced shapes on his back, and no one disturbed them.

When the moon was high and no more light emitted from any of the nearby houses, Evie locked up and took herself and her empty tub back in to the sleeping house.

The light was still on in Charles' room. She got into bed and fancied that she could hear him and Tilly whispering. Only the sound of Netflix, turned up as loud as she dared, drowned out the sound.

Chapter 18

After a sleepless night which etched purple shadows under Evie's eyes, she dressed and got ready for school on auto-pilot. She opted to skip breakfast, her brain unable to deal with anything else.

She had slipped out the front door and down the driveway before the time when she normally stumbled down to breakfast.

If the reporters spoke to her as she passed, their words didn't penetrate the fog in her head. She walked to school, not seeing the journey or thinking much at all.

By the time she arrived in school and stalked through the corridors, she'd reached an internal conclusion that she was done. She was fed up of being made a fool, of being treated like a second-class citizen in her own home and putting herself out for people who didn't appreciate it.

She reached her form room, resolved to stand up for herself and not allow any more pranks at her own expense. Evie swept over to her seat; her hard stare turned on anyone who dared to make eye contact. Her hands shook as she sat down, meeting every gaze as a challenge. Anyone who called her a loser or referenced the video would regret it.

By the time she got her phone out and began scrolling through some reviews, her no nonsense vibes were noted, and no one even looked at her. She concentrated on her phone fiercely until she realised someone was hovering next to her.

She glanced at Roman and turned back to her review.

"Evie, Please. I honestly had no idea. I know it's the second time, and I know you must be really upset. I had a huge fight with Kendall," Roman's voice was low, his tone urgent as he explained.

"Not now," Evie said.

"Let me just say this and then if you still want me to go then I'll respect your wishes. So, a couple of subs on the rugby team were in on it, and they and Kendall worked together to make sure I didn't see my phone and kept me late at training. They purposefully cheated in fitness, so we had to do it all over from the start. They had also left you a note, knowing you'd think it was from me and with Kendall obviously absent. They told me everything, and once they did I had a huge fight with Kendall, I was thinking about how you stood up to her and I followed your lead. Evie I swear, this won't happen again. And when I thought of you waiting for me for hours, it broke my heart and I realised I wish I knew about it because I would have been there in a heartbeat. So, I wanted to ask you directly, so there can be no confusion or pranks involved. Do you want to get dinner with me?" Roman seemed to hold his breath as he finished speaking and waited for her response.

"You're right," is all she said.

"Erm, I'm right about dinner? Or that it won't happen again?" he asked, his brows furrowed.

"You're right that you'll respect my wishes and go when I tell you to. This is me telling you. I am fed up, Roman. It's not your fault, and I know that, but I am over it. I have enough going on as it is and even though I don't blame you, I can't erase how hurt and betrayed I felt when twice now I waited for you. It's not happening, I'm focusing on me and what I need and there's no space for anyone else with me right now." She turned to look him in the eye as she spoke.

She noticed his flinch at the hard stare he received, and the

258

impact of the words was like a verbal punch. He sharply inhaled and colour rose in his cheeks as he listened.

"I like you, Roman. I *like* you a lot. Until recently I wouldn't be able to talk to you without being embarrassed and I definitely wouldn't be able to speak to you about all this. If you like me then you'll give me space and time and if you still like me when I get everything sorted, maybe I'll take you up on that offer for dinner. And thanks, for what you said. You can go now, if you want," Evie said, more kindly as she checked herself and reined in the feelings she had to spare innocent people.

He didn't move for half a minute as the words registered.

Finally, though his face was a little paler, his voice was strong when he said, "Thanks for being honest I guess. You're... harder somehow, Evie. It's a cool thing that you're standing up for yourself but it's a lot. I'll catch you later, let me know when— if things calm down."

Evie smiled and returned her attention back to the phone. She answered her name in the register in a monotone voice and saw yet another film review on a film she'd watched on Netflix. She almost laughed as she read it. Yet another person had missed an obvious foreshadowing and claimed to be utterly shocked by the twist.

As Evie stormed between her lessons, she thought until a plan came together. She already had a strong opener planned and a vague structure.

She was jotting notes down on a scrap piece of paper when her English teacher called on her.

"Sorry, what was that?" Evie asked.

"I said, Evie, that you weren't here last week when we divided into pairs to do the presentation. It needs to be ready to present on Friday, and I'll give you the brief but it's a summary and explanation of one of the chosen texts that we've been looking at. You can choose a pair to join and make sure you catch up, okay? Let me know before the end of the lesson whose group you're joining," her teacher explained.

Evie nodded and returned to her notes. She knew no one would be particularly excited about having her as a partner, and she was notorious for delivering bad speeches. The entire way through school she'd stumbled through public speaking with red cheeks and reading too fast and too quietly. It was torture when someone asked her to speak up, which someone did every time and she'd lose her place and get flustered. Normally this would be her cue to start panicking, but she couldn't muster the energy to care as she usually would. She was just too exhausted.

At the end of the lesson, she weaved her way through the tables until she reached her teacher. As she passed people still packing their bags, a few hissed at her.

"You are *not* invited to join our group, freak."

"Winners only here."

Her steps didn't falter as she heard the words, observed them and then pushed them aside. Her teacher hurried the rest of the class out of the room before she turned to face Evie.

"Have you thought about who you want to work with? And listen, Evie, I know you have a little less time to prepare but even with you missing a few lessons you're doing great. I'm not worried about your grade."

Evie pushed aside the praise and squared her shoulders, adopting a non-nonsense tone she'd heard Charles use a hundred times.

"I don't want to work with any of them. I'll do it by myself."

The teacher blinked a few times.

"Are you… sure, Evie? I know you don't particularly… enjoy presentations," she said.

"An English presentation is the least of my worries," Evie replied as she left the room.

By the end of the day. she had a purpose and the motivation to do it. She'd let Tilly replace her in Charles' life and reject Roman even though it's what she'd been hoping for this whole time and she'd ignore Kendall despite the fact that she ruined Evie's life and was so blatantly bullying her. She'd show them all with her new attitude. Evie breezed through the crowd of students as they poured out from the school and walked in every direction. The majority of them didn't notice her, and a few sixth-formers merely gave her a wary glance before getting onto buses or into cars.

When she got to her road, she noticed only two reporters, and both were sat in their cars. Evie waved as she passed them but didn't stop to enquire where everyone else was.

She slammed the front door and stomped up the stairs to her room. Her parents either worked from their bedroom on laptops or worked in their offices forty minutes away so were out all day. The only time they'd stopped working was the few days when Maria was travelling to and from London and Jason had fancied the trip. They continued to eat separately so she rarely bumped into them. But her sister and great-grandfather were probably home. Once her bedroom door was slammed too, she got her laptop out, smoothed out her scrap paper with notes on and began typing.

For over two hours, she wrote and edited and altogether ignored her family.

She was proof reading her final piece when she heard someone shuffling on the other side of her door. After a few beats of silence, there was a quiet knock.

Evie went still as she listened. Her mother or father would have burst in by now with no care for her privacy. The fact that the door remained closed indicated who it probably was.

She didn't start reading it again until she heard the middle stair with the creaky floorboard sound as he stepped on it.

The relief she expected didn't come. It was like she'd had so much hurt and emotion that her mind was too exhausted to cope and refused to process anything more. She thought about being sad that Charles didn't make more of an effort to check on her but ultimately decided that she didn't care enough to cry about it.

Instead of probing her emotions further, she turned her attention fully to her review. When she felt like she was obsessing over minute details that she'd probably make worse if she scrutinised them, she logged into her email. She picked up a sticky note that weeks ago she'd carefully printed an email address on to and copied the address. She crafted a concise but friendly email and attached the review.

She usually posted on her little blog, never before had she been bold enough to email a big shot company who professionally reviewed films. If they liked her, if they thought she had a bit of skill, then she had a foot in the door.

All of her year group had been working on their UCAS applications, but Evie had no idea where she wanted her life to go beyond working in the film industry, so if she managed to impress the company, she might be able to secure the start of her career. She'd have an edge over anyone her age looking to pursue a career in review writing. All she had currently was half a personal statement, a couple of potential local universities to apply to and a failed blog.

She wasn't going to sit idly any longer, she had a future to plan for and people to prove wrong.

The reply came mere minutes after she sent the review. Her breathing quickened as she hovered over the button. This moment could change her life. This is what she might recount in years to come, inspiring a younger generation to follow their dreams and put themselves first.

She opened it, as soon as she saw how short the reply was, she knew it was going to be painful.

How did you get my email? I am not interested in unsolicited and frankly, unremarkable work. Do not email me again.

Sent from my iPhone.

Suddenly, where her chest and brain had been empty, it was now filling with a pressure that was building and straining.

She needed to get out of the house. Away from the negativity that was suffocating her from every direction.

She pulled on her coat and rushed down the stairs. As she left, she glanced over her shoulder when she heard her name called. Emerging from Charles' room with a look of alarm on her face was Tilly. Charles followed behind, calling her name. She ignored them as she slammed the door and fled down the path, not looking back and not thinking about the fact that no reporters lurked.

She half ran and half staggered as she fled, running faster than she ever had before to outpace her constantly growing stack of problems. Her only thought was to get away from the house and all the bad thoughts that lay in wait for her there. She realised her feet had carried her to the bus stop and she boarded the bus without a second thought when it pulled up as she reached the stop.

Evie paid and stumbled to a seat. Her ragged breathing and the blood pounding in her ears drowned out any thoughts. She decided where she would go, and grimly awaited arriving at her safe haven destination.

Chapter 19

Although the film had long finished, Evie was still at the cinema. She was on her second drink from the café and was busy writing notes and ideas for her blog. She'd been far too distracted lately, and the last rejection, though horrible to receive, was the wake-up call she needed to prioritise her future. She'd written down anything useful to make sure she didn't forget any important details. She needed to write better than ever to gain back her reputation and build up her review blog.

When she ran out of notes to make, she used the time to work on her upcoming solo English presentation. The instruction had been to present one of the chosen texts, and Evie made her life easier by choosing one of her favourites. She'd read it several times over and it didn't take her long to put a speech together. As soon as she was done, she moved back on to her review, outlining her first draft.

She should be glad that Charles and Tilly were so close and had secrets, she thought. It meant she had the time to do what she wanted to do. She didn't even want to know what they were always whispering about. Let her sister step up and share the responsibility of entertaining and protecting Charles. She hadn't done anything she liked to do recently, she'd let her blog go and lost followers as a result. She'd barely watched any films. She'd altogether lost sight of her goals. Evie realised she'd stopped writing and took a sip from her smoothie before she attacked the notes again. She had learned from her rejection, she observed it for what it is and then consumed it as fuel to feed her motivation.

Every so often she'd give her phone a dirty look. It was still on silent from the film, she didn't expect anyone would care about her absence and bother contacting her. Even if they did, it was no one's business where she was. She would be eighteen soon enough and an adult, they had no right to barge in and track her every move. It was infuriating, especially when her sister would go out and not return for several days, and simply reappear with no explanation.

Evie paused again and put her pen down for a minute. Her hand ached from having the pen clenched so tightly. Several people had come in and out since she'd been sat there but no one she recognised. At the moment, there was an elderly couple with a pot of tea and a group of girls giggling into soft drinks probably waiting for a film to start. The staff were chatting as they wiped surfaces and when they all stopped and turned towards the TV that was muted on the wall, Evie followed their gaze. As she turned, the sound was turned up and unmuted by the boy behind the counter.

"Breaking news." The news anchor droned. "Join us live as we report on the latest information in the Everest Eight case. Our regular correspondent Andrea Cabot is unavailable, so we are joined today by Mr Kane Winters who kindly agreed to fill in. Mr Winters, can you share this exclusive information with us?"

"I would be delighted to." Winters drawled, he straightened his tie and turned to stare directly into the camera. Even through the screen, Evie could see how his lips were upturned slightly and his eyes glinted in malice. "Are the dead dying... again?"

A wave of silence swept through the room. The girls were hushing each other as they leaned in, phones already in hands as they furiously typed. Evie's heart stopped dead, stuttered and then began an uneasy beat. She couldn't think of anything except if Charles is okay, if the worst had happened. She willed Winters to carry on, to tell her who was dying.

"Today one of the Eight dropped to the floor and was rushed to hospital where they will remain until further notice. We have on good authority that the rest of them are being contained and isolated. Now, we don't know for sure what caused this, but any intelligent person can consider that these zombies have been frozen, what's to say some archaic disease hasn't been unfrozen at the same time. Who truly knows the effect of being dead for so long? I would imagine anyone would come back with mental health problems at the very least. This only highlights what I've been saying all along – they are not safe. We must take swift action to protect the future for our children. If we're not careful there won't be a future to safeguard for. All for the sake of eight overly ambitious men and women who died before their time for bragging rights to climb Everest and who are now on borrowed time, our time. Now, these are just my opinions of course, but think about it for yourselves. Don't let any freak loving reporters twist—"

"Thank you for that report, Mr Winters. We'll continue following this development as the story unfolds. Now over to the weather..."

Small conversations immediately ignited across the café. The barista boy called someone and began repeating the news report word for word.

"It's already trending, I have to tweet this before someone else does."

Evie took in the scene, seeing and hearing everything in about two seconds. Another second passed.

Evie scooped up her notebook and pen, shoving them into her pocket as she got up and ran from the cafe. Ice cold dread flowed through her veins, hurting her heart with every beat.

She'd gone from being empty and apathetic to panic and fear in an afternoon. She bargained with herself silently as she exited the cinema – if Charles was safe, if he was okay then she wouldn't begrudge any time he spent with Tilly. She would smile and get over it.

As she paced by the bus stop, seeing a sixteen minute wait before her bus arrived, Evie finally turned her phone off silent. She flinched in anticipation of what she might find.

So many messages flashed up, quite a few of them were from Roman, and she deleted them without opening the full message. She clicked into her chat with her sister and saw endless requests for her to call and come home. Evie looked at the bus times again, not even a minute had passed yet.

She couldn't bear to stand there waiting and wouldn't call home when so many people were around and blatantly watching her after she had arrived in such a hurry. She couldn't face receiving bad news so publicly. She was desperate to know that Charles was safe but more desperate to maintain the façade that he was okay, he only wouldn't be okay if she was told he wasn't.

Evie fastened her bag and checked her laces were tied. She took off at a slow jog, painfully conscious of all the eyes on the frantic, running girl. As she jogged, she relished the sweat and tears that blended together on her face. She would never forgive herself if he died and the last contact she'd had with him was storming out the house and ignoring him. If she got home before the bus, maybe he'd be okay. She pumped her arms to speed up.

She didn't notice the car following her. She didn't see the frantic waving from over the steering wheel. But she did hear the horn and reflex had her looking before she had registered the sound.

Tilly was shouting her, the words barely heard over the pounding in her head.

"Get in! What are you waiting for? Evie!"

Evie obeyed and within a minute was in the speeding car heading home.

"Grandad?" she gasped.

"Alive. Upset. Worried about you since you ran away and didn't answer your phone. Not cool, Evie!" her sister replied, not taking her eyes off the road.

Evie was too relieved to respond. Nothing like an emergency to force her to reconcile with her estranged feelings and shove her straight back into family life she thought, as they hurried home.

As they turned into their road, the appearance of more photographers and reporters than she'd ever seen was both a surprise and not surprising at all. There were no familiar faces amongst the group, most likely a representative from all the news outlets had been sent to get some fresh footage to go along with their new story. The news didn't have the name of who had been taken into hospital, so they must have been staking out as many of the Eight as they could until they got something newsworthy.

Evie cringed away from the window, ducking her head while Tilly shook her hair forward as she slowly glided up the drive.

"Do they know he's not with us?" Evie asked tentatively.

"They don't care. They just want the footage. When you get out go straight in, no speaking or looking back. No matter what they say," Tilly said darkly.

As Evie followed the instructions, she looked into the reflection in the window. Behind her, cameras flashed, and people jostled for position. They were chased into the house by a flurry of questions.

"Is Charles sick? Where is he now?"

"Hey kid, tell us where your gramps is?"

"Do you have a relationship with one of the fr—Eight? Is it true what Kane Winters said? How did that news report make you feel?"

"The freaks should be dead, it isn't right and if all you freak lovers feel so strongly, you should follow them back into their graves. Freaks!"

Evie's cheeks burned as she fought to not react. After the door was firmly closed and locked, she looked at her sister.

They were both panting as if they'd run the entire way home. Tilly's body shook as she slumped against the closed door. Her eyes closed and she remained motionless for a few beats as though the mere act of being outside had exhausted her.

"Thank you, for picking me up," Evie said quietly.

"Don't go out again without telling us. Not right now. I need you here," Tilly replied as she pushed herself upwards and into the kitchen.

Evie was about to follow when she heard someone stomping down the stairs.

"Evie! For God's sake! I swear if she riles up the bloody hounds one more time I'll throw her to them myself. I can hardly hear myself think over all this ruckus. Stupid girl." Jason hollered down the hallway to her before he stomped back upstairs.

Evie shook her head and joined her sister in the kitchen. Tilly was busying herself making drinks. Charles sat in his regular seat at the table, with his head in his hands. His cheeks, which were the only part of him she could see, looked paler than she'd ever seen him, and he wore a big winter coat, hat and scarf. He didn't look up as she approached him.

Evie hesitated, she reached towards his shoulder and then pulled her hand back. In the end, she cleared her throat.

"Hi, Grandad. I'm sorry for running out before it won't happen again. I promise. Are you okay?"

Charles' eyes flew open at her voice; he raised his head and then closed his eyes briefly as he mouthed something before he focused on her.

"Evelyn. Thank goodness. I was very worried when that

report came out and I didn't know where you were. I could have done without that, young lady," he reprimanded, but his tone was gentle.

Tilly placed a mug in front of Charles, and another in front of Evie. After she picked up her own drink she settled in the seat on the other side of Charles and took a sip.

"Right, now we've picked Evie up we can get her opinion and work out what to do next. Basically, Evie, me and Grandad have been working on a little project. We're trying to *Unite the Eight*. It sounds dramatic, but it's creating a support system with the only people who have been through this crazy experience. And providing a united front to turn the tide in this media campaign. We hope it'll be like an extended family," Tilly explained.

Evie tried to stifle the rearing thoughts in her mind. She gave a millimetre smile as she pushed her jealousy and frustrations away from her. One thought was constantly springing out. This was her idea, something she'd mentioned weeks ago. The whole secret that she couldn't know was in fact, her own dream and hope for the Eight that she'd been imagining before Tilly deigned to give Charles her time or attention.

"Wow, super. And how's that going for you?" Evie sniped, unable to keep her tone even.

"Now, now. You needn't be upset, duck, it was simply a matter of Matilda being here in the daytime when you're in school and I noticed you had a lot on your plate so I didn't want to add another burden. I know you would have been an invaluable help, but I couldn't bear to give you any more worry. I've got a dreadful headache and a million things to do and sort now that report has hit the front page. If you have any more to say on the matter then do so now otherwise we're putting the matter to bed and moving on," Charles firmly said.

Evie recalled her sister's words in the car. That Charles was upset and worried. She hadn't considered which of the Eight was sick and in hospital, she'd only cared about Charles. She guiltily sent a silent prayer to the other seven and prayers for their recovery and strength for their families.

Evie ducked her head, ashamed.

"No, it's fine of course. I was just surprised. Do you know who it is? Who's sick? Are they okay?" she asked.

Tilly sighed.

"It's all a bit of a mess, to be honest."

"One of the team called me with an update, but I only got the news a little before it went public. It's impossible to keep anything private. Someone videoed poor Frank getting wheeled into the back of an ambulance. His poor family were distraught in the background. But the rest of us are on a watch now, he was right as rain before a sudden illness overcame him. I have to admit, I am rather concerned about the whole thing." Charles wrung his gloved hands.

"If it, if the thing happens to you. We'll be with you every step of the way. Both of us. You'll get better. " Evie told him.

"Yeah," Tilly echoed.

"Thank you girls, but I think I'd be more concerned for both of you than myself. But enough of that type of talk. We've got some planning to do, people to win over and schemes to hatch. If one of you can fetch me a blanket, we'll get started right away."

The three of them spoke long into the night as they discussed and analysed every possible route. At various points, Jason and Maria ventured into the kitchen, but it was like the three of them were in a bubble that was so thick, it created a soundproof barrier.

Before too long Jason stomped out and Maria drifted away. Both had looked disgruntled when Evie reluctantly glanced over.

The clock declared that it was a new day when it chimed

twelve times. They had a rough outline of a plan in place. Tilly was going to make some calls in the morning, Charles was to write some letters and speak to Dexter. Evie had a renewed sense of purpose to *Unite the Eight*. From now on, they weren't going to be alienated and attacked by the media, they were going on the defence and would win over the people who were afraid and upset by the idea of them.

Chapter 20

Before the sun had peeked over the horizon and bathed the world in a fiery orange glow, Evie was roughly shaken awake.

"Get up, Evie. You have to get up. It's important!" Tilly's voice was especially high pitched.

Evie's eyes were burning from the limited sleep that had stretched over several days, perhaps weeks. She rubbed them, knowing they'd be bloodshot and sore for the rest of the day. She yawned widely, her brain was slowly booting up, the only thing she thought about was how inviting and warm her bed was.

"Evie, come on! Grandad needs you!" Tilly implored.

At that, Evie swung her legs out of bed. When they made contact with the cold floor, it was like alertness shot through her like lightning. She reached for her dressing gown and shoved her feet into her slipper boots.

"Okay, let's go," she said.

The girls hurried down the stairs. Tilly didn't hesitate, she barely broke her stride as she opened the door and disappeared further into Charles' room. Evie was hot on her heels and skidded to a stop when she saw Charles hunched in the corner seat. In his hand was his beloved pocked watch and a couple of tears were racing down his cheek.

"Grandad?" Evie asked in a small voice.

Wordlessly, he opened his arms, and she didn't hesitate this time as she walked straight to him and enveloped him in a hug.

"Frank died. He died early this morning. Dexter called me

and told me personally. He was saying the doctors have some theories. They think their—our bodies couldn't cope with current strands of disease and have no immunity to them. It was all antibodies and resistance and science talk, and I don't know what it means or what I should do!" Charles was speaking as though there was no air left in his lungs, and every word uttered was wrenched from his heart.

"I'm so sorry. His poor family, I hope they're okay. I'll try and contact them to see if there's anything I can do. I wouldn't function if we lost you. I can't imagine it," Evie said to his shoulder. She hugged him hard, to remind herself that he was here and safe.

"I'm not going anywhere just yet, duck," Charles said, and he hugged her back just as hard.

"I'm going to make some tea, and maybe some toast. It'll be okay." Tilly hurried out of the room.

Evie finally let go of him and sat on the floor adjacent to Charles. Gradually, the light behind the curtains got brighter. By the time Tilly returned, she could turn the lamp off. She deposited a pile of toast, cut into triangles and generously buttered. She also put down a pot of tea, several mugs, a jug of milk, an apple cut into eight segments and a packet of chocolate digestives.

"I've just got to grab one more thing. Better get started on the toast before it goes cold." And she hurried out the room once more.

Evie didn't feel hungry at all. With all the stress lately, she'd had to remind herself to eat at meal times and she hadn't had the time or desire to go to the dessert parlour. Despite the lack of appetite, she took a small bite of the golden buttery bread and surprised herself with how good it tasted. Before she thought about it, she grabbed another piece and started chewing.

Charles was slow to move. His body seemed heavy as he leaned over to pour himself some tea.

Watching him, Evie found her appetite for toast had evaporated. She shook her head silently when he offered her the pot.

They sat in an easy silence together. Evie was about to go looking for Tilly when the door edged further open and Toby C skidded into the room. A grinning Tilly followed close behind him.

"I wondered who the apple was for. Hello Baby, come to your mummy for a cuddle." Evie crooned to her rabbit. At the sound of her voice, Toby C hurtled over to her, sniffing her leg before he made a beeline for the table. The jump upwards was one fluid motion and before Evie could stand up, he had started on one of the apple slices.

"Please remove this… animal from the table I am eating off girls," Charles spoke stiffly. He held his tea aloft as if he thought Toby C was likely to leap over and try to drink it.

Tilly scooped him up, and the apple as well. She put him down in front of Evie and stroked him a few times before she settled on the sofa and prepared her own cup of tea.

When Toby C had devoured his apple and cleaned his sticky paws and face, he allowed Evie to pick him up and hold him close. He licked her chin a few times and then settled down.

"It is awful, horrible news. He will be greatly missed. I expect it's even worse for you, and you are absolutely allowed to mourn and grieve. But I think this is a turning point. You need to reach out to the others today. It's more important now than it ever was for us to get the media on our side and look after each other. I had a look online when I was waiting for the kettle to boil, and this news hasn't been released yet, but there's already too much stuff about vigilantes and hate groups forming," Tilly said passionately.

"Maybe I should stay here today and make myself useful. Right before I fell asleep, I had some ideas. I think we should arrange for you all to go on TV shows for interviews. Hear me out, if we have you as guests on daytime and late-night telly, they'll be desperate to interview you and you can share your perspective and show them all you're not these satanic unnatural creatures, but real people who could be anyone's grandad or brother or neighbour. That's the main problem, since there's no face to the names or the story, they have all this freedom to speculate and who checks them? Even Dexter's lot can't control the media, and they shouldn't be able to. No one should be able to narrate the story from just their own perspective. But that's what's happening now. Every on air or printed word from Kane Winters is a one-sided, false narrative coming from a place of hatred," Evie told them. Her tired, red eyes were testament to how much research she'd done before she was forced to stop because her eyes had been closing of their own accord.

"No, duck. You need to go to school. I appreciate you helping me on this one, but I don't want it interfering with your school work. I know what you're both saying, and I do think it's time for me and the other seven—six to—to do this. The last thing I want though, is for you two to be dragged along in this crazy journey. And I do expect it to be a long, difficult process. I'd be extremely grateful for your company though, a morning like this when I'm feeling down improves dramatically when you two are around. You both remind me how lucky I am, and why it is so necessary for me to do this," Charles said.

They sat together until Evie glimpsed Charles' pocket watch and it reminded her to check the actual time, and that she needed to leave for school in ten minutes. She said as much as she passed Toby C to Tilly and ran up the stairs.

"I'll drive you!" Tilly called after her, meaning she'd have a little more time.

She washed and threw on jeans and a long sleeve black t-shirt with her black Vans. After running a brush through her hair, she pulled it into a high ponytail. With a quick glance at the time, she realised she had enough to quickly do make up. She did her eyeliner in one, shocked to be happy with the flicks on her first try, usually it took several times of wiping it off and re-doing it for her to deem it acceptable. She swiped mascara across her eyelashes and threw on some lip gloss.

By the time she had gone back downstairs and pulled her coat on, Tilly had put Toby C away and prepared some lunch for Evie. Charles kissed her forehead and they made it to school with two minutes to spare.

"Have a good day, Evie. Thanks for getting up so early. I never know what to do in situations like that," Tilly said, she had pulled over to the side of the road but still looked at the road ahead.

"Are you kidding? You always look super calm, and you don't hesitate or anything. I'm the one who's unsure and awkward all the time. If you were in school instead of me, you'd be a hero, not an outcast. You wouldn't have let the Everest situation turn you into a pariah, I know you wouldn't!" Evie retorted incredulously.

"Sometimes you literally have no idea, Evie. Anyway, you better go in or you'll be late. Later, loser." Tilly smirked and waved as Evie got out of the car and headed inside.

She didn't acknowledge anyone apart from giving Roman a nod. As she took her seat, thinking about how tired she was and mentally pulling herself together, she heard Kendall pipe up.

"So obviously we're still having the dance. It's like the social highlight of the entire year. But, the real question, is if our raised money is going to a genuine cause. I heard that they're all frauds, and Kane Winters was on the news just yesterday saying that they're freaks which we've known all along but why is the money we're working so hard to raise being given to a bunch of zombies? It looks like death is catching up to them now anyway. If the freaks are in hospital, it's only a matter of time before they're all dead. Oh! Is that it—we're fundraising for their funerals?" Kendall said.

To Evie's delight, their teacher told Kendall to be quiet and sit down before she got sent to the head of sixth-form. She was on her last warning. Evie nodded slightly to Mr Scott.

Evie was glad that the news of the death hadn't gotten out yet, although it was only a matter of time. If Kendall was like this now, it was merely a preview of what was to come.

Evie went through her morning, barely noting it. She went from lesson to lesson, dutifully took notes and tried to listen but the whole time her mind was elsewhere.

At lunchtime, Evie opened her bag and found the bag Tilly had presented her with that morning. It contained apple slices, a bag of Maltesers, two ham butties and a mini can of Coke. Evie sent her a text with a smiley face and received an immediate thumbs up in return.

The quick reply and thoughtful lunch left a smile on Evie's face. The lunch hour sped by as she researched daytime television shows. By the time she arrived in English class, she had all but forgotten the upcoming presentation.

Having had no spare time to worry about it, Evie's nerves were stable and under control. By the time her name was called, she had decided to treat it as a warm up. If she was to support Charles on national television and be a champion for the Eight— *seven*, she mentally corrected herself, then she would be speaking to millions of people. Her skin had already had to grow thicker against the words of faceless strangers who wished her ill, so she could certainly handle a room of people she'd known for almost seven years while she presented one of her favourite books.

She breezed through her points, and returned to her seat,

positive she'd achieved the best grade she'd ever had on a presentation and barely caring.

Her teacher complimented her, but the praise bounced off her. It was nice, but she had far more pressing matters to think about. She could hardly remember when public speaking had been such an ordeal, or when snide comments had bothered her. She had no time for either her fear or her feelings to interfere with her plans now.

Now hers was done, she felt as though a lump had settled in her throat. When she would usually be shaking in her seat worrying through everyone else's presentations and comparing them to her own, now she was totally removed from the classroom. She barely clapped at the right times and certainly didn't listen as she contemplated Charles' situation. She figured that she would have to be extra supportive and positive around him, which she could manage knowing that he was in good health and that soon enough they would be left in peace and be able to move into their new home and have some semblance of a normal life again.

As she sat and thought, she suddenly felt very nauseous. The lump in her throat could have been a rock blocking her airway. There was no tangible reason for why she felt so wrong and sick to her stomach, all she knew was that something was very wrong.

Abruptly, she stood up and murmured half an excuse to the teacher and half an apology to the person she'd interrupted. She didn't wait for either to respond before she fled from the room.

Evie raced through the corridors to the school office, and not for the first time this school term, she walked out.

As she crossed the school gates, she noticed Tilly sat in her car, in the exact same spot where she'd dropped Evie off hours earlier. From a dozen feet away, Evie knew her sudden bout of sickness was about to be explained.

Tilly didn't look up as Evie approached the car. She sat with her head in her hands, elbows on the steering wheel. Her shoulders slightly shook, betraying her sorrow even though she was hiding the tears.

Evie knocked on the window before she got in. Tilly jumped and hastily wiped her eyes. They were ringed in red and she was loudly sniffing.

"Evie. I, I was about to go in and get them to pull you from your lesson. How did you know I was here?" Tilly asked between sniffs.

"I didn't. But I felt like something was wrong, so I was going home. What's happened? Is it Grandad?" Evie replied grimly. She knew if Tilly was crying then it must be bad.

"Grandad has, he got sick. Very suddenly and I was sitting with him and I rang an ambulance and they rushed him to hospital. Mum went with him and they told me I can't go and when I asked if he'll be okay, the paramedic—he said, 'we'll see'." Tilly burst into tears again.

As Evie leaned over to hold her sister, she was surprised to find that she wasn't crying as well. She felt like she was on the edge of losing control and surrendering to the panic and sadness. As she held her sister and examined her feelings, she felt her whole stomach lurch, and her lovely lunch and the toast from earlier made a reappearance all over Tilly's car mat. Then the conspicuously absent waterworks were turned on.

They sat there for a long while until Tilly's tears had subsided and transformed into the occasional hiccough. When Evie's tears had finally run dry and they'd exchanged a look that conveyed everything they both felt, Tilly put the car in gear and drove them to the hospital.

Chapter 21

The sisters travelled in silence; the only sound was the tinny voice of the sat nav calling directions. They parked and entered the hospital, feeling younger than they had in years. Evie reached out for her sister's hand, and they held on tight to each other as they mentioned their names and got a personal escort to the bowels of the hospital.

They arrived at Charles' room and stopped before the door.

"It'll be okay. We have to be strong for him, we promised," Evie told her sister fiercely.

"Absolutely, I agree. I just, I don't know what to say. I'm scared, Evie." Tilly's eyes were shimmering.

"We'll be okay. We've got each other. Shall we go in? He'll be worrying about us. I guess Mum is around here too." Evie led her sister into the room.

Tilly glanced at Charles and decided to go and find the canteen, promising to bring back drinks and locate a menu. She smiled at Evie as she left the room, pulling Maria along as Maria had once pulled Evie in a different hospital. Evie didn't think to return the smile until after she'd gone.

The hospital was a slap to the face, reminding Evie that Charles was seriously and undeniably sick when she'd almost forgotten as time had gone on and Charles had settled into the family as if he'd always been there. The whole Everest thing had become so normal, that it was a surprise to recall that he was vulnerable and a sharp reality check that Evie needed to be pragmatic.

But when she looked up, Charles smiled and patted the chair next to his bed. Evie slowly went over, unsure of what she should do. The only thing she could think of was to hold his hand, but it seemed silly when he was awake and talking to her.

She sat down next to him and promptly burst into tears. He patiently sat there and comforted her until her sobs slowed and she swallowed several times.

"Are you... okay?" Evie asked when she could speak.

"Ah, I've been better. You don't need to worry though, duck, at this stage it's a bit of a precaution. I had a dizzy spell and the next thing you know I'm on the floor with a lovely paramedic asking me what year it was. At least I knew the answer this time!" Charles paused, and after a second Evie dutifully laughed, though the sound was forced.

"So, given my situation, they felt it prudent to bring me in to monitor me and to call our friend Mr Dexter and his scientist pals, of whom a car full are racing over. Me and the other Everest folk are causing all sorts of fuss and wreaking havoc for the government types. I feel absolutely fine, but they have to do some testing and find out exactly what is going on inside. You needn't look so alarmed," he continued calmly.

"I-I thought. That maybe...Frank." Evie tried several times until emotion overcame her, and she couldn't voice the words out loud. Even thinking them was too difficult.

She couldn't imagine what Frank's family felt like. How cruel the hand of fate had dealt them, in returning their relative and then reclaiming him in such a short time. In the hours since it happened, Evie had gradually heard all the pieces of the story and put together the full picture.

He had been cooking at the time. His family owned a restaurant and he'd fitted in like he'd never left. He was teaching

282

and learning and so happy to be there. He was fine, until he'd taken ill this morning. It had been very sudden and unforeseeable. He'd dropped a spoon, taken a shuddering breath and collapsed. After being rushed to the hospital, he had stopped breathing altogether and attempts to resuscitate had been successful, but he took a terrible turn in the night and slipped away before the doctors had been able to figure out what was wrong. It was only after that the theories were formed.

"Rest his soul. But this is different, I'm already in the hospital, there's an army of doctors at the disposal of Mr Dexter's team and once they work out exactly what the problem is, they'll figure out a solution. Poor Frank was on borrowed time, same as the rest of us, but he had the misfortune of going first before we had any sort of plan in place."

"It's just so sad. Poor Frank, he was working in his family restaurant and he had such little time…" Evie trailed off.

"Let's dry those eyes, you're almost as big a worrier as my Evelyn was. Almost always you'll look back on all that time spent fretting and realise it was not as bad as you thought and you wasted all that time overthinking it. Now, I'm glad you're here. I need your help with something, and I was waiting for a time when the others weren't around to discuss it," Charles announced, briskly changing the subject.

"Of course, I was wondering when you might ask actually," Evie replied immediately, her voice strong but still sniffing between words.

"You anticipated my question?" Charles looked bemused.

"Yes, of course, it's almost Christmas. I was obviously going to wait until you felt a little better but now is as good a time as any. I'll need to get cracking if I want to get it all done in time." Evie fished a folded piece of paper out of her pocket. She angled it towards Charles so he could see the names of his family scrawled on there, with generous blank spaces under each name.

"Okay, sorry, duck. I have no idea what you are talking about. I was going to propose we decide on the colour scheme and decoration for the new house. What is that paper for?"

"Oh, I assumed you wanted me to pick up everyone's Christmas presents for you. Since you're in here and you're also allergic to online shopping and technology. And I know you found going around the shops a little overwhelming, and it's even worse around this time of year when there's a rush. I thought it would be helpful. I'll even pretend to be surprised at my own present. But I don't have to. You aren't obliged to get us presents of course." Evie was unsure of herself now, she cursed herself for presuming. Now he'd likely feel awkward and guilty like he needed to buy gifts. Which he didn't, she sternly told herself.

"I. Yes. No, what a brilliant idea. You are far more organised than me. Usually, Margaret sorts out the festivities and she always knows, knew exactly what gifts Evelyn would be delighted with. My apologies, we shall discuss both, and spend a fine afternoon choosing things for our future home and our family. How about that?" he proposed.

"That sounds lovely. Which first?"

At the same time, they both said the option the other had suggested.

"House colour first then, since that's the easy stuff. I need time to think about suitable gifts for the family," Charles told her.

They spent hours together as the day grew older. Tilly returned with hot drinks in recyclable cups and was content to sit with them and occasionally offer her opinion. Maria had apparently gone home once Charles was declared stable, she'd mentioned work that needed doing.

Evie knew she was very lucky, she knew visiting time was usually restricted, but in special circumstances such as these, exceptions had been made. Over the rest of the afternoon, several nurses popped in and checked on Charles. Everyone and their nan had an opinion on the colour scheme.

Charles was adamantly against bright colours and paint straight on the wall. He was determined to incorporate the colour brown into the room, and preferably with wallpaper. Evie passionately argued and suggested a compromise of white paint to start with, and perhaps a beige-brown carpet in the living room.

By the time they had negotiated downstairs and designed the entire two floor house down to the glassware and towel colours, it was tea time. After a jacket potato, they agreed to tackle the Christmas side of things.

"One more thing, sweet. Your room is entirely yours. You could choose neon pink polka dots for the wall if your heart desires. And any bedding, furniture, curtains. The lot. Have a little think and maybe a look through the Argos catalogue and then we can start ordering bits and bobs. Now, I am incredibly confused about these gifts. Although I may have something in mind for my esteemed grandson-in-law. Where's that paper?" he asked with a wicked laugh.

Evie and Tilly spent the entire weekend by their grandad's side. Monday came back around and for days, it was the same routine. She'd attend her lessons in school, then either get picked up by Tilly or go straight on a driving lesson. Then after a quick meal, they'd head to the hospital where they'd spend the rest of the late afternoon into evening with Charles. Some days they chatted non-stop and had sore throats after, sometimes they played board games like Scrabble or watched films on a portable DVD player. Occasionally, Charles would be having a bad day, and they'd quietly sit together and take comfort in the presence of each other until the bad spell passed or the day ended, whichever came first. It was a privilege to have a loving, supportive family, the nurses said so all the time. On the bad days, they'd close the curtains and wrap up in fleece blankets and wait for the storm to pass.

As November drew to a close and December loomed, all the trees traded their last golden orange and brown leaves for empty branches waiting to be clothed in the white of freshly fallen snow. With Halloween and Bonfire Night firmly in the rear view mirror, all focus was now on the upcoming holiday festivities. Shops that Evie ducked into to grab a quick drink had Christmas music softly playing. Huge trees were robed in fairy lights and crowned with stars or angels. Bitter winds and cold rains were replaced with weather forecasts for snow and ice.

It was decided that the seven would be kept under medical supervision for the remainder of the winter months. With so many colds and flus making the rounds, it would be too much of a risk to have them out and about. With the seven secure and privately living out of the public eye, the media circus had ground to an ungraceful stop.

Evie had been oblivious to the media for the first couple of weeks Charles was in the hospital. Until he'd been declared in decent health and stable, Evie had paid no attention to the world's judgement. She had later learned that when Kane Winters had tried to capitalise on the footage of Frank being stretchered to hospital, a lot of people abandoned his cause. Poorly elderly family members resonated and won sympathy from the public. Just like that, the fickle public opinion turned and with no new footage or information, many had lost interest.

The shock that had reverberated around the world when Frank had passed away had finally settled and when people realised that these Eight men and women were mortal, the zombie and immortal theories had been put to rest once and for all. These days, Evie didn't even bother checking E8Updates. These days it was just very bored or very lonely people chasing drama, as Charles had once told her when describing bullies. It had been days since the last stubborn reporter had finally called it a day and packed up from the Monroe's driveway. These days people barely mentioned it, unless perhaps to wonder whatever happened to the Everest people. Evie and the nearest and dearest of the Everest folk were sweet-talked, threatened and signed a lot of paperwork swearing that they wouldn't do anything that would shine a light back onto the situation. They all agreed it was in everyone's best interests to maintain low profiles. Evie was also gratified to see the seven had connected and regularly caught up. They were spread out across the United Kingdom, and several were as reluctant to embrace phones as Charles, but somehow they did it and a new support system was created. With Charles in hospital and participating in several tests a day, she knew he enjoyed speaking to the others and comparing experiences.

Evie gradually got used to the new normal. It was almost like before, except Charles lived in the hospital instead of at home. Apart from the location change, there were no drastic changes in her life. They continued to plan Christmas presents and the days passed without much ado.

She even settled into a routine. Tilly would spend the morning to early afternoon period at the hospital, and once Evie arrived from school they would trade. Sometimes they both stayed and ate there, the food changed daily, but the company was consistent. Jason never visited, while Maria only did on occasion, where she would feel obliged to visit and spend some awkward hours making small talk. It was a relief to all parties when the obligated visits were completed.

Everyone, regardless of if they were staff or patient, recognised the sacred time Charles spent with his great-granddaughters. He'd described the never-ending stream of well-wishers and was delighted to listen to other people's stories and share some of his own in return. But they never overlapped with her visits. Evie had hardly believed it at first, expecting Charles to have been embellishing his popularity to ease her worry. She'd later overheard a nurse say that the only time he was alone was in the middle of the night when he was asleep. It made Evie happy and allowed her to sleep better at night knowing how much love and support Charles had, and that he was as happy as he could be in the hospital.

Chapter 22

Evie knew, as she carefully stepped down from the bus, hands thrown out as if she was walking on a tightrope as she slowly moved across the ice-covered pavement, that it was going to be bad. She could barely make out the bulk of the hospital building through the flurry of snow that was turning the world into a snow globe. As soon as she'd woken up and seen the snow, she'd decided to skip school in favour of checking up on Charles. She wasn't far off the Christmas holidays anyway, so she was only missing festive quizzes and films.

Pavements that were usually spotted with dried chewing gum, dog muck and things Evie didn't want to think about were deceptively clean and pure as they were cloaked in white. Before she got to the front door she had to stop and help a lovely elderly lady who was cheerful despite the fall she had just taken that left her on her back looking as though she was about to make a snow angel. Evie supposed that outside a hospital is an ideal place for such an accident to occur, with no shortage of people to help. Though quite a few people merely glanced at them and averted their eyes, earning judgement from Evie. She and two others returned the lady to her feet and escorted her to the main door of the hospital where the floors were marginally safer, if a little damp. The lady was absolutely fine and meandered off into the hospital after many thanks and after she tried several times to give Evie some money, which she firmly declined.

Evie smiled as she went into Charles' room, about to retell

the story to her great-grandad, who would surely be proud of her for helping and amused by the situation.

She paused as she emerged from the lift on Charles' floor, still out of sight of his door. She thought that the snow might trigger some difficult memories and feelings. At the start, Charles had reacted to any words to do with ice, snow or even being cold. Evie recalled a mistake when she used the slang 'chill' and spooked him. Undoubtedly, the first heavy snow of the year would be hard, it was just a question of exactly how hard. The fact that it was only just December and Charles was in the hospital and not at least safe and comfortable at home only made it worse. She'd have to brace herself for anything.

They hadn't had any guidance on what to do in the winter, though they'd been assured a leaflet was to be sent out. With no instruction to follow beyond her intuition, Evie squared her shoulders and headed up to Charles' room.

After greeting the nurses on duty by name and asking about various grandchildren, pets and enquiring about who won the weekly bingo, Evie reached Charles' room and peeped through the door to try to gauge his mood.

Before she'd recognised what she was looking at, the door opened fully and Maria passed her, both of them looked equally surprised to see each other there.

"Hi, I'll uh, see you at home tonight?" Maria asked, not looking her daughter in the eye.

"Sure, I have some sweetcorn and pasta in the fridge, so I'll have that when I'm back. Er, see you later," Evie replied, and stepped aside to allow her mother to pass.

Once she got in the room and closed the door firmly behind, she winced as she saw an IV line disappear into his vein, still not used to it. Charles had seemed quite cheerful the last time she visited when they're whiled away the hours finalising wall colours and décor, which was important since the decorators had started working in the new house. It was a sharp contrast to him today.

Buried under more blankets than she could count, only his arm and the upper part of his face was visible. The overhead light was off, and a lamp had been dragged in, providing a soft light since the window had cardboard covering it. In addition to the radiator in the room, an extra heater was plugged in and aimed directly at Charles. Evie imagined this was exactly what it would feel like to be inside an oven. The air itself was dry and was like sandpaper every time Evie inhaled. She couldn't fathom how Charles was sitting in front of the heat and layered in blankets. He must have been sweating under there. But Evie knew better than to try and coax him out before he was ready.

Evie shook her hair, snow which had quickly turned to droplets of water were flung to the floor. She quickly removed her big coat and woolly hat and scarf. Even just in her hoodie and jeans she was still uncomfortably hot. She gritted her teeth and dealt with it though, she knew without even discussing it that the nearly unbearable heat was crucial for Charles. She then peeled off her hoodie and resolved to not complain, despite the damp patch that was already growing on her back through the vest top she had on.

"Can I get you a drink or anything, Grandad?" she asked him.

A short head shake declined her offer.

"You're not too hot under all those blankets, are you?" she tried again.

This time he slightly rolled his eyes.

"Should we have a quiet day? If you fancy talking about it then I'm ready to listen, but if not we can just sit quietly," she told him.

Evie half expected him to remain silent. She glanced around

291

the room and was internally debating whether she should go to the café two floors above or the vending machine by the maternity ward.

"When I close my eyes, it's like I'm there. I'm on the side of the mountain, and I was so cold, my bones were solid ice. It had seeped into every pore, wormed its way around the gaps in my clothes. I was colder than I had ever been before, and then it started getting hot. All of a sudden, after hours of trying to kindle the tiniest drop of warmth, all I could think to do was pull off my heavy coat and cool down. They told me, in those first few days, that it was a sign I was nearing the end. My death certificate cited exposure as the reason you know. I don't think I will ever be in a position to be that cold again, but I will do everything in my power to never feel cold. That's why it's like we're on the equator, instead of in a hospital in Chester during the first snow of the season," he explained.

"Oh, Grandad. We can have a roaring fire all year round and the heating will always be on. On Christmas day, instead of Christmas jumpers, the house will be so hot that we'll dress like we're on a beach. How about we spend half the year abroad so it's always summer? It'll be okay," she vowed.

"I will endure it because I have to. Because of you and Matilda. But now you know why, and perhaps you will forgive me for it." He broke off, and one hand emerged from the blankets. He was holding his pocket watch, and slowly spinning it in his hand.

In line with his melancholy mood, Charles had serious subjects on his mind.

"My funeral," he started.

Evie was already objecting. She didn't even want to entertain the idea of it, much less plan it.

"Please, Evelyn. I need to do this. I sometimes think about Margaret, she was widowed, and she didn't even have my body to say goodbye to. I used to climb mountains all the time, she always expected me to come home. And I didn't, I left her, and I left my baby, and I didn't have anything in place if the worst happened. One of my many, many mistakes. I will not make those same mistakes. Do you understand that I need to do this? Your mother is refusing to even listen. She visited at my request and left before I even finished speaking." Charles' tone was strangely flat. She could only see his eyes, and they were hard.

"Okay," Evie agreed quietly.

"I don't want to upset you. But I need to say it. In my room is a briefcase, the code for it is the date I got married. Inside it is my will, my instructions and a letter for each of you. I've had it prepared from the very start, and have since added the letters, but now you know where to look. Mr Dexter and the others will be able to provide assistance. My money is to be shared between you and your sister, and a portion donated to charity, especially related to Everest and victims of domestic abuse. It's all detailed in the paperwork, but that's the gist. The house is fully paid for and will be for you girls too. And if it does happen, all I want is to be buried with my wife and daughter. I'm not fussy about the rest of the details, I'd be past caring at that point anyway." His eyes softened a little, they might've glistened in the low light. He paused for a second and seemed to be collecting his thoughts.

"I promise. If—if it happens I'll make sure you're with them. And I'll visit you every day. And I'll miss you every second. Oh, Grandad!" Evie cried as she dived towards him. She dissolved into tears, her head against the approximate location of his shoulder under the blankets. "I don't want to think about it any more. I'll remember the briefcase, so you won't need to worry," she said to his shoulder.

"*Shh*, it's okay, duck. If you haven't realised by now, I'm a

293

fighter. I'm sorry. I didn't intend to have that conversation, but the snow, it makes my brain think of horrible things. If I see the snow falling, I see my own death. It makes me feel like I can't carry on. Like I don't want to carry on. I hate it. I have coping strategies, to observe what's around me and breathe and calm myself and then I feel the icy grip of death hovering over me and there's no point and no hope. Does that even make sense?"

"Yeah, it makes a lot of sense. But you're safe, and you're here with us. Do you want to talk about it? Everest I mean?" Evie offered cautiously, expecting to be rebuffed.

He didn't say anything and turned his face away from her. When he finally turned back, he pulled the blanket from his face and nodded slowly.

"It is extremely difficult to talk freely. But perhaps if you ask me some questions I can answer them as best I can."

"Did you know, at the end? Did you know it was happening?" Evie asked.

He took a deep breath and reached for her hand. She stayed silent, knowing instinctively that he wasn't to be rushed.

"I-I hadn't thought about it. Do you know about the bodies up there? They're like signposts. People walk over them, I walked past them as if it wasn't someone's son, sister, father, friend. They don't even look real, like waxwork figures, not human beings. There're countless people who just look like they're resting, they stopped for a second and never got up. I didn't expect I would join their eternal ranks. I was delirious by the end, I lost all my bearings, got separated from my group. I felt so sick, and my hands and feet and ears and nose were tingling, all I wanted was for the tingling to stop. Until they went numb, and then I wished for any sort of sensation. But I know my final thoughts were of home, though when I pictured their faces,

I truly believed I would be seeing them soon. I think about them a lot, I try to repent, and I would never go back there, but sometimes in my dreams I walk among the frozen souls on that cursed mountain, and I bid each one farewell. Their faces will haunt me for the remainder of my second life."

"You're keeping their memory alive by remembering. But it isn't your burden to carry alone. They took the same risk you did when they went up there. You can be sad, but you can also forgive yourself," she said, every word spoken carefully, as she weighed it before saying it.

"Why me? Of all the people up there. It doesn't seem fair. I dread to think of the other families, who must hate my existence because it could've been their loved ones and it wasn't. I feel guilty, and like I have to make my second chance count. I have to deserve it," he whispered as if sharing a secret.

Evie was glad of the dim lights that would let her tears slide without notice. She sat there and tried to think of what she could say. There was nothing she could say.

"You'll think that I'm awfully selfish for this, but I'm glad it was you," she finally murmured, looking at her feet. He didn't reply and when she finally mustered the courage to look at him, his eyes were closed and his breathing slow and deep.

If it wasn't for his hand still slowly turning the pocket watch, she might've believed him.

Chapter 23

Today was the day the Monroes were celebrating Christmas. Even though the holiday was still weeks away, and advent calendars were still mostly full, they had decided to celebrate early on Charles' request. He'd said something about making up for all the Christmas dinners he'd missed but they were all hyper-aware of the invisible hourglass with sand ever draining away.

The rest of the family had put on their Christmas jumpers and drove over as a three, with the boot and spare seat loaded with pre-cooked food, bottled drinks and decorations. Jason was the only one who didn't pitch in with the cooking or planning, though he begrudgingly agreed to attend and offered snide comments as the day went on.

Evie was taking her own car, almost exploding with pride every time she remembered that she'd passed her test and could finally drive herself around. She was bursting to tell Charles after keeping it as a surprise until she'd passed. Evie could just imagine his shock; he'd try and play it cool and act as though he knew all along, but she'd see his eyes twinkling and he'd probably tell her that he's proud but never doubted her.

Once she'd arrived and parked, only shunting twice before she was neatly reversed in a space, Evie texted Tilly to say she'd meet them up there.

Evie hauled two large bags, one bursting with gifts for her family members, the other containing a festive donation for the children's ward. She picked her way through the car park, still amazed that she had car keys in her pocket as she went in.

Even the jolly decorations and upbeat Christmas music couldn't disguise the fact that it was a hospital full of life and death and miracles and heartbreak. Some of the nurses had tinsel woven into their hair and in almost every office and waiting room artificial Christmas trees were laden with baubles and twinkling lights. But for every laugh there were red rimmed eyes. A howl of pain for every time '*Jingle Bells'* was played or sung. Evie was used to the atmosphere by now, but still hurried with her straining bags as she passed through the hospital. If she lingered too long she wouldn't be able to ignore the fact that underneath it all was a large number of very sick people and not all of them would make it.

Evie smiled as she passed the various doctors and nurses and long-term residents she'd gotten to know from her daily visits to see Charles. She walked the familiar route to Charles' room, not paying attention to the several turns and stairs she was taking, instead looking at the hundreds of hand drawn pictures that covered the walls top to bottom.

As she passed the children's ward Evie put down one of her bags, which contained a lot of her old toys that had been gathering dust in the loft and garage. Although a sentimental person, Evie was glad to know her old beloved toys would be going to good homes and the thick excitement in the air as children of all ages and health conditions sang carols and shrieked in delight as they unwrapped early gifts warmed her heart. She left the bag with the matron as well as a box of chocolates for the nurses and continued on her way.

Evie was so excited to share her news with Charles and have their early Christmas. She hurried, almost jogging as she approached his door. It was closed over, which was unusual, the charming minor celebrity Charles often had a revolving line of people he'd just met who he laughed with like they were childhood friends. His door was always, notoriously open for visitors, unless during a medical consultancy or when his family were there and wanted privacy.

She didn't notice Maria until her mother reached out and gently grabbed her shoulder.

"Evie," Maria started.

Evie was carrying the last carrier bag that was almost overflowing with wrapped up and heavily Sellotaped gifts. She shifted it to her other hand and waited for Maria to continue talking.

"He... he isn't the same as he was yesterday. You need to prepare yourself now so it's not a shock. It won't do him any good to see you upset with all the stress from that other fellow passing away and with it being his first Christmas without his family. Just... try and be strong. Smile. Let's go," Maria guided her in and closed the door behind her. Evie saw her dad and sister first, both sitting in blue plastic chairs. Only Tilly moved when she nodded at Evie from her seat. Jason looked like he wanted to be anywhere else, tension was radiating from the stiff way he sat and glared at the wall. His left foot tapped on the floor furiously.

Evie felt her hands fly up to cover her mouth. Where yesterday there had been a discrete drip and some quiet machines, today he had tubes from both hands and an oxygen tube at his nose and there was a de-fib right next to his bed. Suddenly Evie saw him with fresh eyes, she had not been seeing her great-grandad as he had slowly deteriorated, the minute changes were hard to spot like not noticing a child growing until all of a sudden their jeans are above their ankles and they can reach the top shelf. What she saw hit her like a weight had landed on her chest and was restricting every breath.

His hair hadn't grown or changed, it hadn't the whole time

he had been with them. But the shine was gone, and it hung limp on his head, roughly pushed back. He always wore his hat when out in public, he must have hated not having it to cover his hair. She made a mental note to bring it next time.

Purple shadows bruised his pale skin and made his eyes look huge. His cheeks were hollow and gaunt like he was sucking in his cheeks, but he wasn't. Every rise and dip of the many blankets covering him seemed too long between and rattled a little.

For the first time in a while, it occurred to Evie that he was confined to the hospital because he was sick. One of the Eight had already died, and Charles, tough and strong-willed as he may be, could not defy death for a second time. All of this was thought in just a couple of seconds as she loitered in the doorway. She lowered her hands and fought with every ounce of defiance she had to wipe the horrified expression from her face and remain neutral.

"There's my girl. Come and give me a hug, duck," Charles said, slowly reaching towards her. Even his movement was slow and seemed painful. She couldn't believe she hadn't noticed it. He'd been buried under blankets since the first snow and just her grandad, telling her stories or offering her a game to pass the time.

Evie knew she needed to be brave, she gave Charles a shaky smile and cautiously approached him. Only when her arms were carefully threaded behind his neck, and her face buried in his shoulder, did she let out a silent sob. Her heart was being squeezed so tightly that she couldn't breathe. Although her heart was breaking, she took a deep breath and let go, counting and willing herself to be steel.

"Merry *fakemas,* Grandad!" Evie said, injecting some false cheer into her tone and wincing at how it came out.

"I've decided on some rules for the duration of this false

Christmas for us to follow. First of all, no talk of my health. Including but not limited to asking how I am, fussing over me, or asking any medical-related questions. Also, no crying, exchanging looks, or not enjoying yourselves. It's my first Christmas. My first Christmas back I mean, and it is going to be great fun!" Charles announced.

"And your last," Jason snidely commented. He said it under his breath, but every one of them heard it.

Even Maria jerked around to gape at her husband. Jason was nasty and petty, but to make comments like that in front of a gravely sick man was over the line. Evie saw shock and sadness flash across Charles' eyes, and Tilly bit her lip and looked away. Maria was wordlessly mouthing at her husband.

Evie's shock and sadness erupted out of her. "Get. Out." She spat. "I have never been more disgusted with you in my life than right now. You are a terrible person; you are nasty because you enjoy hurting people and I don't believe you care for anyone apart from yourself. If my mum has any sense this will be the wake-up call for her to leave you and I'm certain she'd be far happier for it. And Tilly, if you have a backbone you'll realise there's only so long you can edge around the bullying and condone his behaviour. You're both welcome to live with me and Grandad, and Jason?" Evie asked, almost sweetly.

Before he could respond, she whispered, "Goodbye." And nothing more needed to be said.

Charles could've exploded with pride as he saw the back of his granddaughter's husband. It was clear from every bone in his body that he was delighted. Charles and Evie had both suspected and discussed that Jason only allowed him to move in the first place because of the heavy government presence and the sheer thrill of having power and knowledge most people wouldn't possess. It was no puzzle to figure out who had been the 'inside source' the press loved.

The door slammed behind him and left a heavy silence in the room.

Evie thought her heart was broken already, but it broke anew when she looked at Charles. He gave her a big thumbs up, but sadness also leaked from his every pore. The words Jason had wielded were too close to home, it very well could be his last Christmas. Already it was ruined, and their dumb fighting had spoiled what should have been a happy occasion.

"Grandad, I am so sorry. He shouldn't have said that. Please, he's so stressed and he didn't mean it. He'll come round when he cools off. We all love you. I'm sorry." Maria's words stumbled across each other. Evie could not believe her mum was still defending him, it seemed she would always revert to the easy option and forgive any transgression of her husband, no matter how awful. It shouldn't be a surprise, Evie told herself. Her mother had never defended her or stood up against Jason.

Evie didn't normally resist against Maria's actions, but this time she couldn't wrestle the emotion into submission.

Right as she was about to let her mother know exactly what she thought of her, Tilly spoke from the corner.

"I'd love to," Tilly said.

"What's that now, sweetheart?" Charles replied after a short pause.

"I'd love to live with you both. More than anything," she said earnestly.

"What?" Maria interjected. "You're not moving out, Matilda. I won't let you."

"Actually, Mum, you have no authority over the matter. I'm twenty-years-old, almost twenty-one, therefore I can legally decide where I do or do not live. And I'm telling you now, I'd

301

rather live anywhere where he isn't. You're hardly better, but I don't hate you for it. I just pity you. Now get over yourself, smile and have a nice day for our grandad." Tilly had never spoken with such venom.

Evie was too shocked to jump in with her own opinions.

She glanced at Charles, and saw his eyes glittering in the stark hospital lights. He held out a hand to Tilly and squeezed her hand with the softest smile she'd ever seen on him. He looked at Evie and extended the same look to her, and it was enough for her to swallow her anger and let it temporarily go.

"Well, that was a fortunate turn of events, since I didn't get Jason any gifts. Now it won't be awkward when he doesn't get any off me." Evie laughed after she said it and was pleased when her words had Charles and Tilly chuckling too. Maria's lips quirked up slightly, but she didn't laugh or comment.

"Presents or food first?" Tilly asked.

"Food!" Charles called.

"Presents!" Evie said at the same time.

There were a few seconds of them looking at each other.

"Food then," Evie countered.

"Presents first," Charles replied at the same time.

They both laughed, genuine belly laughs.

"How about food while we open presents?" Maria offered.

Evie wasn't inclined to forgive her so easily, but Charles made the ultimate decision.

"That sounds perfect, Maria." Charles kindly smiled at her.

They busied themselves filling paper plates with pre-cooked turkey slices, mashed potato, an array of vegetables including sprouts, green beans and broccoli and a pig in blanket each. The heaped plate looked good but was cool to touch after being made and transported all the way to the hospital.

"This looks lovely, my first Christmas meal in a long time!

Thank you, Maria, you did a great job," Charles said after analysing his plate.

"Can you pass me a knife and fork, Mum?" Tilly asked.

A beaming Maria was reaching back into her bag, but at that comment, her face fell.

"Damn! Sorry guys. I forgot the cutlery. I do have something though." She continued fishing in her bag and pulled out a flask.

"Ah, great. You brought coffee? Hot chocolate?" Tilly asked.

"Warm gravy!" Maria announced.

Evie reluctantly noted her mother's efforts.

"I'll gift the lovely nurses *his* portion and see if they have any cutlery to spare for us. Don't take all the gravy," Evie told them as she headed to the door.

The nurses were delighted with the extra snacks and were happy to lend some forks to the party. They had grown quite fond of Evie and Charles in recent weeks. They fussed over Evie now, asking after what had happened since she'd been in the day before.

She was delighted to share her news with them, they were all appropriately impressed.

"Clever girl, I'll see you on the roads!"

"Brilliant, Evie. Oh, your grandad will be so pleased. He talks about you non-stop. He didn't mention you had your test though?"

"Oh, I kept it as a surprise. I didn't want him to worry or be disappointed if I didn't pass you see," Evie explained.

"Sweetie, it took me three times. Sometimes it's bad luck, or you just weren't ready or were too nervous. The important thing is that you worked hard and now you've achieved it. Congratulations! Remind me to get you some chocolates or some air fresheners or something."

303

"Honestly, you don't need to do that. And thank you all! I better go back before the gravy goes cold. Catch you later!" Evie gave them a cheery wave before heading back in.

She decided to wait for a quiet moment to break the exciting news to Charles. Her family knew, of course, they had driven separately after all. Luckily as it turned out, since Jason would have taken his car when he left. She figured she'd wait until after the presents. Tilly had already agreed to go to the café later so she could spend some time with just her and Charles.

"She returns victorious!" Charles announced as Evie distributed the utensils.

In her absence, Maria had produced four glass bottles of Coke and removed the lids ready. On the side table was a chocolate yule log and a selection of chocolate boxes next to a two-foot Christmas tree with battery-powered fairy lights on it and a little angel on top.

By the time gravy had been poured and everyone had taken their first bites, it was a unanimous decision to postpone presents until they had eaten.

The suspense had built by the time the paper plates had only smears of gravy left on them and empty bottles lined the table edge. Although the food had been cold and they'd eaten with paper plates balanced on their knees, it was one of the most enjoyable meals Evie had ever had with her family.

They pulled crackers and everyone gamely balanced a colourful paper crown above their brows and exchanged mini nail clippers and toys.

Maria began collecting their rubbish and tidying up. Tilly stretched and went to the toilet. Evie figured she could use the quiet moment to share her news. She turned to her great-grandad to find him dozing, sitting upright with his head leaned back against the wall behind him.

"Just let him close his eyes for a minute, Evie. He's having a very difficult time right now he must be making a huge effort today to have a normal afternoon with you girls," Maria said softly. "And, Evie, I need to apologise to you—"

"Don't. Don't bring that up now. Just try and have a nice time, please," Evie told her mother.

Maria nodded and excused herself to go and get a hot drink.

Evie sat and looked at her grandad, at how frail he looked as he fitfully slept. She examined her feelings, she truly couldn't afford to lose him, not after getting to this point. Not when she was finally happy and they had so much to look forward to, to do together. Surely fate wouldn't be so cruel as to rip him out of their lives so soon. Her sorrow weighed heavily on her soul, she let herself work through her emotions while no one could see her. When she saw Charles' eyes begin to flutter, she shoved her feelings once again out the way, but silently vowed to address them later, in private.

"Where did everyone go?" Charles asked, confusion clouding his eyes.

"I think they're grabbing drinks. You nodded off for a minute there. It's okay though, Christmas dinner always makes me sleepy too!" Evie answered.

"Oh, duck. I'm so sorry. You should have woken me up! I've been looking forward to today all week and now I've gone and wasted it. Stupid!" Charles looked extremely agitated.

"No one minds honestly. If you need to rest then of course we don't mind! Did you enjoy the food?" Evie asked as she moved to sit right next to him.

"Did I miss presents too?" he asked, still looking heartbroken.

"No, we waited. I got everything on the list you gave me, and I wrapped them. Well, I tried my best to wrap, I'm not very good actually, there's a lot of Sellotape. But when they come back we can swap gifts, I'm so excited!" Evie was desperate to cheer her great-grandad up. The only thing worse than seeing him looking so poorly and frail was the expression currently on his face.

"I have something for you, two things actually. The first is some good news, and the second is this." Evie carefully pulled a wrapped gift from the bag. It was the neatest she'd ever wrapped a present, and since it was a rectangle it was relatively easy. She suddenly felt nerves shoot through her body, doubting if he would like the gift. She remembered the hundreds of potential gifts she'd considered for him before she eventually settled on something sentimental.

"Wow, I thought you said you couldn't wrap!" Charles smiled a little as he carefully unwrapped the layer of silver paper and revealed the frame inside.

He silently turned it over and stared at the photo. His mouth fell open, and one of his machines beeped as he suddenly stopped breathing. A second later he let out a breath and carried on staring. His eyes had glazed over.

Evie held her breath too.

"It's—I—Evie, it's perfect. Thank you, thank you so much. I'll treasure it for as long as I live. Thank you!"

Evie relaxed slightly; it was a high stake gamble that could've gone either way. She let Charles think for a while and didn't disturb him until he put the frame on his bedside table, facing him.

Evie studied the photo. She'd sifted through hundreds of mixed-up photos after Maria had hauled them out of the loft and left them in the living room so many weeks ago. She narrowed them down to a dozen, and then picked the last photo she could find of Charles, Margaret and Evelyn before Everest. It had been printed in black and white, so she'd paid someone to make it into colour and tidy it up a little, so it was clearer. As she glanced back at her grandad, she knew nothing material would have been remotely in competition with this gift. Her shattered heart warmed a little.

"I have something for you too, duck. I want to give it to you now before the others come back," Charles said, he reached out to hold Evie's hand but didn't tear his eyes away from the photo. She suspected he would be drinking in the details for quite some time.

He directed her to his suitcase that was in the corner of the room where she gingerly rooted through various shirts and pants that had been haphazardly folded until she came upon a box.

"Is this it? The latex gloves box size M? I can't see any other box in here."

"That's the one. One of my lovely evening nurses scrounged up the box since I can hardly nip to the newsagents and get it wrapped up all pretty. I hope that's okay," he said.

"It could have been wrapped in toilet roll for all I care; can I look inside now?"

Charles nodded and gestured for her to go ahead.

Evie pulled out some screwed up blue roll and gasped out loud when she saw what the glove box contained.

"Really? You're giving it... to me?" she choked out, overcome with emotion again.

Charles turned and looked away from the photo for the first time.

"Duck. Evie. There is no one in the entire world who I would rather give it to. It's frozen on three o'clock, the time when I— when I died. That was the last time I was in a world where my wife and daughter were alive, and I couldn't bring myself to get it repaired. I won't mind if you want to though, it's yours now. Evie, you are one of the brightest lights in my life. You are kind and smart. You are brave and you make me proud every single day. I love you in this life, and I'll love you in the next. My Evelyn—your nana would have been so proud of you and would have loved you just as much as I do. It would be my honour if you accept this gift and treasure it for the rest of your life, and maybe one day you pass it to your own children or grandchildren. If you're extremely lucky maybe even your great-grandchildren! When you're old and your hair is threaded with grey like mine, you'll realise how special it is to be close to your family and. And—"

His face went slack as he repeated the word seemed to lose his train of thought.

Evie smiled and waited for him to go on. She was so touched; she wasn't sure if she would be able to put her gratitude and pride and love into words.

Charles was mouthing 'and' and then went still. He looked at his photo and then back to Evie.

She reached out for his hand, and he squeezed it.

"Grandad, it's perfect. This is the best, most special present I've ever been given in my entire life. I can't thank you enough. I love you!" Evie told him.

He squeezed her hand again and then his hand went slack.

At the same time, his eyes disappeared into the back of his head and several machines started beeping and flashing lights.

"Grandad? Charles? Grandad!" Evie called, getting more frantic as he failed to respond or react.

She dithered on the spot, still clasping his limp hand. Before she finished the thought, she launched herself over to the panic button and pressed it several times.

Before she'd finished pressing it, a team of doctors hurried in. One started checking his pulse and another pulled the defibrillator closer to him. They were all doing something different and calmly calling numbers and observations to each other.

"Grandad?" Evie said, still clinging to his hand.

When she spoke, the closest nurse looked at her, and gently but firmly unhooked her hand from Charles'. Before she could protest, she was steered out and deposited in the hallway.

"You stay out here sweetheart. Let the doctor's work and one of them will come out and let you know in a little while okay? Is anyone here with you today? Is there anyone you can call?" the nurse asked.

"My—my mum. She was and now she's not," Evie whispered. Unable to process what had just happened. Mere minutes ago, they had exchanged beautiful, thoughtful gifts and were having a lovely bonding moment.

"Evie? You're shaking, why are you out here? Why is the door closed?"

Evie turned to see her mum and sister had come up behind her and each had two hot drinks cups. They all had plastic lids that were leaking steam through the bit where you drink. She saw one of them didn't have the lid on properly and hot chocolate had leaked on the side. As she watched, a drip slid down the side and onto the floor. No one else noticed.

"Evie? What happened?" Tilly tried again.

"He—I—he just let go and then his eyes and she said I had to call my mum!" Evie started at a whisper, but she ended up howling. She sobbed and couldn't catch her breath.

Tilly put the drinks down and wrapped her arms around Evie. A pale and serious Maria ordered them to stay outside and marched to the door. She spoke to someone over the threshold.

From where Evie stood, still shaking in the arms of her sister, she heard a few words drift over to them. 'Coma', 'difficult choice', 'expect the worst'.

After a quick chat, she came back to her daughters. Without saying anything, she wrapped her arms around both her daughters and quietly cried with them.

Evie stood there and watched the hot chocolate puddle gradually grow. In her hand, she held the pocket watch. The smooth silver dug into her palm and she squeezed it harder.

Epilogue

25th December, 2019

Gold and silver and red tinsel danced around the headstones. Some had mini trees and flashing lights, soggy presents resting about six feet above the intended receiver. The cemetery was full of people. Two plots over, a young man quietly cried over a tiny grave. The headstone was in the shape of an angel, white and pure and perfect. Little plush dollies and solar night lights covered every inch of the soil. To the left, a big family arrived between two cars, a baby slung across an elderly lady's hip. She must be the matriarch, there were four other adults and a little girl with pigtails and the baby. The baby grizzled as they trooped over to their grave. I shouldn't be angry; it's a public place and they came to visit someone who is missing from their table and yet I want to scream at them to be quiet and stop disturbing us. I see the old lady look over at me, and I can imagine what she sees.

Christmas day was harder than regular days, losses were so much more noticeable and felt. It was one of the busiest times in the cemetery, there was a constant queue at the tap and the car park was overflowing.

"Merry Christmas. It doesn't feel like Christmas, to be honest. The one we had in the hospital when… well you know when, that was the real one. I'm so glad we did that. I'm sorry, I came over here for a chat and I start crying and can't even get my words out. I just, I—thought, well, even at the worst point when we got the call saying to get to the hospital immediately, I was in denial. I was so sure you'd be okay and we'd be playing Scrabble and eating all sorts of wonderful desserts. I know you'll be looked after up there, but it doesn't hurt any less. Every day, I look to see if you're in the kitchen, my heart skips a beat when the door opens and then it sinks when it's not you."

There was a distant rumble of thunder, the slate grey sky dimming the light and making the world even more gloomy.

"I—er, I got you a present. I brought it here, but I'll take it home with me and look after it for you. You probably think it's silly, but I wanted to do it. The house is full of stuff. People are leaving casseroles and lasagne and curry and various Tupperware that's filled the fridge and mingled into one almighty disgusting smell. To be honest, I think a few of them turned up to be nosey, we were on the news after all. I shut my bedroom door when I know someone is outside. All these strangers offering condolences, and not one of them knew you like I did and knew how funny and clever and kind and thoughtful and—you. They don't know you like I do. Did—"

A pause, it's like there's an invisible barrier around the grave, protecting them and blocking everything else out. The background sound of the other mourners is muffled, as if very far away. The silence is calming for only a moment before it needs to be filled again, before the lack of response builds and all over again it's one person talking to the ground and there's no one to answer any more.

"I know, I'm sure Evelyn and Margaret will have been waiting for you. They'll be looking after you up there. I bet they were desperate to see you and love you and thank you for doing so much good before permanently joining them. I'm sure you had so much to tell them and catch up on. To be honest, I kind of wish I was there too. I know we only knew each other for a few months, but, well it seems impossible to live in a world without you in it. Maria and Jason are avoiding me, they knew how close we are. Were. They don't know how to treat me. They don't know how to treat each other since they separated, we'll see if it becomes a permanent thing. I don't know if you saw, but Tilly has stepped up a bit, she's checking on me and making me eat tasteless casseroles every day. I know she misses you. She's going to come here later to visit, I think she got you a present too, I believe some sort of shimmery hair spray. Oops, sorry for spoiling it. I think she wishes she'd made more of an effort these last few months, I hear her crying at night, and I know I should go and see her, and tell her you loved her and everything, but I can't do it. I'm sorry. I don't want to be so sad; you wouldn't like to look down and see me like this, watering all these flowers just with my tears. Come on."

I raise my eyes skyward, there's that trick that if you look directly into the light that you stop crying. It doesn't work. Instead, I let my eyes look for patterns in the sky, trying to grip my emotions in a vice and stop crying all over the grave. I close my eyes, and when I open them, I see a duck, directly overhead.

It's a cloud, lighter than the sky, lazily drifting. I rub my eyes and look again certain it can't be real. The man to the right stands up, and I grab his arm.

"Do you see that cloud? Right above us? What does it look like to you? Please? Do you see a duck too?" I ask, holding his arm.

He shakes me off, not lifting his eyes which are trained on the ground.

"Please! If it's a duck then it's my sign. They're watching over us I know they are, and they sent me a sign. Please." I'm crying again, frantic for someone to confirm it.

313

The man pushes me, and I stagger back off balance. I turn to look for someone else, and then look back up. It's still there. I know it's a sign. It has to be.

"Quack, quack." I wanted it to be funny, but instead, I drop to my knees, my fingers digging into the fresh mud. I squeeze the mud, feeling my nails break the skin of my palm and I miss you and it's not fair.

"It's not fair. We should've had longer. We should've walked down the aisle together. We both know Jason didn't deserve to. The house was perfect, now I can't stand to look at anything, knowing you chose it, but you are never going to live there. We should have gone on holiday; we could've gone anywhere you wanted. Remember we were going to spend the winter months abroad on a hot, sunny beach somewhere? We were going to do so much and now you're gone! You left me and it shouldn't be like this, I didn't sign up for this. I would trade with you in one second, and then I'd feel bad that I left you, but you deserved to live and to learn and to explore and seize your own destiny with two hands. We had come so far, worked so hard and for what? I miss you and you're gone and what am I going to do now? What's the point?" I'm sobbing, and I'm angry and lonely and lost.

"Excuse me, are you all right? Can I do anything to help?" and the old lady from two plots over has dumped the baby and has her arm around me. I crumble and suddenly I'm sobbing and there's snot on her cardigan and she looks at the new etching on the old gravestone and the freshly moved soil and I see her get it.

"It's hard every single day. You miss them, and you can't believe that you'll never see them again. You'd give anything for one more conversation and one last hug. You loved them so much that your heart hurts to think about it but now they're gone and you're still here. But it will get easier, more manageable, the pain

314

might not lessen but you can learn how to cope a little better and after a while, you adjust to life without them and maybe one day you smile, and it'll be okay." She didn't even know me, but she knew my feelings as well as I did. She stayed with me for so long. In the end, we sat on the cold soggy ground and my eyes ran out of tears, and I stopped shaking and my breathing slowed, and I saw the duck in the distance, breaking into two clouds and I wasn't alone.

It was quite some time before I could manage to speak. I suddenly noticed the baby was gone along with her whole family. I looked around wildly, unable to work out how the sun was now so much lower and the cemetery so much emptier.

"I'll make my own way home later. We don't live far, and I walk here most days to visit my Harold. He's right over there, Harold Robert Johnson, and he's been here for five years five months and one day. It's just since it's Christmas everyone dutifully comes to visit, and they only stay for a minute and it's back to the turkey and the drinks and all that. I'll enjoy the evening of course and the little kids give me a reason to still stick around, but I'll be constantly thinking of him," the kind lady explained when she saw me looking around.

"Thank you. You're too kind," I mumbled, throat sore from the non-stop crying. She smiled and waited.

"This—it's my first Christmas since—" and I break off again.

"Our sixth year separated for me and Harold. The first one was the hardest for me, we were together fifty-seven years, and in that time we never spent a Christmas apart. You just have to keep going. Take it one day at a time. These times of the year, the extra special times, those will be the hardest, but you'll get through it," the lady continued, with a hand on my shoulder.

"I just can't believe she's gone. That I won't see her again. How can I carry on knowing she's not here? I should've died not her. She'd only just passed her driving test, she was bursting with pride. I helped her practice for it. She was driving to the hospital to visit me. And it wasn't her fault, a van skidded on ice and crashed into her. They'd had a few drinks and were speeding, and they got away with scratches but Evie died. She died and she was trying to visit me in hospital. They were sorry, so sorry about what happened but it doesn't bring her back. She's never coming back." My whole body shook as sobs ripped from my chest.

"No, you can't think like that. It's guilt that is, but it's not something you should carry. Unless you killed her. Sorry, that was inappropriate. But you have a hard enough time grieving without blaming yourself. There's always something you should've said or done differently. But you clearly loved her, and she'll have known that. It's obvious to me and I only met you today," the lady continued.

I thought about her words, letting them gently roll around my mind before accepting she could be on to something. I wish we could've moved out sooner, I would've happily taken that rabbit with us, and as I was thinking about the rabbit I smiled just a little. Tilly had been discussing who would take over his care, the poor thing seemed to know Evie wasn't around and was out of sorts. It was only when Tilly said: 'He'd either go straight away or no one would ever want him, only Evie would name her pet after her favourite food place at the time – Toby Carvery.' And we'd both cried a lot and then shared some of our favourite memories and I realised just how much Tilly was hurting too. After that, it was a lot easier to talk and be there for each other. I didn't need to tell her we'd be keeping the rabbit.

I'd almost forgotten the lady was there, but she was quietly smiling and waiting patiently. Once she saw me looking, she began to speak.

"I'm Joyce by the way. I'm sorry to meet you under such circumstances, but I do believe everything happens for a reason and I was meant to meet you today. Please don't blame yourself. If you listen to one thing I say today it's not to hold guilt, it'll only hold you back in the long run," Joyce said. "Anyway, I'll leave you to it. Who knows, maybe we'll bump into each other again, I come here quite a lot. And Charles? Have a Merry Christmas. You can get through this; I know you can. You're incredibly strong." Joyce smiled gently before brushing herself down and heading towards the gates.

I looked at the grave and vaguely wondered how Joyce had known my name. Of course, she'd probably seen my photograph, she'd undoubtedly have heard the Everest story. She seemed like she would have an interactive mobile phone and surf the web. No doubt she'd followed the story. Now I'd gotten better and there was that new fuss about some sort of flu-like new virus, people had quite quickly moved on and left the Monroes alone. The fuss had almost disappeared when they'd all ended up in hospital, but after Evie, the whole story had collapsed. After Evie, no one bothered me. I thought about the lady, Joyce, who had been so kind without any prompt or expectation of reward. It suddenly occurred to me that if I had aged normally I'd be around the same age as Joyce. She looked to be in her eighties.

With a sigh, I scooped up the still wrapped though rather muddy gifts. I bid goodnight to my dear wife, sweet daughter and beloved great-granddaughter and started the journey home, thinking that when I come tomorrow, I'll bring a hand heater to keep warm. I was very impressed with them, with how you could just pop them, and they heated up with chemicals. I would bring some and then I could stay for longer, it was difficult for me to be outside in the dead of winter, in the cold. But for my three angels, I'd come every day no matter what.

As I walked away, I checked the time on my mobile phone, and smiled at the photograph that made up the background. Tilly had caught me looking at it and pressed a few buttons and suddenly whenever I checked the time Evie was there in her polka dot top, smiling at me. I checked the time a lot.